Praise for

Going Through the Notions

"A quaint little village, quirky characters, and a crafty killer—I loved it!"

—Laura Childs, *New York Times* bestselling author of *Eggs in a Casket*

"Cate Price's *Going Through the Notions* has everything I read cozy mysteries for—a terrific setting, a smart plot, and well-rounded, clever characters. Lucky us—it's the first in an all-new series (Deadly Notions)—and I can't wait for the next one!"

—Mariah Stewart, *New York Times* bestselling author of *At the River's Edge*

"A fun, fast-paced debut filled with eccentric characters, quirky humor, and small-town drama."

—Ali Brandon, national bestselling author of *Words With Fiends*

A Dollhouse
to Die For

*

Cate Price

BERKLEY PRIME CRIME, NEW YORK

THE BERKLEY PUBLISHING GROUP
Published by the Penguin Group
Penguin Group (USA) LLC
375 Hudson Street, New York, New York 10014

USA • Canada • UK • Ireland • Australia • New Zealand • India • South Africa • China

penguin.com

A Penguin Random House Company

A DOLLHOUSE TO DIE FOR

A Berkley Prime Crime Book / published by arrangement with the author

Berkley Prime Crime Books are published by The Berkley Publishing Group.
BERKLEY® PRIME CRIME and the PRIME CRIME logo are trademarks of
Penguin Group (USA) LLC.

For information, address: The Berkley Publishing Group,
a division of Penguin Group (USA) LLC,
375 Hudson Street, New York, New York 10014.

ISBN: 978-0-425-25880-4

PUBLISHING HISTORY
Berkley Prime Crime mass-market edition / May 2014

PRINTED IN THE UNITED STATES OF AMERICA

10 9 8 7 6 5 4 3 2

Cover illustration by Ben Perini.
Cover logo *Pin* copyright © Roman Sotola; *Floral Pattern* copyright © LDesign.
Cover design by Diana Kolsky.
Interior text design by Laura K. Corless.

For Owen

Acknowledgements

This book owes an enormous debt of gratitude to a wonderful friend and writer, Eileen Emerson, who was so helpful in so many ways. Let me try to count them. For taking a trip with me to Fabric Row in Philadelphia to impart some of her vast knowledge of fabrics to this non-seamstress, for plot ideas on insulin pumps and remotes, for always being ready to drop everything for a critique, and for unfailing passion for my work. Thank you, Eileen, from the bottom of my heart.

For more medical advice on diabetes, thanks to my forever friend, Cheryl McEntee, and to Lanise Shortell, RN, for the detailed information. Any mistakes in interpretation are entirely mine.

Thanks to Adele Downs, who owned a doll business for many years, for advice on antique dolls and insight into the habits of some extreme collectors.

To the plotstormers with whom I've enjoyed so many lunches, Jeannine Standen, Maria Entenman, Stephanie Julian, Jackie Himmel, and Eileen Emerson. You rock.

Special thanks to Judith Nichols and Gaynor Bosson, childhood friends in England who have always cheered me on, and to Judith's daughter, Chloe, for the creative tips on upcycling sewing cabinets. Thanks to my aunt, Peggy Davies, who writes me lovely notes of encouragement.

To artist Ben Perini, thank you for my beautiful covers, and to artist Robin Carey, who creates amazing dollhouses and features them on her blog, thanks for the inspiration.

I'm grateful for the new friends and readers that I've had the pleasure to meet since *Going Through the Notions* was published, including my very first sale, Gayle Vreeland, who advised me to always be a seeker of the truth.

As always, deep gratitude to my most excellent editor, Jackie Cantor, and my wonderful agent, Jessica Alvarez.

Finally, for my brother, Owen, who is almost more excited about this publishing journey than I am, and who is secure enough in his manhood that he won't mind having a book about dear little dollhouses dedicated to him. Love you more.

Chapter One

As I peered through the windows of the house I'd purchased at auction for two hundred dollars, I realized it was in far worse shape than I'd thought. All the floors needed refinishing, the staircase was askew, and some of the wallpaper was peeling. Most of the boards on the porch were rotted, and a couple of balustrades needed replacing.

Never mind. I smiled as I peeked inside the front parlor, still entranced with my find. I planned to add some sconces on either side of the mirror and a flickering light in the fireplace. A new coverlet for the bed, a dining table and chairs, and perhaps a miniature rocking chair, too.

I straightened up, pressing a hand to the small of my back, and looked down at the pretty Victorian dollhouse with its hand-sewn curtains, real wavy glass windows, and needlepoint carpets.

With a sigh of satisfaction, I left my treasure sitting on a Hepplewhite blanket chest and unlocked the door to Sometimes a Great Notion. My store, a haven of vintage linens and sewing notions in the quaint village of Millbury, Pennsylvania, was a testament to my passion for the past. I specialized in what was called "new" old stock. Like buttons, snaps, and fasteners still on their original cards, and unopened packages of gilt braid, seam tape, and zippers.

I turned on the stereo and soon the sounds of 1940s jazz filled the space. I was about to start a pot of my traditional strong coffee brewing when I saw a gaunt figure cross the main street, on a direct trajectory for my shop.

I groaned and wished I hadn't been in such a hurry to unlock the front door.

Not that I wanted to turn any business away, but Harriet Kunes was a tough customer. She haggled with me on every price, always wanted something thrown in for free, and had a talent for making a veritable root canal out of any transaction.

I pasted a bright smile on my face, but it didn't last long.

"Daisy Buchanan, don't be such a stupid nitwit!" Harriet said a few moments later as she stood on the other side of the counter, glaring at me as she placed both hands on her bony hips.

I glared back. I have many faults, well, *some* anyway, but a lack of intelligence is certainly not one of them. They say the Customer Is Always Right, but in this case, she was sadly mistaken.

"I'm offering you *three times* what this dollhouse is worth!" She whipped off her eyeglasses, as if to better focus the laser power of her stare on me.

"Look, I'm sorry, Harriet, but it's not for sale."

While it was true that I carried some antique children's toys in the store, in addition to the quilts and linens, this one was different. I planned to restore it and give it to one of the best kids I'd ever known, apart from my own daughter.

Claire Elliott was turning ten on Halloween. It might

seem like an expensive birthday gift for a child, but I knew her mother could never afford something like this on her diner waitress earnings. Besides, I looked forward to all the fun Claire and I would have when I babysat.

She was a special kid. One of those old souls who seem wise beyond their years. Like it's not their first time going around this earth. She shared my enthusiasm for antiques and history, and I often forgot she was only nine years old.

And as much as I loved my daughter, Sarah, now twenty-six, she and I were nothing alike. She affectionately dismissed my enthusiasm for the "dusty old sewing things" in the store as simply one more of Mom's funny quirks.

Sensitive Claire and the pragmatic Patsy Elliott were also completely different. But Claire and I would see the magic in this dollhouse and transport ourselves back in time in our imaginations.

Harriet pressed her thin lips together. "You don't understand. This dollhouse is of great personal significance to me."

"Really? Me, too." I wanted to give it to Claire.

"A thousand dollars. My final offer. You know that's an *exorbitant* price."

I almost felt like throwing myself across it to protect it from her avaricious gaze. I'd gone through a lot at the auction to win this particular dollhouse, bidding against another determined, maniacal woman. I wasn't about to let it go now.

Harriet paced up and down in front of the Walker seed counter with its loading bins full of old sewing patterns and unused French ribbons. I could see where she must have been a beautiful woman at one time with her high cheekbones and arched brows, but years of constant scowling had driven deep grooves into her sallow skin. Her hair was a faded blond. Actually not even blond, more like no color left in it at all. Angry suspicion in her eyes leached away whatever spark of beauty remained.

Even though I never wore much makeup myself, I longed

to soften her skeletal features with a dusting of blush. She wore a pale blue bouclé suit, which had to have been an expensive designer outfit when first purchased years ago, but was now so out-of-date it was almost retro.

Harriet's hands reached out as if she ached to grab the house and run. Instead she gripped the edges of the counter. "You must sell it to me," she hissed. "What kind of business-woman are you anyway?"

I shook my head. Some things just weren't for sale.

Calling on my many years of teaching experience, I dredged up the voice I'd used on recalcitrant students and inserted the appropriate amount of steel. "For the last time, the answer is *no*!"

With one last death ray glare, Harriet Kunes stormed out, letting the door bang shut. I winced, praying the old panes wouldn't break.

As the doorbell continued to jangle violently, I stared after her, wondering what the heck *that* was all about.

I'd bought the little dollhouse at the Saturday night auction in Sheepville, from the estate of Sophie Rosenthal, a local woman who'd passed away last February. I admit I'd lusted after it myself when I first saw it, but the sum Harriet had offered me was just plain crazy. Was it really worth more than I'd thought?

Intrigued, I checked comparable items on the Internet again. Nope, it wouldn't fetch more than a few hundred dollars at best in its current condition. It still needed a thorough cleaning, plus all the repairs to the gingerbread trim, roof shingles, and boards on the porch.

Why hadn't Harriet gone to the well-advertised estate auction herself if she wanted it that much? Why the sudden interest?

The whole thing was very odd. Maybe she was just one of those people who, once they decide they want something, have to have it at any cost.

I shrugged and busied myself with arranging some items from a recent yard sale. An accordion-style sewing box I'd picked up for ten dollars would make a great display for the latest notions I'd found, and I arranged them to look as though they were spilling from one drawer to the next. I hung an assortment of tea towels on a wooden drying rack, and grouped a collection of calico needle cases next to a Greist buttonholer attachment.

I also filled some orders off my website. Even though my store was situated in a sleepy nineteenth-century village where time had ground to a halt, I managed to keep in touch with the present day.

Thanks to my business, I'd become quite the estate sale and auction junkie, always on the hunt for unique items to pass along to another good home. In fact, the idea for my store had been born after one of my trips to the auction. I'd bid on an old steamer trunk that turned out to be packed to the brim with a bounty of sewing notions and exquisite fabrics.

And luckily for me, people around here passed their farms and houses on from generation to generation, and when they finally cleaned out their attics and basements, there was a treasure trove of perfectly preserved merchandise that had been sitting in storage for decades.

In only a year and a half, Sometimes a Great Notion had become a well-known destination for collectors, interior designers, and antique dealers.

The doorbell rang again, and some live customers came in next looking for a quilt. There were several hanging on the walls, plus I showed them a few more on the second floor, where I had additional rooms for storage and repairs. They finally settled on a field-of-stars design fashioned from feed sacks in soft colors of mauve, pink, blue, and yellow. I wrapped it carefully in tissue paper and placed it in one of my signature shopping bags with its peacock blue grosgrain drawstring.

After they left, I clambered into the nook in one of the windows that jutted onto the porch of the former Victorian home to rearrange the display. Outside, the sky was darkening, and I hoped it wouldn't rain. My husband and I had dinner reservations at the Bridgewater Inn out on River Road. I pictured us sitting on the veranda overlooking the falls, enjoying the last of the late summer evenings.

Across the main street from me was a shop called A Stitch Back in Time, owned by my friend Eleanor Reid, who restored and altered antique wedding gowns. A CLOSED sign hung on the door. Eleanor opened her store when she damn well felt like it, or had deigned to make an appointment with a client, blissfully immune to the burden of guilt and responsibility that propelled me through life.

Far from the customers always being right, with Eleanor they had to fall on their knees and grovel, but her work was so specialized and immaculate that she was always in high demand. No one was about to trust their grandmother's treasured wedding dress to anything less than an expert.

It wasn't until I was cleaning up the counter at the end of the day that I noticed Harriet Kunes had left her eyeglasses behind.

Great.

I rummaged through my well-worn box of customer index cards. Not very high-tech, I know, but hey, it's what I was used to. I called the number on the card, but there was no answer and no voice mail for me to leave a message.

Joe Daly, my husband, walked through the door just as I was hanging up the phone. I'd kept my maiden name of Buchanan when we married, unable to deal with the concept of going through life as perky-sounding Daisy Daly. Tonight he wore a crisp white shirt, navy pants, and a sports jacket. At sixty-three, he was still a handsome man, tanned, gray-haired, and well-built. Since we'd retired, neither of us dressed up that often, and to see him decked out like this made my heart skip a beat.

I'd also switched my usual work uniform of T-shirt and jeans for a cocktail dress from my collection. A sexy 1950s Christian Dior black lace number that I paired with high-heeled pumps instead of my cowboy boots. I'd twisted my hair up into a decent impression of an elegant knot, although a few wayward brown strands escaped here and there.

Joe's dark eyes took in my appearance. A smile curved his lips, and he pulled me into his arms. When he kissed me, the world spun away, as did the years, and I savored the feel of his firm mouth and the familiar rush of heat and dizzy longing.

I pulled away first, albeit with a smidgen of regret. It probably wouldn't do for Millbury's sewing notions proprietress to be seen making out through the large display windows.

"Do you mind if we make a stop on the way?" I murmured. "Harriet Kunes left her glasses in the store. I know I'd be lost without mine."

"Sure." He offered his arm as we walked down the three steps from the black-painted porch. I smiled at him, feeling the familiar strength beneath my fingers and loving the anticipation of a night out. A real date.

A soft raindrop touched my cheek, and I glanced up at the ominous sky. "Oh, I hope this rain holds off until after dinner."

As we got into the car, I told him how Harriet had seemed desperate to buy my dollhouse. "I'm afraid I wasn't very nice to her, Joe, but she simply wouldn't take no for an answer."

"Sounds like someone else I know." He grinned at me. "Hello, Pot, this is Kettle calling!"

"Ha, ha. Very funny." I pulled the customer card out of my bag and read the address out loud.

Joe took a left at the end of Main Street, and drove up
Grist Mill toward River Road as a crack of thunder sounded.
He had both hands on the wheel of our station wagon to
navigate the twists and turns of the rain-spotted road that
ran alongside the river and canal.

When we got to Swamp Pike, he turned right and then
headed down to the intersection with Burning Barn Road,
where a famous artists' colony attracted painters for week-
long retreats.

It was raining in earnest now, and I sighed. Guess the
veranda was out.

A few minutes later, we pulled up to the Meadow Farms
Golf Club and Preserve. A gold crest adorned each stone
pillar at the entrance, and flags hung on tall poles on either
side. The guard waved us through when we mentioned we'd
come to visit Harriet.

We drove past the clubhouse and attached fitness center,
a beautiful fieldstone complex with a flagstone patio in front.
We'd been to a wedding there once. The clubhouse had an
excellent restaurant and dance floor, and there was an outdoor pavilion next to the pool where the ceremonies were
performed.

The radiant manicured islands on the eighteen-hole
course were surrounded by prairie grass, shimmering ponds,
and copses of trees turning burnt orange and crimson. The
protected open space and the hills in the distance provided
a stunning vista for golfers teeing off.

Beyond the clubhouse and the start of the course was an
enclave of townhomes and single-family houses, bordered
by scenic wetlands and walking trails. We wound our way
through the development until I spotted the sign for Barnstead Circle.

This must have been a premium location when the builder
first sold lots here.

There were only two other black-shuttered brick mansions

on the quiet cul-de-sac besides Harriet's, and hers was at the end that backed up to the woods.

Joe pulled onto the driveway behind a white Lexus SUV. I hurried after him as we dodged raindrops and followed the path toward the front door. There was an impressive porch supported by two white columns and a huge arched window above. I fished Harriet's glasses out of my bag and rang the bell.

We waited, huddling next to each other on the stone step. Lights were on in the foyer, but no one came to the door.

Suddenly I caught a flash of something over to my left.

"Did you see that?" I asked Joe.

"What?"

"I don't know. Something . . ."

It could have been a figure running through the woods, or maybe just a deer. There were so many round here, and the bane of Joe's garden existence, eating his hostas and day-lilies. It broke my heart to see them killed at the side of the road. I was always on the lookout as I drove on some of these country lanes, even in fairly well-developed residential areas.

"Where the heck *is* Harriet?" Joe said. "Her car's here."

I could tell he was impatient to get to the Bridgewater Inn and his favorite meal, the house specialty of roasted rack of lamb with garlic mashed potatoes and almond-mint pesto.

He took a few steps along the path. He peered in another of the arched windows that fronted the exterior of the house and muttered an expletive.

"What is it?" I hurried over and looked into a study crammed with collectibles. Harriet Kunes was slumped over a large dollhouse on a display table.

"Holy smokes. Do you think she's had a heart attack or something?"

Joe didn't answer, but whipped around, his gaze searching the ground.

"What are you looking for?"

He picked up a brick from the path border. "I need something to smash this window." He ripped off his sports jacket and wrapped it around his hand and arm.

I looked over at the front door in desperation. *Hold on.* Was it not quite shut all the way? I ran over and grabbed the knob.

The door swung open, revealing a magnificent two-story foyer with dual staircases, one curving up on each side. Dolls sat on every step, as far as the eye could see.

Joe dashed past me, dropping the brick on the entry mat and heading for the study. I ran after him.

Harriet was clutching the Tudor mansion with both hands as if someone were trying to take it from her.

"Harriet!" I skirted between tables with more dollhouses and displays, trying to find a passageway through.

"Don't touch her!" Joe shouted. He grabbed a Queen Anne chair and shoved it at Harriet like a crazed lion tamer. Her body crumpled to the floor in an ungainly heap.

I gasped. "My God, Joe, what's the matter with you?"

He ignored me, frowning at the dollhouse. "I'll call 911," he snapped. "You start CPR on her, and don't touch *that* damn thing."

With one last jab of his forefinger at the Tudor mansion, he jogged back out to the foyer. A moment later I heard his footsteps clattering on the stairs down to the basement.

Harriet stared up at me with sightless eyes.

Oh, boy.

I kicked off my high heels, hitched up my dress, and dropped to my knees, swallowing against a spike of nausea. Leaning forward, I touched my mouth to her thin, almost nonexistent dry lips and started rescue breaths.

Come on, Harriet. Only the good die young.

A minute later, Joe was back, his face grim. "The circuit breaker was jammed."

He picked up the chair again and knocked out the plug that attached the dollhouse to the wall socket. He frowned as he inspected the back of the house. "Something's wrong with the wiring here."

"How did you know to warn me?" I gasped, looking up at him in between breaths and chest compressions. "How did you know just by looking at her?"

"Some kind of sixth sense, I guess."

Joe had been shop steward for his electricians' union in New York before we retired and moved to Millbury for good. "You know, Daisy, like you can tell if something's a real antique or not at a glance? And how it would all look the same to someone else?"

Sirens wailed outside, and it was with a feeling of raw despair that I moved aside a few moments later to let the EMTs take over. As they bent down to start working on Harriet, I saw the look that passed between them.

It's hopeless.

Joe reached for me and put his arm around my shoulders. "Someone tampered with the transformer that runs the dollhouse lights, Daisy," he murmured. "Harriet Kunes received the full charge of one hundred and twenty volts coming directly from that wall socket."

Chapter Two

We stepped aside to clear the scene, now apparently a crime scene.

A good-looking man, early forties, with gray hair and smoky blue eyes, wearing a black leather jacket and jeans, strode through the front door.

"How're you doin', Daisy? Joe?" he growled, in a New York accent.

Detective Tony Serrano and I enjoyed a pretty good rapport, seeing as I had helped him solve a case not long after he arrived in town. Kudos for Serrano, and for me, a new friend in the police force. The local female population had been whipped into a frenzy over him ever since.

I explained about the eyeglasses and the faulty wiring in Harriet's dollhouse.

"Daisy, sounds like you might have been one of the last people to see her alive."

I stared at him. "Am I a suspect?"

"Everyone's a suspect 'til I figure things out." His expression softened. "Relax. I do need a statement from you, though. You too, Joe."

His eyes scanned the room, as was his habit. I imagined the whir and shutter close of a long-range camera lens. *Click.* Body on the floor, noting position and appearance. *Click.* Number of persons present. *Click.* Condition of the room. Curtains open. Lights on. Any sign of a struggle?

I quickly pointed out that the upturned chair was from Joe pushing Harriet away from the live current.

Serrano shook his head. "Well, this is a new one for me. Someone zapped by a fricking toy house. All right, let's take your statements."

He glanced around as if searching for a good place to sit. The study was crammed, so we moved out to the foyer, and then the opulent living room, where there was also nowhere to sit. Dolls occupied every chair and lined the seat of the Eastlake fainting couch. There was every imaginable style of dollhouse from farmhouse to plantation to clapboard Colonial Revival, either on tables or arranged on the floor. With a pang, I recognized a primitive cradle in mustard yellow I'd sold to Harriet last winter.

"Look at this place. Jesus Christ." Serrano stalked out of the room.

We followed him down to the dining room with its octagonal tray ceiling. A child-size doll sat in every one of the twelve upholstered dining chairs.

"Is it just me, or is that fricking weird?" He sighed. "Let's try the kitchen."

I didn't say anything as I walked down the hall, but secretly I agreed. This was a massive house with soaring ceilings, but somehow it felt claustrophobic.

The kitchen was thankfully the only place that wasn't chock-full of collectibles. It had dark mushroom-colored cabinets with crown molding, a six-burner commercial stove, double wall oven, and a pot filler over the range. The hardwood floor was of black walnut, like the rest of the rooms. This place must have cost well over a million dollars with all the upgrades. Grocery bags were sitting on the granite-topped center island and I ached to put the food away before it spoiled.

As if reading my mind, Serrano said, "Leave it, Daisy. Sit down."

I obediently sat at the table in the breakfast area. Joe took the seat across from me, and Serrano leaned against the island. There was one small dollhouse on the breakfast table—an enchanting Victorian with soft lilac siding and stained glass windows. Beds of flowers cradled a gazing ball in its little garden, and a bluebird sat on the ornate fretwork railing.

I went over the events of the day, while Serrano scribbled in his notebook.

He once told me that he wrote absolutely everything down. Everything, because you never knew which minute detail that seemed insignificant at the time could prove to be important later on.

He dotted his pencil on the pad and turned to Joe. "So what's the deal with the funky wiring?"

Joe leaned forward, elbows on the table. "Well, normally a twelve-volt transformer would convert a household circuit of one hundred and twenty volts down to a lower, safer level for the dollhouse lighting. The wires were skinned back too far though, well past the connection with the screws. The splices weren't soldered, and they should have been wrapped in electrical tape. Wet conditions also reduce resistance, and with the weather tonight, and her hands damp . . ."

"How'd you know the faulty wiring was intentional?" Serrano asked. "She coulda had someone wire it who didn't know what they were doing, or maybe the old girl herself had a go at fixing it."

"That's true, but what about the breaker in the basement?" Joe said. "If it hadn't been jammed, there's a chance it could have saved her life."

The bags on the kitchen island were calling to me. I couldn't stand to waste food. I wasn't sure why I was so worried about it. The dead woman wouldn't be able to use the stuff anyway, but between that and the lilac dollhouse, I was only half listening.

"What's important is the path the current takes through the body," Joe was saying. "If it flows through one extremity and travels across the heart to another extremity, it's much more dangerous than from, say, leg to ground. I'll bet you five bucks right now that the cause of death will be ventricular fibrillation."

I pictured Harriet grasping her dollhouse with both hands.

"But why was she still holding on to it? Why didn't she feel the shock and let go?" Serrano asked.

"A high enough current can cause a spasm that makes the person grip and be unable to release." Joe leaned back in his chair. "You know, it's funny. Guys can sometimes survive a super high-voltage shock, like from a power line, because it throws you back. It's not so much the voltage, but the *current*. Household current is especially dangerous because it exceeds the 'let-go' threshold."

An officer came into the kitchen, and waited patiently until Serrano glanced at him.

"The house is locked up tight, sir, except for the front door. No signs of breaking and entering."

"Thanks."

I thought about Joe almost smashing the window. "So could it have been someone Harriet knew and she let them in?"

Serrano nodded toward two mugs set out on the counter. "Looks like she might have been expecting a guest."

"But she just got home," I said. "And how could anyone mess with the dollhouse while Harriet was here? Even if she went to the bathroom or something, or left them in the study while she went to make tea, I doubt they'd have had time to work on it. Joe, what do you think?"

"It's possible, I suppose, but I don't know how they could have gotten down to the basement as well to mess with that breaker."

After we finished giving our statements, Joe and I decided we were exhausted, and it was too late to go out for dinner. Plus it was pouring now, so the outside veranda wouldn't be open. We headed back to our 1842 Greek Revival on Main Street. It was situated a block down from Sometimes a Great Notion, where the stores stopped and the houses began. It had been our vacation home for thirty years, until Joe convinced me to take early retirement from teaching.

To the casual observer, our house might *appear* to be in reasonable shape, but after three decades of never-ending restoration, it was almost time to start over with some of the earlier tasks. Like repainting the huge living room with its twelve-foot-high ceilings, original millwork, and six-over-six windows. Even when we were younger, it had taken close to a week to finish the whole thing, but now, the prospect of a big job like that was overwhelming. I didn't even want to think about the state of our basement. Fortunately, Joe was very handy around the house, because there was always something that needed attention.

While I set out some honey goat Gouda and creamy blue Stilton on a cedar plank, together with flatbreads, Marcona almonds, and dried apricots, Joe selected a bottle from the wine rack.

Jasper, our goofy golden retriever mix puppy, sat at high attention, his ears pricked, eyes never leaving the board of cheese and crackers. He wasn't technically our dog. He actually belonged to my daughter, Sarah, who'd rescued him off the streets of New York. She worked in film production as a script supervisor, and seeing as she was in Spain on the

set of her latest movie, he was staying with us. Secretly, I
hoped it would turn out to be a permanent arrangement.

Jasper panted and a drop of drool landed on the floor.

"Have a heart, Daisy, give him some cheese," Joe said
as he uncorked the wine.

"Do you have any idea what this cheese *cost*?" I shook
my head, but cut a tiny sliver, put it on a cracker, and held it
out to him. "Ow. Jeez, Jasper. You nearly took my fingers off."

We sat and sipped our wine at the butcher block table
under the glow of the schoolhouse light fixtures. Sometimes
home really was the best place to be.

Joe had remodeled the kitchen a few months ago, inspired
by an unfortunate incident when Jasper chewed up part of
the linoleum. One thing led to another, and now I had new
hardwood floors, cherry cabinets, granite countertops, and
an island for our cookbook storage.

"I never get tired of looking at this kitchen, Joe. It's so
beautiful."

"Hopefully this is the last and final big project we'll ever
have to do in this house."

I crossed my fingers. "Shh. Don't jinx us."

Joe smiled as his gaze traveled over my bare legs. I'd
slipped off my stockings and pumps, but was still wearing
the Dior. "Nice dress. Too bad I didn't get to take you out
to dinner. I was really looking forward to my lamb and
mashed potatoes, too."

He piled a lump of Stilton on top of an apricot and grimaced. "Sorry. That sounds rather petty under the circumstances, doesn't it?"

"It's okay. But poor Harriet. Who the heck could have
wanted to kill her?"

He shook his head. "No idea. But whoever it was, they
went to a lot of trouble. That's a fairly elaborate way to do
someone in."

I shivered. We sat in silence for a moment. For Harriet,

there would be no more dinners, no more celebrations, no more birthdays, no more anything.

After we'd finished our cheese and wine, Joe cleaned up while I quickly got changed. I came back downstairs and grabbed Jasper's leash off the hook on the kitchen wall. "Come on, boy. Let's take a trip around the block. It won't be a long walk tonight. I'm beat."

Once outside, I managed to put up the umbrella while the wind whipped along the street. Jasper ran behind me and wrapped the leash around my legs, but once I untangled myself, we were off.

When I'd first opened my store, the local economy was in bad shape, and most of the buildings along Main Street were vacant. I was lucky enough to get a relatively cheap rent, which was a big help for a start-up business. The lease had expired, and now I was month-to-month. I hadn't requested a new one yet as I didn't want to rock the boat.

Lately several storefronts had been rented, and it was nice to see the street vibrant again. Next door to my place was the new cheese and gourmet pantry shop. Across the street on the corner, a former real estate office had been turned into a garden-themed paradise with planters, fountains, terrariums, and birdbaths. A palm reader occupied the space next to Tony Z's, the barber. The latest newcomer was a chocolatier on the other side of Eleanor, just before the one-room schoolhouse.

I didn't need a psychic to tell me that artisanal cheese and handmade chocolates in close proximity spelled trouble for my waistline.

On the other side of me, and completing the eclectic collection, was the bicycle shop and Sweet Mabel's, the ice cream parlor. Jasper and I turned around at the end of the street and headed back.

Wait a minute. Did I just see a shadow moving inside Sometimes a Great Notion?

My first crazy thought was that it was Harriet, come back to steal the dollhouse, but then I reminded myself that Harriet was dead.

Fried, in fact.

Seeing as I wasn't so stupid to live that I'd try to confront an intruder head-on, I snuck around the back to get a better peek. An alley ran behind the shops, but it was dark now and I couldn't see much of anything. The rain had eased up so I closed the umbrella.

Had I imagined it? It wouldn't be surprising if I was a tad jumpy after everything that had happened tonight.

Suddenly the back door burst open and someone ran out, clad in a black knit cap, bomber jacket, and jeans. He was carrying my dollhouse in his black-gloved hands.

"Hey, you!" I yelled, forgetting to be scared. That was *my* dollhouse, damn it. "What do you think you're doing?"

Jasper, still not broken of the habit of jumping up on people, launched himself toward the intruder, who swerved and slipped on the wet brick path and dropped the dollhouse with a sickening thud.

Crap.

With a muffled curse, he scrambled to his feet and sprinted off down the alleyway.

Whether it was a good idea to follow the guy or not, I don't know, because I didn't have much choice in the matter. Jasper was in full, all-out, enthusiastic pursuit.

I hung on for grim death to the leash, trying to keep my balance on the slippery stones as I sprinted down the alleyway after him. Fueled by anger and adrenaline, my feet barely touched the ground.

There was a corrugated iron fence at the end of the alley. The guy was small and slim, not much bigger than me. When I caught up with the creep, I'd let Jasper have at him first and then whack him with the umbrella. I'd teach him to try to steal a little girl's birthday present.

With one glance back at us, he vaulted up and over the fence in one smooth move and was gone.

Heaving for breath, I stumbled to a halt. As frustrated as me, Jasper hurled himself up against the fence a few times, making the old metal clang and shudder.

I doubled over, praying that I wouldn't cramp up. "Okay, boy, it's over. Stop, Jasper. Stop."

Gasping, I dug my cell phone out of my pocket and called 911. Then I called Joe and asked him to meet me at the store.

A few minutes later, after I'd tried, unsuccessfully, to convince Joe that I hadn't intentionally put myself in danger, Detective Serrano pulled up in his black Dodge Challenger, a throwback to the muscle car of the seventies. He gave me a tight smile when he jumped out.

"I gotta tell you, Daisy, much as I like seeing you, this is getting ridiculous."

"I know, I know. What can I say?"

After the store's front and back doors had been finger-printed, as well as my poor dollhouse, we went inside. Chilled to the bone now, I gave Serrano the lowdown on what had transpired.

"How'd he get in?" Serrano asked. "Again, no sign of forced entry. Did you lock the deadbolt on this front door when you closed up at the end of the day?"

"Yes, of course. I always do." But then I remembered the passionate kiss Joe and I had shared before we left, the raindrops, and our hurry to get to dinner. Had I only turned the bottom lock on the doorknob and pulled the door shut? I couldn't remember. "Well, um, I'm not *absolutely* sure I did tonight."

"So there's no alarm system here?"

"No, there isn't," Joe interjected. It was a sore point between us. He'd wanted one for ages, and I never wanted to make the investment.

"Was anything else taken?"

I quickly cataloged the more expensive items in the store. The French silks, the Amish quilts, and antique jewelry. All still there.

I shook my head. "Not that I can tell."

We stared at the wreck of what used to be a beautiful dollhouse. The plate glass windows were smashed, the chimney was broken, one of the doors was lost in the melee, and the back panel that swung open to reveal the rooms inside was hanging off, damaged beyond repair.

Tears pricked at my eyes, which was sort of funny when I'd been so tough before.

"Don't worry, Daisy. We can sort this out," Joe said, slipping an arm around my shoulders.

Serrano cleared his throat. "So. What's the big attraction with what you say is a relatively inexpensive toy?"

I bit my lip. "I wish I knew."

The next morning, there was a commotion at the entrance to my store. The voluptuous redhead who swept in first was Martha Bristol, my best friend. She was carrying a vintage cake carrier of pink metal with a pinecone design.

"Good God, that doll gives me a funny turn every time I come in here," she said, as she always did, referring to my salvaged mannequin in the corner.

"It's not a doll, it's a mannequin," I responded, as I always did. I'd named her Alice, and dressed her up in clothing appropriate for the season. She surveyed Martha impassively now from under her long fake eyelashes.

Eleanor Reid, my fellow store owner, was next. She wore her usual outfit of all black. Black shirt and black pants. Her white hair was cropped short, and she was almost mannish in appearance, except for her sparkling gray eyes and elegant fingers with a pale pink manicure.

"You guys say the same thing to each other every day,"

she said to Martha and me. "You know that's a sign of getting old, don't you? When you keep repeating yourself?"

Martha dumped the cake container on the counter.
"Damn it, woman. I most certainly am *not* old. And I can
prove it. Ask Cyril who kept him up all night last night."

"La-la-la!" I stuck my fingers in my ears. "Too much
information."

Cyril Mackey was the owner of the local salvage yard,
and Martha's latest renovation project. She'd improved his
toilette, smartened up his wardrobe, and he was now pass-
ably decent. Quite attractive, in fact, compared with his
previous impersonation of a homeless person. Sort of like
Mick Jagger's long-lost cousin.

Yes, they were an odd couple, but when Cupid's arrow
finds you, there's not much you can do about it.

Martha whipped the cover off the cake just as Detective
Serrano strode into the store.

"Well, Detective Officer Sir, you are just in time for treats.
White Chocolate Raspberry Cheesecake. Made by yours
truly." She beamed at him as she cut a massive slice and put
it onto a plate. She was a fabulous baker and brought her
creations into the store so she wouldn't be tempted to eat
them at home. But then she came here and ate them anyway.

"Looks amazing, Martha. Thanks." He accepted the plate
and leaned up against the counter. "How are you doing after
the break-in last night, Daisy?"

"What break-in? What's this?" Martha spun around to
me. "Was anything stolen?"

"No. Only my dollhouse, but I got it back, thanks to
Jasper." I poured four mugs of coffee. "It's a little worse for
wear, though."

Serrano's blue eyes narrowed. "This might *seem* to be a
simple break-in, but it could also be connected to a murder,"
he explained, as he dug into the cheesecake. "Last night's

victim seemed overly interested in this item, and now that person is dead."

Martha frowned, and placed her hands on her ample hips. "What victim? *Who's* dead?" She was used to being the purveyor of news, not the last to know.

"Harriet Kunes," I said. "And she offered me a ridiculous amount for it, and now she's been electrocuted."

"Good God." Martha sniffed. "Well, I know who *my* main suspect would be if *I* was investigating this case."

Serrano's gaze met mine and I hid a smile. "Pray tell," he said.

"Harriet's estranged husband, Dr. Birch Kunes, of course. He wanted a divorce to marry Bettina Waters, his receptionist, but Harriet refused to give him one."

"Wasn't Harriet a lot older than him?" I asked, picturing Harriet's lined, scowling face, and the good-looking endocrinologist with a practice in Doylestown.

"Yes. By at least ten years. She put him through medical school. They didn't have any kids. And get this—even though Birch moved out of the house, he's still renting a townhome in the same development because he wants to belong to the country club and play golf with his friends."

Eleanor wrinkled her nose. "That's kind of weird." She cut a piece of cheesecake even larger than Serrano's and placed it on one of my nineteenth-century Rockingham floral plates.

Martha rolled her eyes at me and cut herself the barest sliver. Eleanor ate whatever she wanted and never gained an ounce, which was a never-ending source of frustration for her friends.

"I gotta agree with you, Martha," Serrano said. "Kunes *is* the number one suspect in my book, but he seems to have an alibi. Says he was at a medical conference for three days and just got back this morning. But a cheating husband is, by definition, a liar. And once a liar, always a liar."

He dinged the tines of his fork against the plate. "I'm going to ride him hard. Make the good doctor account for every minute of every hour of every day. And not just yesterday, but the whole fricking week."

Eleanor shivered. "Ooh. What passion. What dedication."

Serrano glanced at me again, but this time there was more of a plea in his eyes.

I grinned. "So tell me. How does a person get a divorce if their significant other won't give them one?"

"Good question, Daisy. Under Pennsylvania law, Birch Kunes would have had to wait *two years* before he could request the court to finalize a divorce without Harriet's consent. That might just have been two years too long."

"Did you find anything at her house?" I took a bracing sip of the strong coffee. "Any evidence at all?"

He shook his head. "Nah. With the rain, there wasn't much that we could get in the way of footprints. No prints on the dollhouse either, apart from hers. The breaker was wiped clean. Not much to go on at all apart from looking for someone with muddy shoes." He chuckled, but without much humor. "There'll be something though. You know what they say: the guilty party always takes something away, and leaves something behind."

Serrano paused to shovel a section of cake into his mouth while we watched in fond appreciation.

"Fascinating," Eleanor murmured.

He nodded. "It's a tough one. The trick will be to find out *when* the dollhouse was tampered with. And who had the electrical knowledge to work on it? We questioned the cleaning people, who swear the house was locked up tight when they left earlier that day."

Martha cut another sliver of cheesecake. "I don't think Harriet had many friends. And she hadn't spoken to her sister in years."

"Who's her sister?" I asked.

"Marybeth Skelton, the real estate agent. Skelton was Harriet's maiden name."

"Wow, really? I had no idea they were related."

Eleanor set her empty plate down. "Harriet was friends with Sophie Rosenthal, too, right, Martha? I think she used to see her a lot."

"Oh yes, that poor thing." Martha laid a manicured hand across her impressive bosom. "Sophie was an agoraphobic, you know, Detective. They shared a passion for miniatures."

"I never knew her," I said, suddenly sorry that I hadn't known Sophie, seeing as I felt such a strong connection to one of her possessions. The dear little dollhouse.

"Well, not many people did. She used to belong to the Historical Society with Eleanor and me until she shut herself off from the world. You know, it was funny, whenever we visited, she was always perfectly made up, her hair always recently colored and set, whether she was expecting guests or not."

I glanced over to where I'd stacked some vintage train cases, all stuffed full of makeup when I'd purchased them from the same auction as the dollhouse. I'd thrown the contemporary cosmetics away, but kept some of the Art Deco compacts and silver brush sets. I imagined Sophie sitting at a vanity table, carefully applying lipstick for the guests who might or might not appear.

"Well, we used to *try* to visit her sometimes," Eleanor said, "but that miserable old bag Harriet was always there."

"Yes. Made us feel most unwelcome, I must say." Martha sniffed at the memory.

I watched Serrano taking this all in. This must be a long way from what he was used to. I pictured him on the backstreets of New York, tackling drug dealers, running down the mob, and now here he was, surrounded by a bunch of aging, gossipy females.

He stood up and placed his mug and plate carefully on the counter.

"Thanks for the cake and conversation, ladies. Stellar, as always."

We watched him leave. Nobody spoke until he got into his car. It was simply a pleasure to watch him walk, the way he moved, like a prowling mountain cat.

"He certainly is a fine figure of a man, I have to say." Martha made a small sigh of satisfaction.

Eleanor's gray eyes were thoughtful. "That man is a mystery all by himself."

Chapter Three

At ten o'clock, my part-time helper, Laura Grayling, arrived. I'd recently hired her to come in once a week on Fridays so I could attend some auctions and replenish my stock. The business was doing so well, I could barely keep up.

I'd met her at a multi-dealer antiques collective housed in an old barn just outside of New Hope. She made one-of-a-kind jewelry with scraps of Victorian wallpaper, fabrics, buttons, pieces of pocket watches, and the like, and we'd hit it off right away.

With her slender limbs and shy manner, Laura appeared delicate, fragile even, but she was the one who'd had the gumption to ask if I needed any help. In addition to giving her a paycheck, I also let her display some of her merchandise in a corner next to the vintage clothing rack and keep whatever money she made. She was wonderful with my customers, so it was a good deal for both of us.

Instead of the auctions this morning, I planned to head over to Sheepville and see if I could find some replacement parts for the dollhouse. "By the way, Laura, there's a guy coming today to give us a quote for a new alarm system."

"Okay." She set down the battered suitcase that contained her jewelry-making supplies. She wore a long cotton print dress, topped by a crocheted cardigan, and a green scarf that contrasted nicely with her dark chestnut hair.

"You're finally going to spring for an alarm?" Martha said as she gathered up the dessert plates.

Eleanor smirked. "Yeah, won't moths fly out when you open your wallet?"

I slung my pocket book over my shoulder and made a face at her. "Isn't it time *you* opened your store?"

She shrugged. "Suppose so."

"Oh, one more thing, Laura, before I forget. Again." I went behind the counter to grab a box of odd lot jewelry that I'd bought for eight dollars. Apart from a few items I'd taken out to sell, the rest was mostly junk, like broken necklace chains, one earring missing a mate, and brooches without the back clasp.

"Here you go. Work your magic on these."

"Thanks so much, Daisy."

As I reached for my keys, we bumped into each other and the contents of the box spilled onto the floor. I still wasn't used to having to maneuver around someone else behind the counter. Laura apologized profusely, her pale face flushed under her freckles, as she picked everything up.

Martha and Eleanor were busy fixing another pot of coffee.

Nothing like leaving the kids home alone.

I said a prayer for the well-being of my business and walked back to the house. I grabbed the large box containing the beaten-up dollhouse and put it in my Subaru station wagon.

When I got to the end of Main Street, I crossed over the intersection with Grist Mill Road and drove down the dead-end road that led to the salvage yard. The fence surrounding the property was overgrown with weeds and vines, and dotted with rose of Sharon flowers and shiny tendrils of poison ivy.

I parked the car as far inside the enclosure as I could before the piles of rusty junk blocked my way. Among chrome shower doors, radiators, and barbecue grills, I spotted an old carnival wheel with most of its colored paint missing. The kind that you grab the pegs and spin to take a chance. I picked my way through, carrying the cardboard box.

Past a pink octagonal pedestal sink, a portion of ornamental iron fencing, and a copper weather vane in the shape of a horse, a four-by-six-foot Coca-Cola porcelain sign was propped up against the side of the trailer.

The door banged open and Cyril Mackey stood there on the stoop. His hair was straggly and he wore a white T-shirt and gray sweatpants. "Hell's fire! Can't a person eat his jam and toast in peace of a mornin' wi'out someone mithering him?"

"Jeez, Cyril, seems like you're a bit *down in the dumps* today." I grinned at him. "Cheer up. I've brought you an interesting conundrum."

He snatched the box from me, still grumbling, and marched back inside. I followed him into the sunlit kitchen. He acted like a rabid dog, but I'd felt his bark and bite before and survived. Cyril was originally from Yorkshire, England, and had followed a twisting journey over the years through the coal mines and junkyards of Western Pennsylvania to end up here, getting more ornery by the mile.

He'd obviously been working on the day's crossword puzzle in the newspaper, but quickly shoved it aside.

"Need any help with that last clue?" I inquired politely.

"No, ah bloody don't!"

I sat down at the spotlessly clean breakfast table and told him the story about Harriet and the intruder. "Look at this dollhouse, Cyril. It needed a little work before, but it's all messed up now." I blew out a long sigh. "And I so wanted to give it to Claire for her birthday."

"Don't get yer knickers in a twist," he muttered. "We'll make it right as rain."

I knew he would, which is why I'd brought it here. Cyril was a genius at fixing things.

He hefted it out of the box and set it on the table. It was just over two feet tall from the base to the top of the turret, and almost as wide.

"This back panel needs to come off for a start. Not sure I can salvage this. It might ha' to be replaced." He squinted at the house from all angles. "Aye up. Everything's cock-eyed. Staircase is falling down, too. Think I'll have to take roof off and mebbe some outside walls, and start from scratch to make it true again."

I nodded. "Okay. Actually it'll be much easier for me to clean it and fix the peeling wallpaper that way."

He rummaged in a kitchen drawer and took out a petite screwdriver. As he worked, I looked out of the window.

In the field beyond was a graveyard for old cars. A Ford pickup was dark brown with decades of rust. Purple morning glory had grown over the pickup bed and was trailing its way toward the cab. A ray of sunshine stabbed me in the eye, and I turned, cupping my hand against the glare.

In the harsh daylight, Cyril looked tired. Exhausted, in fact.

As if sensing my appraisal, he muttered, "She's going to be the death o' me."

"What do you mean?"

"The woman won't leave me alone. I haven't had a good night's sleep in weeks. I'm completely paggered, I tell you."

He gently pulled off the back panel and set it aside. "And I'm an owd man."

"You're not that old."

He shook his head, his striking green eyes troubled. Cyril, a man of few words, struggled with the handful he allowed himself each day.

"See, Daisy, ah've been used to comin' and goin' as I liked. Don't get me wrong, Martha is a fine lass. More than fine, and at first I was happy as a pig in muck, but now I'm suffocating. She's got tickets for the theater, reservations for a bed-and-breakfast, and God knows what else."

I blew out a breath. I really didn't want to hear any of this. I'd become friends, if that's what you could call our somewhat antagonistic relationship, with him, long before he and Martha started dating. Now it was strange for me to be stuck in the middle. And, well, sometimes you just don't need the visual.

"Let's take a good look at this dollhouse, okay?" I said brightly, to take his mind off things. "Maybe we can figure out why it's in such high demand."

I removed every piece of furniture and we inspected it carefully. We looked in all the rooms and inside the three fireplaces, as well as up in the attic.

Cyril shook his head. "Nowt here, far as I can tell."

He was right. There was no hidden jewelry, no wad of cash, no bag of cocaine. Whatever had caused the fascination with this house, it was long gone.

We did find a secret tower room under the lift-off turret that would enchant Claire, but it was also empty. Still, the dollhouse would be safer here than at the store, at least until my alarm system was installed.

The bay window on one side would need to be replaced and the balustrade for the second-floor balcony was gone. I pulled out a notepad from my bag and made a list.

"Can I leave it here with you, Cyril? I'm going to buy some replacement parts in Sheepville this morning."

"Suit yerself."

While I took some measurements, he ran his hand over the roof. "Those are real hand-painted wooden shingles. Someone must 'ave stuck them on one at a time."

A bunch of them were missing now. I winced at the amount of work it would require. "That should keep you out of trouble for a while."

"Oh, aye?" He grimaced, but he didn't say anymore. I could see he was intrigued with the challenge.

I usually brought him coffee every morning, so I figured I had a few goodwill dollars stored up in my Cyril Mackey bank account. I also thought I'd steal an idea from Harriet's house and paint this one that same soft lilac color with pale yellow on the gingerbread trim.

While Cyril was inspecting the staircase, I slid the newspaper over and picked it up. I would only have a few seconds before it was ripped out of my hands.

Nine across. An eight-letter word. *Consumed by repairs.*

As expected, he snatched the paper. "Be off wi' ye, now."

I was still thinking about the clue as I trudged off to my car. Thoughts whirled inside my head. People obsessing over dollhouses. Cyril always fixing things.

As I backed the Subaru out beyond the fence, I rolled down the window.

"Fixation," I yelled.

Cyril Mackey shook his fist at me.

Next stop was Sheepville, a neighboring town about five miles away, where I'd heard there was a wonderful store that sold miniatures and dollhouses.

It was located in a strip-style shopping center near the center of town. It didn't look like much from the outside, but once I stepped inside the door, I entered a magical wonderland of tiny delights.

There was anything you could want to decorate a dollhouse—from a box of Christmas ornaments to put in the attic to a potluck casserole and candelabra for the dining table. Hundreds of parts in packets hung on hooks along one wall. I should be able to find my missing door and chimney there. Display cases held finished houses and dollhouse kits, and counter cases were full of dolls, teddy bears, furniture, and carpets. The shelves dazzled with all kinds of building components and accessories, from wallpaper and roof shingles to kitchen paraphernalia, plants, and even tiny dogs and cats.

I quickly found out that the owner, Jeanne, loved to talk about her merchandise.

"We have everything here you could possibly think of. Even usable miniature toilet paper for the bathrooms."

"You're kidding me!"

"Nope," she said proudly. Her white hair was cut in an old-fashioned pageboy style, and she wore a T-shirt with appliquéd rosebuds under an open denim shirt and stretchy pants. When she smiled, her dimples deepened into long curves on each pink cheek. "How long have you been collecting, sweetheart?"

"Oh, I don't think I'm a *collector*. I just want to fix up an old dollhouse I bought to give to someone as a present."

"Ah, yes, well, now you see, there are different schools of thought among collectors, from people who gaily mix and match furniture from various periods, perhaps someone such as yourself . . ." Here Jeanne chuckled and coughed lightly. "To those who consider that if it *looks* authentic, it's good enough. And then, of course, you have the historically accurate collector who wants drawers that actually open and close."

She kept talking about scale and historical detail while

I wandered through the store with her. I gave myself a mini-lecture to be patient because I might learn something. I already knew that dollhouses were a one-inch to one-foot scale, although the very old ones didn't always conform.

A whole street of shops and houses that looked a lot like Millbury sat on one long display table. I bent down and peered inside the window of the dressmaker's store, admiring the replica of a vintage Singer sewing machine, the spools of ribbon, pairs of scissors, and the little dress form holding a half-finished dress.

But it was the display in the middle of the store of finely crafted miniature furniture that really caught my eye. "Wow, Jeanne. This is incredible stuff."

Jeanne clasped her hands together. "Oh, yes, aren't they? They're made by Tracy McEvoy, a local artist. Everyone calls her "Mac" though. Aren't they wonderful?"

"I assume they're quite expensive?" The highboy would be perfect for one of the bedrooms of the Victorian, but I winced in anticipation of the price.

"Um, well, yes, I suppose so." Jeanne beamed at me. I couldn't tell if she was truly ingenuous or just a brilliant saleswoman. "Anyway, you don't have to worry about it because Mac is completely backed up with orders. For at least the next year or so."

"A *year*?"

She nodded. "A local reporter wrote an article about her, which gave her more business than she could possibly handle. Plus there's an important dollhouse show and competition coming up tomorrow. Here's a brochure."

As we walked on, Jeanne lowered her voice. "She's been pushed to the absolute breaking point by Harriet Kunes, who *commandeered* her to work on several pieces for the show. Mac's grandfather clock, for instance, takes three weeks to create, and she's had no time to make anything for anyone else. Ardine Smalls was spitting bullets."

Jeanne obviously hadn't heard the news of Harriet's untimely demise. "Ardine Smalls?"

"Oh, she's another collector. They're usually the top two favorites in the competition, don't you know."

I cleared my throat. "I guess you didn't hear. Harriet Kunes was found dead last night."

"Oh, dear." Jeanne straightened the flaps of her denim shirt. "Well, I suppose Mac will probably sell her creations to Ardine now."

I blinked at this rapid acceptance of the news of Harriet's death.

The phone rang and Jeanne bustled off to answer it. I selected the building supplies I needed, as well as some Victorian double doors, gingerbread trim, and window boxes for the first floor. Perhaps a hanging fern for the wrap-around porch, too. I also couldn't resist a tiny toaster oven with two pieces of toast sticking out, and a silver toast rack, because it reminded me of Cyril. Lastly, I picked up some Halloween decorations in honor of Claire's birthday—a little bag of pumpkins, and a spell book with a candle.

Eighty-seven dollars later, I walked out of the store, wondering if this dollhouse was really a present for Claire, or for me.

Chapter Four

"Joe, you know how much I love you, right?"

My long-suffering husband nodded, a wry smile on his face, as we entered the Bucks County Expo and Conference Center on Saturday morning.

The Seventh Annual Dollhouse and Miniatures Show was sort of like Jeanne's shop, but exploded a million times over. Speaking of Jeanne, she had two booths side by side near the entrance, and she waved gaily when she spotted me.

I waved back, but then I grabbed hold of Joe's arm. "Remind me that I'm here to try to find out something about Harriet's murder and why someone would want my dollhouse so badly," I whispered. "*Don't* let me spend any more money."

He grinned. "Come on, you nut. Let's get this over with."

We strolled down the aisles, past traditional dollhouses and one-room displays in a box, all the way down to tiny scenes in a teacup. Some vignettes were in fun containers, like a fruit crate or an old spice cabinet.

"Look at this one," I said. Someone had taken a favorite vacation photo and recreated it in a room box. A bistro on a quaint Paris street, with red umbrellas and a chalkboard sign outside. The actual picture was pinned to the top.

"That's clever," Joe said.

In addition to the displays, there were vendors galore. One made all kinds of mini food items like donuts, pies, and crusty, floury baguettes barely an inch long. Another had fruits and vegetables displayed in boxes like a regular farm stand. I could have stayed there for an hour looking at the glassware alone—canning jars, water pitchers, wineglasses, punch bowls, and candy dishes.

We stopped at a garden display featuring two Adirondack chairs, a tiny lawnmower on the grass, a hose, and a bird feeder. The vendor used real plants—slow-growing dwarf-sized varieties—and Joe soon got into a deep conversation.

Gardening was something he could relate to.

"Hi, Daisy!" Dottie Brown, one of my friends who owned a yarn and fabric store in Sheepville, waved to me from the next aisle over. Her granddaughter was with her.

"I'm just going to say hi to Dottie," I said. "Be right back."

Joe nodded vaguely in acknowledgement as he asked another question about the watering and maintenance of the mini cypress and hemlock.

"You really do have an excellent husband," Dottie said when I caught up to her.

I laughed. "Poor Joe. Yeah, I think I'll keep him. How's Sam?"

"Oh, God, he entered the giant pumpkin contest again this year. You know, it started out as just a hobby. Now he's consumed by it. He spends four hours or more a day in the garden pampering those pumpkins." Her mouth thinned. "Time he could be spending with his grandkids."

I smiled at the little girl.

"I didn't know you were into dollhouses, Dottie."

"I'm not, exactly, but I've started a line of crocheted and knitted clothes for miniature dolls. You know, in this economy, you've got to keep moving or you get swept under by the current. And let me tell you, Daisy, there's *money* to be made here."

Thinking of how much I had just spent at Jeanne's, I could certainly agree.

We chatted a bit more, until her granddaughter gently tugged on Dottie's hand, and they moved on.

There was something about dollhouses that spanned generations. I saw several other grandmothers with grandchildren. I smiled at the wonder on the face of the child, but also at the expression of the older woman who had been transported back in time to her childhood.

I wandered over to check out the competition tables, and marveled at the room boxes with different interpretations based on one standard kitchen design. These were truly kitchens to drool over, with their travertine tile backsplashes, maple cabinets, and pendant lighting. I decided that the best designs looked as if someone had just left the room.

The one with a first-prize ribbon had a salad in mid-preparation on its center island, together with an open bottle of wine and a basket of French bread. I cheered to see the tiny dog bowl in the corner. These people had a dog!

"Prepare to spend a lot of time bent over at this show." The voice was young, raspy, and almost accusatory.

I straightened up and turned around. Too quickly. I sucked in a breath and pressed a hand against the writhing muscle in my back.

The person in front of me was thin to the point of emaciation. Jet black hair framed her pixie face. An unnatural black. She wore olive painters pants, a wrinkled white T-shirt, and a military dog tag necklace.

"You look familiar." She cocked a finger at me. "Didn't

you help solve the Angus Backstead case a few months back?"

"Um, yes, that's me. I'm Daisy Buchanan."

I held out my hand and she shook it firmly with a hand laden with silver rings and leather and braid bracelets. No limp fish there, I noted with approval. So many women didn't know how to shake hands properly.

"PJ Avery. Reporter for the *Sheepville Times*."

She swayed slightly from the ball of one foot to the other as if she were preparing to take a jump shot. It was tough to say how old she was. From her slight figure and the way she dressed, she could be a high school kid, or anywhere into her late twenties.

"Heard about the break-in. Where's the dollhouse now?" she demanded, in a clipped tone.

"At the repair shop," I answered in the same abrupt way, frowning at her. Why was *she* so interested in it?

A very tall blonde in a red halter dress that showed off her toned shoulders and legs strode by. It would have been hard to miss the look of disdain she shot in our direction.

"That's Mac. The chick who makes the furniture." PJ shoved her hands in the pockets of her pants. "She's pissed at me because of all the business she has now from the article I wrote. Go figure."

I shook my head, even as I kept massaging my back. "You know—um—PJ—I have to confess I'm a little confused by that. Isn't more business a *good* thing?"

She shrugged her frail shoulders. "You know. Artists. They're so temperamental."

A microphone crackled as one of the show organizers stepped up to announce the winner of the dollhouse competition. "Please join me in congratulating the winner of this year's show. Ardine Smalls."

"First time she ever won," PJ muttered as a woman hurried to the front of the crowd.

Ardine was probably in her late forties. She had shoulder-length dark hair with wiry gray strands poking through the surface. The kind of hair that had never been colored or straightened. She wore a black-and-white polka-dot dress with padded shoulders and an electric blue belt.

Her face was alight with triumph. I could see this was a Big Deal for her.

"You know, I never realized that dollhouse collecting was such a big business," I said to PJ under cover of the applause. "And people are so competitive. The world of sewing notions seems pretty tame in comparison."

She snorted. "You have no idea what these women are like. They're *obsessed*."

Ardine Smalls was gesturing for her fellow competitors to come together for a group shot. She laughed, but it was a nervous laugh, with her eyes darting from side to side. Two of the women stayed, but the rest drifted away. My heart ached as Ardine's wide smile drooped.

PJ rolled her eyes. "Oh, crap. I gotta cover this. Get some kind of brain-dead quote from her. Hold on a minute."

She pulled a camera with a huge lens out of a tote bag on her shoulder.

A minute later she was back. "Guess I felt like being nice today. I didn't take a shot of the *shoes*."

I glanced at Ardine's scuffed, down-at-heel white pumps and stifled a chuckle. Although PJ didn't have much room to talk. She wasn't exactly a fashion maven herself.

She clicked off a couple more photos of the crowd. "Yeah, so, like, I'm doing a series of articles on collectors. I interviewed Harriet Kunes on Wednesday. Thought it was good prep cuz she was pegged to be the winner." She chuckled without humor. "*That* was a waste of time."

"What did you think of her?" I held my breath.

She lowered the camera and stared at me with eyes that

were almost purple, but again, not the kind of color to be found in nature.

"Harriet was the type of person who went for the jugular," she said quietly. "The type of person who made enemies easily."

I lifted my eyebrows at this quick and effective assessment. She might make a good detective if she ever decided to change her line of work. "And how about Birch Kunes?"

"Don't know much about him, but his future bride belongs to a group of women who meet at the dog park. I call them the 'wine club.' They bring wine and cheese and let the dogs play. You could probably walk your mutt and run into Bettina Waters there."

I regarded her more closely. How did someone I'd never even met know I owned a dog? Although I supposed Jasper and I were a regular sight on the streets of Millbury.

PJ shoved the camera into her bag. "I might do a piece on them next. All these rich bitches who have nothing better to do. If nothing else, it'd be cool to watch 'em all get stoned."

She grinned, and the smile transformed her face from determinedly sour to fresh and alive. She was quite pretty in a tree sprite kind of way.

"Thanks for the tip. I'll check it out."

"See ya." She disappeared into the crowd and I headed back to find Joe.

I passed a few men with their sons, engrossed with a miniature garage, motorcycle shop, or fishing cottage.

Maybe I didn't feel so guilty after all.

He was standing in front of a display with a card in front identifying the furniture as made by Tracy McEvoy.

Joe turned to me, a fierce excitement in his eyes. "Daisy, I could do this." He was a talented carpenter himself and had created or restored many of the pieces in our home. "I'll make a fortune!"

I smiled at him, glad to finally see him so passionate about something, the way I was about Sometimes a Great Notion.

The next afternoon I followed PJ's directions and drove Jasper over to Ringing Springs Park. It was a few miles south of Millbury, near a bucolic neighborhood full of old money, where mill owners had settled in years gone by. Gentlemen's farms, of stucco over stone, sat on pastoral acres with streams, ponds, and mature trees. Some had been built in the mid-eighteenth century and expanded several times over the succeeding years.

I passed long gated driveways, and could just picture the interiors: mellowed pine board floors, deep sill windows, huge wood-burning fireplaces, and gracious formal rooms.

Some were only a couple of decades old, built in the style of a French manor home or an English country estate. Here and there was a heated outside pool and spa, or lighted tennis courts, on professionally landscaped grounds. Inside these mansions would be yards of granite countertops, stainless steel appliances, and custom cabinetry.

Another magnificent place was a veritable compound, complete with guest house, outdoor riding ring, four-story bank barn, and stone creamery building. There was no number on the pillar, just the name. *Sugar Hill.*

But my favorite was a more modest farmhouse, surrounded by cottage gardens, where the slate patio on one side had a built-in barbecue and fire pit, and the rear deck had been constructed around a century-old tree. I could just picture myself sitting out on that deck, reading a book in one of the elegant gray loungers, shaded from the ferocity of the sun by the benevolent old beech.

When we pulled into Ringing Springs Park, I managed

to find a space in the lot, which was already fairly full. Jasper and I scrambled out of the car.

I breathed deeply of the earthy air. I longed to follow the trail that led into the woods where boulders littered the sides of the dry creek bed. In the distance I glimpsed the remains of an old mill.

But it wasn't hard to spot the wealthy-looking women with their coolers and folding chairs in the fenced-in area just off the parking lot.

As soon as we were inside the gate and I unclipped his leash, Jasper, the extrovert, charged toward the other dogs. I watched his easy assimilation into the pack as they happily sniffed each other's private parts.

Some of the women glanced my way, and I smiled and called hello, but they carried on with their conversations. I clutched the leash, standing there uncertainly, hearing the unmistakable pop of a cork. There was a trill of laughter and I told myself I was being paranoid if I thought it was directed at me.

Never mind. It was fun to watch Jasper. I delighted in his joy as he ran free, galloping around with his ungainly puppy stride, followed by a young golden retriever, a schnauzer, a giant poodle, and a couple of shih tzus.

I was about to find a place to sit in the shade near the dry stone wall, when an elderly woman came into the park carrying a backpack.

She bent down and set the bag on the grass, nearly losing her battered straw hat in the process. Out came a red tartan blanket and a carafe of what looked like pink zinfandel.

Her shaggy gray hound came up to me with a stiff-legged gait, gave me a friendly sniff in the crotch, and then ambled off to join the other dogs. With some more rummaging around in the pack, she retrieved some plastic wineglasses and attached a stem to one of them.

"Fancy a drink?"

I smiled at her. "Thanks, but it's a bit early for me."

"Oh, it's five o'clock somewhere." She spread out the blanket, settled herself, and patted the space next to her. "Take a load off. I'm Ruthie. Haven't seen you round here before."

Ruthie looked like she could have led a tour through the Everglades in her youth. Even though I was sure she was quite a few years older than me, her tanned legs were still in good shape. She wore a cotton T-shirt, no bra, khaki shorts, and hiking boots. She tossed the straw hat onto the blanket revealing short white hair, smushed down in places by the hat, and gave her head a quick massage with both hands.

"Nice to meet you, Ruthie. I'm Daisy." I sat down. "I only just heard about this place. A—um—friend of Bettina Waters told me about it."

"Speak of the devil," Ruthie said as a very attractive woman with a Portuguese water dog opened the gate. She wore white shorts, tennis shoes, and a navy V-neck shirt, and carried a camping chair in a bag on her shoulder.

Ruthie waved hello and Bettina waved back, a huge smile on her face. She had an amazing body, with lush dark hair, perfect white teeth, and breasts as pert as a teenager's. The wine club group greeted her and shifted their chairs to let her into the circle.

A little while later, a couple of the women who had been chatting with Bettina strolled over to us. Without asking, they helped themselves to two glasses of Ruthie's wine.

"Suppose you heard about Harriet Kunes, Ruthie." The taller one with patrician features and perfectly coiffed gray hair peered down at us. She wore a pearl necklace with her culottes and striped top, and had a hint of a smoker's growl. Or maybe it was from barking orders at her housekeeper.

Ruthie's eyebrows shot up in question.

"Dead. Massive heart attack." Pearl Necklace slugged down some wine and flicked a glance over me, but didn't introduce herself.

I kept quiet as I didn't want to disturb the flow of this conversation.

"Oh, my," Ruthie said.

"I heard she was electrocuted," said the other woman, who was shorter and jowly, with hair cut higher in the back than the front. One blond bang fell into her eyes, and she kept pushing it back with the hand that wasn't clutching her plastic cup.

"Whatever. It was just as well," said the tall one. "It would have cost Birch Kunes a *fortune* to get divorced. Guess he was willing to pay the price. Or maybe not. Maybe he didn't feel like splitting everything."

"Shh. Don't talk like that." Ruthie took a deep swallow. "Bettina is a receptionist at Birch's medical practice, you know," she whispered to me, her gaze a little unfocused.

"More like *gold digger* is her real job." The shorter one filled up her glass again. There were red curved marks at the corner of her mouth. These two must have polished off their bottle of pinot noir and now were scraping the bottom of the barrel with Ruthie's pink zin.

Pearl Necklace chuckled. "She's had a lot of *work* done, too." She made quote signs in the air with her long fingers.

Whatever it was, it was well done. Bettina was a beautiful woman, without the usual fish lips or frightened expression from plastic surgery. She simply looked well cared for. And just sixty seconds ago, these two had been acting like her best friends.

A cloud passed over the sun and I shivered, even though the afternoon was mild.

Like someone walking over my grave.

Chapter Five

Bettina left the park at that moment, tripping over the dog's leash, her camping chair flopping open. As she struggled to put it back in the bag, she flashed a wide smile at us again. There was a smile on my face, too, as I watched her leave. Even though we hadn't exchanged a word, I liked her. It was sort of endearing that such a beauty was also a bit of a klutz.

"She's a very attractive woman," I murmured.

"Humph." Pearl Necklace peered down at me. "I suppose Birch Kunes is sitting pretty now, too. Don't suppose Harriet ever changed her will. She was always hoping he'd come back to her one day, the dope."

"Maybe if Harriet had cared more about her appearance," said the blonde, blinking against a stray hair in her eye. "She was always more concerned with those stupid dollhouses of hers."

After a while, they drifted back over to the main group

with their coolers that were no doubt full of pricey pinot grigio and chardonnay.

"Who *were* those ladies?" I whispered.

Ruthie laughed, a raucous, gusty sound. "Is that what you call 'em? The tall one is Virginia Axelrod and the blonde is Bobbie Zwick."

"It doesn't bother you that they drink your wine like that?"

"Oh, hell, I got plenty more where that came from. In a box on my kitchen counter. Old Sourface Ginny would die if she knew she was drinking box wine. Sure you don't want some?"

"I'm fine, thanks."

"Everyone shares if someone needs a drink. Anyhoo, I really only come here for Max's sake."

She fondly watched the shaggy gray dog amble after the pack. Jasper was having the time of his life, gamboling around, his tongue hanging out of one side of his mouth.

The sun had reappeared, and I leaned back on the soft blanket, drowsy in the meadow-like setting.

"Poor Harriet." Ruthie filled up her plastic cup. "Wonder when the funeral will be?"

"I don't know," I said. "I guess they're doing the autopsy now."

"Although at least she had a will. Sophie Rosenthal never even wrote one. She was Harriet's best friend, you know."

"Yes, I heard."

"Probate only just closed. Son of a biscuit. These things take so long to settle."

Ruthie shook her head. She leaned forward with her elbows on her knees, looking out into the field, one age-spotted hand holding her wine. "Sophie never married and didn't have any kids. Everything *would* have gone to her brother, but he and his wife died in a car crash about a month before Sophie herself passed away. Terrible. Her nephew got everything. The whole kit and caboodle."

Jasper came over to me now, panting, his ribs heaving, mouth open in a wide grin. He hadn't stopped running for a second since we arrived at the park.

I ruffled the fur on his ears. "Hey, boy. Did you have a good time with all those other dogs?" I made a mental note to bring a bottle of water and a dish for him next time.

Ruthie smacked her lips after draining the last of her wine. "There was a stepdaughter, too, but no one really knew her. Strange girl. Took off after her parents were killed. Supposably to join the Peace Corps. But no one has heard from her since."

"What did Sophie die of?" I asked.

"Overdose of insulin. Diabetic." Ruthie shook the last drops out of her plastic glass and tossed it in the backpack. "Accident or suicide, who knows, but she was real tore up by the loss of her brother. Some say it's the grief that killed her."

Ruthie mumbled that it was time for her to go and I helped her fold the blanket and put everything away. She gave me a little wave and staggered off toward the gate. Even the dog stumbled.

I watched them for a minute to make sure she wasn't going to get into a car, but a couple of minutes later, she trudged up the driveway of an old stone Colonial not far from the park entrance.

I opened up Sometimes a Great Notion early on Monday morning. According to Laura, last Friday had been an unusually busy day, and I'd need to replenish some of the displays. I slipped a Pink Martini CD into the sound system and started the essential pot of coffee.

For a few moments, I leaned on the ten-drawer seed counter, manufactured by the Walker Bin Company, breathing in the store's familiar smell of furniture polish and soothing lavender, and perhaps a hint of wash day from the crisp linens and well-laundered tablecloths and aprons.

The counter had glass-fronted loading bins that housed all manner of sewing notions, ribbons, and hair accessories. Thanks to my recent assistance with a criminal investigation, it now had a nice bullet hole in the front of it.

To my way of thinking, it only enhanced the value. People loved it when a particular item had a story attached. And provenance was key. Not that I would ever sell this prized possession.

Alice, the mannequin in the corner, also had a bullet hole. Right through her left breast. One that was meant for me.

It was carefully covered now with a Bob Mackie–Ray Aghayan dress, a psychedelic, slinky full-length number in a black, white, rose, and orange design of stripes and flowers that came up to her neck in a V-shape, but left her beautiful shoulders and collarbone bare.

I shook off the wisps of bad memories like so many cobwebs with a feather duster and hurried upstairs to fetch a couple of boxes. The main shop was situated in what used to be the front parlor and living room, but thanks to Joe and our friend Angus, the walls between had been opened up to make one space. The dining room served as an office and prep area, and there was a kitchen and powder room in the back.

From one of the boxes I unearthed a stash of Ocean Pearl buttons, still on their original cards. I lingered over a Lady Prim needle book from "Old New York" with a green, gold, and rust design of city buildings.

Next were some exquisitely embroidered linen napkins and a vintage tea towel that I was tempted to keep for myself. I trailed my fingers across its hand-stitched wicker basket of strawberries and wildflowers, but I'd learned early on that I needed to let go of these treasures. I was only their caretaker for a short time.

I came back downstairs and placed them gently in the Welsh dresser that sat against one wall, its drawers open to show a wealth of top-quality placemats, napkins, and tablecloths.

The doorbell clanged and a slim young man with black hair and a well-cut dark suit stepped across the threshold and closed the door firmly behind him. Most men entered this store tentatively, somewhat at sea in the milieu of sewing notions, but he walked straight in as if he knew where he was going.

"Chip Rosenthal." He stuck out his hand to me and I shook it. It was a good firm handshake, but unfortunately his palm was moist.

I stared at him. "Sophie's nephew?"

"That's right."

The nephew who'd inherited everything.

Had he come for the dollhouse, too? I was about to make up a little white lie that I'd sold it, but he slapped the package he was carrying down on the counter.

"Two copies of a new lease," he muttered. "Sign both and you'll get a fully executed original back for your records." His voice was a rigid monotone, only enlivened by a hint of nasal stuffiness, as if he had allergies.

"A lease?" I struggled to adjust to the fact that this wasn't about the dollhouse. "I'm sorry, but what are you talking about?"

He frowned, staring at me with eyes that were set deep into their sockets, so deep they were in shadow. "You know. A *lease*. For this place."

He waved a hand in the air around his head. "You're month-to-month right now. We need to get you back on a fixed-term basis again." He frowned harder, harsh lines prematurely etched between his brows. "Or, I guess you could always move out."

"Do you mean *Sophie* owned this building?" I gasped.

"I had no idea she was my landlord. I've always paid my rent check to the Bucks Mill Company."

He exhaled, as if resenting the waste of precious seconds to explain, and moved over to the center of the store where a collection of wooden crates were stacked together. "They're a property management company. And that's what management companies do—protect the owner's identity."

I watched as he flipped through some fabric remnants, tossing them back into an untidy pile. "I fired them. I have my real estate license. I know how to do this, and I don't feel like paying extra fees." Next he pulled the lid off a yellow Harvey sewing basket. Little wooden dowels inside the round wicker container held nine spools of thread, and it was also filled with notions such as a sock darner, a vintage can of Singer sewing machine oil, bits of trim, buttons, and tailor's chalk.

He took a few spools off the dowels, tossed them back into the basket, and moved on, leaving the lid askew. At the Welsh dresser, he opened up a neatly folded French damask tablecloth, and tossed it down, leaving it lumped in a white mound.

I gritted my teeth. I'd need to straighten up this whole place when he left. I scurried after him, picked up the sewing basket, and brought it back behind the counter.

He waved toward the envelope. "Why don't you open it? *Open it.*" For all that he was well-dressed, his nails were red and raw. Bitten down to the quick.

I picked up the package and pulled out two thick sheaves of paper.

He lifted the lid of the hand-painted Hepplewhite blanket chest and let it fall down with a bang. The rack of vintage clothing was next, and as he swished through the hangers, one of the dresses slipped onto the floor.

With an effort, I dragged my attention back to the lease

and quickly scanned it for the salient points. I gasped when
I saw the monthly rental amount.

"But this is *crazy*! This is three times what I'm paying
now. You can't just raise someone's rent this high and expect
them to suddenly come up with the money."

"Sure I can. You've been paying way below market rent."

"But . . . but look at this village," I stammered, my heart
pounding. "Millbury is miles from anywhere. It's not like
we're in the heart of the downtown Doylestown, for God's
sake."

Chip Rosenthal shrugged. He nodded at the antique quilts
hanging on the walls. "From what I can see, you're making
a decent living." He nibbled at his fingers for a second. "The
ball's in your court. I'm sure you'll figure out a way to make
it happen and we'll have a meeting of the minds."

I sucked in a breath and tried for a calm, rational tone,
even as my adrenaline was raging.

"Look, Mr. Rosenthal—Chip—I've always paid my rent
on time. I've been a good tenant."

"That's really great, yeah." He glanced at his phone and
pounded the keys on the screen. "And we appreciate that,"
and then there was a pause as he finished typing his message, "but it's time for a reality check."

If he used one more buzzword, I'd scream.

He looked up and smiled, as if this was the point in the
conversation where he'd planned to insert one. "At the end
of the day, either you sign a new lease, or you have thirty
days to get out."

"But what about all the work I've done? Refinishing the
floors, installing the display windows, a new air-conditioning
system . . ."

He grabbed a copy of the lease and flipped through until
he tapped on one page. " 'Article 10—Alterations, Improvements, and Trade Fixtures.' All alterations, additions, or
improvements to the demised premises shall on expiration

of the term become a part of the building and belong to the landlord and shall be surrendered with the premises."

He tossed the document onto the counter. "Heard you bring a dog in here sometimes, too. We'll need to up the security deposit."

"Why are you doing this?" I hated the quiver in my voice, but I couldn't help it. "Do you *want* to see me fail?"

He smiled again. "Of course not, but if you decide to leave, I have plans for this place. It's up to you. I'll be back in a couple of days to pick up the executed documents. Let's make it happen, shall we?"

Helpless with fury, I watched the hyper young man, so cavalier about ruining my business and my future, stalk out onto Main Street and slide into his new Audi.

Guess he wasn't wasting any time spending Sophie's money.

Damn it. What kind of businesswoman was I anyway? I should have locked into a long-term lease in the first place, when I opened the store.

But you didn't know how it would all pan out.

Alice the mannequin didn't actually speak, but I could see the compassion in her almond-shaped eyes.

Yes, but I should have been braver. I should have had more faith in myself. And speaking of businesswomen, how could someone who owned commercial property die without making a will?

Oh, Sophie. I wish I'd known you were my landlord, instead of some faceless property management company. Maybe I'd have contacted you earlier and this wouldn't be happening.

I'd never met Sophie, but I'd seen her portrait hanging on the wall of the Historical Society. Jet black hair pulled into a bun, dark eyes with an intelligent twinkle, not as deep-set as Chip's, and a strong, almost Roman nose. Although she was older than Harriet, her downy skin was beautiful, and the slight roundness of her chin softened an otherwise hawkish appearance. A red and black paisley scarf was draped around her throat, fastened with a cameo brooch. In the way of women of her generation, she wore vivid lipstick but not as much eye makeup, which gave her an odd, unbalanced appearance.

I didn't know what happened to the brooch, but the scarf was sitting on top of my Welsh dresser. I picked it up now, a hint of the expensive floral scent she'd worn still clinging to the material.

I was still standing there gripping the scarf, when Martha breezed in carrying the pink metal cake container. She was wearing a wrap dress in a leopard print, stretched to the limit of its elasticity across her generous curves, and an amber necklace and earrings that complemented her fiery hair.

"Good God, I have the most splitting headache, here you go, I made a Madeira cake, do you know a remedy for migraines, I *have* to feel better by tonight, I'm taking Cyril to the Pennsylvania Ballet at the Merriam Theater and—"

Her gaze narrowed on me. "What's wrong?"

"It's the store, Martha." I explained about Chip and the new lease and the hideous increase in rent.

"What are you going to do?"

I shook my head, numb with worry.

"Where's Eleanor?" she demanded.

"I haven't seen her yet."

"Do you think the little creep owns her building, too? Come on. Let's go see if we can catch him in the act."

I hung a BE RIGHT BACK sign on the door and Martha banged the cake tin down on the counter. Eleanor didn't allow food in her immaculate establishment.

We hurried across the street to A Stitch Back in Time. But when we entered, the place was empty. No sign of Chip Rosenthal.

Or of Eleanor either, for that matter.

Her building had taller ceilings than mine, probably twelve feet high. The walls were painted an eggshell shade, and she'd added some Ionic fluted columns for drama throughout, with strategically placed mannequins wearing antique wedding gowns. One wore a dress that had been cut in half with one side cleaned and restored to show the "before and after" effect.

The only decoration was a vase of white roses and fragile greenery adorning the gargantuan mahogany table that served as a place for Eleanor to consult with her clients and inspect the merchandise. On the right was a massive mirror and in front of it, a step stool.

"Hellooo?" Martha yelled.

"I'm back here," came a faint cry.

Martha and I knew enough to take off our shoes before we took another step. We'd been through this routine before. There was also a brusque sign at the entrance demanding compliance and a wicker basket full of crisply laundered white gloves.

We dutifully slipped on the gloves and followed the paper runner as it crunched beneath us, me in my socks and Martha in her bare manicured feet, past the dressing rooms until we found Eleanor. While the front of the store was airy and Spartan in its elegance, the back room was jam-packed, although still impeccably clean.

The walls of shelving held spools of thread, glass jars full of various sizes of pearls and beading, and a plethora of salvaged pieces of fabric, silk, lace, and other trims to repair old garments. Over to the right were four worktables. Some dresses hung on forms near the center of the room, and on one table a silk quilt was awaiting repair.

To the left was a deep double sink, and Eleanor was standing over it, stirring some kind of bath of steaming liquid with a long wooden handle.

"What the hell are you doing?" Martha exploded. "You look like one of Macbeth's witches."

She grinned at us. "Double, double, toil and trouble, fire burn and cauldron bubble . . ."

In spite of *my* troubles, I had to smile back. Dressed in black, with her white hair and sharp features, boiling up her signature concoction to safely take stains out of yellowing antique fabrics, she did slightly resemble one of Shakespeare's ancient hags.

One of the things I'd learned from Eleanor when buying a bolt of fabric was to unroll the whole thing. Brown stains might be lurking inside that aren't visible in the first pristine layer. She'd rescued several items for me with her secret recipe that had something to do with Borax and hot water.

"Eye of newt and toe of frog, wool of bat and tongue of dog—"

Martha waved a hand impatiently. "Yes, yes, never mind all that nonsense right now. Look here. Daisy has a serious problem."

"What is it? What's going on?" Eleanor let go of the handle in the milky brew.

I found that not only was I incapable of standing upright, I'd lost the power of speech. Shaky, and more than a tad dizzy, I sat down at a worktable that held an old Singer sewing machine and a gooseneck desk lamp.

Martha waited a couple of seconds, and then answered for me. "She just found out she has a new landlord who's tripled her rent!"

"What? Who is it?"

"Sophie's nephew. Chip Rosenthal." Martha flipped her red mane of hair over one shoulder. "God, it's hot back here. He says she has to sign a new lease or has thirty days to get out. Do you believe that crap?"

Eleanor swiped a hand across her brow, her cheeks

flushed from the heat of the water. "I never met him, but I always heard he was a twit."

"How about you? Do you rent this store, Eleanor?" Martha asked.

"Hell, no, I bought the building when I moved here. Paid cash for my house *and* the store. I don't have a big home like you guys, but there's no one holding a mortgage or a lease over my head. All done and paid for." She smacked her hands together like a baker brushing off flour. Eleanor had been a former costume designer, and in fact had worked on some of the same film sets as my daughter. She'd made a lot of money and obviously invested it wisely.

I slumped even farther down on my seat. "That's because you're a proper businesswoman. Not like yours truly."

"Maybe you can find another store to rent," Martha suggested.

"Look at this street." I waved an arm in the general direction of Main Street. "It's fully occupied now. There's nothing available."

Sometimes a Great Notion was more than just a store. It was my peace, my sanctuary, my passion. It represented something I had finally done for myself, after years of scrimping, saving, and thinking of others.

Eleanor unlatched a door in the four-door Moroccan storage cabinet in the corner of the back room. "Brandy?"

"Eleanor, it's ten thirty in the morning!" I protested.

"So? Your heart doesn't care what time it is. It just wants to stop racing."

I blew out a breath. Now that the shock and anger had worn off, I could indeed feel the thready race of my heartbeat, together with the peculiar sensation that my body was simply an empty shell. Nothing seemingly substantial inside. None of the usual stuff, like, oh, flesh and bones, for instance.

"Okay," I murmured.

She poured brandy into three snifters, pressed one into my hands, and gave another one to Martha, who raised her eyebrows, but shrugged and accepted it anyway.

"Don't worry, Daisy, we'll think of something," Martha said. "You can't leave Millbury. You're a fixture here now."

"Hey, I have a tidbit of news for you," Eleanor said, as she slugged down a good portion of her drink and then began pounding a piece of cotton backing into submission with something that looked like a medieval torture device. "Birch Kunes and Bettina Waters are getting married next month. She's asked me to restore and restyle her grandmother's gown for the wedding."

I choked on a mouthful of brandy. "Jeez. They're not wasting any time, are they?"

Eleanor smiled, a slow eye-slitted smile that made me think of a cat rather than a witch. "That's because she's *enceinte*." Eleanor liked to drop French phrases into her speech. It impressed the clients.

"On *what*?" Martha frowned at her.

"Pregnant," I said. "Wow, is she really?"

Eleanor nodded and drained the contents of her snifter. "I noticed when I measured her for the alterations. She's not very far along, but *I* could tell."

I sipped some more of my brandy. That was why Bettina hadn't stayed too long at the wine club. Come to think of it, I hadn't seen her drink a drop. That also meant Birch and Bettina had been carrying on their affair for a while—a few months at least.

I gritted my teeth, suddenly sorry for the temperamental Harriet. Even though she had been a difficult character, to put it mildly, nobody deserved to be cheated on.

Especially not with a younger and more attractive woman. No wonder she'd retreated into her safe, familiar world of miniatures and dollhouses.

"Birch," Martha said with disdain. "What a weird name."

"Let me guess, they'll call the kid *Sapling*?" Eleanor snickered.

"Yup. He'll be a real sap." They both roared with laughter.

I stood up to test the waters, and feeling woozy still, leaned back against something that stabbed me painfully in the palm of my hand. "Ow! What the heck's that?"

"Oh, sorry, it's my needle board," Eleanor said. "To iron velvet. You put the fabric nap side down and—"

"Aargh!" I'd stepped forward in my agony and stubbed my toe on something else. "What's *that*?"

"Oh, sorry, it's my sad iron." Eleanor picked up an ancient-looking iron implement with a thick wooden handle.

Martha raised an eyebrow. "Aptly named. It's like a little shop of horrors in here."

I rubbed my sore hands. "Thanks for the drink, Eleanor, but I've got to get back." I hugged them both, left my half-empty snifter on the table, and stumbled back across the street.

Somehow I got through the rest of the day at the store, trying to ignore the queasiness in my stomach, and the malevolent package stuffed beneath the counter. I ate a piece of Madeira cake to soak up the alcohol and took out my calculator. In spite of how well the business was doing, I could only last another six months at that rate.

I called Laura and asked if she could work tomorrow, and after she readily agreed, I called the only real estate agent I knew. Marybeth Skelton. Harriet Kunes's sister.

Chapter Six

Joe enfolded me in his big arms when I got home that night, listening patiently as I blurted out the bad news. "Do you want me to talk to this guy for you, Daisy?"

I sighed. "No, it's okay. I can handle it."

"Maybe when you see him again, you'll get him to see reason." Before we retired, Joe had been the head negotiator for his electricians' union, and he'd never met anyone who didn't warm to him instantly.

"I'm not sure. It was strange, Joe. Like he just didn't care." I thought back to the scene this morning with Chip Rosenthal, and the seeming lack of human emotion, as if he were missing some necessary gene. "He says I need to come up to market rent like everyone else."

"What *is* the going rate?"

"I'm not sure," I mumbled. "I'm seeing a few places with Marybeth Skelton tomorrow for a plan B."

"Well, if you look at other places, you'll know what's

reasonable. Do you *have* to have a brick-and-mortar shop? A lot of your business is online now, right?"

"Yes, but . . ."

It wasn't just that. It was the camaraderie, the coffee, Martha's treats, all of it, that I cherished. Walking into the store each morning was a pleasure that never got old.

As a teacher, I'd spent years working on other people's schedules, on someone else's lesson plans, hours that I wasn't paid for. Now the hours I put in were for myself, and it would rip my heart out to have to let it go.

Joe maneuvered me gently down the wide hallway toward the kitchen. "Come and have some wine, and look at the fantastic stuff I bought for making miniatures."

On the kitchen counter, a mound of translucent sea scallops sat drying on a tea towel, ready to sear in the pan. Joe cooked a gourmet meal for me every night. I recognized his famous potato–celery root purée prepped in a baking dish next to a bundle of bright green asparagus. My stomach rumbled, seeing as it contained nothing but brandy and a slice of Martha's cake.

I poured half a glass of wine and tried not to think about how much the scallops cost.

Joe pointed at the butcher-block table. "See this, Daisy? It's a Dremel Moto-Shop jigsaw-workshop combination. I was talking to that girl Mac at the show, and she recommended I start with this."

I stared at the appliance that was about the size of a portable sewing machine.

"It's five power tools in one. Isn't it great?" Joe was nearly bouncing up and down in his excitement. "And check out this X-Acto Deluxe Hobby Tool Set. There's three knives, eight blades, a coping saw, pin vise, routers, you name it."

I sipped my wine, glad that he'd found something he was so passionate about. The timing wasn't great, seeing as it looked as though money would be tight now, but I didn't know how to begrudge him his dream when he had always been so supportive of mine.

He grinned at me. "Think I still need a soldering iron and some C-clamps though."

Joe was the same way whenever he did a project at the house. Instead of looking in the toolbox for the three nails he needed for the job, he'd go to the hardware store and buy a brand-new pound. If he was painting, he'd buy another paint roller even though the one we had was perfectly fine. Heck, even the roller covers could have been reused if he'd washed and dried them carefully from the job before.

As a teacher on a limited budget, I'd had to scrimp and save to buy school supplies for the kids out of my own pocket. Renting this home out as a vacation place for years and finally having enough to pay it off were a testament to my thriftiness.

"Don't worry, Daisy," he said, as if reading my mind. "Things will work out. They always do."

Things worked out because I made them happen.

Jeez, I sounded like Chip Rosenthal now.

I forced a smile. "Well, I still need a dining table and chairs for Claire's dollhouse if you want to practice."

He clinked his glass with mine. "All right! My first customer!"

The oppressive humidity from August was gone, and the brisk mornings were literally a breath of fresh air. The coolness caught in my throat, and I shivered in delight. Fall was my favorite time of year, but it was always so short. A rush of garden cleanup, preparing for Halloween and Thanksgiving, and before you knew it, it was winter, with its dark mornings, darker evenings, and treacherous roads.

As I put food into the bird feeder in the garden, I heard

the call go out. A rising, chattering chorus from the birds scattered high in the branches of the oak trees.

Breakfast is served! Come and get it!

I fed Jasper and then hurried upstairs to get ready. Marybeth was picking me up at the store, and I needed to go over a few things with Laura before she arrived.

When I came back downstairs, Jasper was hunched on the ground, staring out of the screen door. He could lie there for hours, entranced, watching the little sparrows fluttering around. It must be like television for dogs, tuned to the Bird Channel.

Half an hour later, Marybeth Skelton arrived outside Sometimes a Great Notion in a creamy white Mercedes sedan. As much as Harriet had let herself go, Marybeth was perfectly groomed. Not a gray hair to be found threading its way through the short honey blond, and her eye makeup was simply a work of art. She wore a silky zebra-patterned shirt, a scarf knotted smartly at her throat, camel-colored pants, and black flats with gold buckles.

I'd seen her face enough times staring at me from advertisements on shopping carts and on real estate FOR SALE signs that I'd recognize her anywhere. Admittedly the picture was a few years old, and she was probably in her early fifties now, but she still looked good.

"Thanks for coming, Marybeth, and for setting up these appointments so quickly," I said as I slid onto the leather passenger seat. "I honestly didn't expect you to answer the phone yesterday. I mean, um, you know, under the circumstances and all . . ."

"My sister and I weren't that close. It's just another day to me," she said abruptly, in a way that didn't invite further conversation. She stepped on the accelerator and the car lunged forward.

But one of my faults, or qualities, depending on which

way you looked at it, was that I could never give up on
something once I'd taken an interest. Like the crossword
puzzle I was compelled to finish every day. Eleanor said I
was like a one-eyed dog in a meat factory when I set my
mind to something.

And the murder of Harriet Kunes was still a puzzle that
needed solving.

Marybeth turned the car up Grist Mill toward River
Road. "The bad news is that nothing is available here in
Millbury, so it will probably mean moving to Sheepville,"
she said. "The only street that's zoned commercial is Main
Street and it's fully leased."

"I thought as much." I struggled to sit upright on the
cushy seat. "So, had you seen your sister Harriet recently?"

Marybeth looked at me and gripped the steering wheel
with crimson fingernails. "No. We haven't spoken in years."

She sucked in a breath as she maneuvered the large sedan
around a sharp curve. "The first place we're going to see is
in a nice shopping center near the movie theater. It's available immediately, and in the interests of full disclosure, I
should tell you that I'm the listing agent on this one. It's also
the cheapest one we'll see today."

When we arrived in Sheepville, I trailed after Marybeth
to a vacant retail space that was actually near Jeanne's store,
in the same strip mall. It was modern, one level, and quite
a good value for the square footage, but with none of the
charm of the nineteenth-century Victorian I currently occupied. It was only about five hundred dollars more a month
than I was paying now.

Knowing that commercial real estate agents made their
money on commissions that were calculated as a percentage
of the rent, I appreciated that she was showing me properties
in my price range. She hadn't bought that fancy car outside
by doing dinky deals like this.

"Carlos!" She snapped her fingers at a worker in

paint-stained overalls. "Come here. See these spots? They need another touch-up."

Carlos and I both peered at the wall. It looked fine to me, but Marybeth tapped on it with a long red fingernail, and he obediently applied his paintbrush. The store was one big open space, and I half listened as Marybeth talked about vanilla boxes and the landlord being willing to absorb some of the cost of the buildout.

I couldn't seem to work up any enthusiasm though. Maybe my malaise was due to a lack of caffeine. I would have had several jolts with my compadres by now, but didn't dare suggest bringing a cup of coffee into the pristine white vehicle.

"So. Do you have any idea who might have borne a grudge against Harriet?" I prompted once we were back in the car, heading east on River Road again toward New Hope.

Marybeth sighed. "Oh, Daisy, it could have been any number of people. After all, if she'd screw her own sister out of her rightful . . ."

Her voice trailed off, and her mouth tightened.

"Rightful what? Inheritance?"

She slanted a glance at me from under those perfectly shaded green and gold eyelids. "You're not going to give up on this, are you?"

I shook my head and smiled a fraction. "Nope."

There was a brief silence. To our left was the river and on the right was a towering slope of rock and ferns and rampant wild vegetation. Here and there huge logs lay where they had fallen, like a pile of giant matchsticks. River Road was a two-lane road with a double yellow line, edged in places by a low metal barrier. Sometimes the trees on either side cut out so much of the daylight it felt like we were heading for a shaft of light at the end of a long green tunnel.

"When my mother died, her will said that everything should be shared equally between me and my sister. Harriet took the lead in splitting up the estate. She insisted that I take my mother's little house in Point Pleasant and she would have the jewelry. There was nothing much of value there, mainly costume stuff, apart from her wedding ring."

We passed a weathered barn, a house with pieces of white stucco fallen off in places to reveal brown fieldstone underneath, and a tavern in a three-story Colonial situated on a corner. Black-eyed Susans tumbled over a low rock wall in front. It even had outside seating, if that's what you could call the ramshackle collection of faded green plastic chairs.

"Harriet also got sixty-five acres in the Ohio River Valley that she said were next to worthless. I took her at her word. I knew it was a depressed area, hit hard by the downturn in industrial activity. My mother's house was worth about a hundred thousand back then, so I thought I was getting the better end of the deal. After all, I trusted her. She was my older sister."

I bit my lip as I looked over at Marybeth. Even with my limited experience with Harriet, I had a bad feeling I knew how this story would go, and it wouldn't have a happy ending.

Her lips thinned. "But underneath that worthless land was a thick layer of shale, and six thousand feet below that was a mother lode of oil-and-gas-bearing rock. The energy companies paid three thousand an acre and a twenty percent royalty on production. A windfall for the people in that valley who are getting huge leasing checks now. Harriet received over two hundred grand in the first check alone. I only found out when I received a letter from one of my mother's old neighbors who didn't realize Mom had passed away."

I gasped. "But maybe Harriet didn't know that when she divvied everything up."

"Oh, she knew all right. Turns out Harriet was the one who contacted the lawyer in the first place to put together the association of the landowners."

We came to a one-lane bridge with a stop sign. Marybeth barely slowed down, and I gripped the armrest as the sedan swooped over the bridge. I closed my eyes briefly and prayed for no oncoming traffic. The road bent back on itself in a sharp S-curve and there were only inches to spare between the low stone wall and the side of the car.

"I put myself through school, and now I've made a success of my career. No thanks to my bitch of a sister. It taught me a lesson though. Now I find out everything there possibly is to know about a neighborhood before I sell there. I read the local papers front to back, and I maintain friendships with zoning board members and local developers. I won't let my clients be caught by surprise." She glared at me.

I swallowed. "Great. Good to know."

"Oh, yes. That was the first and last deal where I ever lost money. You expect clients to screw you over, not family. And *that*, Daisy Buchanan, is why I didn't speak to my sister."

I blew out a breath and glanced out of the window. We passed a nursery and a farm stand, and the trees thinned to reveal acres of open land. There was the occasional house, but for a while there was nothing but grass and utility poles, until the two-lane road opened up into four lanes.

The road straightened and the powerful sedan started to cruise at higher speed, carrying me farther and farther away from where I wanted to be.

More homes were clustered together now, with actual yards carved out of the wilderness. It was a curious mix of farmhouses, ranchers, and well-maintained substantial properties. Bales of hay were rolled up next to the road in front of one old white farmstead, plain except for its decorative porch columns. A red barn sat next to it, the wooden slats rotted where they met the ground. Down the gravel-covered side roads were wide potholes full of rainwater.

The only sound in the car was the subtle hum of the

climate-controlled airflow and the occasional click of Marybeth's fingers against the steering wheel.

While it was obvious she was bitter toward Harriet, why
kill her now, years later? And whoever the guest was that
Harriet was expecting that night, it certainly wasn't her sister.

We cut off River Road onto Lower York Road, passing
more signs of civilization—a Dairy Queen, a gas station, an
Italian restaurant, traffic lights, and shopping centers, until
we came to our next destination, just past Peddler's Village.

A nice cluster of one-story white buildings with black
shutters and plenty of parking in front.

"Here's the one I wanted to show you," Marybeth said
as she swung into the lot and parked in front of a freestand-
ing building. "It's a former antiques store, and the other
shops are an art gallery and a saddle and tack shop. This is
a great location, Daisy. You'll capture the tourists coming
from New Hope and Lahaska."

She was right, but the busy thoroughfare didn't quite have
the small-town charm of Millbury.

"This one's not even on the MLS yet. The owner is listing
with me for thirty days first."

The store had large, open rooms and nice display windows, and I could see how it would be a good possibility. I
tried hard to seem interested, and not like a spoilt child who
there was no pleasing.

Next we headed to Doylestown, and a shop on West State
Street. Doylestown was a beautiful town of tree-lined
streets, with a mix of Victorian, Italianate, Greek Revival,
and Federal buildings, some with gloriously ornate
architecture.

Streetlights were adorned with hanging baskets of flowers. It was the county seat, so there were lots of lawyers'
offices, and also upscale gift shops, fashion boutiques, and
chic restaurants.

The shop was about eight hundred square feet, and the

rent was double what I was paying now. It was very pleasant, but it didn't have the soul of my current Victorian either.

"The price includes water, sewer, and common-area maintenance," Marybeth said.

I took a deep breath. "Well, I can see that parking might be an issue, although there's lots of foot traffic."

"Increased traffic means increased business."

On our way through town, we passed the Starbucks at the corner of North Main and West State Streets, and I begged for coffee. It was situated in the Fountain House tavern, an enormous whitewashed three-and-a-half-story building that was over two hundred and fifty years old.

We sat inside and enjoyed our lattes, and I relaxed a little as I felt the caffeine surge through my veins. This was more like it.

"What did you think of that last place?" Marybeth carefully licked the froth off her expertly lined lips.

"It was very pretty, but a bit small."

"But how much room do you really need? Is there any wasted space in your current location?"

I thought about all the stuff upstairs in my shop that I could consolidate.

She tapped a nail on the table. "In my opinion *this* is where you should be. It's a lovely town, with lots of visitors, and you'd do well here."

I had to admit Marybeth knew her stuff. I hadn't given her much notice yet she'd found several places that would have been great for me.

If I wasn't so in love with Millbury, that is.

This would mean a half hour commute each way. Driving to Doylestown would be like entering the workforce again and going to a real job. I wondered how long before I'd resent the trip. The farthest I drove now was the five miles to Sheepville, and that was only once a week for major grocery shopping.

The few yards' walk down the street from our house to
Sometimes a Great Notion was a pleasure, not a commute.

I felt like crying and told myself to stop being such a
baby. It was business, after all.

"The rent is also higher than I'm paying now," I
mumbled.

"Everything's going to be more than you're paying now.
Face the facts, Daisy. You've been paying well below—"

"Market rent. Yes, yes, I know." I tried to wash the irrita-
tion out of my voice. "Thanks for taking me out today,
Marybeth. I just need to think things over a bit."

"Don't take too long. The good places don't last. I'll call
you tomorrow."

After she dropped me back in Millbury, I hesitated on
the street, unsure of what to do next. I should probably go
into the store, but seeing as I was paying Laura for the day
anyway, I decided not to inflict my foul mood on her. I'd go
see the one person who wouldn't care because he was usually in the same frame of mind.

A quick stop inside the house for my bag of dollhouse
supplies and I was off to Cyril Mackey's place.

Past one yard where the homeowner was pushing a lawnmower behind his white picket fence, making one of the last
cuts of the season. The tang of random onion stalks mixed
with the scent of freshly mown grass. Impatiens, tall and
straggly, and basil leaves turned spotted brown all signaled
the final last gasp of summer. A white hydrangea bush
boasted glorious pointed puffs of blooms, bigger than snow-
balls and tinged with a blush of pink at the tips.

I trudged along Main Street, glancing in the store
windows.

Damn all these new tenants. If not for them, I could have
given Chip Rosenthal the finger and moved into another space.

The five stages of grief were denial, anger, bargaining,

depression, and acceptance. I'd done the anger part, but now I was stuck on depression, and definitely a long way from acceptance.

I went into the Last Stop Diner and picked up a couple of BLTs for me and Cyril. The diner operated out of an ancient trolley car sitting on the corner of Main Street and Grist Mill Road. A real old-fashioned diner with sky-high pies, endless coffee, and abusive waitresses.

Cyril seemed almost cheery as he unpacked the sandwiches, stuffed with thick crispy rashers of bacon. The Last Stop got most of its produce from the local farms, and my mouth watered in anticipation.

"So, Cyril, how did you like the ballet?"

He rolled his eyes. "It were all right if you like watching a bunch of blokes poncing about in their knickers."

We sat at his kitchen table, and I gave him the lowdown on the exorbitant new rent for my store and how I might have to move.

"Aye, well, that's why I bought this land outright. I'll never be in debt to no one."

"You sound like Eleanor now." I knew he stubbornly insisted on paying for everything when he took Martha out for the evening, even though she was a very wealthy widow. It exasperated her to no end, but he wouldn't have it any other way.

I rubbed my forehead. I had a splitting headache, whether from worry or hunger, I couldn't tell.

"Here. Make yerself useful. Finish this puzzle." He threw the newspaper in front of me.

I looked up at him, openmouthed. Cyril never even let me see the crossword, let alone ask for my help. I wrestled with the clue while we munched on our sandwiches.

Furniture for some squirrels? Nine letters.

What the heck could that be? *Tree house?* The letters

would fit, but a tree house wasn't really furniture. Perhaps something to do with hoarding? *Cup hoard?*

Oh, jeez, Daisy. Not enough letters anyway.

I frowned as I picked up the last bacon crumb. I'd finished my lunch and still hadn't figured it out. And my headache was even worse.

"All right. Enough o' that." Cyril whisked the newspaper away. "You're mekking yerself barmy o'er it."

He went into the living room and came back wheeling a cart with the dollhouse sitting on top. I could see he'd made good progress already. He'd created a new back panel, fixed the staircase, and repaired the rotted boards on the porch.

"Wow, this looks great, Cyril. Thanks!"

"We can rebuild it. We have the technology."

"Yes, yes, let's just get on with it." I grinned and waved a hand at him, suddenly glad I'd asked Cyril to help. Joe was too preoccupied with his miniatures right now, plus he'd never finish in time for Claire's birthday. I'd had the experience with my husband of projects at the house that mushroomed into giant undertakings when all I'd wanted was a new towel bar. Weeks later, there'd still be no towel bar, but a ripped-apart, unusable bathroom. Oh, it would all get done eventually, and be gorgeous in the end, per Joe's exacting standards, but I didn't have that kind of time.

Cyril was bare-bones practical. Plus he had a soft spot for Claire, too.

I set to work repairing the wallpaper, smoothing it out millimeter by millimeter and gluing it back into place. There was only one patch in a corner that I couldn't fix and I decided I'd put a potted plant there.

I closed my eyes briefly, and thought I could still catch a hint of Sophie's haunting floral scent, clinging to the dollhouse as it had to the paisley scarf.

While I cleaned, Cyril stained the double doors in

preparation for installation on the porch. In companionable silence, we repaired the windows with new glass panes and before I knew it, a couple of hours had passed and the light was fading outside. Dusk was coming earlier these days.

I'd been so lost in the world of the dollhouse, I'd completely lost track of time.

"It's getting dark, I'd better go. Thanks, Cyril. Thanks for everything."

He nodded. "Aye up."

We still had a lot to do, but I felt better, knowing we'd finish on schedule now. There were a few projects left: fixing the rest of the roof shingles and the outside trim, painting the exterior, installing the lighting, and putting the furniture back. The fainting couch, carved rosewood bed, marble-topped parlor table, and Chippendale desk.

Hey, wait a minute . . .

"Cyril! Where's that newspaper?" I grabbed it and scribbled in nine letters. "Ha! Chip 'n' Dale. Get it?"

He looked blank.

"Oh, I forgot, you were probably still in England at the time. It was a cartoon from the fifties about two little chipmunks. Chipmunks are a type of squirrel. So . . . furniture for some squirrels. Chippendale. Chip 'n' Dale. See?"

Cyril just shook his head in disgust. "Be off wi' ye now."

I trudged down the long overgrown potholed road from the salvage yard toward the main road. As I got closer to civilization, I caught a whiff of singed-meat smoke in the air. Someone must be grilling steaks for dinner. I walked a little faster, shadows falling across the pitted tarmac. It was still warm enough that I could wear sandals during the day, with no need for a coat or sweater, but the nights were deliciously cold, down into the fifties. I'd snuggle up to Joe, comfortable under the covers, but with the bedroom windows open, listening to Jasper's light snoring and occasional close-mouthed barking as he replayed chasing rabbits and squirrels in his dreams.

T he next morning, before anyone came into Sometimes a Great Notion, I called Warren Zeigler.

"Hey, Warren, could you turn off your lawyer meter for five minutes, please? Look, I need some advice, but I can't afford a big bill. How about I buy you lunch next time I see you?"

He sighed, and I pictured the diminutive attorney taking his round spectacles off and rubbing his eyes like a sleepy dormouse.

I quickly explained about the lease and the huge rent increase.

"Ah, yes, I heard probate finally closed on the Rosenthal estate," he said.

"Is there anything I can do? And before you tell me that I should have renewed the lease before now, I'm already kicking myself."

"As to your business acumen, I couldn't possibly comment," Warren said, with a slight cough. He had a sense of humor drier than one of Eleanor's Beefeater martinis. "But if you're on a month-to-month basis, then yes, I'm afraid the landlord can give thirty days notice if he wants to, and you're out. Have you tried negotiating?"

"Have you ever *met* Chip Rosenthal?" I thought I heard a faint chuckle on the end of the line. "Well, I might try that again, if it's my last resort. And if I have to move, I'll ask you to read things over this time before I sign. But what I don't understand is that Sophie died in February, and I bought the dollhouse from her estate auction in June. How could any of her stuff be sold before probate closed?"

"Pennsylvania laws are more lax than most. They would probably let him settle some personal effects ahead of time.

Seeing as there was only one heir, it would make things that much simpler."

"Speaking of which, I heard that Sophie's brother also had a stepdaughter." In the back of my mind was some half-baked idea that I might try to find this girl and appeal to her for help.

"Stepchildren are not eligible to inherit when a person dies intestate," Warren said, one step ahead of me.

"Really? That doesn't seem fair."

"Quite possibly. But without a will, there are rules of succession. Sophie Rosenthal *could* have written a will and specified how her estate was to be divided if she was concerned."

The doorbell jangled, and Martha and Eleanor came in. I thanked Warren, and he said he would look forward to his three-course lunch at the Bridgewater Inn.

I chuckled as I hung up the phone. I'd been thinking more along the lines of an egg salad sandwich at the diner.

Martha laid a flat rectangular container on the counter and whipped off the lid with a flourish. "Ginger Brandy Snaps. These are a labor of love, let me tell you."

"Oh, thanks, Martha. I know they're a lot of work, but the customers go crazy over these." I hugged her and admired the mountain of delectable delights.

Eleanor edged closer and slid a brandy snap out from the side of the stack. "Daisy, remember how Detective Serrano made that crack about looking for someone with muddy shoes? And you know how I make everyone take their shoes off at the door?"

"We know," Martha said, with an arch look at me.

"Well, when Bettina Waters came for her fitting on Monday, she was wearing sneakers. When I moved them to one side, I noticed they were damp." She paused for dramatic effect. "And it wasn't raining that day."

Obligingly, I gasped. "Do you think she washed them? To get the mud off?"

Eleanor shrugged as she palmed two more of the brandy snaps. "Who's to say? They looked very clean though."

"Might I point out that these are for the *customers*?" Martha snatched the box away as Eleanor stuffed the treats into her mouth. "Good God. Did you see that, Daisy? It's like the woman unhinges her jaw like a *snake*."

The doorbell rang again and the reporter PJ Avery sauntered into the store.

"How'd you make out with the wine club?" she said to me, by way of greeting.

She was wearing the same outfit as on Saturday. Olive painters pants, and a T-shirt that looked like it had been tossed into a laundry basket straight from the dryer and never folded.

I smiled. "Okay, I guess. It's an interesting group."

PJ eyed the plate of delicate ginger crisps stuffed with whipped double cream.

"Have one, dear." Martha proffered the plate.

"Thanks. I'm so hungry I could eat myself." PJ murmured in appreciation as she licked out the cream and crunched through the rolled wafer-thin spicy cookie. "*Holla*. These are bangin'. Where'd you get them?"

"I made them."

PJ Avery stared at Martha with those strange purple eyes that had to be due to colored contacts. "Are you kidding me right now?"

"No. I really did. Have another." Martha beamed at her. She loved to feed people and watch them eat. Well, everyone except Eleanor.

PJ needed no further encouragement and grabbed one more. "Man, this is great," she said between bites. "Do you guys eat like this every day?" She yawned and stretched her arms above her head and the shirt rode up, revealing a stomach as hard and flat as a young boy's.

"I thought you said they were for the cust—" Eleanor

sucked in a breath and I couldn't be sure, but I think Martha was standing on her foot.

"How about some coffee?" I filled another mug to the brim.

PJ took it with a nod of thanks and downed a large swallow. "This is awesome. I don't usually get a chance to eat much with being on the road all day. Definitely beats gas station slushies and microwaved breakfast bagels."

I pictured her apartment. A full ashtray on the coffee table, a bottle of vodka in the freezer. In the cupboard perhaps a half-empty bag of stale pretzels and an opened box of cereal. The fridge would contain a lone Chinese take-out container, but no milk.

Martha shot a horrified look at her and nudged me. "Don't you have a sandwich in your fridge, Daisy?" she hissed.

"Yes, but that's my lu—"

"Hand it over. Can't you see the poor little thing is starving to death? You can always run home and make another."

While I retrieved my sandwich of crusty French bread, roasted turkey, fresh sliced tomatoes, and romaine lettuce, together with a pot of Joe's delicious homemade basil mayonnaise from the fridge, I stole a glance at Eleanor.

She had the air of an Olympic champion who sees the younger, faster rival nipping at their heels. There's a hint of impending defeat, but being the champion that she is, she won't give up the title without a fight.

PJ pointed toward a Hawkeye Refrigerator Picnic Basket. "Can I look inside that?"

"Please do."

She lifted one of the two hinged lids. I noticed a silver skull ring on her thumb.

"How does it work?" she demanded.

I showed her the metal-lined removable ice compartment inside the woven rattan basket. "You would put ice on this side to keep the food cold."

"Neat. Hey, you could use this at your wine club." She closed the lid carefully.

"They're not *my* wine club."

"When was it made?"

"I would guess in the early 1900s."

And so it went, through the entire store. She wanted to know what everything was, what it was used for, how it worked. She reminded me of the best students I'd had, the ones who always questioned, who were never satisfied with a pat answer. I showed her the passementerie—the tassels, ornamental cords, rosettes, elaborate trimmings, and fringes. She wanted to know the provenance of the quilts and the needlework samplers, the value of the vintage evening bags, the age of the antique spinning wheel and the cobbler's rack.

It was refreshing to see it all through her eyes, and I made a mental note of the things she was drawn to, noticing treasures I'd almost forgotten. A new arrangement to place them front and center would make the customers notice, too.

Now I beamed at her, just as Martha had done.

What really caught PJ's attention, though, was the box at the back of the store. I'd hung a former post office sign that said MAIL, except I'd crossed it out and written MALE. Underneath sat a wooden toolbox that Joe filled with treasures for the men, all priced at five dollars. Today it held things like a watch, a belt buckle, antique postcards, and a poker chip caddy. She finally picked out a Ronson "Tuxedo" lighter from the 1930s with an attractive green enamel Art Deco design. The front of the lighter swung open with storage for cigarettes inside.

"This is way beyond cool." She fished out a crumpled pair of one-dollar bills from the back of her pants, and after she'd searched her pockets in vain for another couple of minutes, I couldn't stand it anymore.

"Take it. It's on the house."

"Awesome. Thanks."

"There *is* something you can do for me in return, though. Tell me what you know about Chip Rosenthal."

She rubbed at her eyes as if the purple contacts irritated her. "Not much. I know Harriet Kunes didn't like him."

I sighed. "Damn it. I wish Sophie had written a will. Then maybe Chip wouldn't be the owner of this building."

PJ frowned. "Actually, during our interview Harriet said that Sophie *did* write one, but no one knows where it is."

"Really? Wouldn't there be a copy filed with Sophie's lawyer?"

"No, there isn't, but I did some research. In Pennsylvania a holographic, or handwritten, will is still legal."

"I guess working as a reporter makes you an expert in a lot of things."

Her strangely colored eyes sparked with intelligence. "Trust me, I know more now about collecting miniatures than I ever wanted to know."

"Why didn't Harriet say anything to the authorities?"

PJ twirled a bundle of German button mushrooms with toffee-colored stems as she paced to and fro. "She didn't want to tip her hand. She wanted to find it before Chip did, because she knew he'd destroy it."

It was as if a swarm of mosquitoes were after her and she had to keep moving to avoid being bitten. I was feeling slightly seasick and had to avert my eyes. No wonder she was so thin. It was all that nervous energy. "Do you have any idea what the will said?"

"No. I wish I did," she said vehemently. "Harriet was getting ready for the show, and I made some comment, and she suddenly goes, *Of course! Why didn't I think of this before?*"

"Well, what did you say?"

"No idea."

I told myself to muster my meager supply of patience. "*Think*, please."

She arched an eyebrow at me as if to say that's all she ever did.

"I was looking at her Tudor mansion—so perfect and proper just like her. I mean, it was beautiful and everything, but there was no soul to it." PJ glanced around Sometimes a Great Notion and ran a hand through her jet black hair. "Not like this place. This has character, you can *feel* it. You can tell something about the owner the minute you walk in the door."

I looked at my eclectic collage of merchandise and Alice the mannequin in her psychedelic dress and bit my lip. What the heck did my store say about me?

"Kind of how a book says a lot about its author, even though the writer might think they're not revealing anything personal about themselves?" Eleanor said.

PJ gave her an odd look, and I wondered again what went on in that lively brain.

"Yeah. Something like that." She snapped her fingers. "Hey, that's it! I talked about how a house tells a story about the homeowner, and Harriet stares at me and goes, *My God, it's the only place I didn't search!* And then she quickly ended the interview, and I assume, came rushing over here."

I blew out a breath. "Well, if Sophie Rosenthal wrote a will, she definitely didn't hide it in my dollhouse. It's been taken completely to pieces, with all its secrets revealed."

"Oh, yeah? Well, there's more." PJ looked around as if to make sure there were no customers in the store. "Something else I'm working on . . ."

She clicked her lighter a couple of times, making us all jump. "Harriet thought that the housebound Sophie was murdered."

"*What*?" Martha clapped a hand to her chest. "Murdered! Why on earth did she think that?"

"Cuz Sophie had been sad over her brother's death, but certainly not enough to kill herself."

"Did Harriet say anything to the police?" I asked.

"Nope. She had no evidence. She seemed pretty sure, though."

Eleanor cleared her throat. "Martha, as fascinating as this is, we have to go."

Martha rolled her eyes at me. "Meeting of the Hysterical, whoops, I mean, *Historical* Society this morning."

Eleanor was the president and Martha was the secretary. They hurried out, with the hyper reporter close behind them, pumped full of a thousand calories of cookies and untold milligrams of caffeine.

After they left, I stood in the middle of the store, deep in thought.

Did Chip kill his Aunt Sophie to inherit, knowing there were no other eligible heirs? And had he heard that a will did possibly exist, and was *he* the one who came into my store and tried to steal my dollhouse?

If there was a chance that Chip Rosenthal was not really my landlord, I was more than motivated to find that will.

Chapter Seven

I was in the midst of rearranging the displays that afternoon when a man burst into the store, looked around wildly, and grabbed my arm. "Daisy, help me! I've gotta hide. Please, I'm begging you, don't tell them I'm here."

"Go upstairs, Serrano. I'll cover for you."

Odd. The handsome detective was the type to stand in front of me and take a bullet, not leave me to face dangerous pursuers alone.

He'd barely made it to the top of the stairs when I noticed a group of women staring through the front display windows. One of them hurried inside. I thought I recognized her as one of the wine club.

"Hi, can I help you?"

"I'm just looking, thanks."

A board squeaked upstairs, and I coughed.

"What's that?" she snapped, on the trail like a bloodhound in heat.

"Oh you know these old houses, how they creak and moan."

She gave me a suspicious glare and prowled through the entire space, looking behind the vintage-clothing rack and peeking into the prep room.

I didn't have to be the psychic from across the street to be able to read her thoughts. *Where the hell is he?*

I put on my best professional smile. "Can I help you find something in particular?"

"This is a nice bag," she said, barely looking at the item nearest her, one eye on the stairs. It was an Edwardian silver mesh evening purse. "How much is it?"

I told her the price. It wasn't cheap, but after she'd made a few more circuits around the shop and lingered as long as she could, she whipped out a credit card and signed without question. I wrapped it in tissue paper, tied a bow around it with my peacock ribbon, and placed it in one of my signature shopping bags.

With one last piercing look around, she picked up her purchase and swept out.

A couple of minutes later, I announced that the coast was clear and Serrano crept down the stairs.

"Hey, Tony, I could get a lot of sales this way. Thanks!"

"She's stalking me. And it's not just her. There's a whole fricking pack of them."

I hid a smile. A single, attractive man in a small town is automatically fair game, and a haunted male who also seems in dire need of a hug is an especially deadly combo.

Today he was wearing a faded denim shirt and jeans, with a hint of stubble on his face. I couldn't decide which was sexier—the suave, elegant Serrano, or this slightly dissipated version.

As usual, my heart rate kicked up a notch in his presence. I was a happily married woman, and I might be fifty-eight, but hey, I wasn't dead yet.

I stole a quick look in the mirror. I'd recently colored my hair, so the gray streaks were temporarily gone from the dark brown. I was even wearing a little makeup. Thank God.

"They keep baking me stuff. I must have put on at least ten pounds since I got here." He rubbed his flat stomach, and nodded toward the window. "And I found *that* piranha waiting for me in front of my condo when I got home last night. She won't leave me alone."

Serrano rented a place in Quarry Ridge, near Claire and Patsy Elliott.

"Why don't you just arrest her for harassment?"

The detective rolled his eyes. "Daisy, do you have any idea how the guys at the station would have a field day with that one? I'd never hear the end of it. The only way Serrano can control his women is put them in handcuffs?"

I smiled. "I see what you mean."

"Besides, that was my first mistake. I'd heard about some women sucking down wine at the park, so I stopped down there to check it out. Make sure no one was drinking and driving."

I busied myself with carefully straightening up the already neat pile of shopping bags at the end of the counter.

"Turns out most of them live nearby, so they walk, and the ones who don't have a designated driver. One woman even has a limo that picks up a whole bunch of 'em. *And* the fricking dogs." He blew out a long, shuddering breath. "When I asked to be transferred to Bucks County, PA, I thought it would be a nice, quiet existence." He shook his head. "Thank God for you. And Martha and Eleanor, too, of course. The only sane females in this town."

"Ha! That's pretty sad, considering how crazy we all are." I chuckled as I went over to the Welsh dresser and picked up two corners of a Wilendur yellow tablecloth with a lily-of-the-valley design. Customers were notorious for inspecting linens and not refolding them properly. Or at least not to my standards. Without being asked, Serrano took the opposite ends and we worked together to fold it into a perfect rectangle.

I'd never asked what he was doing out here in the back of beyond, but I wondered for the hundredth time—what deep, dark secret was he hiding?

"So. Thought you'd like to know Joe was right," he said as he followed me over to the vintage-clothing rack, where I picked up a velvet jacket that had fallen to the floor. "Our guys checked Harriet's dollhouse over and the wiring *was* tampered with."

He straightened the dresses on the hangers, one by one. A Bob Mackie mint green strapless gown of pleated silk, a light blue taffeta number with matching bolero jacket, and a black chiffon evening dress. "Apparently the main power cord should only be connected to the primary winding. If it's connected to the secondary, the way it was, it can produce an extremely hazardous voltage when it's plugged in."

He pulled the green dress out from the rest and draped it across one arm, as if picturing a dancing partner's body inside. "This is a very well-made garment."

"Well, it is a Bob Mackie, after all."

Watching his tanned fingers slide slowly down the silky material, I could almost feel that hand against my own waist and I shivered involuntarily.

"Harriet Kunes had some lighting added to the house in preparation for the show," he continued. "According to the electrician, Larry Clark, he showed her how it operated in front of some other customers at his shop. It worked fine then, and didn't fry anyone. Clark was really shaken up about the whole thing when we questioned him."

He frowned and switched the hanger holding the black chiffon gown so that it was next to the other two black gowns on the rack. "These should all be together. Right?"

I stifled a smile. "Sure. That's fine. Now, Harriet came

to my store when I'd just opened. Did she pick up her doll-house right after that?"

"Yeah. Then she brought it home. The cleaning people from The Dazzle Team said it was just after they got there, around noon. She left them in the house and went to Tracy McEvoy's place to pick up some custom pieces. Interestingly enough, Mac was the one who recommended that Harriet use Larry Clark in the first place."

"Hold on a minute. Why couldn't one of the cleaning people have messed with the dollhouse?"

"They could have, except Harriet put the fear of God in them to never, ever dust the collectibles. They all swore they never touched it."

I pictured Harriet coming in with her groceries late that afternoon, not even stopping to put them away, bursting with anticipation to check out her perfect dollhouse, and install the finishing touches that she was sure would win her first prize in the competition.

I frowned, remembering the mugs and the bags on the counter. "What time did it say on her grocery receipt?"

Serrano grinned. "Nice, Daisy, you'll make a good detective yet. 4:32 p.m."

I smiled back. I'd felt a sudden kinship with him the moment we'd met, and it wasn't just because we were both transplanted New Yorkers. Joe and I had lived in the city for most of our lives, until we sold the condo to Sarah and retired to Millbury.

I appreciated the fact that Serrano trusted me with con-fidential information, and I considered my role of his sound-ing board as providing good community service. Although I didn't know whether to be flattered that he valued my friendship or mortified that I was apparently so old and safe that he felt comfortable with me.

He flicked a glance toward the window.

"Let's go into the prep room," I suggested. "No one can see us there from the street."

He followed me and sat down at the maple two-piece dovetailed workbench that had a recessed portion in the middle for sorting and separating items.

"According to the guard at the gate, Harriet arrived home about twenty minutes before you and Joe," he said. "There were no other visitors."

I flashed back to the scene outside the house and I gasped. "Wait a minute. I forgot to tell you this before. I saw a movement in the woods when we were standing outside. I only caught a glimpse—it could have been a person or a deer—I'm not sure. But that could have been our perp."

"I hate to break it to you, Daisy, but real cops don't say *perp*."

"Oh. Well, what do you say, then?"

"Just *the guy*." There was a bag of vintage buttons on the bench from a recent box lot I'd bought at auction, and while he talked, Serrano didn't seem to be able to help himself. He tipped the bag out, and started moving the Czech glass with their iridescent finishes to one side, the ivory buttons to a separate pile.

"As far as alibis, Birch Kunes was one of the featured speakers at the medical conference he was at, so it's easier to account for his movements, but his girlfriend might have had the opportunity to drive back and forth. He got kinda prickly when I brought it up, though. He's real protective of her."

I was concentrating on the cut steel and the Bakelite, but I looked up from my button sorting. "Did you know she's pregnant? I mean, I probably shouldn't say anything as I don't know for *sure*, but . . ."

"Interesting." Serrano's gaze narrowed. "Cheating bastard."

"How about Chip Rosenthal?"

"What's he got to do with anything?"

"Well, Harriet thought that Sophie did in fact write a will. Maybe whoever killed Harriet did so to stop her talking? Someone who wanted the fact that Sophie died intestate to prevail. Like Chip Rosenthal, for instance."

Serrano grunted as if he thought I was grasping at straws. "Okay, I'll check on him. Harriet's sister, the real estate agent, was showing houses that day, and has clients who can confirm where she was. That strange woman who was her main competitor—"

"Ardine Smalls?"

"Yeah. She'd already installed her dollhouse at the Expo Center. People saw her fussing with it all day. The only one without a real alibi is Tracy McEvoy, who was alone in her studio. Apart from when Harriet visited to pick up her stuff, that is."

Serrano ran a hand across his closely cropped salt-and-pepper hair. "I gotta tell you, Daisy, these collector biddies are too much for me. Could I ask you to keep your eyes and ears open for any relevant information, seeing as everyone congregates in this place anyway?"

"Sure. No problem."

Once the buttons were sorted, I did a quick reconnoiter outside to see if the coast was clear before he gingerly exited Sometimes a Great Notion.

The weather degenerated into a gray funk, and a fine drizzling rain misted over the village. An annoying rain, as it was too warm for a raincoat. The humidity was back, with days in the seventies. Typical of the fickle Philadelphia area climate in the midst of September.

It had been raining the night of the murder, too. Why did

Harriet park on her driveway? Why not drive into the garage and enter the house that way?

I knew that Joe would tell me to mind my own business and let the police handle things. After I almost got myself shot this summer, he was still a little sensitive on the subject. But Serrano had practically given me a gold-plated invitation, hadn't he? Besides, just gathering some useful clues wouldn't be that dangerous.

I rearranged a display of various boxes—an orange five-finger Shaker box, a Kingsford Silver Gloss Starch wooden crate, and a wonderful trifold Victorian sewing box with a writing slope covered in its original blue velvet.

Marybeth Skelton called to say she was lining up a few more places for us to see. I thanked her with as much enthusiasm as I could muster. After I hung up, I realized I hadn't told Serrano about the Ohio Valley land and her resentment toward her older sister, Harriet.

Because you don't want to see your real estate agent arrested until she's found you another place?

I glared at Alice. "Now, that's not fair."

Her eyes with their long lashes slanted speculatively toward me, and I gritted my teeth.

It was a slow morning at the store and an even slower afternoon. My only sale all day had been Serrano's stalker, and I was considering closing early when the phone rang.

It was Angus Backstead, the auctioneer. My best friend in the world, apart from Martha and Eleanor.

"Daisy, I need your help."

"Sure, what is it?

"Birch Kunes wants to clean out Harriet's house in preparation for a sale. He's going to send the collectibles to auction. I've had some dolls through the auction house from time to time, but I could use your help with the appraisal. I'm going over there tonight."

"Well, I'm no expert either, but between the two of us, we might be able to wing it."

"I'll pay you."

"Don't be silly. God knows I owe you, after all the work you've done around here. But how can he start selling her stuff? Doesn't he have to wait for probate?"

I felt like I was becoming an expert in the ways of estate settlement.

"Apparently the house was titled in both their names, so it automatically rolls over to Birch. She never changed her will, so everything else goes to him, too."

When I got to Harriet's house, the only vehicle there was Angus's Ford F-150 pickup. I parked behind him on the street, ran over to the passenger side, and hopped into the cab, just as I'd done so many times before on our picking adventures.

"What's up, Daisy Duke?" Even though it was a big truck, Angus seemed to fill it up with his shock of white hair and mountain man physique. His meaty hands rested on the base of the steering wheel, and he wore his usual plaid shirt, jeans, and work boots.

I grinned at him. "Not much, Burger Boy."

"Kunes is running late. He's on his way."

This past summer, Angus had been wrongly accused of a murder, and I'd done my best to get him acquitted. He hadn't been much help in his own defense, appearing confused, belligerent, and frankly, like he was losing his marbles.

It turned out he was suffering from a brain tumor, which thankfully was benign. Since the surgery and his prison experience, Angus had radically changed his lifestyle. He was still a big guy, but now that he wasn't drinking, he'd slimmed down and looked younger than his sixty-something years. His cheeks were no longer ruddy from Irish whiskey, but healthy and tanned, and the beer belly was almost gone.

"Thanks for coming, kid. Want some?" He held out a plastic baggie of wheat crackers and carrot sticks. This snack would have consisted of a couple of chili cheese dogs, a large order of fries, and some beef jerky a few months ago.

"No thanks. I'll wait until I get home."

"Joe cooking one of his gourmet feasts?"

"Expect so."

"You're a spoiled brat, you know that?" Angus punched me gently in the shoulder and shook his head. "My Betty's taking a knitting class tonight. I hardly ever see her anymore."

Betty Backstead, always dependent on her husband to take care of everything, had found a measure of independence during his incarceration.

I rubbed at my shoulder and hoped he hadn't left a bruise.

He pointed a carrot stick at the view through the windshield of townhomes clustered around the golf course. "You know, I remember when all this was farmland. Shame that so much of the open space is gone now."

In Bucks County, many of the old farms had been sold off for redevelopment. The builders had moved in and offered the farmers what must have seemed like a fortune and an opportunity to leave a hard life of relentless work behind.

At least this one had had some green sensibility in its development. The township had negotiated for a park preserve of fifty acres out of the three hundred.

As we waited, I brought him up to speed on the circumstances of Harriet's death, the fervent interest in my dollhouse, and how Serrano considered Birch Kunes to be his number one suspect.

Angus grunted. "Speaking of Kunes, where the hell is he?"

At that moment, a white Land Rover came racing up.

Here's the cheating bastard now.

Angus got out of the truck first, opened an umbrella, and came around to my side. It wasn't raining hard, just the type of rain that clung to my hair and turned it into a frizzy mess.

Birch Kunes hurried up to us. He was tall, with dark blond hair, and still tanned, even though summer was over. Sort of what the all-American college preppie should look like a couple of decades after graduation.

"God, sorry I'm late. You know how it goes."

The gorgeous effect was spoiled however by his rumpled shirt, and a stain of what looked like spaghetti sauce on his tie.

At least, I hoped it was.

"I'm not sure how much help I'll be to you. I don't know that much about dolls, but I'll do my best."

I couldn't smile back. I could barely look at him. *The boyish charm is wasted on me, pal.*

Angus and I followed him into the house. The arched window above the front door that spilled light into the foyer was matched by one at the top of the grand curving staircases. I glanced over at Angus, seeing the same startled reaction in his eyes as I'd had when I first saw the dolls lining every step.

"Right. Well, let me show you around." Birch coughed. "Um, sorry, I guess you were already here once, right Daisy?"

A faint flush colored his face under the tan. "Let's start with the garage." He walked to the right of the foyer and opened a white six-paneled door.

The cavernous space that could have held three cars was completely filled. Stacked from floor to ceiling with a mountain of cardboard boxes and totes. Through the clear plastic sides of the totes, I glimpsed dolls in their original boxes and hundreds of doll accessories and pieces of dollhouse furniture.

I sucked in a breath. *So that's why Harriet didn't park inside the garage.*

Birch hung back in the house, while Angus and I maneuvered our way into the narrow passageway that led to the garage doors.

"Holy smokes, Angus," I whispered. "Harriet was a hoarder!"

He stared at me. "Hell, yeah." He opened a few of the nearby crates. "This is crazy. We're going to have to move all this stuff to the auction house before we can even begin to catalog any of—"

A phone rang and Birch appeared on the threshold. "Would you both excuse me for a moment?"

He strode off down the hallway toward the kitchen, his voice a soothing murmur to whomever was on the other end of the line.

Angus and I did our best in the garage, but it was only a guess as we couldn't get to most of it. We then itemized everything in the living room and dining room while Angus scribbled furiously on his pad, and Birch was still missing in action.

Finally we moved over to the study.

I swallowed hard, seeing the space on the rug where Harriet had lain. The display table was empty now, the Tudor mansion taken away to the police station for evidence.

"You okay, Daisy?"

Poor Harriet.

Not even dead for a week, and already the rapacious widower, the one who'd been desperate to be her *ex*-husband, was getting rid of her prized possessions. Not just getting rid of them, but about to make a very nice windfall.

I gritted my teeth. "Yes. Let's get on with it."

Angus had filled five sheets on his legal pad, and we'd nearly reached the top of the stairs, counting dolls all the way, when Birch caught up to us.

"Sorry about that. Duty calls, you know?"

I concentrated on examining a pair of vintage Raggedy Ann and Andy dolls, awake on one side, asleep on the other. These were the real deal and should fetch a pretty penny.

Angus and Birch reached the top of the stairs ahead of me and I scrambled after them.

The finishes on the second floor were as upgraded as downstairs, with crown molding and five-inch baseboards throughout, or what little I could see of them. I'd thought the first floor was crammed, but it was nothing compared with this. A wide hallway had been whittled down into a slim lane by the dollhouses arranged along its length.

We walked into the first bedroom, with its custom drapes and high-end light fixtures. I trailed my fingers across the brushed nickel handle and glanced back at Angus, catching his almost imperceptible nod. It was like we were picking again, and we could read each other's minds.

This door handle alone probably cost fifty bucks.

The room was stuffed with dolls. French dolls in gorgeous clothes that would make any collector's mouth water. There were German dolls, too, but without the same fancy attire. Those were often sold naked or with a simple shift, the idea being that the German child would learn to sew.

I stared at a whole row of French "Bebe" dolls from the 1880s, with their jaunty hats, soulful brown eyes, and bisque heads. There was about thirty thousand dollars sitting on that one shelf alone.

"Some of these are German," Birch said. "Simon and Halbig, I think? There's plenty of those, and then she got on a Jumeau and Bru kick."

Birch actually knew more than he realized. He reminded me of my daughter, Sarah, who professed to have no interest in the store, but unconsciously absorbed information by osmosis when she became immersed in my world for a while on one of her infrequent visits home.

A group of boudoir dolls sat on the bed, as they were designed to do, seeing as they were not meant to be played with by children. I was inspecting a porcelain doll with bushy bangs and a smug expression when Birch's phone rang again.

"Whoops. So sorry," he whispered, and disappeared into the hallway.

As I'd told Angus, I wasn't an expert, but I could tell these dolls were really old and really unusual, which is the key with most collectibles.

"Angus, there's a *fortune* in this place," I murmured.

He set the notepad on the bed and flexed his fingers. "This is going to take a couple of weeks to pull together. I'll tell you Daisy, this could be the biggest auction Backstead's has ever had."

I nodded. I could see people coming from hundreds of miles away, eager to add a rare doll like one of these to their collection.

"I'm fairly sure they're real, but you may want to consult an expert once you get them back to the auction house." I picked up one of the Bebe dolls. "Look at the body for a start to check for fakes. Someone might be able to duplicate the face, but an older body is harder to do." I showed him the numbers on the back showing the mold mark and size. "Often the heads and bodies were made in different places and this helped match them up."

"Yeah, I had one of these at auction last May," he said as he took it from me.

I smiled at the sight of the fragile figure in his massive, but gentle grasp. "The closed-mouth ones are twice as valuable as the openmouthed," I said.

Angus nodded. "Yup. I can see why Kunes is anxious to get his paws on the cash from this lot."

We cataloged the rest of the room and moved down the hallway to the second bedroom.

A veritable sea of dolls crowded the bed and the carpet
and ebbed up to about three feet from the door. A multi-
faced one sitting on the windowsill seemed like it was staring right at me. A fine sweat prickled my forehead. It wasn't
an especially warm evening, but suddenly I wanted to get
this over with as soon as possible.

Angus snorted as we hovered in the entryway. "Damn.
Guess ol' Harriet wasn't planning on having any guests sleep
over. This place is *stuffed* with stuff!"

I steeled myself to edge inside. In this room was more of
a variety. Kewpie dolls, Madame Alexanders, and Izannah
Walker cloth dolls from the 1870s. I bent and picked up a
tiny World War I era doll with a body of papier-mâché, a
bisque head, mohair wig, and painted-on shoes.

"Jeez, Angus. Some people are only interested in a cer-
tain kind of doll, but it appears Harriet was an equal opportunity collector."

"She sure knew how to spend money, I'll give her that."

There was even a first-edition Barbie doll in her zebra-
striped bathing suit, still in the original box. I smiled rue-
fully to myself as I thought about Sarah's Barbies; their
golden ponytails restyled into choppy bangs with a pair of
scissors and barbed wire tattoos added with a black marker.

Angus did his best to make an inventory, and I called out
as many different dolls as I could spot.

Next was the master bedroom and adjoining sitting room
with their high tray ceilings. There was one very large doll,
about three feet tall, sitting in a rocking chair, and numerous
others covering the bed. It was tough to see how Harriet
could have slid in between them to sleep, no matter how
skinny she was. While I inspected a Victorian tin dollhouse
near the bathroom, and Angus was busy counting the dolls
on the bed, Birch Kunes finally caught up to us.

I didn't look at him, but I sensed his appraisal.

"I don't know what you must think of me, Daisy," he said softly.

Was my contempt that easy to read? And why should he care what I thought of him, anyway?

"I did love her once, you know." He gestured to a silver photo frame on the dressing table. It was a picture of Harriet, a younger Harriet, and I caught a glimpse of the woman he must have fallen for. She was on a boat, wearing a black maillot swimsuit, her body slender, not yet painfully gaunt. She was laughing at him, her blond Adonis, with her hair swept back in the breeze. Even though she was ten years older than Birch, I couldn't see much of a difference between them in this picture.

Wow. Harriet had aged rapidly. And badly.

"After we tried unsuccessfully to have a baby early on, she shut me out. She became obsessed with her collecting, with no room for anything or anyone else in her life. Literally."

Birch ran a hand through the now artificially streaked blond hair. In the unforgiving light shining up from the table lamp, I could see the bags under his eyes, and the lines around his mouth showed his four-plus decades on this earth. He looked more like a distracted scientist than a successful doctor.

He frowned slightly, not from anger it seemed, more like he was pondering a puzzle. "We moved to Meadow Farms about five years ago. I'd hoped it would be a fresh start for us, but unfortunately nothing changed. She managed to fill this place with junk in a relatively short period of time."

Very expensive, very collectible junk.

Birch sighed and straightened the picture frame. "After a couple of years, I guess I finally gave up. That's when I met Bettina."

He brightened at the sound of her name, the lines of

exhaustion disappearing for a moment. "She was a patient.
She was getting divorced at the time and needed a job. Even
though she didn't have a medical background, she made a
great receptionist. Not only was she warm and friendly, but
being diabetic herself, Bettina could sympathize with my
patients, especially the younger ones who had just been
diagnosed. Diabetes is tough for anyone to deal with, but
especially kids, when they're with their friends who want
to go to the Dairy Queen . . ."

His voice trailed off and out of the corner of my eye I
could tell he was still carefully watching my expression.

My heart rate sped up again.

Come on, Angus. How long was this going to take?

"Harriet and I had been living separate lives for a long
time before she died, and long before I ever started a romantic relationship with Bettina."

He shoved his hands into the pockets of his khakis. "I'm
not quite sure how it happened, but my wife became an
absolute bitch, through and through. Don't think I'm an
awful person, will you Daisy, but I can't say I'm sorry Harriet's gone. Maybe I'll have a chance at some happiness now.
Do you know what it's like to live with someone who's
completely obsessed?"

I bit my lip as I remembered the other bedrooms and my
near panic attack.

"She took great pleasure in telling me she would never
give me a divorce. Deliberately stonewalling me and not
letting me get on with my life."

There was a moment of silence while he swallowed so
hard I could see his Adam's apple move in his throat. "Bettina is so different, so sweet. She's pregnant. Did you know?
Not quite what we'd planned, but I couldn't be happier."

If he'd killed Harriet, he seemed unusually open and
willing to talk. He was obviously proud about the pregnancy,
but in a quiet way.

Grudgingly, I felt my anger at his cheating fade somewhat and I looked at him for the first time that evening. "Will Bettina be okay? I mean, being pregnant with diabetes? Isn't that a risk?"

He swallowed again. "She'll be all right. She deals with her condition very well, and we'll monitor her carefully."

"I'm sure she's in good hands," I murmured.

Wait a minute. Diabetes. "Did you know Sophie Rosenthal?"

"Yes, Sophie was my patient." He slid his glasses off and rubbed at his eyes. "I'm still upset that I didn't realize how depressed she was. Perhaps I could have helped her more."

"Could it have been an accidental overdose?"

"Suppose so, but it's doubtful. Sophie was a type 1 diabetic, and had been for most of her life. She was very familiar with how to administer insulin correctly." He slipped his glasses back on and blinked a few times. "Would you excuse me?" He gestured toward a row of wax dolls. "I've never liked those. Something funeral-ish about them. I'll meet you guys downstairs, okay?"

After he disappeared, Angus and I made our way to the last guest room, which was full of nothing but bisques.

"Angus, these are Bru dolls. There's about fifty of them at a quick count. They can go anywhere from a couple of thousand each to twenty, thirty, or more, depending."

Angus scratched his head. "I'm running out of zeros on my calculator."

I felt an overwhelming sadness. This type of manic spending was a sickness, even as beautiful as this vast collection was. "I have to get out of here soon, Angus."

"Me, too. If I were still drinking, I'd go have a shot and a beer after this."

There were four bedrooms upstairs, and two and a half baths. Much too big for one person, unless, like Harriet, they had enough merchandise to fill a chain of retail stores.

We found Birch Kunes downstairs, sitting at the kitchen table, staring morosely at the pretty lilac dollhouse.

Angus explained that he could give Birch a more exact presale estimate once everything was back at the auction house and he could go through the items from the garage.

"I trust you, Angus. I don't even know what the hell is in there anyway."

"The garage alone will take a full day even if I bring a couple of guys with me. We'll tag and inventory everything and give you a complete list for your records. My company is fully insured and bonded—"

Birch waved a hand impatiently. "Yes, yes. That's fine."

"It'll be a specialized auction," Angus said. "Give me some time to advertise in all the trades."

"I don't care when the auction is, as long as I can start marketing the house for sale," Birch said. "But I need to get this crap out of here first."

I had to agree. I'd heard real estate agents advise clients to declutter, but this was ridiculous.

"It's a beautiful property," I said. "It should sell quickly. But wouldn't you want to live here? It's such a great location—one of the best in the development."

"God, no. Bettina would never agree to that." He looked up at us. "I just want to hand over the keys to Marybeth and let her do her thing. I need to buy something else before the baby comes."

I stifled a gasp. He was letting Harriet's estranged sister list the house?

"Why don't you guys go on out the front door and I'll lock up."

As Angus and I walked down the brick path, I hissed, "Angus, don't you think that's a bit weird? Harriet and Marybeth Skelton *hated* each other."

He shrugged. "Well, she is the best real estate agent around here."

"True enough. I just think it's odd that Harriet's husband would have no loyalty to his dead wife."

"Yeah, and he's on a real tight schedule, ain't he?"

When we reached the end of the driveway, I looked back. Through the open garage doors, I watched as Birch set the alarm.

"It's also funny that he still has a key to her house, and she obviously never changed the alarm code after he moved out," I whispered.

Birch Kunes hit the garage door closure and made an athletic crouching run under the descending door like he'd done it a thousand times before.

Chapter Eight

It was a strange moon tonight. A full moon, but hazy and out of focus. Like a cracked meringue of the palest blue, tinged with rust.

It was close to eight o'clock when I trailed into our Greek Revival. I stood in the foyer and inhaled deeply.

My favorite game. Trying to guess what Joe was making for dinner.

I only had a moment, though, before Jasper came barreling down the hallway, showing no signs of slowing down or veering off course. I stepped to one side, barely escaping being bowled over. I dropped to my knees and submitted to a tongue licking that left my whole face slightly damp. It might be a bit messy, but this was pure, unconditional love, and after my depressing experience at the Kunes place, I didn't mind one bit.

"Okay, boy." I stroked his silky head and then dragged

myself to my feet. I found Joe in the kitchen, wearing a striped apron, with a massive pile of chopped vegetables on the counter in front of him.

"Daisy, you're just in time. I'm trying out a new recipe. Hot and Sour Chicken. You're gonna love it." Joe kissed me, too, albeit not as sloppily as Jasper.

I hugged him, reluctant to let go.

"Tough day?"

"Yeah."

He poured me a glass of Riesling. I slumped in one of the kitchen chairs, put my feet up, and gave a sigh of thanksgiving that he accepted my one-word response without question.

Dear Joe.

I sipped the wine and watched him cook. He sloshed some sesame oil into a wok and when it was hot, added pieces of chicken. Next came fermented black beans and red pepper powder.

I had to monitor Joe with the spices because sometimes he got carried away if we were talking and would forget he already added the menu's required allotment. And like the home repair purchases, he bought exotic ingredients that he'd probably never use again. There was a new bag from the hardware store on the table, too.

Joe and I would need to have a discussion about his spending habits, but not tonight.

Tonight I was too tired to say anything.

I thought about Harriet's house and all those rare, expensive collectibles and wondered where my little dollhouse would have fit in. It wasn't in the same league at all.

Joe gaily threw piles of green peppers, bamboo shoots, carrots, and celery into the sizzling wok. He finely chopped some fresh garlic and ginger, and then added soy sauce, vinegar, and wine.

I knew Birch Kunes was numero uno on Serrano's list, and while I had also been more than ready to blame the good-looking but slightly nerdy doctor, too, he didn't seem to have any real animosity toward Harriet. He didn't even seem that concerned about how much she'd spent. More like simply worn out by her obsessions, and consumed by a desire to get on with his life.

Of course, now he was infatuated with Bettina.

Birch had said that if he and Harriet had had kids, things might have been different. When they couldn't, that was the turning point, and she'd become addicted to miniatures. Before Sarah, I'd miscarried our first child and I'd become just as neurotic about our only daughter, trying to control every inch of her life until I learned that she could manage quite well on her own.

It took both of us nearly getting killed this past summer for me to realize just how strong she really was.

I drank more wine. Martha was obsessed with Cyril, Serrano was gunning for Birch Kunes, Sam Brown was passionate about his pumpkins, and the wine club woman was crazy about the hot detective. And me? I couldn't stop thinking about Chip Rosenthal and the future of my store.

I shook my head.

"You okay, babe?" Joe glanced at me as he stirred some cornstarch into the mixture in the wok.

"I'm just sad for Harriet, I guess." How many other women were out there, my age, whose husbands cheated on them with younger women?

There, but for the grace of God, go I.

And here I was, worrying about Joe buying some fermented beans, for Pete's sake. I was an ungrateful wretch, that was for sure.

I got up, put my arms around him, and held him as tight as I could.

* * *

On Thursday afternoon, after a long day of looking at balance sheets and not much else, I decided I was sick of worrying. Some fresh air would do me good. I hung a CLOSED sign on the front of the store, went home and picked up Jasper, and drove to Ringing Springs Park.

Maybe I'd run into Bettina Waters and have a chance to chat. However beautiful and nice she seemed from a distance, she certainly had the motive to get rid of Harriet, the woman who had spitefully obstructed her future. She'd also had the opportunity to slip away from the medical conference, but what did she know about wiring a dollhouse?

I'd make those other snotty women say hello to me this time, too, including the terrifying Virginia Axelrod.

As it turned out, I found someone much more interesting to talk to.

I arrived at the dog park enclosure just in time to see a few of the wine club members, quite literally, turn their backs on Ardine Smalls.

She stood, unmoving, her hands shoved into the pockets of the camel hair coat she must have owned for decades, her head with its nest of wiry hair bowed against the cold.

I let Jasper off his leash and he bounded joyfully into the center of the pack. I moved over to stand next to her. "Which one is your dog?" I asked.

She looked around for a split second, almost comically, as if sure that I must be addressing someone else. Up close, her skin was pitted by years of long-ago teenage acne, and a dusting of dandruff powdered the shoulders of her coat.

"That one." She pointed to a scruffy terrier type whose bottom teeth stuck out, making him look like a miniature boar. "He hates me."

I glanced at her in surprise.

"He's horrible, but I can't get rid of him. He belonged to my mother. She passed away two years ago."

She showed me the scars on her hands from bite marks. "I'm really scared of him."

My lips thinned as I watched the nasty little brute. This dog needed some serious discipline. He snapped at Jasper, who danced away, taken aback by the unexpected aggression. Jasper was a bit like my husband, who'd never met a living thing that didn't instantly adore him.

I recognized the two wine mooches, sour-faced Ginny Axelrod and floppy-haired Bobbie Zwick, sitting in the chairs among the array of coolers. There was another, matronly woman wearing a headband, long denim skirt, and red golf shirt. I bet the golden retriever belonged to her. The schnauzer with the permanent scowl was probably Ginny's, and the two shih tzus had to be Bobbie's, if the old adage that dogs looked like their owners was true.

Ruthie wasn't here today, and neither was Bettina. A younger woman in tennis whites arrived towing a giant poodle, and an aristocratic older woman joined in with a pair of pugs.

Again, I was reminded of the cliques in high school. Me, Ruthie, and now Ardine were definitely *not* the cool kids.

As I watched Jasper gallop around, sticking his nose up everyone's butt, I winced. If dogs' personalities also matched their owners, then I was somewhat goofy and more than a little intrusive.

"I've brought some cider," Ardine said, gesturing to the plastic bag she carried. "Would you like some? I don't drink much myself."

"Well you don't *have* to drink in order to bring your dog here, you know." I smiled at her as I held out my hand. "I'm fine, thanks. I'm Daisy Buchanan. I don't think we've met. But I did see you win the dollhouse competition on Saturday. Congratulations."

Ardine was wearing purple mittens with woolen balls hanging off the cuffs. "Were you there? Wasn't it so exciting! I'm just sad that Mother wasn't around to see me finally win."

When Ardine talked, it was like the top of her mouth was fixed and immovable and the bottom half could hardly move either.

Her bright expression dimmed. "Although even if she *were* around, she would say the only reason I won was because Harriet Kunes wasn't in the competition."

"Well, I thought your dollhouse was terrific."

"Really?"

"Yes. I saw Harriet's Tudor mansion. Rather gaudy. I know you would have won anyway." I didn't know that for sure, but if it made her feel better, it was worth it to see the big smile reappear. "I'm refinishing a dollhouse myself at the moment. For a little girl's birthday present. It's an 1860s Victorian."

"Ah! You know, those early dollhouses had a very rough notion of scale." She chuckled and shook her head. "They didn't worry about the typical one inch to one foot. Many old examples look ludicrous when you compare objects in the same room."

Ardine's eyes darted from side to side as if it was hard for her to look directly at me. "They'd have a two-inch-scale cup on one-inch-scale table, and so on. The important thing to remember is that it isn't so much *what* the scale is, but that everything is in the *same* scale." She waved her mitten-covered hands for emphasis.

Jasper came over to check in with me. Ardine reached out gingerly and patted him on the head. He sniffed her in a friendly way, but without his usual enthusiasm. I ruffled his ears and he galloped off again to crash into the pack of canines.

"Sometimes you look at the size of the bed, and you realize the person would have had to be a high jumper to get into it." Ardine giggled, and I chuckled along with her. "Chairs reach halfway to the ceiling, and chandeliers were so low, a person would bang their head every time they stood up."

Now she was gasping for breath because she was giggling so hard. I felt my smile becoming slightly frozen.

She glanced at me and quickly composed herself. "But for a child, you're creating something that will be fun to play with, not like the dollhouses of the seventeenth and eighteenth century, which were intended to be seen and never used."

"Do you want to sit down?" I gave up on my plan to ingratiate myself with the wine club. I could learn a lot more right here.

"Okay." Her face lit up and my heart ached for her. It was the same pain I'd felt when I'd encountered students who were bright, but came from such hideous home environments that their surroundings obliterated their potential. As a teacher, you could only do so much to change the world, but I'd certainly tried.

Even though Eleanor had been a geek in high school, she'd developed confidence as she got older, whereas Ardine Smalls never had.

There was a bench in a sheltered spot by the wall and we made ourselves comfortable.

"You see, there are different schools of thought in doll-house construction," she continued. "Should they exactly duplicate full-sized versions? Should drawers and doors open? Should mortise-and-tenon joint construction be used?" Ardine was talking faster now, as if I was a mirage that might disappear at any minute. "Some people say yes— miniatures should be formed down to the minutest detail whether visible or invisible. Others, like Mrs. Thorne and Eugene Kupjack, say it's not necessary."

I had no idea who these people were, but from the

reverent tone of her voice, I gathered they were icons in the field and I didn't want to interrupt her train of thought.

Intrigued, I watched as she warmed to her subject. She was a good teacher. I could recognize the quality in another and found myself thirsty for knowledge, hanging on her every word. I wished I had a notebook with me.

"Miniatures are a wonderful way to preserve settings for all time. I know people who have recreated their house, say, before they moved, down to the exact detail, even the wallpaper."

"The wallpaper?" I said.

"Oh yes, there are companies that make custom wallpaper. You could replicate the antique wallpaper in your dollhouse if you wanted."

The wallpaper. Was there some kind of clue in the design on the walls? Like a treasure map or something? Some kind of hieroglyphical clue? I'd go over to Cyril's first thing tomorrow and check it out.

"What did you think of Harriet Kunes?" I asked. "What kind of collector was she?"

"Harriet was fanatical about being accurate in every detail. She was very scornful of those who mix and match items from different time periods."

I bit my lip as I thought of my modern toaster oven.

"We used to argue about it all the time. When we were speaking, that is."

"You were friends?"

"Oh, well, we were best friends once. In fact, I was a nurse at the same hospital where Birch did his residency. I introduced them."

"Really?" Curiouser and curiouser.

"But Harriet changed. It's sad. She became so competitive, she antagonized a lot of people." Ardine played with her knotted dog leash. "In fact, I'm sure Harriet's the one who sabotaged my entry at a show once by putting cockroaches inside. They scurried out when the judges opened the front panel and my chances of winning were doomed."

"Wow. I can't believe she'd do something like that."

She looked directly at me for the first time. "You have no idea what those competitions are like."

"And would Harriet be the type to confront a killer if she found something awry?"

Ardine frowned. "Not sure what you mean, but yes, Harriet was very confrontational."

A few raindrops spattered on the bench, and she scrunched up her nose as she looked skyward. "We'd better get going."

The wine club was busy packing up their coolers, and I smiled at the golden retriever owner who smiled back. Maybe they weren't all bad.

As Ardine struggled to put the leash on her annoying terrier while he snapped at her, Jasper suddenly wrestled him to the ground. He looked at me, his huge paw still pressing down on the little dog's shoulder, as if to say, *Sorry, Mom, but I couldn't take it anymore.*

Silently I cheered, but said, "Stop it, Jasper!"

"It's okay, Daisy, this dog needs someone to straighten him out." Ardine grinned as she clipped the leash.

She put up her umbrella. One of the spokes was broken. "Thanks for being so nice to me."

I watched as she hurried to her car, the umbrella flying up in the rain.

Chapter Nine

The next morning, Mother Nature provided a taste of impending winter. It was lashing with rain so hard that the storm sewers couldn't keep up, and there was standing water on the street corners. Jasper loved it—the wetter and muddier the better—but I cursed as I struggled to manage the umbrella and the leash. When we got home, it took longer to dry him off with a slew of old towels than it had taken for the walk.

As it was Friday, Laura was managing the store, so I stopped at Cyril's to check on the progress of Claire's present. He was working on the roof, painstakingly attaching the shingles, one at a time. I handed him a cup of coffee from the diner and hid a grin when I spotted a library book about building dollhouses.

"Aye up, you can snicker, but look at this. Queen Mary's dollhouse. It were a right grand place." He opened a page and pointed at some photos. "Four years to plan and build. Elevators from basement to top floor. Door handles that close and clocks that tick. It even had water pumped up from the basement."

I marveled over the description of water running into the tub and the marble-topped sinks in the king's bathroom. The details were incredible: the wine cellar with its honeycomb walls that held a hundred dozen bottles of wine, a strong room for the crown jewels, the tiny piano equipped with real strings, hammers, and ivory and ebony keys. In the library, each minuscule book bound in leather and embossed with gold leaf was actually readable.

No expense had been spared. The kitchen was constructed with thousands of tiny sections of oak, rooms were paneled in rosewood, and there was silver and porcelain throughout.

"Ah'm worried about this 'ouse being historically accurate," Cyril said.

My eyes widened as I stared at him.

He jabbed a finger toward the front porch. "Ah don't know about these here winder boxes."

"It's okay, Cyril. It's for a little girl to play with. I know what you mean, and we'll do our best, but only to a point. I still want my toaster oven."

He looked unconvinced.

"Look. Think of it like a real Victorian house, bought by a person who loves the period and wants to preserve the beauty of the home, but lives there in the current day and needs modern conveniences."

He grunted and attached another shingle. "Did tha find another store to rent yet?"

"Not yet. Marybeth is setting up more appointments."

I'd have to ask Laura to work an extra day. The familiar panic at the thought of leaving Millbury twisted inside me and I made a sudden decision. "You know what, I'm going to call Chip Rosenthal today and see if we can work something out. Get him to see reason."

"Mebbe you just got off on the wrong foot before."

I blew out a breath. "And maybe he's the one who murdered miserable Harriet because she knew that her best friend Sophie did, in fact, write a will. And maybe he's the one who came to my store that night trying to steal the dollhouse because he thought the will might be hidden inside."

Cyril pulled the lid off the coffee and stirred in a couple of creamers. "Getting a bit carried away, Daisy?"

"I don't think so. And I'll see you Harriet's murder and raise you one. There's a possibility that Sophie was murdered, too. And guess who benefited most from dear old Aunt Sophie's death?"

He nodded. "Young Chip."

"Exactly. Serrano is convinced that Birch Kunes killed Harriet, but I have a bad feeling these two deaths are connected, and the linchpin is my new landlord."

Suddenly I remembered Ardine's comment about the wallpaper. I got up and peered inside, inspecting the walls for a clue, but as hard as I looked, nothing seemed like writing to me. It was simply a classical Greek ornamental design.

"Ah'll fix the broken chimney today, and the balustrade on the second-floor balcony. We're going to need more shingles to finish the roof."

I broke the news to Cyril that I wanted to paint it, too, but to my surprise he didn't explode.

I had a feeling he was getting into this as much as me, sharing my fascination with the perfect little world inside the dollhouse.

Not like the messy real one, with its evil landlords, murdered women, and cheating husbands.

O n my way to Sheepville, I had to swerve around several downed trees that were partially blocking the road. I cursed as one car driving too fast in the opposite direction kicked up a huge wave of water, dousing my windshield while I drove blind. Some yards were already completely underwater, and ROAD CLOSED signs were up on the side streets that crossed over the creeks.

When I got to Jeanne's, I pulled out my cell and called Chip Rosenthal. He wasn't in, but I left a message saying I'd like to discuss the lease, and asking if he could meet on Monday.

I picked up the shingles I needed and spent a few minutes admiring the displays. In the attic of one house was a myriad of enticing items—ice skates, a Victorian pram, some luggage, a bare light bulb in a socket with pull string, and a wood violin with bow and velvet case. Even a mousetrap.

I couldn't resist the bare light bulb for Claire's attic. I selected a three-tier petit four stand for the dining table, and was lingering over some tiny kitchen utensils when Jeanne came up to me.

"Aren't these darling?"

"Yes, Jeanne, but before I get too carried away, I want to try to stay as authentic as possible."

She smiled. "Don't worry about it too much, sweetheart. Just have fun."

Ardine Smalls came around the corner of an aisle, carrying a box. "Yes, you don't have to worry about it unless you're going to be the next Mrs. James Ward Thorne." She giggled, showing those uneven teeth.

"Who *was* this paragon?" I asked.

"She created remarkable rooms in the early twenties. They're at the Art Institute of Chicago now. Totally historically accurate through five centuries, from the sixteenth to the twentieth. She designed all the textiles inside, too."

"You've discovered my little secret, Daisy," Jeanne said as she pointed at the box Ardine was holding. "Ardine designed a lot of the displays here in the store for me."

"They're beautiful."

Ardine beamed at me. "I love doing them. It's kind of like interior design and stage design rolled into one."

She set the box down and I peered into an open-plan kitchen and living room. On the kitchen counter, I saw a bowl of batter and balls of chocolate chip cookie dough set out on a baking sheet. It was so clever and realistic, I felt my mouth water.

In the living room, there was authentic clutter—projects in progress, a bookshelf crammed with books, and a coffee table holding some knitting, a sewing pattern, and tiny needles.

"It's good to suggest movement and a sense that someone has just left the room." Ardine bent down next to me. "Look at your composition from every angle. Also think of where the traffic lanes are."

I felt myself zooming down to one inch tall. I would have simply positioned the furniture in my dollhouse wherever it looked good. But could I really pass between the parlor table and the fainting couch?

"This is fascinating, Ardine. I had no idea that so much went into it."

We both straightened up, although it took me a little longer.

"And the most important thing?" Ardine waggled her finger. "A room has to have a *personality*. Finding the rhythm in a room is a subtle thing. Like music, you have to get it just right."

I nodded and picked up a steamer wardrobe travel trunk. I knew that was proper Victorian detail and would appeal to Claire, too. She could pretend the occupants of the house were packing for a journey. Speaking of which, they would need toiletries. I added a bar of soap and a hot water bottle to my pile. There was even a chamber pot, but I passed on that. I chuckled as I imagined Claire's reaction. *Ew!*

"Oh, and I need to pick out some paint," I told Jeanne. I

scanned the shades on the wall, but couldn't seem to find quite the right one. She showed me a catalog with more selections, and I finally found the perfect pale lilac hue.

"If I order it for you today, it should come in Monday or Tuesday."

As I paid for the items, I thought of getting mad at Joe for spending money on his tools.

You're such a hypocrite, Daisy Buchanan.

But it's for Claire, I protested to my inner voice.

Jeanne had a quizzical expression on her face and I wondered if I'd spoken out loud. I was getting too accustomed to my conversations with Alice the mannequin. I mumbled good-bye and told her I'd see her next week for the paint.

My cell phone rang just as I walked outside.

It was Angus. "Hey, Daisy, we're going to need help appraising all this stuff. These dolls look authentic, but I have a reputation to uphold. We need an expert."

I rolled my eyes. Hadn't I already told him that?

Never mind. I peered through the store window, where Ardine was still at the register, talking to Jeanne. "I think I know just the person."

On Saturday morning, Joe said he was going to see Tracy McEvoy.

"I was talking to Mac at that show, and she said she'd give me some tips on making miniatures. Told me to stop by today if I wanted."

I remembered the statuesque blonde in the red halter dress and my stomach tightened.

"Want to come with me?"

"Sure. Okay," I said, as casually as I could.

When Angus was wrongly accused of murder, I'd spent a lot of time investigating the case before Serrano arrived in town. It had all worked out well in the end and I'd found the real killer, but Joe, patient to a point, felt neglected, to say the least. We were still feeling our way back to the former closeness we'd enjoyed.

We headed out toward Forty Acre Road, where the houses were few and far between, and where my friend Joy David owned an upscale bed-and-breakfast called the Four Foxes.

We missed the turnoff to Mac's place a couple of times until I finally spotted the sign for Deerpath Road, almost hidden in the trees on the corner of a narrow country lane. It was another few hundred yards before we came to the mailbox for number nine Deerpath.

A gravel driveway led up to a cedar-shingled high-peaked contemporary house. There wasn't a weed in sight, in spite of the length of the drive. The grass was recently cut and a gorgeous crimson and gold Japanese maple in front was pruned and well mulched.

The studio was behind the house, in the same contemporary construction with floor-to-ceiling glass windows and a brick patio. We parked where the driveway ended with landscaping timbers set against the grass.

A black cat darted across in front of us and disappeared into the woods.

A magical place.

The wide Craftsman door to the studio opened and Mac stood there, wearing paint-spattered jeans and a ripped T-shirt exposing her toned arms. I didn't want to stare at her chest, but I thought I could make out a logo for Temple University. The shirt must have been red at one time, but was now a dull rose. It was probably round-necked originally, too, but she'd slit it down into a V-neck and ripped the sleeves off.

"You made it." Her gaze swept over me, but it was a neutral appraisal. I couldn't decide if she was irritated that I was along for the ride, or if she couldn't care less.

"Come on in."

We followed her into a light-filled space with natural oak floors. Wood beams lined the swooping curves in the roof, and the walls were off-white. Easels held paintings in progress, and finished works hung along the wall to our left.

I stopped to admire one in particular. "Hey, these are really good. I think a friend of mine has one of your paintings." Eleanor had a similar one hanging above her fireplace, of a barn at sunrise and a man walking across snow-covered fields with his dog.

"I don't sell many. I'd rather keep them."

I stared after her as she strode through the studio toward the carpentry workbenches, the jeans that encased her long legs worn pale in places.

I hadn't realized she was an accomplished artist as well as an expert in miniatures. *Jeez.* She had more business than she knew what to do with, a fabulous workspace, and obviously boatloads of cash. The paintings were simply a way to express herself, not to make money.

A display stand in the center held examples of the magnificent craftsmanship that was in such demand—an inlaid walnut bureau, a Queen Anne highboy with finials, a lowboy of cherry wood, a Chinese Chippendale cabinet, a four-poster bed.

"How did you get into making miniatures?" Joe asked.

"I was a carpenter for full-size furniture before I started this business. I made every stick of furniture in here. Built the house and this studio, too."

"*You* built it?" Joe looked around with wonder. "By yourself?"

"Yes. Well, I had some help with pouring the basement and the roof, but I did the rest."

"And the plumbing and electrical?" I asked. She was so tall I had to lean my head back to look up at her.

"The plumbing, yes, but Larry Clark did most of the electrical. I know a little. Enough to be dangerous."

Mac nodded toward a bank of windows at the end that provided a peaceful view of the woods. There was a deck at ground level and French doors to the right. "I lived in a mobile home out there for a year and a half."

"You're quite the girl, aren't you?" It would be hard to miss the look of admiration on Joe's face. "Well done."

At last, here was a hint of a smile on her face.

I wondered if what *little* she knew about electrical was enough to rewire a dollhouse. Did she have a reason to kill Harriet? With that, I reminded myself that I wasn't just here as my husband's chaperone. After all, Mac was the one who'd recommended Larry Clark to Harriet in the first place.

"I took shop in high school before it was acceptable for girls to do so." Mac stuck both hands in the back pockets of her jeans. "Yeah, I was never into sewing, or girly stuff like that."

I gritted my teeth. "Your work is exquisite."

"Thank you," she said, but with no smile for me. "I studied art in college, and worked in a restoration shop part-time. Just got into it, I guess. Bought some tools, and here I am."

She picked up a tilt-top tea table and turned it over to show Joe the construction underneath. "This table was originally made in Philadelphia around 1770. It's walnut, over a birdcage support." She ripped a tiny piece off a sheet of finishing paper and began sanding. "It'll get five coats of shellac with sanding in between. Lastly a good rubbing with paste wax of French polish."

I stared in awe at the precise baluster turnings, and the three carved cabriole legs with snake feet. The detail was incredible for something so small.

"Harriet was the one that got me into the miniatures in the first place. She commissioned me to create a Windsor

chair. I discovered I liked the challenge." Mac blew gently
on the table and inspected it. "She was an opinionated bitch,
but so am I, so we got along." The faint smile reappeared for
an instant until her face scrunched up in concentration again.

Joe sank down on a stool. I stood behind him.

How old was she? That shirt had to be at least ten years
old, so perhaps she was mid to late thirties. Her body was
in such good shape, it was hard to tell.

"Here's a sample of the grandfather clock I made for this
last show. It actually runs. Solid mahogany with box inlay,
and the clock face is hand-painted paper over metal. Except
Harriet's was bigger, of course. It nearly drove me to drink,
but I finished at the last minute. I was up for twenty-four
hours straight getting it done."

Joe never took his eyes off her, hanging on to her every
word. I couldn't exactly blame him. There was a lot to look
at, with the tight jeans and the top that hung loosely on her
toned frame. When she bent over slightly to set the clock
down, I caught a glimpse of pale breast and red bra.

"Harriet came over here to pick it up?" My voice sounded
as raspy as the scratch of the sandpaper.

Mac frowned. "Yeah. And I already told that annoying
cop everything. What a pain in the butt he is."

Was Mac the only female on the face of the planet who
was immune to Serrano's innate sex appeal? Heck, I ramped
up the air-conditioning in the store whenever he stopped by,
no matter what the weather. Was she gay? Was Harriet?

Suddenly nervous under her glare, I chattered on about
my dollhouse and how I was fixing it up and having trouble
choosing what to put in because there were so many choices.

She eyed me closely. "Many miniaturists allow one style
to predominate. But in real life, people often have a variety
of pieces they've inherited and accumulated. If you're trying
to document an historical record, it's probably best to keep
the same period together, but otherwise, do what feels right."

I pictured our house, with its mix of modern, antique, and what was actually authentic for a Greek Revival. The old steamer trunk in the study, the butcher-block table in the kitchen from the turn of the century, and the modern leather couches.

She turned to Joe. "The fine-grained woods are best. Oak is too coarse, so you want to use birch to *look* like oak." She gestured to the tools on the bench—the pliers, files, tweezers, and chisel. "You have these, right?"

Joe nodded eagerly. Like me in my conversation with Ardine the other day, I could see that he was trying to soak it all in.

She showed him some drawer pulls made with a jeweler's lathe and carvings done with dentist's burrs. "These tools are delicate enough for the most intricate work. It would probably be good for you to take a jewelry class at some point."

Oh, great. Something else to spend money on.

She slipped on a pair of head magnifying glasses. "You need a hell of a passion for detail to do this type of work. You might be able to get away with an imperfection in a larger piece, but not in miniature."

"I don't know if my big old fingers will get in the way," Joe said.

Mac grinned at him, and as she worked, she relaxed even more. "You could specialize, too, Joe, depending on what you're drawn to. One guy I know makes ship models, another woman only makes wing chairs. The world of miniatures uses almost every craft from pottery to textiles."

"Why were you mad at PJ for writing that article about you?" I asked. *Nice transition. Smooth, Daisy.* I could practically hear Serrano's mocking voice in my ear. "Um, it's just that I would have thought more business was a good thing."

"I was mad because I specifically asked her not to," Mac

said, slowly and carefully. "She went off and wrote the damn thing anyway. I don't like having to turn customers away."

I blinked. This Amazon struck me as someone who wasn't afraid of saying no.

"Many craftspeople have more orders than they can handle." She nodded at Joe. "In fact, I have some leads I can turn you onto when you feel you're ready."

Joe smiled at her, his dark eyes glowing.

"But it was the fact that PJ plowed ahead like a steamroller, intent on her own agenda, that pissed me off. The fact that she didn't take no for an answer."

I winced. She could have been describing me. I didn't dare look at Joe. I knew the corners of his mouth would be turning up.

"She just gets into everyone's business, she's nosy, and—"

"Okay, okay, I get it," I snapped.

Mac raised an eyebrow, but made no further comment.

I shifted on my stool. "Um. I was thinking about adding some lighting to my dollhouse. Do you know anything about that?"

"Some purists say that since light can't be scaled down, it shouldn't be used at all." Mac smiled at me for the first time, and I wondered if she was just humoring me. "But the simplest technique is to use a regular bulb and splice the bulb socket directly to the line cord that plugs into the wall. I wouldn't recommend it, though." She paused and blew a fine layer of dust off the table. "Not unless you want to commit suicide, that is."

I sucked in a breath, while Mac and Joe discussed why toy train transformers were also dangerous to use. I backed away and wandered around the studio, ostensibly to look at the paintings, but my mind was in a whirl.

Had Harriet killed *herself*? No one had even considered that possibility. Why not? She could have been depressed over her husband leaving. She'd certainly seemed on edge when she came into my store.

Because she'd never give Birch Kunes the satisfaction, that's why not.

And if someone was planning on doing themselves in, why would they make elaborate preparations for a competition the next day?

"A ten-volt doorbell transformer should be okay," Mac was saying, "and it can light some wheat-of-grain bulbs. Then you can hide it behind a wall or inside the ceiling. But make sure the bulbs are well ventilated."

Joe smiled benevolently at her, as if he hadn't spent most of his life as head of an electricians' union.

She'd explained everything so carefully. Would she really reveal all this knowledge if she was the killer? Or maybe she was being extra clever to divert attention away from herself. But what would Mac have against Harriet?

"It sounds like Harriet was a good customer," I said. "Did she ever keep you waiting for payment? Did she owe you for the pieces she'd just commissioned?"

Mac laughed, a short hacking sound. "Oh, no, she always paid on time."

I could feel Joe's eyes on me, silently pleading. *Stop playing investigator, Daisy.*

After another twenty minutes or so, Mac announced that she had a lunch appointment, so Joe and I got up to leave.

"This was fantastic," he said. "I learned so much. Thank you."

"Feel free to stop back anytime."

I'd bet my last dollar that the invitation did not include me.

Chapter Ten

On Monday morning, after a restless night, I took Jasper out early. It was still dark. Actually more like a strange half-light in the diaphanous transition between night and day. We hurried down Main Street, where the streetlights were still on and the wind whipped stray leaves in tumbling circles alongside us.

I mentally rehearsed my pitch to Chip Rosenthal as I trudged, glad of my warm gloves and scarf. I would be calm, pleasant, and persuasive, and I'd get him to see reason. The more I practiced, the more my confidence grew. I wasn't leaving this town without a fight.

A bread truck passed us on its way to the diner. In the distance I could see the yellow glow from the old trolley car, already serving meals to the night shift.

Joe had spent the rest of the weekend down in the basement, putting his new ideas to work, inspired by our visit to Tracy McEvoy's. Mac had been a female version of Cyril—gruff and off-putting—but Joe didn't seem to notice. All the way home in the car, he kept saying what a great girl she was.

Suddenly I gasped, the dry air biting the back of my throat. I stood stock still on the street while Jasper looked back at me in surprise.

I should have asked her about Sophie. If Sophie was as avid a collector as Harriet, I'd bet Mac had done some work for her, too. And seeing as Sophie was agoraphobic, she may have had to go to Sophie's home. I wondered how I could approach her to find out. Mac had erected such a wall between us, I wasn't sure I'd ever manage to scale it.

I headed toward the south end of Millbury, and found myself walking past Dottie Brown's house. To the right of the above-ground pool that was covered now for the winter, Sam had created his pumpkin patch. It encompassed almost half of the backyard. Bet Dottie was thrilled about that.

There were three large pumpkins growing amid a vast bed of waist-high dark green leaves. Sam had erected wooden shelters above them, presumably as protection from the wind, and in the chill of the morning, they were also lovingly covered with blankets. The largest was snuggled under a Thomas the Tank Engine comforter.

Sam waved and came over to the split-rail fence when he saw me and Jasper.

"How are the pumpkins coming along, Sam?"

"Oh, well, you know, it's a full-time job, what with watering, fertilizing, and weeding. You have to watch them all the time."

"They're amazing. I can see where it could be quite a project."

"I've developed a new program this year. Molasses, fish kelp, and milk." He held up a canister with a sprayer attached. "They say the reason punkins split is because they're calcium deficient. I bathe them every day with my secret recipe."

He lowered his voice and leaned closer. "Think I might have a chance this year though. Especially with Georgia over there."

He pointed toward the biggest pumpkin.

"She's a beauty. Good luck, Sam. See you later."

Jasper and I headed home, and like a montage in a movie, we gradually walked into morning. The daytime sky was now a wintry white.

When I opened up Sometimes a Great Notion, a message from Angus was on the answering machine saying Ardine Smalls was doing a fabulous job. She'd been at the auction house with him for most of the weekend, writing up descriptions of each item for the auction catalog. I smiled as he raved about her vast knowledge of collectibles, and how she'd given him lots of contacts to advertise the event.

Marybeth also left a message asking if I was available to visit some more retail locations.

I sighed. A very deep sigh.

Alice, over in her corner, gazed at me sympathetically.

"I know, Alice. I'm trying to keep an open mind, but my heart's just not in it."

With the weather turning colder, I'd need to change her outfit soon. Or at least add a jacket to cover up those bare fiberglass shoulders. "See, I want to keep the store but I don't want to go through our entire savings to do it. Joe's doing a good job of that all on his own."

I decided I would only turn on the lamp on the Welsh dresser and the one by the register. No sense wasting electricity. I should start riding my bicycle more, too.

"Why the hell is it so dark in here?" Martha asked as she came into the store a few minutes later, with Eleanor on her heels.

"I'm trying to conserve energy."

"For God's sake, don't be so cheap."

Fine for Martha to say. She'd never had to worry about money. Teddy Bristol had spoiled her for years and then left her very well-off. She didn't have to work—apart from her volunteer activities and the Historical Society.

Eleanor winked at me. "Daisy, I need some of your vintage lace."

While I pulled some pieces out of the dresser drawer, I told them about my visit to Tracy McEvoy's studio with Joe.

"Brilliant artist, but buying a painting from her was next to impossible," Eleanor said. "She can be pretty tough to deal with. Almost rude, as a matter of fact."

"I couldn't agree more, but you know how Joe gets along with everyone. Apparently she's his new best friend and mentor."

Eleanor picked up one of the yards of lace and held it up to the stark light near the window. "And he's still a good-looking guy."

"Yes, very handsome." Martha sniffed. "You want to watch your back there, Daisy. She's probably one of those babes looking for a father figure."

I thought back to the self-contained young woman who had built a house by herself, seemingly unaware of her primal allure even in an old T-shirt and jeans. "You know, I don't think she's looking for *anyone*."

I poured coffee into three mugs. "And Joe's purchased every tool under the sun for this new hobby of his, even though he knows money will be tight. Although from the way Harriet Kunes carried on, maybe he's not so bad."

Martha removed the lid from the rectangular tin she carried to reveal stacks of honey madeleines.

"I've brought you something, too." Eleanor fished in the tote bag she carried and brought the sad iron out with a flourish. "Figured it owes you. You can sell it and keep the five bucks."

"Gee, thanks." I grinned at her as I set it down on the ground. "I think."

"We can't stay long this morning," Martha announced. "We have another excruciatingly boring meeting of the Hysterical Society. These things only used to be once a month. Now it seems like it's every week." She shuddered. "Oh, I can't wait to go to the B and B with Cyril. I need to get away from all this hustle and bustle."

Eleanor and I looked out of the display windows to where the Main Street of Millbury slumbered like an old-time picture postcard. There was not a soul to be seen.

"We're staying at the Four Foxes. But Cyril says he can't see the point of paying money to stay in your own backyard." She picked up a French carriage parasol of duck egg blue cotton with ivory lace and twirled it around. "I don't know what's going on with him lately. He's been acting kind of funny."

The front door jangled and Dottie Brown came bustling in. "Morning, all. Daisy, I brought you some flyers about my next class starting October first."

In addition to running the yarn and fabric store in Sheepville, Dottie also held knitting classes at night. "I could use some more of your business cards, too."

I handed her a stack. Dottie and I appealed to some of the same clients, and we supported each other as much as we could. "I saw your husband this morning," I said. "Those pumpkins are really something."

"Oh, those damn things! You should have seen him in July when it came time to pollinate. He borrowed some of my stockings to cover the female blossoms so some stray bee couldn't accidentally screw things up, pardon the pun."

Eleanor snickered.

Dottie shook her head in despair. "And you should see my water bill these past few months. I bet he's using a hundred gallons a day or more. But I suppose it keeps him out of trouble while I'm busy with my knitting ladies. See you all later."

As she was leaving, the front door opened again and Laura Grayling came in, carrying her green suitcase.

"Laura! What are you doing here?" For a moment I wondered whether I had my days mixed up.

"I have to replenish my display." She opened the suitcase and brought out a velvet pouch. "I sold so many things last week."

"I'm glad you're selling well. You deserve the success."

She flushed faintly under the freckles. "Thanks, Daisy."

"I might need you for an extra day on Wednesday if you can. I'm supposed to see more places with Marybeth."

"Sure, no problem. Here's what I made with some of the stuff you gave me."

We admired the collection of necklaces and earrings. One in particular caught my eye. It was a long chain with green glass beads and vintage enameled buttons, featuring a gold monogrammed heart with the initials MAJ.

"I don't remember seeing this heart before," I said. "It's very pretty."

After fixing up her display, Laura left, telling me she'd see me on Wednesday. We were just settling down with our coffee again when the front door banged open.

Chip Rosenthal strode into the store with the same bullet-like trajectory as before.

"Got your message. Are you ready to sign?" he said, coming up to me, and ignoring everyone else.

Martha planted both hands on her ample hips, and if Eleanor were a dog, the hair would be standing up on the back of her neck.

I cleared my throat. "Actually, I wanted to talk to you about that . . ."

I struggled to remember my carefully prepared speech that had sounded so good in the first light of morning, but now fizzled from my brain like early snow landing on warm pavement.

"You see, Chip, um, well, you know I've been a very good tenant and—"

"Yes, yes, I believe we covered that already." He pushed against a child's rocking chair from the late nineteenth century, with high sides to guard against drafts. It creaked painfully back and forth against the wooden floor. "Are you willing to re-up or not?"

"It's too much of an increase. Can't we work something out? I can't afford such an astronomical rent."

He took a deep mucus-laden sniff as if to clear his sinuses. "If you don't want to sign, that's fine. I'm thinking about opening a wine bistro in here anyways."

"A wine bistro!" Eleanor's face lit up, and then she quickly sobered as she caught my eye.

Chip glanced around, as if already picturing the store cleaned out, and my quilts and linens replaced by wine barrel tables and bottle racks on the walls. "I think a restaurant is badly needed around here. Should prove much more profitable than some crappy old sewing store."

His phone rang and he whipped it out of his pocket. "Rosenthal. Yeah, let me call you back."

He reminded me of some students I'd had in my classes over the years, the ones who found history boring and had no respect for the past. Well, if you didn't learn the lessons of the past, you were bound to repeat the mistakes.

He clicked the phone off. "So, yeah, I don't really care if you stay or not. Your choice."

Martha picked up a vintage Chinese paper fan and started waving it in front of her face.

I glanced at Eleanor and saw the answering alarm in her eyes. An overheated or hungry Martha was a very bad sign. A combustible situation to be avoided at all costs.

Danger! Danger! I visualized flashing sirens going off

inside the store and opened my mouth to interject, but it was too late.

Martha strode forward and poked Chip Rosenthal in his chest. Hard. So hard that he staggered back a step.

"Now listen here, you little pipsqueak. How dare you waltz in here and speak to my good friend Daisy like that? You need to learn to mind your manners."

To his credit, Chip recovered quickly. He glared at her and straightened his tie. "I have no idea who you are, ma'am, but this is between me and my *tenant*. This lease is nothing to do with *you*."

Martha tossed her mane of fiery red hair. "Well I'm making it my business, snot nose."

"Oh, for God's sake." Chip fumbled with his cell phone, as if hoping it would morph into some kind of Taser to zap her with.

"Hey, I have a good idea." She thrust her not inconsiderable chest out and towered over him in her leopard-print pumps. "How about you take your dumb lease and stick it where the sun don't shine?"

I finally found my voice. "Martha, please . . ."

"Zip it," Eleanor muttered, coming up and elbowing her sharply in the side.

Two bright spots appeared on Chip's sallow cheeks, and he pointed the phone at me. "You can call off your pit bull now. Either sign the lease or be out by the end of the month." He spun around on his shiny brogue shoes and stalked out.

The door crashed behind him, and we stood there in shock until the bell finally stopped jangling.

Eleanor was the first to speak. "*Mais oui.* I think that went well."

"Sorry, Daisy, but he just made me so mad." Martha picked up the fan again. "I might have gone a bit overboard, though."

Eleanor snorted. "No kidding, Captain Obvious."

I ran a hand through my hair. "Do you think he's serious about a bistro? Is *that* why he wants to push me out?"

She shrugged. "I'm not sure he'd get approval for it. Martha, do we know anyone on the zoning board? Don't worry, Daisy, we'll find a way to squash it. Make sure he never gets a liquor license."

Suddenly I remembered Marybeth talking about making it a point to stay friendly with zoning board members and developers. "I can ask Marybeth Skelton. She has some connections."

"What's her motivation to help you?" Eleanor asked. "If you stay where you are, she gets nothing in commission."

"Oh, jeez, you're right. Well, I'll offer to pay her a fee."

"Bribery?" She picked up two of the honey madeleines.

"No, no, I mean for the work she already did. For taking me out to the places she's shown me. For her time."

I knew it would be more a matter of pride with Marybeth anyway. She was a savvy real estate agent who knew that if she took care of me, I'd recommend her to others or use her again someday. Real estate wasn't a one-off kind of business.

At that moment, PJ Avery bounced into the store like a skinny female Tigger. "Hey! What's goin' on? I was just passing by."

She frowned as she looked at us. "What's the matter with you guys? Did someone else take a dirt nap?"

"No. No one died," I replied in a dull voice. "Well, not unless you count the death of my business, that is."

"Buck up, Daisy," Martha said, with a worried glance at Eleanor. "That doesn't sound like you. You're usually Miss Glass Is Half Full."

My friends filled PJ in while I poured her a cup of coffee and proffered the biscuit tin.

"This is becoming a habit," Eleanor said. "Like feeding a stray cat."

"I know," PJ said, her eyes closing briefly as she took an appreciative gulp. "I *love* this place."

I was sure she was smart enough to pick up on Eleanor's sarcasm, but chose to ignore it. She must figure that if Martha and I wanted to spoil her, she'd be a willing participant.

"Daisy, I almost forgot. I did some digging on the Rosenthal case," PJ said. "According to my sources, it sounds like that stepdaughter was Sophie's main caretaker, and after she left, Sophie's health deteriorated rapidly."

Eleanor placed herself between the reporter and the madeleines. "It's ironic that the person who looked after her the most was the one person who couldn't inherit."

"Yeah, although actually I just found out she died abroad," PJ said. "Some kind of tropical disease. Sad."

"What kind of disease? Where?" I asked.

She picked up a brass egg-shaped thread holder with thimble attached and inspected it closely. "Not sure. Doesn't really matter anyway, does it?"

For someone who was supposed to be a reporter and in the business of getting facts and details straight, she seemed a bit vague.

PJ sucked down more coffee. "So, like, maybe you could close this place, work online for a while, wait until one of the other tenants leave, and then take over their space?"

"That's not a bad idea, except I'd lose a lot of business. I'd have to start all over again." I walked back to the counter and promptly stubbed my toe on the sad iron I'd left sitting on the ground. "Ow! *Ow!*"

Martha glanced at Eleanor. "We'd better get to the meeting."

"Yes. See you later, Daisy."

I couldn't speak, just waved as they beat a hasty retreat, with PJ close behind. When the throbbing in my toe subsided and I could walk without gasping for breath, I tried to think clearly about what I was going to do.

I still had money in the store's bank account, and a lot of valuable merchandise to liquidate. If I closed Sometimes a Great Notion now, I could walk away with a nice chunk of change, instead of risking it all on a new location and a higher overhead.

"Alice, what do you think? Should I quit while I'm ahead?"

Alice stared back at me, an uncharacteristically stern set to her mouth.

I sighed. "You're right. That's not like me. I never give up."

The next morning, I decided to ride my bicycle to Jeanne's store to pick up the paint. She opened at 9 a.m., so if I got there on the dot of nine, I could still be back in plenty of time to open mine at 10 a.m. It was only two small cans and I could put them in the basket on the front of the bike.

With the price of gas these days, I'd be saving the money it would take to buy the paint.

Pleased with my logic, I set off.

Sheepville was only about five miles away, but some of the turns and hills on River Road were a challenge. It felt good to push myself physically, to work off the tension and stress of the past weeks. The traffic was heavier than I was used to, with kids being back in school, and there wasn't a whole lot of room for a bicyclist.

It was a beautiful morning, with the temperature forecast to be in the sixties later on. As I cycled, my muscles warmed up and the bike hummed along. The more I rode, the more my mood improved. No matter what else happened, I was determined to finish this dollhouse, and I grinned at the thought of Claire's reaction.

After I stopped at Jeanne's, I was feeling so good that I decided to swing by Meadow Farms before I headed back to Millbury. I didn't have much of a plan in mind, except an urge to ride by Harriet's house one more time.

I pulled up to the guard house and gave the elderly sentinel my brightest smile.

"Good morning. My husband and I are thinking about joining the country club. He's such an avid golfer and he wants to teach me. I wonder if I can go in and check it out?"

He looked dubiously at my ancient bicycle, but after having me sign in and show some identification, he let me in.

I rode toward the clubhouse complex. Several golfers were already out on the course. It was a great day for a game. Not much wind and a clear sky. The trees were all turning color now, and the riotous mix of scarlet, burgundy, orange, and yellow was breathtaking with the hills in the distance.

A couple of women drove by over the greens in a golf cart, and I nearly fell off my bike.

I was pretty sure that they hadn't seen me, but what the heck were my real estate agent, Marybeth Skelton, and the artist Tracy McEvoy doing here together?

Chapter Eleven

What an odd couple. I would never have connected the two as friends, although I supposed they were from the same Easter basket in many ways. Both tough, competent, self-made women.

Real estate and miniatures must certainly be lucrative to afford memberships here.

I rode up to the clubhouse, and when I glanced back and saw the guard was busy checking someone else through, I sprinted toward the road that led to the residential area. I slowed down once I was around a corner and out of sight. Also because my heart was heaving painfully in my chest.

Maybe Mac was the one who had done the dirty deed on Harriet? She had the electrical expertise, plus Marybeth Skelton was more the type to hire people to do stuff for her, not get her hands dirty herself. With those long fingernails, she could barely dial a phone, let alone handle intricate wiring.

Harriet would know Mac and would let her in. Mac could have made up some story about bringing more miniatures over for her to see. And although the guard had said there were no other visitors except me, Joe, and the cleaning people that day, Mac wouldn't even have to say she was visiting Harriet. She could just flash her membership card like she was going to the clubhouse, and who would be any the wiser?

I reached Barnstead Circle and cycled slowly down the cul-de-sac. I took a quick look around and wheeled the bicycle across the grass and leaned it up against the side of Harriet's house, nearest the trees.

As I walked into the woods, the noise of the world faded away except for the chirping of birds high above and the sound of leaves crunching underfoot.

What did I expect to find? A monogrammed scarf conveniently caught on a tree branch perhaps, or maybe Chip Rosenthal's wallet that he'd dropped as he ran from the scene?

Get real, Daisy.

The police had scoured this area, I was sure. I went as deep as I could before the brush blocked my way, trying to imagine I was mowing grass, making straight overlapping lines back and forth. As I made another route back toward the house, I caught my breath. A young deer stood staring at me, only about six or seven feet away. There was a moment when neither of us moved, and I drank in the sight of its liquid brown eyes and soft fur. A bird cried out, and suddenly spooked, he crashed away in a flurry of spiky legs and white tail.

It had probably been a deer that night, too. So much for my overactive imagination.

A minivan with a logo saying THE DAZZLE TEAM zoomed down the street, radio blaring with some kind of joyous music with a throbbing drumbeat. It ground to a halt in front of the house across from Harriet's.

I slipped behind a tree and hoped they wouldn't notice my bicycle. Four women tumbled out of the van, laughing and chatting. I watched for a few minutes, as they went in and out of the house with cleaning supplies.

Harriet's house must have been sort of a sweet deal, come to think of it. Only one person living there, with no pets. They would only have had to vacuum a narrow pathway through the hallways. Most of the bedrooms were inaccessible, being stuffed to the gills with collectibles, which they were forbidden to dust anyway.

As I hid behind the tree, wondering when I could make my getaway, I saw the garage doors rise, and two of the women, one wearing a bright red bandana around her hair, pulled the trash cans to the curb for pickup next morning. They went back inside the house, leaving the garage open.

Was *that* how the killer entered the house? It wouldn't be too hard to slip inside, and hide somewhere that the cleaning people wouldn't go, like the unfinished basement. Or heck, even in Harriet's garage, if they squeezed behind one of those towering piles of totes and boxes. Once the crew left, it would be a simple matter for the killer to tamper with the dollhouse, hit the door closure, and scoot under the garage door, just the way Birch had done.

I checked my watch. Damn. Already 9:45 a.m. I'd need to haul it back to Millbury. No doubt I was going to be late opening the store. The question was how late. As I swung my leg over the crossbar, I had a bad feeling I'd overdone it. What had seemed like a great idea suddenly seemed reckless, if not plain stupid.

I rode along Burning Barn Road, thigh muscles aching, and toyed with the idea of calling Joe to pick me up.

A car was coming from the opposite direction, and I gasped as the one behind me suddenly passed, leaving barely six inches between its mirrors and my handlebars. I swerved, the bike wobbled, and I fell off into the undergrowth by the side of the road.

I lay there for a minute, praying that my bike wasn't covered in lilac and yellow paint.

Lights flashed in my peripheral vision. I groaned as I twisted around and saw an unmarked police car with Serrano at the wheel.

I sat up as he sauntered over to me. He was wearing a dark gray suit with a sky blue tie that matched the color of his eyes.

"Whatcha doin', Daisy?"

Looking like an old fool. "Saving money."

"By getting run over and ending up in the hospital?" He held out a hand and I grasped the steely warmth as he pulled me gently to my feet. "What are you doing in this neck of the woods anyway?"

"I just bought some paint for my dollhouse." I picked up the cans. They were a bit dented, but thankfully intact.

"At Meadow Farms?"

I sucked in a breath. "Look, Serrano, I think I know how the killer got into Harriet's house." I explained about seeing the cleaning women leaving the neighbor's garage doors open.

"You can't see that particular street from the gate."

I gritted my teeth. "All right, all right. I may have talked the guard into letting me check out the clubhouse."

Serrano shook his head, whether in exasperation or admiration, I couldn't tell.

"See, someone could have snuck in when the cleaners were busy, rewired the dollhouse, and then exited through the garage, the same way Birch Kunes did."

"You have a point there," he said. "Most people leave the door unlocked from the garage to the mudroom or kitchen, and leave that alarm zone turned off. But what about the front door being ajar?"

"When Harriet got home, she was probably so excited about seeing the dollhouse, she forgot to close it properly." Now that I'd stopped cycling, I could feel my leg muscles cramping up again and I rubbed a hand against the small of my back. "We assumed it was from someone running out, but maybe not."

"Want a ride?"

I nodded. *To heck with my pride.* "Yes, please."

Serrano picked up my bike, slipped the front wheel off, and slid it into the vast trunk of the Crown Victoria. I was worried about him getting grease on his suit, but before I could even voice my concern, it was completed with one smooth movement. The way he did everything.

I pulled a leaf out of my hair before I got into the car. Serrano didn't need to know that I had been poking around in the woods. God forbid he'd infer that I didn't think the police could handle their jobs.

The passenger seat was well-worn and comfortable, and I relaxed against it as the cruiser ate up the miles between the environs of Sheepville and Millbury.

"Hey, guess who I saw golfing together?" I said. "Tracy McEvoy and Marybeth Skelton. What do you make of that?"

"There's no law against playing golf, Daisy." There was a weary note to his voice.

I frowned. He wasn't taking this seriously at all. "But one of them, most probably Mac, could have been the person that Harriet was expecting that night. As members of the club, they wouldn't have had to sign in as her visitors."

"Or it could have been Kunes," he said. "He knew the code, and was used to running under the garage door. He rents a place in the development. He wouldn't have to sign in as a visitor either. And he has the best motive of all the suspects."

"I don't know, Serrano. He seems like a nice guy."

"Sometimes the obvious suspect is so for a good reason.

And it's often the guys who are too nice, too helpful, that you need to consider."

"Look, I really think you're barking up the wrong tree here."

He made no answer. Serrano was as immaculate as ever today, but there were fine lines at the corner of his eyes, and he was so perfectly shaved, it was as if he'd taken extra trouble with his appearance.

"Do I look okay?" he inquired.

I blushed. "Yes, you look very nice."

He exhaled. "God, I'm tired. I found a strange woman waiting for me in my bed last night when I got home."

He looked so glum about it that I had to cough against the laugh that rose up in my throat.

"She was wearing nothing except high heels and a frilly black apron, and she was holding an apple pie."

"An *apple* pie?"

He frowned. "Yeah. Why?"

"Well, I would have thought chocolate mousse was sexier." A grin escaped that I couldn't hold off anymore.

Serrano shook his head, but there was a trace of an answering smile as he glanced at me. "All right, Ms. Buchanan, you can mock, but it was a severe invasion of my privacy."

"How'd she get in?"

He sighed deeply. "She told the cleaning people that she was my sister, and seeing as burglars usually don't bring pies, they let her in. My Spanish is limited, but I think I got through to them not to do it again."

"Did you arrest the woman?"

"I told her to get dressed and then I escorted her out of the development. Then I went home and washed the sheets."

There was silence in the car as we swung up onto Sheepville Pike.

"So, did you ever check out where Chip Rosenthal was on the day of Harriet's murder?" I asked.

"In his office mostly, but there are gaps of time when no one can confirm his whereabouts," Serrano said, reluctantly. "When we tried to interview him, he refused to answer any questions without his lawyer present. Sniveling and whining the whole time. Pathetic."

"You see? Guilty!" I cleared my throat. "Um, do you think you could take a look at the file on the recluse, Sophie Rosenthal? There's some talk that she may have been murdered, too."

He raised an eyebrow. "I don't suppose you have anything substantial to back this up?"

"Not exactly, but you know how lazy Ramsbottom was. It's unlikely he conducted a thorough investigation." The detective that Serrano had replaced was not only slipshod, but had in fact been suspended for questionable activities.

Serrano pulled up in front of Sometimes a Great Notion. As he hoisted my bike out of the trunk and attached the wheel again, I asked, "Why are you gunning so hard for Birch Kunes? Why are you so convinced he's the guilty party?"

"Just have a real problem with guys who cheat. Long story. There's something else," he said, lowering his voice, "and this is just between you and me, Daisy. We've discovered a sizeable payment from Birch Kunes into Marybeth Skelton's bank account. I gotta wonder if this guy's some kind of serial cheater, or what?"

"Maybe he felt guilty over how his wife treated her younger sister, and he's trying to make amends."

Serrano's expression was grim. "Or maybe it's payment for a job well done."

The next morning, before I even got out of bed, I knew I'd be paying the price for yesterday's adventure. I moved slowly, stretching muscles that were determined to punish me for the unaccustomed vigorous exercise.

I took Jasper for a walk, wincing as he pulled on the leash and my back cried out in protest. Piles of leaves lined the sidewalks and he dove, burying his head underneath and then coming up for air, shaking them off like so many water droplets. After the oppressive humidity of summer, he'd found renewed vigor in the crisp fall.

The tree in front of the one-room schoolhouse had exploded into a fiery burst of burnt peach, smoky lemon, and spicy lime. Halloween decorations were already up on some of the houses, and I admired the arrays of mini pumpkins and mums lining the doorsteps. Ghosts made of white scarves swung from the eaves of porches, and the dried stalks and pods of summer flowers made a spooky display. We passed one place with plastic gravestones planted in the yard, and Jasper gave a startled bark as a motion detector set off an eerie chuckle of laughter.

At Sweet Mabel's, pumpkin ice cream was the special of the day, and a sign invited customers to COME IN AND SIT FOR A SPELL.

I hoped Serrano had taken me seriously about reviewing Sophie Rosenthal's file. Maybe a clue had been overlooked. Some small detail or photo that would give a hint as to the real cause of her death.

We walked past the Browns' house, and I slowed down, enchanted at the sight of the giant pumpkin. Like a scene from a fairy tale in the foggy quiet of the morning. It was far bigger than the other two now. I could picture mice turning into coachmen and vines swirling up around it to make carriage wheels.

In spite of the early hour, Sam was already working in the patch, pulling up weeds.

"Georgia seems like she grows every time I see her," I said.

"Oh, yes, giant punkins are incredible when they get going. They can grow thirty to forty pounds in a day."

We both stared at it, and I fancied I could see the pale monstrous fruit swelling before my eyes.

"The right seed is the key," Sam said as he came over to me. "This year I crossed a 1472 Meklin with a 1323 Ames. Walter Ames won last year with a fifteen hundred pounder. I don't expect to equal the real heavy hitters, but I would like to get above a thousand pounds before I die."

He smiled at my expression. "You think I'm crazy, but you should see some of these guys. I know one guy who has his punkin attached to all this monitoring equipment. He can tell you how much it grows every hour. He's got graphs, pollination records, and a seed collection like you wouldn't believe. And some of them have huge fields on their farms. I'm just doing it in my backyard."

I smiled back. I'd always thought of Sam Brown as an amiable, if rather dull sort of man, but in talking about his pumpkins he was transformed, his eyes alight, the energy fairly crackling from him.

I'd always been fascinated by people who were fully engaged with something, whatever it was. So many people never found their passion in life.

Marybeth was due at 10 a.m., so I said good-bye to Sam and hurried home to get ready. But when I opened Sometimes a Great Notion, there was an apologetic message on the machine. Apparently she'd tried to line up a couple of places, but one of them had just rented, and the owner of the other decided it wasn't ready to show.

I gritted my teeth. Marybeth probably just wanted to go golfing again.

When Laura arrived, I explained that I wasn't going out, but I could still use her help. We set to work cleaning out the upstairs bedrooms, which was one of those projects I'd been meaning to get to, but never had.

Numerous yard and estate sale purchases were piled up

against the wall, mainly things that needed repair or were missing a match. I cheered to discover some vintage post-cards from an auction I'd attended in the spring. Somewhere in this mess was a collection of old valentines, too, and I'd planned to display them together.

It was so much faster and nicer with someone to share the job. Laura was always so amenable and willing to work hard. I promised myself I'd do whatever I could to take care of her, no matter what happened with the store.

Although she came to an abrupt halt when she picked up a pale green glass plate.

"Laura? What is it?"

"Sorry. This reminds me of my mom." She ran her fingers lightly over the intricate beaded pattern.

It suddenly struck me that I didn't know that much about her. She'd never revealed a lot about her family or her back-ground. Who *was* Laura Grayling?

"Your mother collected sandwich glass?" I asked gently, aware of the brightness in her eyes.

She nodded. "I don't remember that much about her. She died when my little brother was five."

"That must have been hard for you." I thought of my wonderful, quirky daughter, off on a film set in Spain. Sarah had been adored and spoiled her whole life and still gaily complained about anything and everything.

Here was a girl who'd had a lot more to deal with and had still found her way.

"I expect you had to grow up fast, taking care of your brothers and sisters."

"Yes, but I didn't mind. We're very close."

She didn't seem to want to say any more, so I said briskly, "Okay, let's move some of this stuff downstairs for sale."

As I set out some postcards from the turn of the last century on the Welsh dresser, the terse inscriptions made me smile.

One from Weatherly, PA, sent in 1916, said, "This town is much nicer than I thought. Wish you were here. Your wife, Elsie." Another from the Devil's Pool, Wissahickon Creek, Philadelphia, was inscribed simply, "Having a fine time," and signed with the sender's initials.

The lost art of letter writing.

I found a boudoir dresser scarf in another box, and knew immediately where it had come from. There was that elusive scent of Sophie's again, still clinging to the navy silk. The scarf was hand-embroidered with baskets of roses and lilacs at each end.

Now I remembered why I hadn't displayed it right away. The metallic trim had separated in a couple of places, but it was an easy fix. I sat down right then and there with a needle and thread. There was no sense in leaving this exquisite scarf languishing in a cardboard box a moment longer.

As I sewed, I wondered what had happened to the regal, intelligent woman who owned all these lovely things? In spite of the fact that I'd never met Sophie, I had to admit I was much more interested in learning the truth about her death than the spiteful Harriet's.

Laura uncovered a set of wooden alphabet stamps, and we set them next to the postcards. She also found a Victorian necklace of a real butterfly mounted on mother-of-pearl. The chain was broken, which was why it had been stored upstairs.

"I can fix this, Daisy. No problem."

Little by little, over the course of the next few hours, I coaxed more memories out of Laura, especially about her mom. She wasn't the type to open up right away, and patience was not my strong suit, but eventually she relaxed.

At the end of the day, I was amazed at how much we'd done, and I hoped that the telling of long-buried stories had helped her in some small way.

"Thanks so much, Laura. I think we accomplished a lot today."

I left her to close up and took Jasper to the park.

I found Ruthie on her old tartan blanket, holding court with a couple of the wine club members. One was the matronly golden retriever owner and the other was so unbelievably thin, Martha would have wanted to take her home and feed her a plate of spaghetti and meatballs.

"Glass of wine?" Ruthie asked.

"Actually, yes, thank you, I will." I sat down on the blanket next to her. "It's been a long week already."

I smiled at the other two. "Hi, I'm Daisy Buchanan."

The golden's owner was the first to hold out her hand. "I'm Alice Rogan. Nice to meet you."

"Alice! Hey, I have a—um—another friend called Alice," I said, but I didn't elaborate.

Before the second woman told me her name, she cried out, jumped up, and ran into the pack of dogs to pick up a snarling Chihuahua.

"That's Caroline," Ruthie said. "She's always doing that, because she's afraid her dog's going to get hurt, but he's the one who starts most of the fights."

It hadn't taken me long at the park to realize it wasn't the dogs you had to worry about, it was the owners. A nervous, insecure human invited aggression by making his or her pup feel as though it had to step up and take charge.

I sipped the zinfandel. It was sweeter than I liked, but hey, it was wine.

"Doesn't Bettina Waters come to the park anymore?" Alice asked. "I haven't seen her in ages."

"She's preggers, you know." Ruthie glugged down the rest of the pink liquid in her glass. "At least he's going to make an honest woman of her. I hear they're getting married next month."

Alice made a harrumphing sound. "She's a nice girl, but she—well, she can be rather odd at times."

"What do you mean?" I asked, my ears pricking up.

"My husband and I had a dinner party once, and I found her in my family room, going through my photo albums. Apparently she's so self-conscious about the way she used to look that she removes her old photos when she visits people's houses."

Was there some deep dark secret that would jeopardize Bettina's upcoming marriage to Birch if he found out? She had a motive to kill Harriet, but why Sophie, too? Unless Sophie had some incriminating evidence against her. But would a person really commit murder over an unflattering photo?

Ridiculous, Daisy. Have some more wine.

Caroline came back with the tiny dog in her arms. "I am *so* not speaking to Ginny Axelrod," she declared. "You know how hard it is to find good cleaning people? She just stole the woman who works for my good friend Rachel."

She sat cross-legged on the blanket, balancing the wriggling dog and her glass of wine. "My husband likes my girl— too much so for my liking. He says he's not attracted to her, just her laid-back personality. But I'm keeping Angel. She's the best I've ever had, and no one's going to steal her from me." She gave a derisive nod in the direction of the other clump of wine club participants. "So, *too bad*, people!"

Ruthie leaned closer to me. "There's always a battle going on to find the best, and they all poach from each other."

"The one I had before Angel?" Caroline continued. "Ohmigawd, if I told the woman once, I told her a thousand times. Put the forks in the dishwasher with the tines up and the knives pointing down! How hard is that to remember, I ask you? She never stacked the dishes right, either. She'd put plastic on the bottom, shove pots and pans in there, she did everything wrong. It drove me *crazy*."

"Cheese and crackers," Ruthie muttered in my ear. "I have the same cleaning woman as Marybeth Skelton. *She's* the best. I pay through the nose, but it's worth it to keep her. Don't tell this lot," she whispered as Caroline commiserated with Alice Rogan about the paid help who used Tilex on travertine tiles, and were seemingly oblivious to smears on stainless steel appliances.

I zoned out a little as they talked about the correct way to fold laundry.

Would there have been any reason for Bettina to go over to Sophie's house the night she died? Perhaps with an emergency supply of insulin? Could a patient order insulin to be delivered directly from a medical supply place, or did it have to go through her doctor? I didn't know how that worked, but made a mental note to find out.

Alice was delivering a monologue about her four grown children and grandchildren, as if she were in charge of every aspect of their lives. I envisioned a massive whiteboard in her house dotted with multicolored Post-it notes where she kept track of it all, like a detective's situation room in a murder investigation.

"What about The Dazzle Team, the cleaning company that Harriet Kunes used?" I asked Ruthie. "Are they good?"

"Heck, yes. They also clean the Historical Society buildings."

Well, there was proof that they were completely trustworthy. No one would dare cross Eleanor.

"Speaking of Harriet," I said, "did you ever hear about her sabotaging other competitors' dollhouses? Like she did to Ardine Smalls?"

"Oh, you mean the old cockroach story?" Ruthie barked with laughter. "Not sure if that's urban legend or not, but I heard it was the other way around."

Was Ruthie confused? In her rosé-soaked reality, it might be tough to keep things straight.

She got up and picked up her backpack. "I'm taking the RV to Florida in the morning. Max and I will be there all winter."

I grinned as I got up and helped her fold the blanket. I hoped I had half her spunk when I reached her age. "Have a good time. Drive safely. See you in the spring?"

"If you're lucky." She winked at me. "I don't buy any green bananas these days."

I noticed a woman with a Great Dane heading off toward the woods, towing it slowly behind her like a small pony. "Where's she going?"

"Oh, didn't you know?" Alice said. "That path takes you all the way to Millbury. It comes out near that house with the big pumpkin patch. It's about a mile and a half walk if you're up to it."

"That's great." I wouldn't have to take the car anymore and use precious gas. Why hadn't I figured this out before? Grist Mill Road twisted around on its route from Millbury, but I could see now how this path could cut straight through.

Today I'd have to drive the car back, but next time I'd give it a try.

I got up, gave Ruthie a hug good-bye, and called to Jasper.

More of the wine club drifted over, including Ginny Axelrod, who ignored me as usual.

"Heard that Marybeth finally found a buyer for the Rosenthal place," she said to the group. "It's always tough when someone died in a house. Turns buyers off."

I bent down, pretending to adjust Jasper's leash.

"With the age of the places around here, there's a good chance that *someone* died in them at some point in time," Alice pointed out in a reasonable tone.

"Where did Sophie live, anyway?" someone else asked.

"Up on Cook Hill Road. A Tudor-style house," another woman replied.

Thanks for the information. I stayed in my half-crouched position. I think they'd forgotten I was there.

"Yes, Marybeth is doing very well for herself," Ginny said. "Apparently there's a new waterfront development in the works and she'll be the broker of record."

The talk moved back to cleaning services and the troubles with their particular employees. I straightened up, one painful vertebra at a time, and strolled to the car with Jasper.

As I was pulling out of the road that led from the park, I jammed on the brakes as a black Audi came flying by, with a white Mercedes on its tail, both occupants driving like maniacs.

"Jeez. Coincidence?" I said to Jasper. "I think not. Where are those two going?"

I followed as closely as I dared, hanging back on the corners like I'd seen in the movies, and when Chip Rosenthal and Marybeth Skelton pulled onto Cook Hill Road, I kept going past the street and then doubled back.

A minute later, I drove down Cook Hill, keeping a constant speed and slumping down in the driver's seat as I passed Sophie's house, where Marybeth was already attaching a SOLD banner to the sign on the lawn. In my rearview mirror, I saw Chip jump out of the Audi. He was wearing a black knit cap, gray hoodie, and black sweatpants.

I banged a hand on the steering wheel when I saw the knit cap. *Gotcha.*

Once I was far enough away, I made a U-turn and parked in the shade of some trees growing close to the road.

"Jasper, I'll be right back. Be good, okay? Just for a few minutes?"

He panted at me and began whining. As I opened the car

door, he gave a sharp bark. "Oh, come on then, but please keep quiet. Good boy."

We crept slowly up the road, lingering behind a privet hedge on the next-door neighbor's yard. I strained to hear their conversation, but it was hopeless. I was too far away.

Okay, genius. Now what? What would Serrano do?

The property was a fine old Tudor, but in need of some major landscaping and TLC. There was a huge oak tree to the left side of Sophie's house, its great branches almost touching an upstairs window.

As I crouched there uncertainly, Chip and Marybeth disappeared inside the house.

"Come on, Jasper." I sprinted for the old tree, and the dog, delighted by my unaccustomed speed, bolted with me. Once I was behind the trunk that was wide enough to hide us both, I realized I was no better off. The windows were shut. I could see them in the downstairs living room, but couldn't hear a thing.

Marybeth stroked a long red fingernail down his chest, while Chip, who was facing my way, looked as if he was about to choke.

Suddenly he strode toward the window and my heart lurched in my chest.

He threw up the sash and leaned out a little, sucking in air. "God, it's stuffy in here. Sophie always kept this place locked up like a tomb."

"Well, it's sold now, and you know how I can't wait to get started on our next project together, Chipper."

"For the last time, don't call me that." He gritted his teeth. "And I already told you, things are right on schedule, so chill out. The site plan's been reviewed by the county planning commission. It's at the township for approval."

She shook her head. "I still can't believe it. Good old Sophie owning all those prime acres along the Delaware River."

Aha. Guess I could kiss any help with the zoning good-
bye. Marybeth was snuggled up in bed with Chip, and would
have his best interests at heart. Maybe that's why she'd been
so accommodating to try to find me another location.

"The bank has assured me financing won't be a problem,"
Chip said. "As soon as we have the building permit, you can
start taking deposits."

Jasper was pulling on the leash, so I fumbled in my
pocket and found a single dog biscuit. I broke off one minute
crumb at a time and fed it to him. He looked at me as if to
say, *I knew you were cheap, Daisy, but this is ridiculous.*

"This development will be an asset to the waterfront, and
the township knows it," Chip said. "Plus we're improving
the roads and adding connections to the public sewer, which
should keep everybody happy."

Jasper nudged my pocket and gave a muffled whine, and
I searched frantically for another treat.

"Did you hear that?" Marybeth came to the window and
scanned the yard while I gently cupped my hands around
Jasper's mouth. Sweat beaded on my forehead.

"What?" Chip's cell phone rang. It was the theme from
Pink Floyd's "Money," and the sound of cash registers and
falling coins drowned her out.

The window slammed shut, and soon after that I heard
the sound of the front door closing. I waited until both cars
had driven off down the street before I headed back to the
Subaru.

Could the unholy alliance of Chip and Marybeth have
killed Sophie to get the prime commercial land, and then
Harriet, too, to shut her up about the will?

Nothing like killing two old birds for one condo development.

Chapter Twelve

On Friday, I was at Sometimes a Great Notion, looking through my auction listings when Eleanor walked in. "What are you doing today, Daisy?"

"There are a couple of auctions I'm interested in, but I'm not sure I should be buying more merchandise with the way things are going. Where's Martha?"

"Shopping for her big romantic getaway. And *you* need a day off to forget about your troubles. Come with me to Fabric Row."

I grinned. "Now that does sound tempting."

"Come on. It's the best offer you've had all week and you know it."

My mouth watered at the idea of silk chiffon and vintage buttons.

Eleanor tapped her foot on the floor. "Blessed are the flexible for they shall not get bent out of shape."

"Okay, okay, I'm coming."

When Laura arrived, Eleanor and I hurried out of the store, but I stopped in dismay when I saw the red Vespa parked outside.

"Oh no, I'm not riding to Philly on the back of that thing. We'll take my car."

Eleanor shrugged. "Suit yourself."

We walked back down Main Street toward the house. Across the street, a sign in the psychic's window advertised palm readings for ten dollars.

"I wonder how long a psychic can stay in business here at those prices," I mused, visions of vacant storefronts dancing like spots before my eyes.

"Have you ever gone in there? Had your fortune read?"

I clicked open the locks on the car. "Not sure I believe in that stuff."

"You'd be surprised," Eleanor said, giving me an arch look as she slid into the passenger seat. We made a quick stop at the diner for coffee to go, and we were off.

Just under an hour later, we were wandering down historic Fabric Row in Philadelphia, situated roughly between South and Catharine Streets. At the turn of the twentieth century, there would have been pushcarts trundling along here, where Jewish immigrants plied their trade and eventually opened brick-and-mortar establishments.

It was full of dressmakers, upholsterers, costumers, and drapery workrooms. One shop sold nothing but bridal accessories. Another was just for sewing notions, and others sold blinds and shades, bedding and pillows.

We entered the first shop, enjoying the familiar sight of bolts of fabric crammed together, and battered cardboard boxes with yards of rayon cord valance, piping, and beaded trim spilling out over the tops. There was a long row of cutting tables in the back and, as usual, a wizened proprietor perched on a stool somewhere in the shadows.

"God, I'm exhausted," Eleanor said. "That maniac, Tony

Z, decided he has a crush on me. He's been singing outside my bedroom window at all hours of the night."

Tony Zappata, the barber, had a beautiful operatic tenor voice with which he entertained clients as he gave them a short back and sides.

"He really has a very nice voice," I murmured.

"Not at three o'clock in the morning!" she snapped. "I finally called the police and had him arrested for disturbing the peace."

"Ah, poor Tony. The perils of unrequited love."

"It's not funny, Daisy. You try listening to 'Una Furtiva Lagrima' when you're trying to sleep."

I was about to make a joke about catching some z's, but after glancing at the grim set of Eleanor's mouth, I decided against it. I felt sorry for Tony. The little barber was perennially sunny-natured, and it wouldn't be a bad match.

Okay, he was rather short, but Eleanor wasn't that tall herself.

What the heck was going on in Millbury? Was there some kind of aphrodisiac in the water supply?

We browsed as much as we could, although this particular store was so stuffed with fabric piled to the ceiling, it wasn't easy. If you knew what you wanted though, chances are they had it stashed somewhere.

We walked back out on the street and continued our prowl.

"My grandmother was a milliner," I told Eleanor. "I used to wander around the Garment District in New York with her looking in dusty windows just like this." As a child, I was hypnotized by the towering displays of French ribbons, pearl buttons, glass beads, and velvet and satin passementerie that were used to trim hats.

The next shop had gold lettering on its display window proudly stating it had been in business since 1919. It didn't look like much from the outside, but inside was a wondrous textile emporium.

A seamstress's dream.

Eleanor made a beeline for a bolt of white gauzy material. "I need some of this English bridal net. It's fantastic. Actually I'll need lots of it."

It struck me for the first time that Eleanor worked with brides-to-be all day long, yet she'd never been married. I knew she had a fiancé who had died at the very tail end of the Vietnam War. But at this point, it didn't look like she'd ever get to wear one of her beautiful creations.

She was always so self-contained, yet how much pain did that prickly façade hold?

Even though Martha and Eleanor were both my good friends, I was probably closer to Martha. But of the two, Eleanor was the one who understood the thornier, crueler side of life.

We also shared a love of history, and a wedding gown could hold a wealth of stories and meaning. It truly was a piece of the past that needed to be conserved. Eleanor had a master's degree in textile science, and sometimes gave lectures to local colleges on fabric preservation.

True bridal net crackles satisfyingly against your fingers, and I played with it while she picked out some seed pearls. Eleanor paid the forbidding old man at the counter for her purchases, getting the customary ten percent trade discount, and we moved on to the next store.

"I'm experimenting with different herbal teas to dye lace," she told me. "I need to get an exact match on that lace I bought from you to repair some missing sections on Bettina Waters's wedding dress. Apple cinnamon seems to work well, but I'm anxious to try orange pekoe."

"How's the dress coming along?"

"Almost done, and not a minute too soon, as a matter of

fact. The woman had a complete meltdown in my shop the other day."

"What do you mean?"

"Well, when she was getting changed, I commented on the beautiful gold cross necklace she always wears. Apparently she's extremely religious and it's vitally important to her that the baby is born legitimate."

"What would she have done if Harriet hadn't conveniently died?"

Eleanor looked at me, her gray eyes somber. "Exactly. She told me how frustrated she was by Harriet's refusal to grant Birch a divorce, and then she burst into tears. I mean, she went completely *hystérique*, screaming about how she couldn't possibly wait two years. I fully expected her little head to turn around three hundred and sixty degrees."

"Do you think it's just pregnancy hormones?"

She shrugged. "When I reminded her that she was, in fact, getting married next month, and assured her that the dress would be ready in plenty of time, she calmed down. But it was touch and go there for a while."

"Wow."

Eleanor picked up some changeable silk, or shantung, of raspberry and chartreuse woven together. "Feel this, Daisy."

"It's gorgeous." There was an almost guilty pleasure to the sensual slide of the fabric against itself.

"Better than sex, right?" she murmured.

"Well . . ."

"No, you're right. But better than chocolate?"

"Not sure about that either, but I can picture the stunning lady's evening jacket this would make. And there's only one person who could carry it off."

"Martha!" we both said at the same time.

I held on to the beautiful material. "Eleanor, I have a proposition for you."

"God, it's been a long time since I heard those words. Makes me feel like I'm back in the sixties again."

"Look, I'll buy the fabric and you make the evening jacket. It could be our Christmas present to Martha. I've been wanting to do something for her for a while. She always brings treats into the store and never lets me pay her back."

"What about you? You feed us coffee every day."

"Well, yes, but it's my store, and I benefit. A lively atmosphere attracts customers."

I let the smooth silk slip beneath my fingers. Every time Martha moved there would be a hint of raspberry beneath the shimmery lemon and green.

It would be the perfect foil for her vibrant hair.

When we arrived back in Millbury, Eleanor hurried over to A Stitch Back in Time to brew up the tea to color the lace.

It was still only 4 p.m.

I stared at the psychic reader's shop. It didn't have the typical neon sign hanging outside. That would never be allowed by Millbury's zoning codes. Instead there was an elegant purple and gold wooden circle: PSYCHIC ADVISOR, TAROT CARD, PALM READINGS.

There was also another sign, for Halloween, that said, WITCH PARKING ONLY, ALL OTHERS WILL BE TOAD.

At least this medium had a sense of humor.

What the heck. As if my feet moved of their own accord, I crossed the street and peered in the window, where silver stars hung from silver threads. Hippie tapestries were tacked to the walls, and I spotted a wine bottle where numerous candles had dripped down its sides, forming a colorful stalactite. It looked more like a dorm room from my college days than a retail establishment.

I opened the door and entered the dim interior. Candles burned on top of the bookshelves lining both walls and on the round table near the back.

"Hello?"

No one appeared, so I browsed through the books, which were mainly on witchcraft and how to read the tarot. More candles, mortar and pestles, and silver pentagram jewelry were displayed for sale on a table in the center, and cinnamon brooms were propped up against it, the spicy scent competing with incense sticks smoldering in a jar on the counter.

Talk about being back in the sixties again.

It was smaller than my place, but like Marybeth said, I probably didn't need all the room I had now. With some consolidation and careful space planning, I could make this work.

Suddenly beads on a hanging curtain clacked together and a robust woman materialized, her face a mask of pancake foundation that was practically orange. Her head was wrapped in a tie-dyed bandana, but what little I could see of her hair was platinum blond.

She pointed a long purple fingernail at me. "You are here because you vant my store!"

"What?" I stifled a gasp. Was my avaricious intent so easy to read on my face?

"No? You have come for reading?" Her eyes, heavy with black eyeliner, almost disappeared as she squinted at me.

"Um. Yes, I think so."

She motioned for me to sit at the table. Once we were both seated, she moved the crystal ball in between us and placed both her hands on top.

Here we go. What a crock.

She was silent for a few moments until slowly her hands moved across it, as if she were feeling each minute imperfection of the glass.

"I see a man, no, two men, surrounding you. Both have vhite hair. Both are loving you. One is larger than the other."

Angus and Joe?

"Here is another man—a dark and dangerous man." She paused, frowning as she stared into the ball.

I drew in a breath. That must mean Serrano.

"He lives his life in the shadows. But this is the one you really vant. Yes?"

My heart started tripping. It was true that I was attracted to the good-looking, tormented detective, but I was a happily married woman.

Wasn't I?

"And a fourth!" She eyed me speculatively and then peered closer into the globe. "This man has long hair. Looks a bit like . . . Mick Jagger . . . ?"

I jerked my head up in time to see the twinkle in her eye before she burst into uproarious laughter.

"I'm just joshing with ya." The semi-Russian accent was gone, replaced by a South Philly dialect broader than Tony Z's. "I know who you are, and I heard about your troubles with that dirtbag landlord of yours. Figured it wouldn't be too long 'til you stopped in."

She held out a hand with its purple talons. "How're ya doin'? I'm Ronnie. My last name is Polish, and no one can pronounce it, so I just go by Ronnie. Or Madame Ronnie, if you wanna be formal-like."

"Jeez, you had me going there for a minute, Ronnie." I grinned as I took her hand. "So you can't really read minds, or see the future, then?"

She shrugged a plump shoulder. "I dunno. Sometimes I do get a feeling, sort of, but a lot of it is intuition and good old life experience. When you grow up on the streets, you learn to size up people and situations real fast."

I nodded. It was as I'd always thought. These psychics were just clever students of human behavior.

"But seriously, what is it that you want?" she asked.

I stared into her eyes, so dark brown they were nearly black. I felt myself being sucked into their enigmatic depths.

"To stay in Millbury."

"At any price?"

I nodded slowly. In that moment, I decided I'd do whatever I could to get Chip to agree to let me sign a new lease, but only for a year. If I was very careful, I could make it, even at the ridiculous rate he was asking.

I'd ride my bike more, drink cheaper wine, curtail Joe's spending. It would buy me some time, in case someone else moved out and I could take his or her spot on Main Street. Or if nothing else, a year to adjust to the idea of moving to a different town.

Even if Chip went ahead with his bistro plans, he'd need time to get the zoning approval and apply for a liquor permit, and he would probably welcome another twelve months worth of significant rental income.

It was as if I could suddenly breathe again. Making a firm decision on what to do instead of all this uncertainty constantly buzzing around in my head felt like an elephant had stepped off my chest.

I pulled out my wallet. "Thanks, Ronnie. This is the best ten bucks I ever spent."

She nodded and tucked the bill into her bra. "Who knows how long I can make it here anyway."

Now she really *was* reading my mind.

"There's plenty of people would like to see me fail. Brings down the standard of the neighborhood, they say."

"I'm sorry. People can be so mean and thoughtless."

"Tell you what, if I'm not going to renew my lease come July, you'll be the first to know."

"Thanks, Ronnie. I appreciate that."

We shook hands again. Suddenly her fingers tightened around mine, so hard that I couldn't break free.

My heart rate accelerated and I stared at her. "What is it?" I whispered, but she didn't answer, her eyes unseeing and almost opaque.

The skin touching mine turned ice-cold. I knew she wasn't faking it, and my heart beat even faster. She was silent for so long, my hand was freezing by the time she finally let go.

"*What?*"

Ronnie shook her head, looking as shaken as me.

"Something. I don't know what. But you're in danger, Daisy Buchanan, there's no doubt about that. Watch your back."

On Saturday, Angus held the auction for Harriet Kunes's vast collection. We all agreed to help out because he could use the extra hands on deck.

Martha and Cyril volunteered to man the snack bar, Eleanor said she would check people in and assign bidder numbers, and I offered to help move merchandise up to the stage. Betty Backstead would be logging in the winning bids on her laptop.

Joe had promised to come, too, but on Saturday morning when I was ready to leave, he decided he was too busy with his miniatures. After a brief, tense exchange, I walked out of the house, slamming the door behind me.

The auction building was situated on three pastoral acres just outside of Sheepville, across from the Backsteads' white stucco farmhouse. It was a low corrugated metal building, and I was glad the weather had turned cooler because there was no air-conditioning inside, only a few ceiling fans. With the way some auctions and some bidders heated up, it could get brutal in there.

As I pulled into the lot, I glimpsed Eleanor's red Vespa zooming up behind me in my rearview mirror. Cyril's pickup truck was already parked outside. Eleanor and I walked into the auction house together, past the reception area to the snack bar, where Martha was setting up two large slow cookers.

"I've brought my famous buffalo wings and spicy meatballs today. That should keep the men happy."

"Oh, aye? Tha's a right spicy meatball tha sen," Cyril growled, appraising Martha from the rear as he turned the coffee urn on to brew.

Eleanor made the motion of sticking a finger down her throat, and I chuckled as I walked on through to the main auction space. Rows of wooden folding seats that Angus had salvaged from an old theater sat in the center of the concrete floor.

"Yo, Daisy!"

I turned around as I heard the familiar husky voice of Patsy Elliott. She and her daughter came rushing up to me, and I bent down to give Claire a hug. She clung to me, unwilling to let go. I sometimes thought that even though we weren't technically related, these two meant more to me than some of my real family members.

Patsy was tall, with dark curly hair and blue eyes, and lean curves that generated lots of tips at the diner. The classic healthy freckle-faced Irish girl. Claire had dark hair and would be tall, too, when she grew up, but that was where the resemblance ended.

Her heart-shaped face and huge eyes under arched brows would almost be too exotic for Millbury when she eventually blossomed into womanhood. Angus had nicknamed her "Legs" because she had the longest legs compared with her nine-year-old body.

"Sorry I haven't stopped in your store in, like, forever," Patsy said. "I've been run off my feet with waitressing, and helping with the auctions. Plus, do you have any idea how much freaking homework they give kids these days? I'd like to smack some of these teachers."

"Daisy used to be a history teacher, Mom." Claire grinned at me, her dark eyes shining.

"Oh, God, sorry again. Forgot about that. And I haven't gotten around to sending out invitations yet, but will you come to Claire's birthday party? It's the night before Halloween."

I smiled at Claire. "I wouldn't miss it for the world."

"Mommy said we wouldn't do it on my *actual* birthday, because all my friends would be trick-or-treating."

"That's true. And besides, you deserve your own special day. Can't wait until you see what I got you. It's a special present from me. And from Cyril, too."

"Ooh! What is it? Can I guess?"

"Nope." I exchanged a glance with her mother. *Especially not here, surrounded by dollhouses. Too many clues.* "You'll just have to wait and see."

Patsy winked at me. "You know, Daisy, Angus has been just awesome. I'm helping out more and more here lately. Thanks again."

When Angus had been in prison, and then in the hospital, I'd suggested that Patsy step in and handle the bid calling in order to keep the business going. Betty Backstead was too nervous to get up on the stage herself, but Patsy turned out to be a natural auctioneer.

"In fact, I might be able to quit the diner one of these days and get that little place we've been dreaming of."

"That's wonderful."

Patsy and Claire lived with Patsy's sister at Quarry Ridge, in the same development as Serrano. They had the whole finished basement to themselves, but it wasn't the same as having your own house.

Patsy put an arm around her daughter's shoulders. "Well,

kid, let me get you that soda I promised you before the action starts. See you later, Daisy."

They headed toward the snack bar and I spotted Ardine Smalls making last-minute adjustments to some of the doll-houses on display. I went over to her, and we walked around together during the presale inspection. She seemed to have a story about each one. Which competition it had won, and in which year, or at which auction Harriet had outbid her to buy that particular house.

The hall was filling up quickly, so I told Ardine I'd catch her later. I recognized some of her gray-haired compatriots from the competition milling around. There was so much to be sold tonight that Patsy and Angus were going to trade off the auctioneering, an hour at a time. I brought Claire back-stage with me. We'd be in charge of lining up the dolls in the correct order for the assistants to carry out to the podium.

Once the auction began, I started marking my catalog with the winning bids, but after a while I gave up, stunned by the huge amounts. They were already way over what I'd thought, and the reserve prices Angus had established. Although as he'd often told me, it's the marketplace that sets the market value, not the auctioneer. Ardine had spent a fortune herself by buying five of the bigger dollhouses.

During a break in the action, I went outside for some fresh air. The lot was jammed full, with cars spilling onto the surrounding fields. There were license plates from New Jersey, Maryland, Delaware, even as far away as New York and Ohio.

As I passed the snack bar on my way back inside, there was a long line of men laughing and joking with Martha as she served up the wings and meatballs as fast as she could go. Cyril was glowering and pouring sodas and hot coffee.

He stepped out from behind the snack bar when he saw me. "Could I have a word?"

"Sure, Cyril."

I summoned my meager supply of patience as he worked his way up to whatever it was he wanted to ask.

"It's me cat," he said finally. "Martha and I are going to a bed-and-breakfast, or some such nonsense next week." He looked as morose as if he'd said he was going to Dottie Brown's knitting class.

"Could you look after the little feller? He has a cat flap so he can take off whenever he pleases, but if you could stop in every other day or so and make sure there's food and water down, that's all ah ask."

"Of course, no problem."

"I'll give tha a key."

I nodded slowly. "Okay."

This was a Big Deal for Cyril. As far as I knew, Martha didn't even have a key to his place.

"Don't you worry about a thing," I assured him. "Just enjoy yourself."

He grunted and went back to serving coffee.

The auction, which started at 1 p.m. and was supposed to end at 5 p.m., finally wrapped up around 6:45 p.m., leaving us all exhausted and aghast at the fierce bidding. In addition to the packed auction hall, there had been lots of online action, which contributed to the astronomical winning prices.

I'd never seen Patsy Elliott cry in all the years I'd known her, but her eyes were full tonight as she ran over and gave me an even tighter hug than her daughter had earlier.

"Pats, what on earth's the matter?"

She gulped in some air. "Angus told me before we started tonight's auction that he was giving me a cut of the commission . . ."

Here she stopped and sucked down more air. "But I never dreamed we'd fetch prices like this. Those were *crazy* numbers. My God, Daisy, I think it's enough for a down payment on a house. I can't freaking believe it!"

As I hugged her, I felt tears coming to my eyes, too. Angus had confided to me that he was grooming Patsy to take over the place someday. There was a five-year survival rate for the type of tumor he'd had, and I hoped it was a hell of a lot longer than that, but you never knew.

"Why are you crying, Mommy?" Claire wrinkled her nose as she looked up at us.

"Because I'm happy."

Claire shook her head at me and smiled. "Grown-ups are so weird sometimes."

At that moment, I spotted Serrano at the entrance, so I excused myself and hurried over to him. Tonight he was in his casual, but chic mode. Black leather jacket, jeans, and white shirt.

"Are you here to bid on a dollhouse, Detective? Or perhaps a charming French bisque?"

"Very funny. I'm on my way home after my shift. Figured I'd stop in and see how things went. Where's Joe tonight?"

I bit my lip. "It's a case of 'be careful what you wish for.' I hoped he would find a hobby that he'd enjoy, but now all his time is taken up with making miniatures. He says he's getting so many orders, it's tough to keep up."

I started to tell Serrano how amazingly well the auction had gone when his attention shifted to something behind me. I turned to see Bettina and Birch talking to Angus. They looked relaxed and happy, as Birch shook Angus's hand and clapped him on the back. There was a brightness of spirit emanating from Bettina that even being around the wine club hadn't tainted. They didn't seem like guilty killers to me. Just a couple who were very much in love.

Serrano's eyes narrowed as Birch placed a hand gently on her stomach.

"By the way," he said, never taking his eyes off the father-to-be, "we checked Harriet's phone records. Apart from your call that afternoon, there was one more. From a cell phone belonging to PJ Avery."

"Well, I know she'd been interviewing Harriet for a series of articles on collectors."

"That's what she said. And she was supposed to meet up with Harriet that night, which might explain our two coffee mugs, but when she saw the flashing lights and commotion, she turned around and left."

I frowned. "Isn't that a bit odd? As a reporter, wouldn't you think she'd want to be in the thick of the action? Getting the story?"

Serrano nodded, but he was still watching Birch Kunes. I felt like I was talking to a teenager engrossed in a video game.

"Serrano, there's something else I need to tell you. Chip Rosenthal has some kind of major development deal going on. Apparently Sophie also owned prime waterfront acreage along the Delaware River. It blows my mind that she was a commercial property owner, yet never wrote a will."

I made a mental note that I needed to nag Patsy to write one for Claire's sake. I knew that mine and Joe's left everything to Sarah, but what if she was gone, too? I should update it with a provision for Jasper, leaving a portion to Eleanor. She would take care of him.

I felt Serrano start to move on, and I touched his sleeve. The well-worn leather felt cool under my fingers. "Chip's hired Marybeth as the broker for the development. I mean, inheriting my store was one thing, but this is big time. More motive for murder, wouldn't you say?"

"You're really stuck on this guy, aren't you?" He looked at his sleeve, and I could feel my cheeks grow warm. I dropped my hand.

"I checked the file again, Daisy. Nothing suspicious about the old lady's death. No forced entry."

"Well, there wouldn't be if it was Chip. He lived there."

"There *was* one thing, though . . ."

"What?"

"I couldn't find an obituary of that stepdaughter who died abroad. No mention at all. It's like she vanished off the face of the planet."

At that moment, everyone else crowded around us. Martha groaned and pressed a hand to her back.

"Tired?" I asked.

"Tired isn't the word for it. I think I've lost the will to live."

"Fancy a drink, Detective?" Eleanor bestowed her best cat smile on him.

Serrano smiled back, a lazy smile, and I felt my heart twist. "Well, I was off duty as of 6 p.m., so yes, I will accept your intriguing invitation."

"I do have some rather special absinthe back at home, as a matter of fact."

He laughed. "I'll just have a beer, thanks."

Eleanor slipped her hand into his. "Then come on over to the dark side."

I winced and said a little prayer for Serrano's safety as she drew him toward the exit.

"And I'm starving," Angus announced. "Let's go out for pizza."

Ardine Smalls was standing at the edge of our group, twisting the handles of her large old-fashioned black purse between her fingers.

"Smalls, you coming?" he barked.

She hesitated for a moment, the way she'd done with me, as if she couldn't believe he meant it.

Angus strode over and threw an arm around her shoulders in a crushing half hug. "Pop's Pizza and a cold beer would hit the spot right about now. Come on, missy."

A smile that illuminated her whole face was his answer. Twenty minutes later we were installed in a booth at

Pop's. I was squeezed in between Martha and Cyril, and facing Angus and Ardine.

I took a grateful sip of my cold beer. Nothing had ever tasted so good. "I can't decide which hurts more—my back or my feet."

"It's the back," Martha moaned. "No, it's the feet. Good God, what a night."

Cyril drained half of his beer glass in one swallow. "All that money on a bunch of dolls? I'm fair gobsmacked."

Angus rubbed a hand across his thick white shock of hair. "I can't believe it, either. Did you see the price that that Thomas Edison talking doll brought? Jesus, I thought those two old biddies were going to come to fisticuffs."

Ardine sipped her Coke through a straw. "It's because you hardly ever see them on the market, not in that condition, except once in a blue moon."

He made an exaggerated show of peering out the window. "It's almost a full one, but I dunno about the blue part."

She giggled, hiccupping on her soda.

Good old Angus. Like me, I knew he thought Ardine was an odd duck, and sometimes she tried a bit too hard, but he was always kind, no matter what. Angus often talked about karma when we went picking. Treat people right and it would repay you many times over. Treat them badly and you never knew what would turn up.

He grinned at me and then nudged Ardine with his huge shoulder.

"You spent a bundle, too, tonight, didn't you, missy?"

Ardine rushed to explain, embarrassment making her stumble over her words. "I know, but you see, I make quite a good living selling medical supplies, and, well, the house is paid for and, well—"

He roared with laughter. "I'm just kidding with ya."

"Ardine, this is a tough crowd," I said, smiling. "You shouldn't take too much notice."

Tonight was just like old times. Except not quite. Angus was drinking soda, too. This time last year, he would have had a whole pitcher of Bud to himself.

"How's that beer?" he asked, ogling my glass. "Tell me it tastes like crap."

I stuck out my tongue. "Ugh, it's terrible. Like soapy dishwater. Blech!"

"You're a terrible liar, Daisy Duke."

"I know." I reached across and took his meaty hand in mine. "But you're doing great, Angus. I'm so proud of you."

After we'd polished off two large pizzas, two sodas, and a pitcher of beer, we headed back to the auction house. I'd promised to help Ardine bring her dollhouses home. She could fit two on the backseat and one on the front, but the other two were too tall to fit in the trunk of her car, so I put them in my station wagon.

She lived on the outskirts of Sheepville, not far from Hildebrand's garage, owned by Betty Backstead's brother. Right where the zoning changed from commercial to residential, which was a mixture that stripped the existing homes of much of their comfort zone.

Ardine's house was a plain rancher on a corner lot, painted a light green, with a rusted wire fence and a statue of the Virgin Mary in the center of the front yard. There were no flowers, no bushes, no landscaping at all.

Ardine gave me a shy smile as I got out of my car. "Would you like to come in for a minute?"

"I'd love to."

Nothing going on at home anyway.

I picked up one of the dollhouses and followed her inside. "Where do you want it?"

"In this back room." Ardine led me to a tiny sunroom off the kitchen. "I'd like to display some in the living room, but there's nowhere to put them. I haven't changed anything since Mother died."

We went back for another load, and when we came back inside, I stood for a moment, surveying the living room. The furniture was huge. Monstrous, in fact. A wraparound beige sectional sofa encompassed almost all the available floor space, and a massive entertainment center crammed with knickknacks dwarfed the wall facing the front door.

I knew from the rooms she'd created for Jeanne that Ardine had a good sense of design. Quite an elegant sense of style actually, which one would never guess from her appearance. Or from this space.

"Horrible, isn't it?" Ardine came up behind me.

"Do you really need all this furniture? Can't you get rid of some of it?"

She gasped at this heresy. "Oh, no, Mother picked it out, and it's only ten years old." There was a pause while she chewed on her bottom lip. "But what do you think?"

"I could see one pretty love seat and two armchairs in here, and there would still be plenty of room for a display table in front of the window."

I could almost see Ardine's mind working. I knew from her buying spree at the auction she must have plenty of money, and she'd probably saved a lot by living with her mother all these years.

"You could always sell this sectional or donate it to the church for needy families," I suggested.

She brightened. "The church is a good idea. I don't think Mother would mind that as much."

"I think she'd just want you to be happy."

She shook her wiry gray head vigorously. "Mother disapproved of me spending money. I always had to make do. That's probably why Harriet won the competitions."

Ardine walked out of the room and I followed. She stopped at the base of the staircase that led upstairs and jiggled the banister. "I need to get this fixed." She stared at me. "That's how she died, you know. She leaned on it and lost her balance. Fell down the whole flight of stairs. I found her unconscious when I came home. I called the ambulance, but it was too late."

She pressed a hand to her mouth.

"Oh, Ardine, I'm sorry. I shouldn't have started talking about your mom. I really need to learn to mind my own business."

"It's okay, Daisy. And you're right. She's been gone for two years now. It's about time I redecorated."

We went back into the sunroom and she showed me one of her completed houses.

"You need to train your eye to see one material as another. Like this." She held up a flowerpot, which I realized was actually a wooden thread spool. "This table is made from a poker chip, and the chandelier is made of toothpicks, beads, and bits of jewelry."

"That's very clever. They should have given you marks at those competitions for creativity."

Ardine bit her lip with her protruding teeth. "Harriet looked down her nose at it. Sophie, too."

"There's nothing wrong with saving money," I said firmly. "Nothing at all."

"I'm always on the lookout for common objects that I can repurpose. This pedestal base is a chess piece. This oriental rug is a piece of a paisley scarf."

"This is great!" My mind was whirling with possibilities. "Hey, these would be fun projects to do with Claire. I must have tons of stuff at the store that I can use—buttons, thimbles, ribbons, and other odds and ends."

"That's great, but don't overdo it. The art of miniaturizing is to use only what's needed to complete the setting." Ardine tapped on the side of one house. "This family doesn't get along with the family in the Vermont country house next door. It all started when Mr. Murphy cut down Mrs. Johnston's hollyhocks by accident." She shook her head sorrowfully. "Mrs. Murphy would like to make up, but her husband wouldn't approve."

Thankfully, I managed to stop myself from rolling my eyes.

"Here's a new dinner service that Jeanne gave me for the last room design," she said, showing me a Staffordshire china set. "I think I'll give it to the Johnstons to make up for the hollyhocks. You know, then maybe Mrs. Johnston might invite the neighbors over for dinner. This could be a new start for everyone."

Suddenly I saw how real this had become to her. As a teacher, I knew that playing with dolls was a way for children to be in charge. But what did it say about a grown woman? It seemed a bit weird for someone her age, and then I pictured me playing with Claire and making up stories. But that was different.

Oh, yeah? How's that?

"Ardine, you really know your stuff. Have you ever thought about teaching?"

There was that brief, bright smile. Like a student that glowed under just a little attention and positive reinforcement.

"I mean it. I think you'd be great. You have so much knowledge to share."

"Oh, Daisy, you're so nice. Your friends are so nice, too," she said. "I'm so glad I met you."

Chapter Thirteen

When I got home, Joe was still down in the basement. I called hello, and he answered, but he didn't come upstairs, so I grabbed Jasper's leash and headed out for a walk with the dog.

I found myself going down to the south end of Millbury and past the Browns' house. Sam was sitting out in a rocking chair on the porch, and he jumped up and waved to me.

"Come on in, Daisy. Come and see Georgia."

Jasper and I went through the gate, and we walked over to where the pumpkin sat in all her peach-colored glory, swelled to the bursting point and glowing in the moonlight. Like a fairy princess who'd sunk to the ground with her ball gown puffed up around her.

I held Jasper back while Sam hovered over her like an expectant father. "You know, you get real attached to them," he said, stroking her skin. "Like a child or a pet. From starting the seed to the final weigh-in at Doylestown, it's a nine-to-ten-month process."

Like a pregnancy. I thought of Bettina growing larger by the day with Birch's baby.

"Until the day comes that you have to cut the vine to take it to the show. You hold your breath until you get the punkin on the truck. It's like cutting the umbilical cord. It won't grow any more after that. In fact it starts losing weight."

"But how do you know how much it weighs before you go?" I asked.

"You don't. You just have to estimate by measurements, but it's not exact, and you don't know what's going on inside." He rubbed a hand across his weathered face. "I had one that went down last year. Damn squash borers got to it and ate a hole through the side. I cried like a baby."

I swallowed. Somehow I'd developed an attachment to the giant fruit, too. I prayed that this one would make it.

"Then there's the woodchucks. Don't even get me started on those. I seen one creeping round here the other night. I'm ready for him though. Got me a twenty-two rifle. I'll get the little bastard."

I glanced at him in alarm and hoped he wouldn't shoot any unsuspecting walkers with their dogs.

Sam held a finger to his lips. "Ssh. I shouldn't talk like this around the punkins. That's why I don't let Dottie near 'em. She's got bad energy. It stresses them out."

We turned and strolled back toward the house. "Sometimes I play music for them," he said. "Brahms mostly, but the romantic tunes, not his melancholy stuff."

"So the pumpkins like music?"

A seed of an idea was sprouting in my brain.

He nodded vigorously. "I know it helps them grow. I can almost see the leaves move."

"Sam, have you ever heard Tony Zappata sing?"

* * *

On Wednesday morning, before I opened the store, I trudged up to the salvage yard. It had been raining, and I probably should have taken the car, but I was still on my kick of trying to save every penny I could. I picked my way around deep puddles along the muddy road, past green wooden shutters with crackled paint, and Victorian iron gates and fencing. There was a new stack of rusty radiators near the trailer and a gap where the carnival wheel used to be.

Cyril looked glum as he met me at the door, once he saw that I'd come without coffee from the diner. I followed him inside and he made a big production of filling the teakettle and banging it onto the stove. The phone rang and he glared at it.

"Aren't you going to answer that?"

He shook his head and sighed deeply. "Ah know it's Martha. She's called three times this mornin'. Ah can't even splash my boots wi'out her asking me what I'm doing."

I winced, and pressed a finger to the corner of my eye, which was beginning to twitch. "Maybe some quality time alone with you will help her relax."

Or maybe he needed a vacation from Martha.

He still looked unconvinced. "Here's tha spare key."

I stowed it carefully in my bag.

"His Nibs won't stay inside, but don't worry about it. He's used to roaming around at night, but he comes back in t'morning. Just put food and water down and he'll be all right."

The cat was as eccentric as its owner, and had an unnerving habit of hiding in strange places and then suddenly flying across the room like some feline ninja.

Cyril set out two mugs and sighed again. "Hopefully we'll be straight in, straight out, just like the Special Forces."

I bit my lip. I knew Martha would be heartbroken if things didn't work out. I wondered if I should say anything to her about backing off a bit and giving him some space. Or maybe I should just mind my own beeswax.

There was no question they were a strange match. As far as I knew, she'd never even set foot in this rusty place of his, but they really did care for each other. Hopefully some time away would do them both a world of good.

"What do you think o' this?" He brought out the weather vane I'd seen outside last time. It was beautifully polished now and the copper horse and brass directional arms gleamed in the sunlight. "Thought ah might give it to her for a Christmas present."

He wouldn't meet my eyes, but I smiled at him anyway, and breathed a sigh of relief.

"I think she'd love it."

If he was already planning ahead to Christmas, that was a good sign. The ornate weather vane was a bit over-the-top, but then so was Martha, and so was her huge Victorian house, with its elaborate gingerbread in various shades of pink, rose, and cream.

Next he produced the dollhouse. The roof was complete, the porch repaired, the trim attached. Everything was perfect. And he'd painted the whole thing, too. It was as beautiful as Harriet's house, only better.

"Ah wanted to get as much done as I could before we went away."

I walked around it, lost in wonder. "Oh, Cyril, this is fantastic. I can't believe you did it so quickly."

"All that's left to do is to put the furniture and the rugs in. Maybe Joe can tackle the lighting. I'm no expert, and after what happened . . ."

I nodded quickly, forcing the image of the electrocuted Harriet out of my mind.

We spent the next half hour installing rugs and furniture,

gluing books on shelves and anchoring ceramics and other tiny accessories with florist's clay.

I was about to put the framed pictures back on the living room wall when I choked on my tea. "Wait a minute! I think these are actual photos of the Rosenthal family." I peered at one of them. "Yes, here's Sophie." It was a tiny version of her portrait on the wall of the Historical Society.

I handed the minute frame to Cyril. "Here's another. This couple must be Sophie's brother and his wife." I picked up the last one and studied it.

It was a picture of a young blond girl, presumably the stepdaughter. There was something familiar about her, but what was it? The picture was so tiny, it was hard to make out any details.

"There's one missing," Cyril muttered.

I gasped. He was right. The picture of Chip Rosenthal.

Did Sophie have time to pull his photo down from the wall to finger her killer before she died?

After I'd thanked Cyril effusively and promised him coffee every morning for the rest of his natural-born life, I staggered back to the store with the dollhouse safely cushioned in a cardboard box. By the time I made it inside the front door, my arms were shaking. With the last of my strength, I put it in the upstairs storage room.

I covered the top of the box with a pile of quilts and stacked some bolts of fabric in front of it. I still hadn't given the alarm company the go ahead to install a system, seeing as I didn't exactly know what my plans were, but it should be safe enough. I'd make sure I locked the deadbolt when I left for the day.

The doorbell tinkled and I hurried down the stairs. A young woman in a black peacoat and rose-colored scarf looked up at me and smiled. A real live customer!

"Hi. Do you have any vintage needle books? My aunt is a collector, and I wanted to get her one for her birthday, but I had no idea where to find something like that until someone in Sheepville told me about your store."

"You came to the right place." I happily pulled out my needle book collection. Nowadays they were utilitarian affairs, but decades ago, they were truly works of art.

Gorgeous pictures adorned the covers and inside was a jewellike array of colored foils to hold the needles and threader. Bright green, pink, gold, red, and purple foils, some embossed with an intertwining spiderweb design to symbolize the industrious seamstress.

I showed her my "Sewing Susan" needle books, from the thirties through the fifties, featuring the same group of women sitting around, laughing and sewing.

"See how the women changed over the years? In the later books, they used brighter colors, with different hairstyles. Even the painting changed in the background."

Sometimes a Great Notion was a wonderful opportunity to combine my interest in antiques and history with my passion for teaching. People loved to hear stories about the things they bought so they could pass on tidbits of knowledge when they showed off their purchases to their friends.

"That's interesting," she said. "I know absolutely nothing about sewing, but these are really neat."

"Some of these were produced as promotional giveaways to advertise insurance companies and supermarkets and the like. The travel theme was popular, too." I showed her one in the shape of an ocean liner, and another with a view of mountains from a train window. "Probably because sewing was something you could do to pass the time on a journey."

She picked a book with a picture of a woman sewing in a garden surrounded by pink rosebushes. "This is pretty. I think I'll take this one." On the reverse was the same woman inside a drawing room, sewing with a child, and looking out of the window at those same pink roses.

"That's what we call 'new' old stock," I said. "More often than not, the books have some needles missing or the cover has some wear and tear, but there are a few here that have never been used."

I helped her put together a nice selection of five needle books for her aunt. After she left, delighted that she'd found a thoughtful birthday present for under thirty dollars, I put the rest back on display. I picked up one of the Sewing Susan books again, musing over the pictures of the women on the cover.

That picture of the stepdaughter in the dollhouse. Whom did it remind me of?

It was like the thread of a dream that you remember when you first wake up, but the harder you try to think about it, the more awake you become and the further it disappears from reach.

What I needed were more pictures of the Rosenthal family.

I called Debby Millerton, the librarian over in Sheepville, and asked if she could help me locate some microfilm of the newspaper reports of Sophie's death and also the accident that had killed her brother and his wife.

Next I called Chip Rosenthal and left a message that I had an interesting proposition for him and would he please call me back as soon as possible.

It was a busy day at the store, and when the last customer left around 5:30 p.m., I raced over to the Sheepville Library.

I called the house on the way but got the answering machine. I left a message for Joe that I would be late and not to worry about making dinner.

The library was an attractive two-story brick building on the corner of Main and Porter Streets. It had tall white Palladian windows on the first floor, and soaring wide arches inside formed impressive entryways between the various rooms. It was once the borough hall, and had served briefly as a polling place and senior center. It was actually quite a large library for a town the size of Sheepville.

Debby met me in the lobby, where there was a fireplace and comfortable couches to sit and enjoy a good book. She brought me back through the reading tables and endless aisles of bookshelves, through the used-book sale area, and finally to a back room, with beige filing cabinets and a table holding the microfilm reader. "We only have a limited collection of newspapers, but I think you'll find what you need. I've pulled out the *Sheepville Times* for the dates you asked about."

I sat down in front of the reader, and she showed me how to set the reel on the spool and feed the film through the guide.

"What's going on, Daisy?" she whispered, even though no one else was around. "Are you involved in a top-secret investigation again?" Her eyes sparkled. Debby was a film buff and everything was dramatic and exciting if she could make it that way. She'd been writing a romance novel in her spare time for the past five years, but she'd never let anyone read it.

I shrugged. "Don't know yet. Just one of my hunches." I looked around and lowered my voice to a whisper, too. "No one knows if Sophie's death was from an accidental overdose of insulin, or if she killed herself because she was depressed over the death of her brother. I was hoping to find some clues in these articles."

"Well, it's strange that Sophie Rosenthal renewed her library books online the day before she died if she was planning to commit suicide."

"Really?" I stared at her. That wouldn't be enough of a clue for Serrano, but as far as I was concerned, it was another nail in the coffin for Chip Rosenthal.

Debby left me alone then, and I settled down to read.

Apparently Charles Rosenthal, his wife, and stepdaughter
had gone to a New Year's Eve party. Driving home, their
car skidded on some ice on Swamp Pike and crashed over
the barrier, plunged down a hill, and slammed into a tree.
Charles Rosenthal and his wife were killed instantly. The
only survivor was the girl, who had been thrown from the
car, but miraculously sustained only cuts and bruises and
managed to crawl up the snow-covered hill and flag down
a passing car for help.

I enlarged the photo that was captioned "Margaret Jane
Rosenthal." She was a beautiful, if slightly chubby blonde.
I shook my head, catching that wisp of a remembered frag-
ment of a dream again.

Margaret Jane Rosenthal.

A picture of the monogrammed heart Laura had used for
her necklace flashed into my mind. But the initials were
MAJ, which didn't fit.

I gritted my teeth and scrolled through more of the
microfilm. I read all the accounts I could find on the accident
and then changed the reel for one brief account of Sophie's
death, but there was no additional information there.

I stared at Sophie's photo. The arched brows, the promi-
nent nose. A steely look in her eye that was tempered by a
softness to her smile. Definitely a moneyed air about her, and
I could see where she might have been a high-maintenance
chore for the stepdaughter.

The grainy images on the screen were making my eyes
water.

I switched off the microfilm and started searching on the
Internet. I typed in *Charles Rosenthal* and found news items
about his various business deals over the years. I was just
about to give up and head home when I stumbled across
their wedding announcement.

Charles Rosenthal to Dana Avery. Apparently Margaret's

mother used to be married to someone with the last name of Avery, before he died and she married Sophie's brother.

Margaret Jane Avery. And wasn't Peggy sometimes a nickname for Margaret?

With shaking fingers, I reinstalled the reel of the date of the accident. I adjusted the magnifying lens and enlarged the photo as much as it would go, of the blond girl with scratches across her face and badly bruised eyes.

I squinted, trying to imagine her without the mass of blond hair and thinner, to the point of emaciation. I then added purple contacts, cut her hair, and dyed it black.

PJ Avery, the *Sheepville Times*' star reporter, stared back at me.

Chapter Fourteen

I hurried out of the file room, at what I hoped was a digni-
fied fast walk past the people sitting at the reading tables.

Debby was at the reception desk. She read my body lan-
guage instantly, dropped the books she was checking out
for a startled patron, and rushed over to me.

"You've done it! You've cracked the case, haven't you,
Daisy?" Her voice was hoarse in its whispered excitement.

I grabbed her hands. "I don't know yet, but thanks for
your help. I've got to run now. Call you later."

With that, I broke into a real run, out of the heavy front
doors and hell for leather along Main Street to the intersection with Sheepville Pike. It was faster than moving the car
and trying to find another parking spot.

The sergeant on duty was singularly unimpressed with
my frantic plea to see Detective Serrano on a matter of grave
importance. He finished making notes on his pad in what
had to be the worst cursive in the world, and took his time

dialing Serrano's extension, while I paced up and down, panting.

Too bad that monogrammed heart wasn't the right letters. So close, but no cigar.

Suddenly I gasped and almost slapped my forehead. "Oh, silly Daisy! The initials *do* fit." On an old-fashioned monogram, the center letter signified a person's last name. "So MAJ is Margaret Jane Avery. And she must have been the one who broke into my store that night."

The sergeant gave me a quizzical look, and I realized I'd spoken out loud.

Finally he opened the gate and gestured for me to go down the hallway toward Serrano's office. It wasn't really an office, more like a corner of a large room, but it looked a lot different from the last time I'd been here. Back then I'd had to run the gamut of detectives lolling around, chatting, some giving me curious once-overs as I hurried to where the former detective in charge, Frank Ramsbottom, reclined in his chair in slothful splendor.

Now the walls had been repainted, desks straightened up, and this crew looked like they were auditioning for the pages of *GQ*. They were on the phone, on the computer, all on point.

It was true that management style trickled downhill.

Even though Serrano was as immaculately dressed as his men, the haunted look in his eyes was more apparent than when I'd seen him outside Meadow Farms. I hoped one day he would trust me enough to tell me about the demons that tortured a man who seemed to have everything else going for him.

"Serrano, I found a picture in the library of Charles Rosenthal's stepdaughter. I'm convinced it's PJ Avery."

My words tumbled over each other as I explained to the bemused detective about bumping into Laura with the box of jewelry remnants and how she'd picked everything up off the floor, including the monogrammed necklace. "PJ must have lost it while trying to steal the dollhouse. At first I thought it was Chip who broke in, because he has a black knit cap, too, but then I realized the person I saw that night was too short and too thin to be him. It had to be PJ."

"So what do you wanna do, Daisy? Arrest this chick for breaking and entering?"

I sighed. "Not really. I just want to find out what's going on. I mean, why would someone go to such lengths to conceal their identity? And by all accounts, she was the one who took care of Sophie the most. She would have known the ins and outs of her insulin routine."

Although I hoped against hope that PJ had nothing to do with Sophie's death. I'd grown fond of the quirky reporter.

Serrano frowned at his pencil. "I heard she did some time in the Peace Corps. Wonder if she picked up some electrical training there? And perhaps some B&E skills, too."

Now it was my turn to frown. "It might make sense that PJ would kill Sophie, assuming she thought the woman planned to leave her something in her will, but once she found out there wasn't one, it doesn't make sense to do away with Harriet as well. After all, Harriet was trying to find the proof that might make PJ the heir, and not Chip."

I slumped back in my seat.

There was silence between us for a few moments.

"So. Did you have a good time at Eleanor's the other night?" I asked.

I held my breath as I waited for his reply.

The lazy smile flashed, but only for a moment. "She's an interesting woman. Very interesting."

When I got home, there was a note from Joe on the kitchen counter saying he'd gone with Tracy McEvoy to her studio so she could help him finish up an order. He advised me not to wait up, and that she would give him a ride home.

I glanced at the clock. It was 7:30 p.m. I let Jasper outside and he peed for about two minutes straight. "Poor puppy," I said, gritting my teeth and taking the leash off the wall.

Would it have been too much for Joe to call and let me know that he wouldn't be home to let the dog out?

"Good boy. Let's go for a walk."

Jasper and I took what was becoming our regular route toward the south end of Millbury and the Browns' house, the giant pumpkin calling me like a siren. I'd miss it when it went off to the competition.

A couple of blocks away, I heard the singing.

If I wasn't mistaken, it was the aria from *Roméo et Juliette*, when Romeo sings up to his love on her balcony.

I stopped in the shadow cast by the side of the house. In the twilight I saw the diminutive barber standing in the middle of the pumpkin patch, surrounded by leaves the size of dinner plates, his hands held up to the regal fruit in supplication. Above him, dark spikes of high tree branches pierced the indigo sky, and the moon was a milky blur behind the clouds.

His soaring tenor resonated around the garden with gorgeous, lush tendrils of sound, and I fancied I could almost see the leaves trembling. Even Jasper sank unbidden into a sitting position, his ears pricked and head slightly cocked to one side.

I closed my eyes, the melody washing over me, sometimes tender and soft, sometimes heartbreaking in its passionate entreaty.

"*Bellissimo*," I whispered.

If that didn't encourage Gloria to thrive, I didn't know what would.

When we got home, Joe was still out. I watched television for a while, but finally went to bed. It was close to 10 p.m.

by the time I heard a car pull up outside, the front door open, and the stairs creak as he made his way upstairs.

I slipped out of bed, drew on my robe, and met him in the hallway.

He took a step back. "Oh, Daisy, you're still up? Thought you'd be asleep by now."

I swallowed, hardly knowing where to start.

"Look, Joe, I don't know if you should be spending a lot of time alone with that woman. I'm not sure I'm comfortable with it."

His face was in shadow in the dim hallway and I had trouble reading his expression.

"Why not?" he said. "You hang out with Angus. You meet up with that playboy Serrano whenever you like. I don't get jealous of that, do I?"

I opened my mouth to protest, when I spied the smile playing around his lips, and I released the breath I was holding. "It's just that there's something a little creepy about her. And she could be a killer!"

Joe hugged me to him. "You're a nut. You and your imagination. Come and see what I have for you."

He pulled me into the bedroom, turned on the overhead light, and patted the bed. "Sit. And close your eyes."

Obediently I climbed onto the bed and felt him place something wrapped in a soft cloth into my hands. I opened my eyes, unwrapped the package, and looked up in wonder.

His face was flushed with success. "It's the dining table for Claire's dollhouse."

"Oh, Joe." The mahogany table had delicately carved spiral twist legs, and there were eight tiny side dining chairs and two armchairs. His usual perfectionism had been zoomed down into exquisite miniature. It was magnificent.

"That's what I was working on tonight with Mac. It also has two extra leaves to seat up to ten people."

"It's so beautiful. Thank you." I swallowed hard and

smiled up at his dear face, anger and insecurity evaporating in the warmth of my love for him. "Cyril finished the painting and repairs on the dollhouse, so we're almost done."

"I can handle the lighting for you."

"Are you sure?" I asked. "You have so much else going on."

His mouth was firm. "Yes. I need to know it's done right. For Claire."

I got up, wrapped my arms around his neck, and drew him back down onto the bed.

The next morning, I was standing in the kitchen spooning coffee into a filter, when a drop of water landed on my head. I looked up to see a small wet patch forming on the ceiling.

I ran upstairs to see Joe coming out of the bathroom, a towel wrapped around his waist. "Joe, there's water coming through the kitchen ceiling."

"Hmm, okay, I'll take a look at it."

He didn't sound particularly motivated. I knew he was anxious to get down to the basement and work on his projects, and after last night, I didn't feel like nagging. I wanted to prolong the relaxed afterglow as long as I could.

After he jogged downstairs, I took a quick look at the bathroom floor. Joe was a sloppy bather. Sometimes he forgot to close the shower curtain all the way, or he jumped right out, splashing water everywhere. Oddly enough, it looked dry today. I shrugged and hurried to get ready for work.

I'd barely opened Sometimes a Great Notion when Martha swept in with Eleanor and Debby in her wake. She was wearing a beige traveling suit, with a creamy-colored tank top underneath, and miles of pearls and gold chains around her neck. Her red hair was twisted up into a chic knot.

"Cyril and I are leaving within the hour," she announced.

"I've baked you extra goodies. You can freeze these bars and brownies and take them out as you need them. Same with the cheesecake."

I grinned and gave her a big hug. "Thanks, Martha. I was worried I was going to lose those last ten pounds while you were away." She'd stocked me up. Not just with the treats to put in the freezer, but with shortbread and gingerbread in airtight tins.

"How did you sleep last night?" I said to Eleanor as I handed her a mug of coffee.

"Like a baby, as a matter of fact." She wrinkled her nose. "Strangely well, now that you mention it."

"No Tony Zappata singing outside your window?"

"No," she said, and then she gasped. "Oh, God, is he all right?"

"He's fine. Look, Eleanor, I'm not quite sure how to tell you this, but I think he's found a new love. Her name's Gloria, she weighs about eight hundred pounds, and she's orange."

"*What?*"

I told her about my brainwave to have him sing to the giant pumpkin.

Martha and Debby roared with laughter.

Eleanor pouted in mock dismay. "I don't know whether to be relieved or insulted. Passed over for a pumpkin!"

"I walked by the house this morning," I said. "She must have put on another fifty pounds overnight. I think Sam Brown stands a very good chance in this year's competition."

"Daisy, you never called me to tell me what happened after you left the library yesterday," Debby said, dancing up and down in excitement.

"Oh, I'm sorry, there's been so much going on."

"Like what?" Martha narrowed her gaze at me. "*What's* going on?"

"Well, get this. I figured out that PJ Avery is really Margaret Jane Rosenthal, or actually Margaret Jane Avery,

Sophie's long-lost relative. I imagine she's down at the Sheepville Police Department as we speak."

Martha's mouth dropped open. "*Well.* It's a fine thing when people don't confide in their best friends, I must say. The whole town probably knows by now."

"Oh, no, I don't think anyone else knows," Debby assured her.

I winced as I saw a flush creeping up Martha's neck, and I moved in between them to protect the innocent. Eleanor and I knew enough not to answer back. "Look, Martha, this only just happened yesterday. I haven't had a chance to tell anyone."

"So what's this all about? Why did she hide her identity?" she demanded, hands on the hips of her elegant suit.

"That's what I'd like to know. But I hate to think she might have had anything to do with Sophie's death."

Eleanor shook her head. "Serrano said her passport was date-stamped two weeks before Sophie died. She was out of the country, so there's no way she could have done it. He had nothing to hold her with, seeing as you didn't want to press charges about the break-in."

Martha swung her attention to Eleanor. "And *you.* What the hell are you doing with that young detective? There has to be a twenty-year difference in your ages at least."

Debby stared at Eleanor with what looked like a mixture of disbelief, jealousy, and awe. She was always dreaming of a white knight to sweep her off her feet and carry her away. Serrano fit the bill perfectly. "Oh, my, he could put his slippers under my bed any day," she sighed.

"It's ridiculous." Martha smoothed a stray hair back into her bun. "This isn't like a May-December thing. More like January to December. You're not even a cougar. More like a ratty old mountain lion."

"Or a honey badger?" I offered.

"He's not as young as you think," Eleanor snapped.

"Besides, we're just friends. He appreciates a mature woman who can sit and have an intelligent conversation with him instead of hiding behind a tree with an apple pie."

I'd seen Eleanor in action with men before. She had this mysterious appeal to the opposite sex. Something remote, yet attractive, like the push/pull of a magnet.

It was the way she carried herself, I decided. That kind of been there, done that, world-weary attitude, like nothing would surprise her, yet she seemed ageless, with a quirky way of expressing herself.

"I learned a long time ago that people will think what they want, regardless of the facts. Just live your life so you can look yourself in the mirror every day. That's my motto. We enjoy each other's company, and apart from that, it's nobody's business."

Debby helped me carry the baked goods back into the kitchen. "Do you suppose they, you know . . ." she whispered to me. "Serrano and *Eleanor*?"

"Let your imagination be your guide," Eleanor called. She might be in her early sixties, but there was nothing wrong with her hearing.

As I put some of the brownies in the freezer, I mused that when I was young, I thought sex must end at forty. I simply couldn't imagine older people doing it. Boy, was I wrong. In some ways it was even better as I got older—slower, yes, but more in tune, more relaxed, more *fun*, in fact. Although I preferred to believe that Eleanor and Serrano were just friends.

"Have you figured out what to do about the store?" Eleanor asked as I came back up to the counter.

"I'm staying. Or at least, I hope I am. I need to convince Chip Rosenthal to let me sign a lease for twelve months. I've left him a couple of messages, but he hasn't called me back yet. If I'm careful, I think I can make it, even with the crazy rent. And a lot can happen in a year. Maybe something else will open up on the street."

"Sounds like a plan."

I didn't tell them about Ronnie. I wasn't a very good liar, and with my luck, I'd spill the beans on what she'd said about my infatuation with the hot detective.

Martha twisted the chains around her neck. "God, I can't wait to get away so Cyril and I can reconnect," she burst out. "I haven't seen him since Saturday. He never answers his phone. He could be dead for all I know."

"Oh, I saw him yesterday. He's fine," I said blithely until I was forced to suck in a breath because Eleanor was treading on my right foot.

There was a tense pause.

"You know, because he asked me to watch his cat," I managed, through clenched teeth. "He had to give me a key." Desperate, I picked up the carafe. "Would anyone like some more coffee?"

Debby held out her mug, Eleanor stepped back, and I rushed over to fill it.

"Aargh!" I stubbed the already injured foot on a hard, immovable object on the floor, and looked down to see the sad iron. "That damn thing!"

I'd set it on the counter, but Laura must have moved it back to the floor.

"Jeez, would you look at the time?" Eleanor said, glancing at her wrist although she never wore a watch.

Martha sniffed, still quivering with injured pride. "Yes, I must be going, too. I just hope Cyril arrives to pick me up."

"Have a good trip," I said as I hugged her, even though she was only driving six miles away. Debby said she had to go, too, and they all hurried out. I had just finished cleaning up when the door to the store banged open.

A sullen PJ Avery stood on the threshold.

Chapter Fifteen

"Thanks a lot, Daisy." She scuffed her way toward the counter, glaring at me with eyes that were now a greenish hazel, no longer the ugly purple. "Thanks for ratting me out to the freaking cops."

From force of habit, I opened my mouth to apologize. My daughter, Sarah, had trained me well throughout her teenage years to tread lightly around angry, emotional people.

But the events of this past summer had taught me that the fear of confrontation could actually be worse than the standoff itself. I took a deep breath. "Hey, you should be thankful that I didn't press charges for breaking into the store and smashing up my dollhouse. How did you get in here, anyway?"

PJ shrugged one thin shoulder. "Didn't take much to pop the lock on that old door. Just used a credit card. You really should get an alarm system."

"Yes, yes, I know. Thank you *so* much for the information."

She sighed and slumped down on the counter with her elbows propped on top. I saw her gaze travel to the coffee carafe.

"Look, PJ, what the heck is going on here?" I said, my voice softening. "Why did you leave? Or more important, why did you come back in disguise?"

I poured her a mug of coffee, and she reached out to snatch it with both hands.

"I came back to pay my respects. Chip never even bothered to let me know that Sophie had died, the jerk, so I missed her funeral."

"And no one's recognized you this whole time?"

She slugged down some coffee, and glanced up at me, her eyes still cold and wary. "Nope. No one except for Harriet. She used to see me when she came over to the house to visit Sophie, so perhaps she knew me better than most."

Or maybe she was used to paying attention to detail from working with the miniatures.

Her mouth hardened. "Chip passed me on the street in Sheepville the day I arrived. He didn't even give me a second look."

I offered the tin of shortbread, but she shook her head.

"Then I talked to the lawyer to see what Sophie left in her will. I mean, I expected Chip would get most of her estate, but I thought I'd get *something*. I couldn't believe she never even wrote one. And, as a result, zip for me. Nada. After everything I'd done for her."

She lapsed into a brooding silence.

I poured some coffee for myself and waited. Even though patience wasn't one of my strong points, I've learned that most people can't stand the quiet and feel compelled to fill it. I didn't have long to wait before PJ obliged.

She pushed away from the counter and began her usual pacing.

"At first I thought maybe I could reason with him, make

him see what's fair, but when Harriet told me how Sophie died, I got a bad feeling. She wasn't the type to kill herself. I was sure it wasn't an accident either. That's when I decided it might be better to go incognito."

She grabbed one of the shortbread fingers on one of her flybys past the counter.

"Harriet came up with the idea to dye my hair. She hooked me up with her optician for the colored contacts and paid him enough to keep his trap shut. Getting the job at the *Times* was easy enough. I'd done some reporting abroad, so I showed them writing samples and they hired me on the spot. Being a reporter, I figured I could get into places that I wouldn't otherwise. Find out what happened to Sophie."

"But you're so much thinner now than in the photos. How did you do that so quickly?" *Was she taking drugs, or what?* "Did you really run away and join the Peace Corps?"

PJ paused for a moment. "Not the Peace Corps. Too structured for me. It was just a nongovernment volunteer place in Nicaragua, where we brought tourists on hikes round the volcanoes. We raised money to keep kids off the streets and give them some education. Four to six hours of hiking a day, most days a week. It was a workout, trust me."

She swiped another biscuit from the tin. "And you should see what they eat there." She stuck her tongue out. "Cow's udders, bull's testicles, pigskins—yuck. I stuck to the fruit, and sometimes rice and beans. I lost a ton of weight without even trying."

"And you left in the first place because . . . ?"

"I left because I was upset." She glared at me, waving the shortbread in the air. "Jesus. My mother had just died two weeks before. My stepfather, too, although he was a useless waste of space. Not awful like Chip, just useless. He spent all her money on his idiotic schemes."

She blew out a shaky breath, and I had to sip my coffee and wait until she was ready to talk again.

"We went to a New Year's Eve party. My mother insisted we go, although I don't think Charles wanted to. When we left, it was snowing. I told them it was stupid to drive, and the people who had the party said I could stay, but I didn't want to be left behind in that house either. Bunch of old people, and one old fart who kept leering at me." She paused as if seeing that winter's night tableau in front of her. "Charles took a corner too fast and the car spun around on the ice. Last thing I remember is my mother screaming. Then nothing."

My heart ached for her and I wanted to hug her, but she was on the move again.

"Sophie blamed my mother for the accident, of course, even though it was her brother who was driving. A couple of weeks later, Chip and I got into a huge fight, and Sophie took Chip's side. It was so unfair. Even though he treated her like crap, she stuck up for him because he was her flesh and blood. I'd had enough of the whole stupid family. There was nothing keeping me here, so I took off."

"Weren't you worried about leaving Sophie?"

PJ rolled her eyes. "She wasn't as bedridden as she made out. She could cope pretty well on her own. She just liked the attention and being waited on hand and foot. Plus she had Harriet coming over every day."

"What happened to her? To make her shut herself away from the world like that, I mean."

"She got mugged. When she was shopping in downtown Philly one afternoon. The guy beat her up pretty bad. Her cheekbone was crushed and had to be rebuilt. She looked fine, but she was always self-conscious about it, and she was afraid to go out in public again."

PJ concentrated on finishing the shortbread. "Sophie could be difficult in her own way," she mumbled, mouth full. "Demanding, clingy, but she wasn't half as bad as that witchy Harriet. I can see why they got along. I was on my way over to Harriet's that night to make plans to get your dollhouse back. It was lucky I didn't go in or I might be zapped now, too."

I took a sip of my coffee. "Do you think Chip would know how to rewire a dollhouse?"

"Not sure. He's not exactly handy. He could have hired someone to do it for him, I suppose." Her hazel eyes flashed, and she punched a fist in the air. "I do know he's a soulless jerk. Sophie kept asking him to arrange for the lawyer to come to the house so she could write a will, and he kept promising, but he never did."

She looked straight at me, intense and unwavering. "Now he's screwing you, too, with raising the rent on your store. Yet another example of what a creep he is. But I'm going to find a way to fix him."

"PJ, please don't do anything illegal."

"Don't worry about it, Daisy." She grinned at me with a touch of the old cockiness. "Hey, I'm just glad I don't have to wear those freaking contacts anymore."

After she left, I decided it was time to sort out my future once and for all. I called Warren Zeigler and asked if he would intercede for me with Chip Rosenthal, who wasn't returning my calls. After the last fiasco, maybe it would be better to let a professional handle it. Not only was he a very good lawyer, but if anyone could finesse Chip without ruffling his feathers, it would be Warren, with his quiet old-fashioned courtesy.

"I was going to be in Millbury today, anyway," he said. "Do you want to take me to that nice three-course lunch at the Bridgewater Inn you promised me and we can discuss?"

"Um, how about the diner?"

He chuckled. "That's fine, too. See you at noon."

Warren arrived precisely at twelve o'clock, and I hung a CLOSED FOR LUNCH sign on the door and we walked up to the Last Stop Diner. I normally didn't like to leave the store, but desperate times called for desperate meals.

The former trolley car was doing a roaring business, but we found a booth near the back, and slid onto the lumpy red vinyl seats. I tried to perch on a spot where I didn't sink down into a hole. Warren looked bemused by the menu that was six double-sided pages long.

"Yo, Daisy, Warren. What can I do you for?" Patsy came up to our table and leaned against the side of his seat. Her face was slightly flushed, and people were still coming in and lining up at the front counter. There would be no time for idle chitchat today.

"Egg salad on rye, please," I said. "And a side of curly fries and an iced tea."

"Is the corned beef exceptionally lean here?" Warren asked.

Patsy raised an eyebrow. "Are there mustaches in Mexico?"

"That's fine, then. With a dab of mustard, not too much. And plain water to drink, please. No ice."

She rolled her eyes at me, scribbled on a green pad, and swept away.

I asked Warren to request a year's extension at the higher rent, and he agreed to contact Chip. He also suggested building options into the lease that I could exercise if I wanted, but that weren't automatic renewals.

Our lunch arrived in about ninety seconds and I thought back to that morning at my store, and how this whole thing had started with Harriet trying to buy my dollhouse.

"You know, Warren, I'm wondering if Sophie even wrote a will at all. Harriet Kunes seemed convinced she did, but maybe she never got around to it. But let's say that a will does turn up. What happens then?"

"Probate could be reopened, I suppose, although there might be a statute of limitations. Probably a year." He peeled back the bread, inspected the corned beef, and apparently satisfied, picked up his sandwich. "Actually, and this is in the strictest confidence, Daisy . . ."

I held up three fingers. "Scout's honor."

The corners of his mouth quirked up. "Sophie Rosenthal contacted me shortly before her death. Said she was thinking about changing lawyers. She seemed convinced her attorney couldn't be trusted anymore." He took a delicate bite. "I thought she sounded a bit paranoid at the time, but who knows?"

"Was Chip trying to get power of attorney over her or something? Manipulating her somehow?"

Warren shrugged his slender shoulders. "She didn't say. It was as if she was afraid someone was listening in on the line. She abruptly said, 'Never mind,' and hung up."

I dunked a curly fry in a pool of ketchup. "I wonder if these two deaths could be about something else entirely, and not Sophie's estate at all."

"It's possible, but as it turns out, there's an awful lot of money involved, what with Sophie's house, your store, and the waterfront acreage." Warren sipped his water, his eyes solemn behind the round spectacles. "If I had to hazard a guess, and a conservative one, I'd say we're talking close to three million dollars."

The next day, Friday, I hurried out of the store as soon as Laura arrived. Warren had promised to contact Chip today, and I was confident that by early next week, I could put the matter of my lease renewal behind me. Which still left the puzzle of what happened to Sophie and who had rigged Harriet's lethal dollhouse.

I considered my list of suspects. Who was the only person with a concrete connection to both victims?

Birch Kunes.

I decided I needed to educate myself on the subject of diabetes, and see what else I could find out about Birch's relationship with his patient, Sophie Rosenthal. My efforts to run into Bettina Waters at the dog park had proven fruitless, so I grimly got back on my bicycle, for what promised to be over an hour's ride in my current out-of-bike-shape to Doylestown.

I wasn't quite sure what I'd say when I got there. In the back of my mind was some half-baked plan about saying I had an elderly relative who'd recently been diagnosed with diabetes and I wanted to learn as much as possible about her condition.

At first, my muscles were tight and sore, but surprisingly after about twenty minutes on the road, I felt better. It was one of those glorious fall days where the sky is a cloudless blue, and the air is cool, but not frigid. Leaves were turning color more and more now, and the red maples were ablaze. Majestic sycamores with their towering trunks and peeling bark like beige camouflage spread fiery orange crowns overhead. Delicate river birches sprinkled the ground with pale yellow confetti.

As I headed down Sheepville Pike, not far from the Wet Hen pottery studio, I passed Ardine Smalls running in the opposite direction. She waved at me, and I risked letting go of the handle bars for a second to wave back.

I wouldn't have pictured her for a runner, but she ran in the same nerdy way she did everything, with arms flailing, and legs almost going in circles as she went. Her sneakers were so old they were retro. I'd bet a hundred dollars they were the same ones she'd had in college.

I kept going, past the cornfields and The Paddocks riding stables, a smile on my face.

I took the back roads to avoid heavy traffic as much as possible, and about 11:15 a.m. I rolled into Doylestown.

I parked the bike close to Kunes's medical practice, and locked it to one of the antique black gas lamps. His office was on State Street, not far from the hospital.

I opened the glass door and walked into a large, open,

and very modern reception area. The light fixtures were like flat neon spaceships overlapping on the ceiling. Orange and aqua armless sectional seating curved through the space in long wavy lines. What appeared to be a glass partition around the waiting room was actually a row of fish tanks, as tall as a man's body.

I could imagine the same two words coming out of every kid's mouth that came in here for the first time. *Wow. Cool.*

"Hi, Daisy!" Bettina was at the circular front desk and she stood up and gave me a broad smile, showing those impossibly white teeth, with a hint of dimples. She was wearing a long black cowl-neck sweater and regular dress pants. If I hadn't known, I wouldn't have been able to tell she was pregnant.

"Wasn't the auction so much fun? I'm still pinching myself at how well it went. I talked Birch into keeping a couple of the Barbie dolls, just in case we have a girl."

She laid a hand across her stomach, the very picture of health, with glowing peach skin and thick, shiny hair. "He's hoping it's a girl, but I don't mind, either way."

I smiled back. "Yes, it was a great success. Have you found a house yet?" With the amount they'd made on the auction, they probably wouldn't even need to wait for Harriet's to sell.

"Yes. One that just came on the market. It's a lovely farmhouse near Ringing Springs Park. It has a deck in the back that's built around an old tree."

"Hey, I know just the one you mean. That's a gorgeous house."

"You'll have to come over in the summer. I'm sure we'll do lots of entertaining out there."

"I'd love to." *Assuming your husband isn't in jail by then.* "And how are the wedding plans coming along?"

"It's a very small affair. Just a couple of people from this office, a few close friends, and my parents. Sixteen of us.

We're having dinner at a private room at the Bridgewater Inn."

"You're not inviting the wine cl—I mean, the ladies from
the park?"

She smiled and shook her head. "No. We're keeping it
very low-key." She paused, as if trying to figure out if this
was just a social call. "Birch is over at Meadow Farms with
Angus right now doing the final clean-out of the house."

At that moment, a teenage boy came up to the counter.
"How are you doing, Jason?" she said. She handed him a
small device and promptly knocked over a pile of files.
"Whoops." Bettina laughed at her own clumsiness as she
gathered the papers together.

"I'm good," he said, grinning at me. Jason was probably
about sixteen or seventeen, with a hint of acne, and showing
the slim, muscular build that would develop into a powerful
physique when he matured.

Bettina picked up the mouse and glanced at the computer
in front of her. "Only the nurse practitioner is here right now,
Daisy. Did you need an appointment?"

"No, actually, I, ah, you see, I have this relative with
diabetes and I was hoping to find out a bit more about it.
You know, so I can help her out."

I crossed my fingers inside the pockets of my windbreaker and hoped my good intentions would outweigh a
little white lie.

"You should tell them to get a pump with a remote, like
I have," Jason said to me. "They're awesome. Especially if
you play sports."

"Let me guess. Football?" With his blond hair and all-
American good looks, I bet he drove the girls crazy at school.

He grinned again. "Yeah. It's so much better than having
to inject yourself all the time. It connects to a cannula under
the skin. See? Here's my site." He whipped up his shirt and
quickly reconnected the device. "The pump has a disconnect

port so you can take it off to shower, or if you're not allowed to wear it when you play. You just program it to give a tiny dose every few minutes. It's easier to maintain your glucose levels 'cause you can adjust your basals on the fly."

I smiled at him. Far from diabetes putting a crimp in his style, it seemed like he really got a kick out of his high-tech gadgets.

"You can hook it up to your computer, too, to see patterns of when you might need a higher basal. Then when you come into the office, the doctor downloads the pump data to see how your plan is working for you."

"Um, I'm sorry, but what's a basal?" I asked.

Bettina pushed the fall of her glossy hair over her shoulder. "There's a basal dose that's delivered continuously to maintain your blood glucose in target. A *bolus* dose, which is an extra amount, is given to cover the rise in glucose for meals or snacks, or because of a high reading. You can also use the remote to administer it."

She smiled at Jason. "These remotes are great. I have one myself."

"You do?" he said.

"Yup. I was diagnosed when I was younger than you. Although they didn't have cool stuff like these pumps back then. Just remember, don't stay disconnected more than one to two hours without any insulin."

She showed both of us how her remote had features like a low-cartridge warning and a safety lock. "And don't forget to carry your emergency kit at all times, Jason. It has quick-acting glucose tablets and spare batteries."

I hoped Jason was paying attention. He looked a little lovestruck.

Bettina touched his shoulder gently. "I know it's a lot to deal with, but you're doing really well, and you have such a great attitude."

"Thanks, Ms. Waters."

I swallowed, seeing his face light up with a smile that could break a young girl's heart. I didn't know much, but I knew one thing. There was no way that Bettina Waters was a murderer. I'd stake my own life on it.

After Jason left, I cleared my throat. "Bettina, I was wondering what would kill a person with diabetes."

She gave me a startled look.

"God, I'm sorry, that was a very indelicate question. It's just that I'm so concerned about my—um—relative. She's an older woman. Like Sophie Rosenthal, for instance, who died from an insulin overdose. You know how older people get things mixed up, and I can see that the treatment can be complicated. Could it have been an accident?"

"Not for that amount. It had to be suicide. What killed Sophie Rosenthal was a bolus—a big push of insulin she told the pump to deliver. Normally it would be because of a high reading during waking hours. Or at meal times. Not at 2 a.m."

A shadow crossed her face. "Birch still blames himself. He thinks he could have done more for Sophie if he realized how close to the edge she was."

I picked up the remote to inspect it, but Bettina quickly plucked it out of my hands with an apologetic smile. "Sorry. Just don't want you to give me a bolus by accident, Daisy."

"I understand. Don't press the proverbial red button, right?" I chewed on my lip, thinking hard. "Hey, is it possible that someone could have stolen Sophie's remote to deliver that fatal dose?"

"It's possible, I suppose, but they'd have to be close. Like in the same room."

She gave me that kind, sweet smile.

"Diabetes can be a tricky thing, Daisy, especially for someone who's had it for a long time, like Sophie. Even though I'm very careful, I had an episode myself back in February, right when she died. It gave me the shivers, let me tell you, when I heard what happened to her."

Chapter Sixteen

I got back on the bike and headed toward Sheepville. I cursed myself that I hadn't brought my phone with me. I could have called Serrano, instead of having to ride all the way to the police department. Plus it wasn't too bright of me to be out on the road without one.

As I rode, I wondered how the heck I was going to prove, months later, that Sophie Rosenthal had been murdered. She was dead and buried, the house cleaned out and sold, and her best friend, the only person who might have shed some light on the situation, pardon the pun, had been electrocuted.

The desk sergeant took one look at me and dialed Serrano without being asked this time. I hurried through the back room toward his desk, conscious of my leggings, windbreaker, and sneakers in the midst of all these male fashionistas.

Serrano leaned back in his chair. "What's up, Daisy?"

I tried to control my breathing. "Can you pull the file on Sophie Rosenthal, please? Now? It's urgent."

He let the chair fall forward onto its legs with a crash and ran a hand over his close-cropped hair. "Why the hell did I ever ask for your help? I must have been mad. Or delirious from lack of sleep."

"Come on, Serrano. I need to see the part that talks about her insulin pump and remote."

He exhaled and subjected me to that penetrating blue gaze.

I stared right back.

"You realize this is highly irregular," he said, but he picked up the phone anyway.

When a sergeant brought the file, Serrano quickly flipped through the pages. "This shows that she gave herself a large dose at 2 a.m. Coroner said hypoglycemic shock and then brain death. Apparently when the blood sugar drops too low, a person simply never wakes up." He read further in silence, while I squirmed on my chair. "They assumed suicide, but there was no note."

"Yes, so what if someone stole her remote to give her the fatal dose?"

Serrano ignored me and kept reading. "She was also taking sleeping pills. A prescription from Kunes to help after the death of her brother. Sometimes those sleep aids make you do weird things. You ever hear of people sleepwalking, making breakfast, going for a drive, and they have no recollection afterward? She might not have known what she was doing when she gave herself that bolus dose."

"Do you have a picture of Sophie's house in the file?" I asked.

He shook his head.

"Marybeth Skelton listed it for sale. I bet we can find it on the Internet."

Serrano sighed, but tapped some keys on his computer. I scooted around to his side of the desk and we both stared at the pictures on the real estate listing.

"What are we looking for, Miss Marple?"

"Look! See that tree?" I pointed at the screen and the huge oak tree to the left side of the Tudor house, its great branches close to the upstairs window. "Was that Sophie's bedroom? The killer could have climbed in through the window and stolen the remote."

"That's a lot of supposition, Daisy. Here at the police department we need to deal in cold hard facts."

I sucked in a breath at his condescending tone.

"Plus a person would have to be pretty athletic to climb a big tree like that, shimmy along a branch, and pop in through a window."

I thought of PJ Avery, hiking and climbing rocky cliffs up the sides of volcanoes in Nicaragua, but pushed the thought from my mind. Anyway, her passport stamp put her in the clear. "Does the report say if a remote was found on the scene or not?" I couldn't help the hint of impatience that crept into my voice.

Serrano raised an eyebrow, but gestured to one of the detectives on the other side of the room. "Dodson. Come here."

I recognized the detective who ambled over. It was one of Ramsbottom's old cronies. Serrano had cleaned house when he took over, but Dodson was a holdover.

"Sophie Rosenthal," Serrano said. "Insulin overdose last February. Remember seeing her remote anywhere? It isn't mentioned in the report."

"Yeah, it was there. On the bedside table." Dodson splayed his legs apart and crossed his arms.

"Could someone have come in while she was sleeping?" I asked.

"Negative. The house was locked up tight."

"Was the room cold when you went in? Colder than the rest of the house?"

"Yes, but—" Dodson blew out a breath, his eyes dark and glittering. "Look, I already told you. The house was locked up tight. Windows, too."

"Who found the victim?" Serrano asked.

"Harriet Kunes tried to call her that morning and couldn't get an answer, so she dialed 911. The victim's nephew was away in Boston on business, so we had to break the door down."

"Was there a visiting nurse or anyone else who might have had access?" I asked.

Dodson shook his head. "Sir, is that all? I'm kinda busy right now."

I bit my lip. Sophie Rosenthal had died alone, in a locked-up house. Being an agoraphobic, she wouldn't have gone into the outside world where someone could have had the opportunity to tamper with her insulin paraphernalia. The only people who had keys—PJ and Chip—were either out of the country or three hundred miles away.

"Where's the stuff from the crime scene?" I demanded.

The husky cop glared at me. I probably wasn't his favorite person for helping to put his old boss Ramsbottom in the slammer. He'd had a nice, cushy existence back then. Now he was actually having to put in a full day's work.

"It wasn't a crime scene," he snapped. "There was no reason to suspect foul play, so we didn't take anything."

I slumped back in my chair.

Dodson smirked at me. "That Kunes woman helped the nephew clean a lot of the personal stuff out of the house. But she's a goner now, too, so I guess you're outta luck."

As he ambled away, I grinned widely at Serrano.

Being the pack rat that Harriet was, there was still a chance. A slim one, but a chance, none the less.

"Oh, Christ." Serrano sighed and stood up. "Come on. I'll go with you."

When we got outside, he slipped the front wheel off my bike and installed it in the trunk of his Dodge Challenger. "This is becoming a habit, me driving Ms. Daisy around."

"Hey, I have good intentions."

I clung to the armrest as he drove, even faster now he was in his own car. "I know why Harriet helped Chip, even though she despised him. It was so she could look for that missing will. Cross your fingers she kept something else that will help."

We swung through the gates of Meadow Farms a few minutes later.

Angus's pickup truck was parked outside the house, and a large van was backed up to the garage.

"What are you doing here, Daisy?" Angus asked as he came out onto the driveway.

I ran past him into the garage.

It was completely clean. Just a cavernous, bare concrete space. My heart sank down into the tips of my well-worn cowboy boots. As I stood there in despair, Angus and Serrano came up behind me.

"I was hoping that Harriet might have kept some stuff from Sophie's house. Like an insulin pump?"

Angus shook his snowy head. "Don't know as I saw anything like that in here."

"Well, we didn't touch the basement yet." Birch Kunes walked into the garage, more rumpled than ever in his jeans and a pale blue pullover with a moth-eaten hole on the chest. "We had to clean out the garage first to be able to carry things through, but there's still a bunch of stuff downstairs. Go take a look if you like."

I hurried into the foyer, but paused for a moment, hardly recognizing the place. The staircase was bare, and across the foyer, all that was left in the study were two armchairs by the fireplace, an oriental rug, and a floor lamp.

"Marybeth said it would be better to leave some furniture

here for staging purposes." Birch's voice echoed around the foyer.

Ardine appeared at the top of the stairs, carrying a cardboard box packed with tissue paper. "Hi, Daisy. I'm helping pack the rest of the collectibles, now that the dolls are all sold."

I mumbled hello and rushed toward the basement door. I clattered down the long flight of stairs into a vast unfinished space that ran the length of the house. I cheered inwardly to see rows and rows of cardboard boxes and totes lining the far wall. There was still hope.

Birch switched on a couple more lights and everyone came down into the basement. We began inspecting the first row of boxes, one by one. Christmas decorations, Tupperware, boxes of letters and postcards, heavy plastic crates full of hardcover books.

"Oh, this one says, 'Mill Creek Road,'" Birch said, looking at the writing on the outside of one cardboard box. "She must have never unpacked from our last move."

I glanced quickly at him, but all I could read was a wistful remembrance of better days gone by. He opened the box and began slowly inspecting each photo that he pulled out, one by one.

I gritted my teeth. Birch was not operating at the necessary speed.

"Working with Angus is so much more fun than my regular job," Ardine whispered to me, as we waited for Angus and Serrano to pull the boxes down off the top of the next row. "I have about six weeks of vacation time coming to me, so when he asked for my help, I didn't think twice."

I had to smile at her in spite of my anxiety. I recognized a fellow busybody when I saw one. "Plus it's fun looking around other people's houses, too, right?"

Poking through the most intimate possessions of her old nemesis must be particularly sweet.

She gave me that toothy smile and took the box that Angus handed to her. "Basements are so much less scary in a newer house like this. Mine is horrible, all dank and dark. I never go down there if I can help it."

Fifteen minutes later, we had gone through the second stack and were working on the last row against the wall. This was it. If we didn't find anything soon, the mystery of Sophie's murder would die with her.

Come on, Harriet. Help me out here.

"Here ya go, Daisy." Serrano held up a box that said 'Sophie's House' on the side in Harriet's spidery handwriting.

He pulled a handkerchief out of his pocket and lifted some items out, one by one, onto the folding table next to the washer and dryer. Eventually out came the insulin pump and then, to my dismay, the remote.

I stared glumly at the killer device, obviously left at the scene of the crime. I explained my theory to Angus, Birch, and Ardine that maybe someone had stolen Sophie's remote, but now I was stumped because the house had been locked up tight when the body was found.

"We can check it for fingerprints though, right?" I asked Serrano.

He nodded, almost imperceptibly.

There were a few moments of silence while Birch flipped through some more photos with a bittersweet expression on his face and I paced up and down in front of the washer and dryer.

Wait a minute. "Hey, what if there was a second remote?" I said. "Is that possible?"

There was a pause while we all stared at each other.

Birch roused himself from his trip down memory lane for a moment and shook his head. "The problem is that you can only pair one remote to one pump."

Ardine chewed at her bottom lip for a moment, deep in

thought. "Well, it *is* conceivable, although the second one would have had to be in the presence of the pump at some point to synchronize them. You have to confirm pairing on the pump first and then on the remote."

I stared hard at the washing machine, picturing the tree outside Sophie's house, and imagining the inside of her bedroom, while the surroundings in the basement faded away.

"So, let's say the killer gets into the house," I said slowly, "and sets up the new remote with the pump, when Sophie has it disconnected while she's in the shower or something. Once that was done, he leaves, and then Sophie locks up the place before she goes to bed."

"Daisy, you're so clever," Ardine said, admiringly. "You're so good at figuring things out that even the police can't."

I didn't dare look at Serrano. "That oak tree is pretty close to the house. He could have been on a branch just outside her bedroom window. Later on he sends the signal to deliver the fatal dose."

"You may have something here," Birch said. "They can work up to about ten feet away. You don't even need a direct line of sight as long as it can read the RF signal. It works on the same kind of frequency as your cell phone."

"Birch, can't you download the information from this pump and see if the serial numbers of the pump and remote match?" Ardine asked.

"Hey, that's a great idea. I'll get my laptop." He jogged upstairs while it was my turn to gaze at Ardine in admiration.

"I forgot you sold medical supplies. You're the genius, not me!"

"She's our guru for all things now," Angus said.

She flushed with pride. "Just glad I could help."

"Wouldn't there have been some kind of warning for an unusually high dose like that, though?" Serrano asked.

"Some kind of audio signal?" He reached over and plucked a stray hair off Ardine's coat.

I frowned at him. God, he was anal. And just because he was considered some kind of sex symbol in these parts, it didn't give him the right to be so familiar with any woman he chose.

But Ardine only nodded eagerly. "Yes, there should have been. But the remote can clear alerts and warnings from both devices."

Birch came back, attached the pump to his laptop, and I held my breath while the download processed. He peered at the screen. "Well, I can tell you that her last dose was definitely initiated from the remote and not from the pump. What's the serial number on that one?" he asked.

I read the numbers off the remote sitting on top of the washing machine.

Birch glanced up, his face pale. "According to this data, that's not the one that sent the final command."

Angus scratched his head. "And no one picked up on anything funky at the time?"

"Well, it probably wouldn't have seemed significant to the police, whether the dose came from the pump or remote," Birch said. "By the way, we were never asked to help. We just assumed the police knew what they were doing."

Again, I winced and refused to look at Serrano.

"One thing's for sure," Angus said. "I reckon if you find that second remote, you've found your killer."

Chapter Seventeen

When I got home, there was no sign of Joe, and no note. I let Jasper out for his favorite game of chasing squirrels. As soon as they heard the door open, they hightailed it down the yard, and Jasper, in full-out pursuit, nearly crashed into the trees at the far end. He'd never caught a squirrel yet, but he never tired of the game either.

"Almost, Jasper. Maybe next time," I called as he sniffed around the garden shed, christening the corner of it with a long stream.

"I'd better go and feed Cyril's cat now," I said when I brought him back inside. "I'll have to take you for a walk later. Don't think he'll show himself if you're with me."

At Cyril's place, I filled the cat's bowl with fresh water and topped up the dry food in the dish. I took a good look around at the top of the fridge and the cupboards, on guard for the little dive-bombing feline, but there was no sign of him. I locked up the trailer and scanned the piles of junk.

He was probably checking me out right now from behind a rusty hubcap.

Cyril had said not to worry, but I'd have felt better if I'd at least caught a glimpse of him.

It was kind of creepy being out here alone. I'd never noticed it much when Cyril was at home, but it really was a long way from the main road. I definitely wouldn't fancy staying here at night by myself. I walked faster, imagining I was being watched, but it was probably just the cat.

I broke into a run as I got closer to the intersection of Main Street and Grist Mill, breathing a sigh of relief when I could see Millbury again. Cowboy boots aren't the ideal running gear, and I slowed to a hobble. But I didn't even make it to Sometimes a Great Notion before Eleanor rushed across the street to meet me.

"Daisy, did you see the paper today?" Her face was pale and serious, with none of the usual wry humor.

"No, I've been out all day. Why?"

She simply handed me a copy of the *Sheepville Times*.

My blood ran cold as I spotted my picture on the bottom of the front page with the caption "Chippy Did the Dirty on Me."

"I'll give you the CliffsNotes version and spare you reading the whole sordid thing. There are *quotes* throughout from Daisy Buchanan, basically talking about what an ass he is," Eleanor murmured.

I ripped open the pages and scanned the vicious article anyway, with the byline PJ Avery. I cringed at the pointed inferences from one Daisy Buchanan that Chip Rosenthal had perhaps knocked off his aunt to reap the benefits of her estate, callously leaving his penniless stepsister out in the cold. It also talked about the mysterious demise of his aunt's best friend, the person who'd raised inconvenient questions about the possible existence of a will. Now he was acting the part of the deadbeat landlord, with his usurious and untenable rent increase, ripping off an upstanding, elderly member of the community.

I gritted my teeth. *Elderly*?

I'd barely finished reading when a black Audi came screeching up beside us. Eleanor took a step back onto the sidewalk.

"How dare you?" Chip Rosenthal screamed as he jumped out of the car. He was wearing a black Lycra slim-fitting workout top and shorts, showing his skinny, but quite hairy legs. His face was unshaven and beet red, whether from fury or because he'd just left the gym, I couldn't tell. I bet he'd been reading the paper on the treadmill and almost fell off when he saw the article.

"Look, I never actually said those things," I protested, although my voice was missing some of the necessary conviction. How many times had I spouted off about how he was my prime suspect to all and sundry, trying him in the court of public opinion?

There you go again, Daisy Buchanan. You and your big mouth.

"Never mind raising the rent, I'm not renewing your lease now at any price!" There was a hysterical, Mickey Mouse note to his voice.

"But Chip—"

"You have until this time next Friday to get everything out. Screw *you*."

He threw himself back into the car and tore off while we watched the taillights disappear into the distance.

"Jiminy Cricket, there might be another murder in town soon," Eleanor said. "I should have let Martha have at him when she had the chance."

I blew out a breath. "Well, I guess that's it. No choice in the matter now."

"Fancy a drink?" Her gray eyes were full of sympathy.

"Thanks, but I think I'll go and break the news to Laura. May as well start packing, too."

"I hate this, Daisy."

I nodded, but couldn't say another word.

When I walked into the store, Laura was in the midst of selling one of her vintage button bracelets to a customer. I watched her, while I swallowed against a pang so sharp it physically hurt.

God, I'd miss this place.

Once we were alone, I explained the situation, assuring Laura we'd figure something out, but when she left, I ran upstairs and into the room containing the box with the doll-house. I pulled the covers off my treasure and collapsed in front of it, while tears streamed down my face.

Too bad I could never set foot inside. Within its rooms was a perfect little world with hand-sewn curtains, exquisite furniture, and permanent sunlight. A world where nothing could go wrong and nothing was out of place. A world where ceilings never leaked, dinner was always on the table, and people couldn't say bad things about you and completely mess up your life.

Finally, after about twenty minutes of this, I was getting on my own nerves, so I struggled to my feet and headed downstairs. I would have to come to grips with the fact that I'd have to shut down my beloved store. A tiny part of me, a very tiny part, was glad I hadn't shelled out money on a new alarm system, but the biggest part of me was one big, wrenching heartache.

Over in the corner, Alice surveyed me in her usual enig-matic fashion.

Buck up, Daisy. Other people in the world have real problems. You still have your health, your friends, your wonderful husband.

I stared at her. "You're right, as always. And don't worry. You'll be coming with me."

I made sure to lock the deadbolt when I left for the day and headed down Main Street toward home.

When I opened the door to our Greek Revival, I stood for a moment, imagining that Joe was cooking dinner for me, like in the good old days before he became obsessed with his miniatures. What could I smell? Boeuf bourguignon or some hot buttered crab, perchance?

Nothing. Just the usual woody, antique smell of a house that was over a hundred and fifty years old.

Jasper scampered up to me and stuck his wet nose into my hand.

"Oh, yes, and the best part when I'm counting my blessings? My dog." I fell to my knees and threw my arms around him. He blew a warm breath into my ear and pressed his head against my shoulder. Jasper gave the best hugs.

Next, I found Joe in the basement and gave him the sad news.

"Don't worry, Daisy. You should see all the orders I have to fill. I'll make plenty of money to keep us afloat."

"That's not really the point, Joe."

He smiled at me above the whine of the table saw.

I trailed up the stairs into the kitchen, fed Jasper, and then looked in the fridge, hoping against hope for some tasty leftovers. There was a carton of eggs, a fruit drawer with two wizened apples in it, some vegetables, a gallon of milk, and a few condiments.

"There's nothing to eat in here."

I smiled wryly at the echo of my words. I sounded like Sarah in her teenage years.

Well, why don't you make something, Daisy Buchanan?

I pulled out a cookbook for the first time in a long time, searching for comfort food. I found a recipe I remembered from years ago, when Joe and I were first married and counting pennies. After some scrounging around, I found a cabbage in the fridge, a packet of chicken-apple sausage in the freezer, and a couple of cans of white beans in the pantry.

"Yes, Jasper, we can do it! We have the technology!"

He gave me a high five with his paw, which he considered merited a treat. I slipped him a dog biscuit, washed my hands, and set to work.

Half an hour later, I was stirring a big pot of nourishing soup. I ladled out a bowl for Joe and carried it on a tray down to the basement, where he was engrossed in constructing an Empire chest of drawers. He murmured his thanks, although the appetizing smell didn't even make him look up. As I walked back upstairs, I wondered if he would eat it before it got cold. I had an even stronger sense of what Birch Kunes must have gone through.

I'd saved a piece of the cooked chicken-apple sausage for Jasper, who devoured it, seemingly without the need to chew first. I ate a cup of the soup myself, and then put the rest into several plastic containers and stuck them in the fridge.

As I was wiping down the counter, a drop of liquid fell on my head. I looked up to see that it wasn't just a small wet circle anymore. It was a large patch that was ballooning out and threatening to burst.

"Joe!" I ran to the top of the basement steps and yelled. There was no reaction. Gritting my teeth, I ran all the way down. "Damn it, Joe, we have a *situation*. Can you please pay attention for one second?"

He gazed up at me. "Yeah?" He hadn't eaten any of the soup.

I grabbed his sleeve. "Just come with me."

Joe took one look at the kitchen ceiling and headed for the upstairs bathroom. He felt around the base of the toilet and along the edge of the bathtub. "It's dry here. I have a bad feeling that the leak's coming from behind the wall. It must be the sewer stack."

"What's that?"

"The main drain that runs from the bathroom all the way down to the basement. We'll need to get a plumber out here tomorrow."

And with that, he disappeared downstairs again.

"Tomorrow?" I said to Jasper, who waved his plume of a tail at the sound of my voice. "That doesn't sound like nearly soon enough for us, does it, boy?"

I called the local plumber, Wayne Troxel, but got his answering machine. Emergency service wasn't always in the vernacular of the Millbury tradespeople. I left an urgent message, and then called Angus, who said he would retrieve the plumber from his customary stool at the Sheepville Pub.

Next, I placed a call to the insurance company, who said they would try to get someone out tomorrow, or more likely on Monday. However, the policy only covered whatever it took to gain access to the pipe and the resultant water damage from the leak, not the pipe itself. The deterioration of a hundred-and-fifty-year-old cast-iron drain was considered normal wear and tear. They advised me to get an estimate for the dismantling and replacement of the cabinets, to take pictures, and to save a piece of the sewer stack to show the adjuster.

Great.

Twenty minutes later, Angus and Wayne arrived, the latter reeking of alcohol and cigars.

Wayne scratched his striped shirt over a bulbous beer belly that reminded me of the giant pumpkin. He hitched up his pants and cleared his throat.

"Oh, yes. We're going to need to rip out this here entire wall to be able to get to it. All these here cabinets will have to come down 'cause it's right behind here." He banged on the wall for emphasis. "You're looking at a very expensive repair here. Oh, yes."

I closed my eyes briefly. My beautiful recently renovated kitchen would be ruined.

Wayne got down on his knees and inspected the drain under the kitchen sink. His jeans, no match for his belly even when vertical, gave up the ghost and slipped halfway down his wide rear end.

"What else could go wrong today?" I said to Angus.

"Isn't that what they always say in those B movies before someone bites the dust?"

I rolled my eyes and tried not to look at Wayne's substantial plumber's crack.

The next morning, in spite of Wayne's condition the night before, he was back first thing with a contractor who would handle the dismantling of the cabinets. I took pictures of everything before he started, and by the time the insurance adjuster arrived in the afternoon, all the cabinets were down, the wall cut open, and the ancient cast-iron pipe exposed.

I handed the adjuster the contractor's quote of $2,953 to remove the wall cabinets, countertop, dishwasher, and base cabinets to gain access. He would also patch the walls as needed, repair the basement concrete floor, reinstall everything, and clean up.

The adjuster nodded. "This sounds reasonable. I'll make my own calculations and send you a final estimate of approved damages on Monday. Less your deductible of five hundred, of course."

"Of course." The cost to replace the sewer stack itself was $3,712, which would come out of our own pocket.

"Don't worry, Daisy," Joe said, as he made a brief appearance upstairs. "I'm telling you I'm going to make money with these miniatures."

"Oh, well, seeing as I won't be paying *store rent* anymore, we'll have extra to spend on *sewer stacks*."

"That's my girl, Daisy." Joe squeezed my shoulder. "Way to look at it as the glass half full." And with that, he disappeared back down into the basement.

Angus and I stood there with our mouths hanging open.

"Jeez, Angus, he doesn't even realize when I'm being sarcastic anymore."

My best friend of the male variety shook his head sadly. "If you need to take a shower, come on over to my place, but you can use this downstairs powder room to wash up in the meantime. The leak in the pipe is above this level, so it'll be okay. I'll help Wayne replace the stack on Monday. He's knocking off for the day now."

"Miller time?"

He nodded.

"Thanks so much, Angus." I gave him the biggest, tightest hug I could manage around his mountain man physique. He was helping with the work purely out of the goodness of his heart in order to make the project go faster.

After Wayne and Angus packed up their stuff, I slumped down at the kitchen table, depression gnawing at me. I'd have to get my merchandise out of Sometimes a Great Notion soon, as I wouldn't put it past Rosenthal to change the locks before the deadline, but I couldn't bring myself to go to the store now.

I decided what I needed was a good long walk.

I put on my hiking boots, down jacket, and woolen scarf. It was another cold, but bright and sunny afternoon, and Jasper danced along beside me, delirious with excitement. He was going to miss these country adventures when Sarah finished filming and brought him back to the city. I bit my lip, not wanting to think about that now, on top of everything else.

We took the path through the end of the Browns' property, saying hi to Georgia, who was basking in the sunlight, and plunged into the woods, walking along trails covered in a thick bed of rust-colored pine needles. Ferns lined the way, and there were enough smells from hidden wildlife that Jasper was a sniffing machine, dragging me along as if I were holding on to a ski tow.

There wasn't another soul on the path. Out of the sunlight, the temperature dropped at least ten degrees, and I was glad of my warm coat. We passed the ruins of someone's long-ago house. A piece of one fieldstone wall was still standing, and the stone slabs on the ground showed the base of a fireplace. I wondered who had lived out here in the middle of the woods. Perhaps an artist looking for solitude, one of the many for which Bucks County was renowned. Or maybe it was one of the old mill worker's homes.

The terrain sloped up, and I fought for breath as we negotiated a rocky slope. Jasper, who had dragged me nonstop along the flat, now walked obediently at heel. I gritted my teeth as we crested the top, and headed down the other side, past boulders littered over what might have been a lake bed at one time. The trees thinned out and I could hear the creek.

When we reached it, we walked alongside the swiftly moving water, where piles of twigs and branches had washed up along its sides. In an eddy formed by a couple of gray boulders, I watched the water lap over the mossy rocks beneath. I bet it would be fun in the summer to sift through the mud here and see if there were any remains of broken pottery from the mill. One tree had fallen into the creek, and lay with its roots half exposed, but amazingly, still alive.

Lastly we came to the crumbling mill itself with its accompanying outbuildings, now nearly engulfed by climbing vines. The holes where the windows used to be were like sightless eyes that let me see straight through the stone walls to the trees behind.

It was late by the time we got to Ringing Springs Park. A mile and a half in country terms sure felt like a lot longer. I wondered if Alice had just guessed at the distance, or had ever actually walked it herself.

The wine club was already packing up their coolers and throwing a few bottles into the recycle can. Jasper said hello to several of his friends and then, too soon, it was time to turn around and go back.

The light was fading, and I'd need to hurry it up, despite

my aching legs. I didn't fancy being alone in the woods in the dark. Despite the precarious state of my finances, I wished I'd brought the car. I dug in my pockets, but of course I hadn't remembered to bring my cell phone either. All I had were a few dog treats and some empty grocery bags to take care of Jasper's business.

"Come on, buddy. We can do this." He looked up at me, his red tongue hanging out, and I walked him over to the water fountain where I took a drink and then cupped my hands to let him have some.

There was one empty wine bottle that had missed its target, lying in the grass. I picked up what was formerly a quite expensive white burgundy and tossed it into the recycling can.

I stretched, exhaled, and headed back toward the path.

We had just reached the old mill buildings again when I realized we weren't alone.

Chapter Eighteen

Chip Rosenthal stepped around the corner of the mill and came toward me, wearing black workout gear and a black knit cap, his face unsmiling.

Holy smokes.

My heart raced into overdrive.

I knew that even if I turned and ran back to the dog park, all the wine club women would be long gone. Even Ruthie's house was too far to hear a cry for help, and she was in Florida anyway. And that was assuming I could run faster than a guy in his late twenties, which I sincerely doubted.

I dropped Jasper's leash. If he wanted to defend me, I wasn't going to stand in his way.

Ronnie the psychic's warning echoed in my head, and I wondered if this is what she'd seen when she touched my hand.

I glanced at my dog, expecting to see the hair standing up on the back of his neck, but his golden tail began to wag.

He trotted up to Chip, who bent down to pet him with nails that were bitten to the quick.

"What are you doing here, Chip?" I managed, hoping he'd think the quaver in my voice was due to exertion from the brisk walk.

"I come here to think sometimes. It's peaceful." He glanced around at the still forest, its only noise the faint ripple of the creek. "You hardly ever see anyone else around."

Even though Jasper seemed to be okay with him, I hung back, on guard for the slightest hint of aggression, seeing as I was out in the middle of the woods with a temperamental lunatic.

He pulled off his knit cap and rubbed at his sweat-dampened hair before jamming it down over his ears again. "I know that newspaper article was Margaret Jane's doing. I was angry and took it out on you. I'm sorry."

I was so taken aback I couldn't speak for a moment. *Who are you, and what have you done with the real Chip Rosenthal?*

"Guess I was shaken up to find out she was still alive and skulking around town in disguise. I'd heard she died in some jungle somewhere. And all that questioning by the police stirred up some bad memories."

"About the accident?" I ventured.

He breathed in deeply, whether to clear his sinuses or stop himself from crying, I wasn't sure.

"I'm trying to handle things better than my father, you know." He focused that hooded gaze on me. "I won't drop the ball, and I won't go from one get-rich-quick scheme to another. I'm going to stay with something long enough to make a success of it."

I didn't really know what he was talking about, but I nodded, my heart rate still jumpy. "Okay. Absolutely. Persistence is the key in any undertaking. I think you have the right attitude there."

Chip sighed and sank down onto a fallen log, his hands on his knees. Jasper sat down next to him and leaned against his leg.

"God, I'm tired. Some idiot set off the alarm on my car last night. I can't wait to get out of that crappy apartment and into a new waterfront condo."

I shoved my hands in my pockets and took a step closer.

"When he was married to my mother, my father lost all their retirement savings in a spec deal. Sometimes I wonder if he engineered the fights just so he could divorce her and move on to greener pastures."

He put his arm around Jasper and stroked his silky chest. "You name it, he tried it. Equity trusts, foreign-exchange markets, pyramid schemes, no-money-down deals, trading strategies that promised triple-digit annual returns . . . I swear it was almost like an addiction with him. It's frightening to think how much money he lost over his lifetime."

This was finally a glimmer of understanding into the puzzle that was Chip Rosenthal. But why did my store have to be the target of his steamroller strategy?

He ruffled the fur around Jasper's ears. "Come to find out, a lot of these gurus lie about the money they make anyway. They profit from seminar fees and selling start-up packages to the suckers. Most get-rich-quick schemes deal in intangibles. That's why I love real estate. It's something concrete, something lasting."

My gaze traveled to the crumbling mill behind him, and I raised a quizzical eyebrow.

The first smile I'd ever seen on his face appeared as we shared the little joke.

"And your mom?" I asked gently. "What happened to her?"

"Oh, she had the last laugh. She opened a home-care company for seniors who want to stay in their homes instead of going into assisted living—doing their grocery shopping, taking them to doctor visits, arranging for housecleaning, paying the bills. Now she's franchised it and is making more money than she ever dreamed of. But she did it by hard work and by using her brain. Not like my dad. It drove him crazy to see how successful she was. And then he married Margaret Jane's mother."

"How did you feel about that?"

Chip stared up at the trees. "At first I resented the fact that my father remarried, but Dana was such a sweet lady and well, you couldn't hate her. Then he started going through her money, too."

His mouth thinned. "Right before the accident, he asked to borrow funds from me for one more surefire idea that was going to make him a millionaire. I refused, so then he went to Sophie. That's when I put a stop to it."

Now he stood up and began pacing, kicking through the pine needles, his face flushed. "He'd already lost his own money. I'd be damned if I'd let him lose my only chance at an inheritance. I told the lawyer to stay away and that Sophie wasn't allowed to sign anything."

Here was a glimpse of the temperamental Chip I knew and loved to hate.

I also saw the grieving young son, the person he was desperately trying to hide, who had been let down by the one person who should have set a good example. It wasn't hard to see the toll it had taken on him and the resultant well of bitterness.

"And PJ? I mean, Margaret Jane?"

"We got along okay at first, but I'll admit, I came to resent her relationship with Sophie. It was *my* aunt after all. She just took over—you know, with the womanly things—helping her do her hair and her makeup. Stuff like that. When Sophie's health started going downhill, I got worried.

Margaret can be very persuasive when she wants to be. I could just see her talking my aunt into donating the whole estate to a refuge for wild turtles, or some such crap."

Jasper came back over to my side and I casually picked up his leash.

"Money doesn't mean much to Margaret," he said. "When she finally settles down and stops traipsing around the world, I have money set aside to help her buy a house. She thinks she's so tough, but she's gullible, like her mother. I'm protecting her interests, whether she realizes it or not."

He stopped pacing and faced me. "By the way, I talked to your lawyer. I was thinking, how about a one-year lease at double what you're paying now? Would that be acceptable? That *is* fair market rent, you know."

I gasped. "Wow, yes, that's great, thank you very much."

From my recent experience, I knew that was exactly what I should be paying to be in line with the market.

We shook hands and I decided to end the conversation while things were still on a relatively even keel. "Okay, well, it's been very nice talking to you, and I look forward to a pleasant relationship over the next year."

I hesitated for a moment before I walked away. "I don't know if you'll think this is impertinent of me, but I think you have a lot of potential, Chip Rosenthal."

He smiled shyly at me and I felt as if I was back in high school, talking to one of my students. "You're well on your way to being successful, not just in business, but in your life."

"Thank you." He nodded, his gaze serious.

I walked off in the direction of Millbury, leaving him standing by the broken-down mill.

When we came out onto the end of the Browns' property, Georgia was covered up and tucked in for the night, resplendent in the grass. The sight of her plump body, motherly and welcoming, was like coming home.

* * *

By some miracle, Joe had roused himself from his miniature making long enough to call for a pizza, which had just been delivered by the time I walked in the door, chilled and starving.

He opened a bottle of Shiraz, and ignoring the ripped-apart kitchen as best as we could, we headed for the study carrying our impromptu picnic of the pizza, a handful of napkins, a couple of glasses, and the wine. We snuggled up on the leather couch, and while he poured, I told him about my adventure in the woods.

"I still can't believe it, Joe. I'm trying to wrap my mind around the fact that I'm going to be able to keep the store and not have to pack everything and move out."

"That's great, Daisy."

We clinked glasses.

"By the way, I have some news, too," he said. "I signed up for a jewelry-making class that Mac recommended. It's going to be held at the artist's retreat on Burning Barn Road, two nights a week."

Two nights a week, eh? And no discussion with your wife before you made that kind of commitment?

I sighed. As much as I didn't want to spoil the mood, now was probably as good a time as any to have a discussion with Joe about his spending habits and the amount of time he was devoting to his new hobby.

I drew a deep breath. "Look, Joe—"

"No, *you* look, Daisy."

I stopped in surprise at the sharp tone in his voice.

"I've been as supportive as I possibly could about Sometimes a Great Notion, letting you do your thing and whatever else you wanted." Joe jumped to his feet. "Now it's the time for me to do something *I* enjoy. To be a little selfish for once in my life."

I stared at him, my mouth open. Dear, dependable Joe was standing over me, dark eyes intense, his mouth firm, the very picture of resolve and purpose.

"Okay," I whispered.

"And I do enjoy it, you know, more than I ever thought possible," he said, his voice softening.

I took a sip of my wine for courage. "I know, Joe. I know you deserve your passion, too. It's just that money is going to be tight if I'm—I mean—if *we're* going to be paying twice the amount of rent at the store."

"Well, I just sold a dining table and chairs like the one I made for Claire for eight hundred dollars."

I nearly lost my mouthful of wine. "You're kidding me. That much?"

"Yes, that's what it's worth. When you add up all the hours I spent . . ."

"I know, but *eight hundred dollars*?"

He nodded. "And I have orders for three more."

"Wow." All I could do was stare at him as he sat back down, picked up a slice of mushroom and pepperoni pizza, and grinned at me.

"And the Empire chest of drawers? Already on order for a customer who's paying four fifty." He took a large bite of the pizza.

I was quickly doing the math in my head. His miniature sales so far would almost pay for the whole pipe replacement.

"I can see your wheels turning, Daisy Buchanan," he said as he wiped his hands on a napkin. "Don't worry, this new income will all go toward our house bills and the store."

"It's going to be a huge help, Joe." I set my wineglass down with trembling fingers. "I'm so proud of you."

He pulled me into his arms. I leaned deeper into his embrace and sighed in delight. He lowered his lips to mine and kissed me, slowly and tenderly, until my bones began to melt into the couch. Suddenly I remembered how much I enjoyed kissing.

"Your pizza's getting cold," he whispered against my mouth.

"I like cold pizza," I said and felt his lips curve against mine.

I drew back so I could look into his eyes. "I know I've spent a lot of time at the store this past year, Joe. Too much. I was thinking that I could give Laura more hours if she wants them. And I could make dinner for us on the nights that you have your class."

He smiled slowly. "And I'll only take as many orders as I can finish during daylight hours."

"Deal."

We reached for our wineglasses and toasted again.

"Oh, I almost forgot," Joe said. "Sarah called today. The shoot wrapped in Spain, and they're heading home tomorrow. Everything went well. She sounded on top of the world."

"That's great," I said, glad for the news of my daughter, but my heart sinking at the thought of her coming to take Jasper back to the city.

He was sprawled out in front of the fireplace now, the fun-loving golden-haired puppy who had wrangled his way into my heart and become such a big part of it I couldn't imagine him not being here.

Even the tantalizing smell of pizza hadn't been enough to keep him awake after his three-mile trek through the woods. His eyes were closed, but he was barking in his sleep, a curious muffled sound, like he was dreaming of chasing squirrels all the way to Ringing Springs Park.

"Did she—um—say anything about when she might be picking him up?" I cocked my head toward Jasper, not wanting to say his name and disturb his slumber.

"No, she didn't. Not quite."

Joe frowned as he savored another swallow of wine.

"She asked about him, of course, but honestly, Daisy, I got the feeling that she's hoping we would offer to keep him permanently. And I've got to say, I think his life here is so much better than he'd have in New York. Here he's got lots of fresh air, exercise, a regular schedule, a big backyard to play in . . ."

Suddenly I remembered Sarah trying to talk her parents into getting a dog when we'd first moved to Millbury, but we'd always resisted the idea. I shook my head in wondering affection, and also in the sneaking suspicion that Joe and I had been had.

By my very beautiful, very clever, very conniving daughter.

I grabbed a piece of pizza and grinned at my husband. My kitchen might be wrecked, my store rent doubled, but who the hell cared. Things were definitely looking up.

The next morning, I woke up early. Very early. I rolled over and glanced at the alarm clock. Only 5:45 a.m., but I was bursting with energy and the pure joy of being alive.

All the stress I'd been living under for weeks had magically disappeared. It also might have had something to do with the night of tender lovemaking that followed a hearty mushroom pizza and a bottle of Shiraz.

I lay there for a few minutes, luxuriating and stretching under the covers. I knew I'd never go back to sleep now, and not wanting to disturb Joe who was still sleeping peacefully, I slipped out of bed.

I grabbed some clothes, dressed quickly in the guest bedroom, and padded down the steps. Poor Jasper hadn't even come upstairs at bedtime. He'd slept in the study all night long. Maybe I'd overdone it a bit with him yesterday. I needed to remember he was still a youngster.

I'd go for a walk and pick up breakfast and coffee on the way home from the diner. The dishwasher had been pulled out from the wall as well as the cabinets, and the less dishes to wash in the powder room sink, the better. I'd call Eleanor later and see if I could take a shower at her place.

Jasper roused himself and yawned, still so sleepy that his tongue fell out of one side of his mouth.

"Want to go for a walk, boy?" I whispered. He dragged himself to his feet and I knelt down and hugged him. "Poor little tired puppy. You could stay here if you like." But he was already panting with excitement and looking up to where his leash hung on the hook on the wall.

The morning was cool and foggy, and there wasn't another soul around on Main Street. I walked past the store, my heart swelling all over again at the realization I'd be able to stay in Millbury.

Sometimes a Great Notion was going to live to fight another day.

Soon we were down in the south end, making our usual pilgrimage to say hello to the giant pumpkin.

As we neared the white picket fence surrounding the Browns' property, I frowned as I saw a glimpse of peach through the mists. I could have sworn Georgia was covered up when we passed by at the end of our walk yesterday afternoon. There was a dark streak across one side of her. I stopped and peered, trying to make out if it was just a shadow or perhaps the blanket had slipped off to one side.

Was that a prone figure lying across her expansive flesh?

"Oh my God. Sam!" He must have had a heart attack or something.

I fumbled with the latch for the gate and ran toward the pumpkin patch with the dog bounding alongside, yelling for Dottie.

When I got closer, I saw that it wasn't Sam at all.

Chip Rosenthal lay across the pumpkin at an awkward angle, his head brutally smashed in.

A broken wine bottle lay on the ground nearby.

Chapter Nineteen

I swallowed hard and gripped Jasper's leash to hold him back. Chip was still wearing the same workout gear from yesterday, minus his knit cap. His Lycra pants were saturated with dew as if he'd been lying there all night. I closed my eyes briefly against the sickening sight of his blood-streaked face.

I fumbled for my phone, thanking God that I'd had the foresight to put it in my pocket today. I ripped my gloves off, shoved them in my pocket, and dialed 911.

After I'd been assured that the police were en route, Jasper and I ran toward the house. My screams and banging on their front door finally roused the Browns, and Sam came stumbling out, with Dottie close behind. A young man also ran over from next door just as sirens sounded in the distance.

With a strangled cry, Sam charged toward the patch.

"Stop, Sam! Don't go any closer, this is a crime scene now," I called.

The young neighbor grabbed him and held him back while Sam tried his best to wrestle free. I came up behind them for a better look at the hideous tableau.

Chip must have fallen on the pumpkin in the final throes of death, perhaps scrambling to get away from his killer, and the weight of his body had ripped the thick vine away from the enormous fruit, depriving Georgia of her life-giving food source.

All those countless hours, days and weeks of caring for her, lost in an instant.

"That *bastard*! Let me at him. I'll kill him." Sam was beyond distraught at the devastation, tears streaming down his face.

"For God's sake, Sam," Dottie cried, "he's already dead."

Tears filled my throat, too. Georgia's swollen skin looked like it was actually weeping from the wound.

I wondered what kind of awful thing it said about me that I was more upset about the loss of a giant pumpkin than a human being.

The sun broke its watery way through the haze, lifting the dense fog. The first officers to arrive had already begun marking the area with crime scene tape and asking us to move back when Serrano came roaring up in his Dodge Challenger. He strode over to the body, giving me a "wait right there" signal as he passed.

I pulled out my phone again and left a frantic message on the machine for Joe.

Ronnie the psychic ducked under the tape and came hurrying up to me, wearing a silk floral robe and purple pajamas. "I knew it, Daisy! Didn't I tell you something bad was going to happen? I had one of my funny turns again. I couldn't sleep a wink last night."

Without the orange caked-on makeup, she looked prettier, even in the harsh light of day. Older, but prettier. Her hair was wadded into blond clumps where she'd slept on it.

Jasper snuck his nose under her robe and breathed deeply.

"I don't believe this." Serrano stalked back and addressed the officer near me who had a roll of tape in his hands. "This is supposed to be a crime scene. Ever hear of securing the area?"

"Sorry, sir." He waved his hands helplessly. "But it's a whole punkin patch."

"I can see what the frick it is. Just do it."

Eleanor slipped through the space between the two men and stepped into the garden. She wore a white T-shirt, gray yoga pants, and her feet were bare.

Serrano ran a hand across his head.

"Oh, well, now it's a fricking party. Anyone *else* out there want to come in?" he yelled as he made an exaggerated show of looking up and down the street.

"*Bonjour*, Detective," she said, with a sly glance at me. "My, my. You seem a little testy this morning."

Over where the Browns and their assorted neighbors had gathered near the pumpkin, Sam's anger swiftly turned to inconsolable grief.

Eleanor raised a finely arched eyebrow. "*Zut alors. Quelle commotion.*"

The wailing was approaching operatic proportions, a monumental screeching dirge of despair. I finally understood what the word *caterwauling* meant. Like a vociferous feline with its tail caught in a door.

"Jesus *Christ*." Serrano motioned to one of the officers. "Get that guy out of here. Or in exactly sixty seconds, I'm going to take out my department-issued firearm and shoot the sonovabitch."

I hurried over to the Browns.

"He says he'll never forgive me, Daisy," Dottie shouted to me over the din. "I made him go to our granddaughter's dance recital with me last night. Lucy was sleeping over afterward, and when we got home, I insisted Sam stay inside and play games with us instead of going out to the patch."

She looked at me, despair in her eyes. "He's convinced this never would have happened if he'd been here."

I wasn't sure whether she meant the murder of Chip Rosenthal or the death of the pumpkin.

"It's not your fault," I yelled back. "I think he just needs time to grieve."

Lucy took her grandfather's hand. "It's okay, Grandpa Sammie." Sam fell to his knees, buried his face in her little neck, and sobbed some more.

Once he'd quieted down somewhat, I went back to find Serrano and gave him a quick rundown of meeting Chip in the woods the afternoon before and then finding him in the patch this morning.

"You know what, Daisy, I gotta tell you, this is very interesting," he said, pushing his elegant suit jacket back across his hips and slipping his hands partway into the pockets of his pants. "See, I have this rule. The best suspect is usually the last person to see them alive, or the first person to see them dead. In this case, you're both. *Again*."

I stared at him and sucked in a breath. His eyes were ice blue with none of the usual amusement when he looked at me.

"I need to talk to you. Alone this time." He motioned to the back of the Challenger. "Let's go."

Joe came running up. "Daisy, what's going on?"

Serrano nodded at him. "Take the dog, please."

I handed Jasper's leash to Joe without a word and got into the back of the car.

I stared out of the window as we sped away, even as my pulse accelerated. I wasn't really in trouble, was I? Why the heck was Serrano acting like this?

He didn't speak to me on the ride to Sheepville, only to the other officer in the front passenger seat. When we got to the station, we didn't go toward his desk, but to a small interrogation room.

I slumped down at the table and looked around at the bare beige walls. I needed a shower big time, plus I had a severe headache from caffeine withdrawal.

"God, I'd kill for a cup of coffee," I muttered.

Serrano glanced sharply at me.

"I'm kidding, Serrano. It's just a figure of speech. Jeez."

"Officer Spinelli, please get Ms. Buchanan a beverage."

When the officer came back, and I'd accepted a Styrofoam cup from him with a grateful smile, Serrano clicked on a tape recorder. "Start at the beginning."

I took a deep breath and repeated everything I'd told him at the pumpkin patch, except in greater detail, hoping I was making it crystal clear that there was no lingering animosity between Chip and me regarding the article in the *Sheepville Times*. I finished my account with describing walking Jasper this morning, seeing the body, and calling for help.

"You didn't try to revive the victim?"

I shook my head. "It was obvious he was dead. He'd been there all night."

"Let's leave that up to forensics, shall we?"

I glared at the detective that I thought was my friend. What the hell was the matter with him?

Did someone get up on the wrong side of the bed this morning or what?

I bit my lip as I wondered *whose* bed. He'd shown up awfully fast. Eleanor, too, come to think of it.

"It doesn't sound like you had a very high opinion of the victim, according to an account in the local paper yesterday," he continued in that same cold, clipped fashion. "He was making life difficult for you. Maybe you'd have liked to see him out of the picture. Sounds like a plausible theory to me."

"Well, sometimes your theories are all wet!" I snapped.

Those icy blue eyes turned positively glacial. "Ms.

Buchanan, are you seriously mouthing off to a senior member of the police force?"

At that moment, there was a knock at the door, which Officer Spinelli answered with alacrity. He came back to their side of the table holding a large plastic baggie with a broken wine bottle inside.

"Ah. The wine bottle that was found near the body," Serrano said. "Probably the murder weapon."

I gasped, suddenly recognizing the elegant black and yellow label on the bottle. A 2009 Pouilly-Fuissé from the Mâcon region of France.

Just like the one I'd thrown in the recycle container.

"What is it, Daisy?" Serrano leaned forward, searching my face.

It had to be the same one. How many bottles of pricey white burgundy would be hanging around Millbury? *Oh, God.* Would my fingerprints be on it? Like it wasn't enough that I seemed to be in a sticky situation already.

As if reading my mind, Serrano said, "It's been dusted for fingerprints. You don't mind giving us yours, do you?"

I swallowed.

It wasn't really a yes or no question. I tried to remember if I was wearing gloves yesterday.

"Do you know who drinks this particular type of wine?" he asked.

"No. I'm not exactly in the clique, as it were." I took a slow sip of coffee while my mind raced. *Everyone shared wine down at the dog park. There could be a whole bunch of fingerprints on that bottle.*

An hour or so later, Serrano decided he was done with me and the other officer left the room.

"Come on, Daisy, I'll give you a ride home."

I got up, tight-lipped, and trailed after him out of the building. *You're in big trouble, mister. I don't appreciate your attitude in class today.*

He opened the front passenger door of the Challenger for me and I got in without a word. There was a frosty silence between us until we took the left turn onto River Road.

Serrano was the first to break it.

"I know you're pissed at me, Daisy, but here's the thing. I have to set an example for my men. Do everything by the book. They need to know that I'll always do what's right, regardless of the personal feelings involved."

I turned away and stared out of the window.

"The fact is, the day before he died, you and the victim had a very public spat. In the press, no less."

"I didn't say all that stuff!" I exploded. "PJ made it up. And I told you, Chip and I had worked things out."

"You know, this murder is different, though," he said, as if I hadn't spoken. "The other two victims sort of killed themselves. Murders from a distance, if you will. This was a hands-on, full-out act of passion." He sighed. "How many fricking killers am I dealing with here?"

Serrano looked like he could use a cup of coffee, too.

"Maybe some kind of affair gone wrong?" I suggested.

"With one of the wine club women?"

I thought for a moment. "Not sure about that." I pictured the usual crowd down at the dog park. There were a few women in their thirties, but most of them were older. "I think they were all a bit long in the tooth for him."

"Don't discount the mature woman," Serrano said as he smiled at me. *Finally.*

"PJ Avery would have been my first choice of suspects," he continued, "but she was covering a charity dinner last night, which Birch Kunes and Bettina Waters also attended. The medical examiner pegged the time of death somewhere between 7 and 9 p.m. They were all there until well past 10 p.m."

"Birch is no more a killer than Jasper," I said. Although if the murder victim was a squirrel, I couldn't swear to it.

"Marybeth wouldn't have done it, either. He was her meal ticket to major commissions. I can't think of anyone else Chip might have known, but with the way he carried on, I'm sure he alienated more than a few people."

Serrano pulled up in front of my house. "Do me a favor. Try not to find any more dead bodies for the rest of the day. It *is* Sunday, after all."

I smirked at him and got out of the car.

After I reassured Joe I was okay, I called Eleanor and asked if I could use her shower. Angus had offered the use of his facilities, too, but she was closer, plus I thought I'd be more comfortable at her house.

I packed a bag with a towel, shampoo, soap, and a change of clothes and set off. On the way, I stopped at Cyril's place to feed the cat. I still couldn't see the little guy, but the food was gone from the dish. He was still alive, somewhere. I filled it to the brim with dry food and put fresh water in his bowl.

When I stepped out of the trailer, I suddenly spotted him, peeking from around an old bathtub. I knelt down, and softly whispered for him to come closer. He stared at me for a moment as if weighing his options, then decided better of it and was gone.

Patience, Daisy. At least he was showing himself now.

Eleanor lived in a pretty Victorian on a side street called Henrietta's Alley. The house was a very pale blue, with white shutters, white front door, and rosette and ribbon detailing on the gable. She'd completely redone the whole house inside, and painted it a soothing mix of light and dark grays, creams, and white.

She opened the front door before I even had a chance to knock, and I followed her past the dining room, where there were always fresh flowers on the table even in the middle of winter, past the French country-style kitchen, and down the hallway to the back staircase.

We walked up to her airy master bedroom that had gray
walls and a wrought iron bed layered with soft antique quilts
and white linen sheets. It was topped with hemp pillows
decorated with French quotes in elegant lettering.

A stack of old valises served as a side table and the dressing table was salvaged and repainted white, with the addition
of vintage glass knobs. The floors were whitewashed, and
an armoire of the palest celadon stood in one corner.

It was the same minimalist, uncluttered décor as the
downstairs level. Quirky, but elegant. Kind of like Eleanor
herself.

"Well, I'll leave you to it," she said. "There are towels in
the bathroom for you. Feel free to use anything else you like."

Eleanor shut the door, and I lingered there for a moment,
enjoying the peace of the romantic retreat.

I wandered into the adjoining dressing room, which was
probably another bedroom at one time, and was now fitted
with custom shelving and rods.

Eleanor didn't have a lot of clothes. What she did have
were hung neatly, with space in between the wooden hangers, not all squished together like mine. The original shallow
closet set into the wall held her neatly arranged rows of
shoes.

The dressing room led into the bathroom, which again,
must have been an architectural redesign from the original
Victorian layout. It had rectangular white subway tiles on
the walls and tiny black-and-white tiles in a checkerboard
pattern on the floor. A wrought iron hay rack on the wall
held rolls of fluffy white towels. Another door provided
access into the hallway.

I found myself checking the room for any sign of male
occupancy, but the toilet seat lid was down and there wasn't
a single whisker in the immaculate white pedestal sink. The
bathtub was also spotlessly clean. I brought my dollar store
bottle of shampoo in with me, but as I stood under the rain

shower nozzle, I inspected Eleanor's selection of toiletries with interest—a bottle of luxurious European bubble bath with a pine forest scent, the kind of shampoo they sell at the hair salon that must have cost about ten of mine, lemon-basil body wash, and an expensive razor.

I used my own shampoo and towel, but once I was out of the shower, I couldn't resist a dab of the rich buttery body cream from Provence that was sitting on the marble countertop.

Eleanor lived simply, but very, very well.

When I came back downstairs, clean and refreshed, I found her in the kitchen, standing by the stainless steel cubby that housed the espresso and cappuccino machine.

"Feel better?" she asked.

"About a thousand percent," I said as I sat down on an industrial metal chair at the old pine table. "You don't realize how much you rely on things like water and electricity until you have to try to do without them for a day or two."

Eleanor set a latte in front of me. She'd drawn a fleur-de-lis design in the froth.

"Showoff." I grinned at her and took a long, appreciative sip. "Yum. Thank you, Eleanor. Honestly, it's been a hell of a morning. Our favorite detective was a tad peevish with me, to say the least."

She pulled another cup from the machine. "Absinthe hangovers can be a bitch."

I narrowed my gaze at her. *Don't you have something you'd like to share with the class?*

She looked at me and laughed. "Oh, Daisy, your eyes are full of questions! No, I didn't sleep with him, if that's what you want to know."

Taking her latte, she slid into a chair opposite me. "At my age, it's enough to be able to enjoy a friendship with a good-looking younger man. There doesn't have to be any more to it than that."

"Did he ever tell you what he's doing here? Out in the back of beyond?"

I held my breath while Eleanor regarded me steadily with her dark gray gaze.

"I know you won't repeat this, but he simply needed a place to heal. His older sister died last year after a long battle with breast cancer, his mother suddenly and unexpectedly passed away soon after that, and he was trying to escape his grief, I suppose. Not that anyone can. That's just geography."

I felt a spike of irrational jealousy that Serrano had told her his story. I should have been the one to hear it. I swallowed another gulp of my latte as I tried to swallow my disappointment, reminding myself that I didn't hold any kind of rights over him. He wasn't mine.

"I guess you can stay in the store now that the charming Chip is gone?" she asked.

I sighed. "I don't know what the heck's going to happen now. The funny thing is that Chip and I had worked things out. We'd come to an agreement that we could both live with, pardon the pun, except now he's toast, and someone did him in before I could sign a new lease."

Eleanor made a murmuring sound. "Well, let's hope for the best. Where's Joe today? Does he need to use the bathroom, too? He's more than welcome."

"No, actually he went to Angus's to shower. On the way to see Tracy McEvoy."

"How do you feel about that?"

"Not exactly comfortable, but what can I do? I trust him."

Eleanor took a careful sip of her latte. "Of course you do."

Chapter Twenty

On Monday morning, Angus, Wayne, and a couple of his helpers arrived at the house bright and early to work on the kitchen. Wayne assured me that as long as all went well, he could get the main stack replaced and the base cabinets and dishwasher reinstalled by the end of the day. He'd probably have to come back on Tuesday for the rest of the cabinets and paint touch-ups, but at least we'd able to use the plumbing tonight.

I thanked them all and strolled down the street to open Sometimes a Great Notion.

Once the coffee was brewing, the music turned on, and the front door unlocked, I sat down on a stool behind the counter.

I hated to consider it, but Serrano's first instinct might be right. Of all the possible suspects, PJ was certainly the one with the best motive to kill Chip. She hated him with a passion he could only dream of, and like Serrano said, this was a crime of passion.

Although how could she be in two places at once?

Unless the medical examiner's estimate of the time of death had been off. Maybe once the autopsy came back, there might be more clues. I pictured Chip's poor beaten body. Someone had really done a number on his head and face. But wouldn't the killer have had to be a man to do that kind of damage? And someone tall? PJ was tough, but she was slightly built and shorter than Chip.

I hopped off the stool and took some of Martha's chocolate walnut brownies out of the freezer and unwrapped them, setting them on a majolica maple leaf cake stand.

It seemed so quiet here without her. I hoped that she and Cyril were having a good time. They say absence makes the heart grow fonder, but I was already fond of Martha. I just wanted her back.

Although once she found out what she'd missed, she'd probably be hell to live with.

I straightened a length of antique feed-sack fabric with a purple and white morning glory design and wondered if Chip had prepared a will. He was young, but he struck me as the type who might have taken care of something like that, especially after what had happened with his aunt. Which brought up another question. Who would get Sophie's properties now? And who was my new landlord? I guessed it would be Chip's mother.

I sighed and poured myself a cup of coffee. What a mess.

The door swung open and Serrano strode in. "Am I in time for the morning coffee klatch?"

I saw the teasing light in his eyes, and I breathed out in relief. Things were back to normal. "Coffee yes, but the treats are still frozen."

"That's okay. I need to lose a few pounds anyway." He

rubbed his flat stomach and accepted the cup that I poured for him. "Thought you'd like to know that you were right all along, Ms. Buchanan."

"I was?" I stared at him, openmouthed. "About what?"

"About our boy, Chip Rosenthal. We found the second remote that killed Sophie Rosenthal. In his apartment. He didn't even bother to hide it, the gavoon. It was sitting right there in his bathroom cabinet."

He took a deep slug of his coffee. "That's Sophie's murder accounted for, anyway. We still don't know who killed Harriet."

I sank back on my stool while I tried to marshal my scrambling thoughts.

Serrano smiled at me as I frowned in concentration. "*Now* what's the matter?"

"I don't know." I shook my head. "Somehow this all seems too pat, too convenient."

He eyed the brownies on the cake stand as if willing them to defrost. "What if PJ made up the story about that will that Sophie might have written? All we have to go on is what she's fed us from her supposed conversations with Harriet. What if she planned to kill Chip all along and concocted this whole story to throw us off the track?"

"I can't believe that PJ is a killer. Plus she was out of the country."

Serrano wasn't giving up. "Okay, so what if knocking off Sophie was a plot between the two of them? But then Chip reneged, kept all the money. She got her revenge and also figured out how to stick him with the blame."

I bit my lip. "I don't know, Serrano. I know that I'm naïve sometimes, but I just don't see it."

"And how about Harriet? You don't think ol' Chip could have rewired the dollhouse?"

I thought for a moment. "He was more like Marybeth,"

I finally said. "He was the type to have other people do things for him. So yes, if he hired someone to break into Harriet's house and rewire the dollhouse, I could buy it."

But Birch Kunes was suddenly popping back into my mind, with his casual run under the garage doors, the password that Harriet never changed, and his urgency to sell the house.

"Oh, crap, none of this makes any sense," Serrano said. "It's a month after Harriet's death and we're no closer to finding out who killed her and now there's two other murders."

"Hey, if it was an easy job being a detective, everyone would be doing it." I smiled gently at him. "You know, it's ironic. I was convinced that Chip was the guilty party for the longest time, and now I'm not so sure. Now I'm actually leaning toward Birch Kunes."

Serrano shook his head. "Think I might have had tunnel vision in that respect. I've got this thing about guys that cheat. But I don't think he did it." He drew a deep breath and settled against the counter. "There's something I've never told you, Daisy."

I held my breath, too, knowing he was about to tell me his story, except I'd already heard it from Eleanor. I schooled my face to look like this was the first time I'd heard the information.

"About a year ago, my older sister got breast cancer. She was fifty years old and perfectly healthy up until that point. She didn't smoke, hardly drank, it was a complete shock to all of us. But she was brave, Daisy. She went through the surgery, the chemo, the radiation, the hair loss, all of it, without ever complaining. She was my hero."

I swallowed and nodded.

"But while she was going through hell, her scuzzball husband was carrying on an affair. As she lay there suffering, with chemo ripping through her veins, he was banging his secretary."

Serrano jumped to his feet as if the memory charged him with adrenaline. "I found out about it, and I have to admit, I went a little crazy. Beat the crap out of him. It didn't do any good, though. It didn't make me feel any better. And Shelly died a month later. And then my mom, too."

"I'm sorry," I whispered.

He paced up and down. "I went even wilder. Drinking, getting in fights, almost losing my badge, until one night I made a mistake that nearly cost me my life. I knew that was when I had to get out of New York. Figured it would be nice and quiet here, and I could get my act together."

Serrano smiled wearily at me. "You can see how well that worked out. And why I've been so focused on Kunes. I've let my prejudice blind me to other possibilities."

I touched his hand. "We all do that from time to time. And we seemed to have switched suspects. I was always so convinced that Chip was the bad guy. Now I'm not so sure."

He grabbed one of the brownies and took a bite. "Nearly thawed out. I'm off to take a fresh look at this whole situation, Daisy. See ya."

And with that, he was gone.

As I was cleaning up the kitchen after dinner, the phone rang.

"Hullo, Brat, what are you doing tomorrow?"

"Hi, Angus. I'm working. Like I usually do on a Tuesday."

"And what *else* happens on Tuesdays?"

There are no stupid questions. Only stupid answers. But the glass of wine I'd had with my shrimp risotto was dulling my tired brain. "I give up. What?"

"It's the Swamp Pike Flea Market!"

The market was held year-round on Tuesdays and Saturdays, although Tuesdays were the best with a livestock auction and more of the Amish vendors in attendance.

"Come on. Take the day off and go with me," he begged.

"Look, I can't just close the store."

"Please, Daisy? I—ah—really need to talk to you."

I took a sip of my wine. I could use a break myself, if truth be told. "Okay, okay. Let me call Laura and see if she can cover for me."

"I already called her. And I'm paying her for the day, too, so we're all set."

"Jeez, Angus." He could be a bit pushy sometimes. "Fine. Well, we don't have to get there at the butt crack of dawn, do we?"

"If we don't get there when it opens, we might miss the good deals. And you know how I hate driving around looking for a parking space."

The market didn't open until 7 a.m., but I'd been through this routine before.

I sighed. "See you at six. And for God's sake, bring some coffee."

Joe grinned as he put away the rest of the risotto in the fridge. "Picking with Angus tomorrow, I take it?"

"I agreed to go in a moment of weakness. It must be your fabulous cooking that softened me up." I kissed him, put the pan in the sink, and poured in warm water and soap.

"He has been a huge help with the plumbing," Joe said.

"I know, I'm just kidding. I'll try not to wake you."

At 5:45 a.m., I dressed quickly in my jeans, red thermal shirt, boots, and windbreaker and was ready when Angus pulled up outside. I hopped into the truck, glad to see he'd remembered the coffee.

He made small talk as we headed along River Road and then down Swamp Pike for a couple of miles.

Patience wasn't my strong suit, but I figured I'd wait until Angus was ready to tell me what was weighing so heavily on his mind.

"Have you finished cleaning out Harriet's place?" I asked.

"Yeah. It was funny, though. Ardine and I showed up the other day, and the lockbox was gone. I guess Marybeth put the place under agreement already."

"Wow. So what did you do?"

"Oh, it was okay. Ardine figured out the code to the garage door."

"She did? How on earth did she do that?"

Angus chuckled. "Apparently she used to work for Kunes, back in the day. He never changes his passwords. It was the same damn number he used for his office voice mail password years ago."

I frowned as I sipped my coffee.

"You know, Ardine's kind of a weird gal, but I like her," he said.

"Me, too. And I think she's very happy to have found some friends around here."

Part of the market was housed inside in an old hairpin factory, where there were about fifty stores, a bathroom, an ATM machine, and two small restaurants. The main attraction was outside, however, with over three hundred tables selling everything from vintage jewelry to organic vegetables. A century ago, it was just a livestock auction, but over the years, the flea market sprang up and was now an institution. People came all the way from New York and northern New Jersey to combine early morning browsing with a day out in New Hope or Lambertville.

We found a parking space relatively easily, although the grounds were already half full. Angus and I wandered down aisles of tables where the vendors were setting up glassware, books, tools, and old records. There was furniture for sale, too, including complete sets of dining chairs, Tiffany lamps, oil paintings, clocks, and chandeliers.

Angus usually went for the rusty stuff and I stayed on the lookout for vintage linens and sewing notions. These days it was getting tougher to find the real bargains. Online auction sites had made everyone an entrepreneur and antiques expert. Or at least they thought they were.

I spotted a bag of skeleton keys on one table among some coins, stamps, and baseball cards. "I know Laura can do something magical with these," I said, as I paid three dollars and stuffed them in my tote bag.

The clouds above us were a dark peach and light gray. Like a fresh bruise against the face of the sky. An occasional breeze blew scattered leaves across the tables.

It might rain later, but with any luck it would hold off until we were done. In the summer it could get ferociously hot on these forty acres, but in this soft, cool dampness, I felt like I could walk all day, reveling in the joy of the hunt.

"I'm so glad you asked me out, Angus. It's helping to take my mind off everything that's been going on. Too much drama lately."

Angus glanced at me, his expression somber. "Speaking of drama, I've got some news."

Here we go.

I moved off into a grassy opening between the aisles and he joined me, shoving his huge hands into the pockets of his jeans.

"I'm getting a divorce."

"What?" I gasped.

"Well, Betty says she wants one. I don't."

We stared at the table across from us, filled with comic books, cookie jars, and lunchboxes from the sixties.

"You know, when she never came to see me in prison, that should have been my first clue," he said.

I bit my lip. After the first time we'd visited the Bucks County Correctional Facility, Betty had been too intimidated by the whole experience to face it again, not even for Angus's sake. The visits had been left up to me from then on. In fact, sometimes I'd felt like I was the only person in the entire county who still believed in him.

"She says she's found her independence. Said I'm too domineering, whatever that means," Angus mumbled.

After a summer spent on her own, his formerly mousy wife had finally discovered she had a backbone.

"Well . . ." My voice trailed off as I thought about how he had practically commandeered me away from my store for today's adventure.

"Hey! Whose side are you on, Brat?"

I mustered a wan smile. "What about counseling?"

"It's too late for that. She's already moved out."

"Wow. I'm so sorry, Angus."

"Yeah, well, I haven't lost hope yet. Maybe if I let her spread her wings, she'll come flying back one of these days."

I wasn't so sure. His wife had done a radical transformation. A total three-sixty. Sometimes people who knew the "old" you could never reconcile themselves to the person you'd become. I'd be willing to bet she knew in her heart that Angus could never accept the new and improved Betty Backstead.

"I'm going to hire Patsy full-time now to work at the auction house," he said.

Even as I silently cheered that Patsy Elliott would be able to quit the diner and work at something she loved, my heart went out to Angus. My boisterous, bossy, exasperating, but bighearted friend.

"Well, I'm sure Pats will be a huge help," I said. "She adores working with you. In fact, that last auction for Harriet's dolls gave her enough money to hopefully afford a house for herself and Claire."

"Yeah, talk about irony. Betty said it's that same damn auction that gave her the idea to leave me."

"*What?*"

"She knew that night that I'd made enough money to buy her out of the house and the business, and that she was finally free to go."

"Jeez." I shook my head at how one event could trigger so many others.

How often did I take Joe for granted? It didn't matter how old you were, nothing was ever permanent. People changed, and the marriage needed to keep up. It was a work in progress. Something to be cherished and protected and nurtured. Always.

"Check this out, Daisy." Angus, apparently done with the heart-to-heart, strolled over to a table that looked like it held the contents of an attic. He picked up an antique duck decoy. "These things are worth a fortune," he whispered in my ear. "He's asking $185, but that's still cheap. I'm going to offer a buck and a half."

After a little haggling, Angus tucked it under his arm and winked at me.

For my part, I couldn't resist a vintage hand-sewn tea towel that said "Home Sweet Home Cooking" with a farmhouse that looked like so many of those around Sheepville, surrounded by various red-stitched chickens and other farm animals. It would sell in a second. If it ever made it out of my house, that is.

I was drawn to another table with Victorian paper dolls, antique toile, and lace trim. A yellow Vaseline glass vase from around 1900 that sort of resembled a squid caught my eye. I knew it wasn't anything to do with sewing notions, but it was so quirky and unusual, I had to have it for the store. I'd never not sold anything I'd picked up this way.

Angus and I made a trip back to the truck and unloaded our stuff.

"Fancy a hot dog?" Angus asked. "To hell with my diet."

Suddenly starving, I nodded. "I'll take two."

We stopped at a stall and bought chili cheese dogs. Angus slathered on every condiment on the counter and I did the same.

Just like the good old days.

The food stalls were over near the sellers with merchandise like designer-style handbags, airbrushed T-shirts, and handmade woolen socks. Produce, garden accessories, Amish meats, and baked goods were also on display.

"This is the newer stuff." Angus wiped his mouth with a napkin. "We need to head back in the other direction."

I followed him to a table near the factory building that was filled with license plates, vintage cameras, lodge pins, motorcycle kidney belts, a train set, and even a brass spittoon.

The vendor had a display of sterling silver forks with all the tines bent down except for one. If the tines were fingers, the one sticking up would be the middle finger. They were advertised as pickle or olive forks.

"I *have* to get one of these for Eleanor," I told Angus.

After I paid, I wandered over to where he was sorting through a stack of automotive and oil promotional signs propped up against the brick wall. These old signs were like catnip for Angus. He pulled out a dented red and black metal one.

"Oh, yeah, I remember this," he said. "This shop used to be where Jake's Hardware is now. Fred Smalls. Ardine's father. He was the only electrician in town for years."

I peeked over his shoulder. The sign said SMALLS ELECTRICAL.

"Angus!" I gasped. "How come you never mentioned this before?"

"What?" He craned his head to look up at me from his kneeling position.

"The dollhouse that killed Harriet Kunes. My God, don't you remember? Someone messed with the wiring!"

Angus eased himself slowly to his feet and scratched his thick shock of white hair. "I know what you're thinking, Daisy Duke, but you're dead wrong."

I blew out a breath, trying to control my exasperation. I had to remind myself that not everyone was trying to do the police department's job, like me. "But don't you think it might be just a *tad* relevant?"

"I dunno. There's lots of electricians round these parts, let alone their kids. They can't all be murderers."

Yes, but it only takes one.

Chapter Twenty-one

When Angus dropped me off at home, I hurried toward the sunroom at the back of the house where I had a corner workstation and laptop setup. I stopped for a moment to admire the kitchen, where Wayne had obviously finished the final touch-ups this morning.

Apart from his invoice on the counter neatly marked "Paid," it was hard to tell that anything had ever been torn apart. It was perfect, and a welcome relief to have my kitchen back. There was also a note from Joe that he'd taken Jasper out for a walk.

I smiled, shaking my head in exasperation. Joe could never quite get used to the idea of leaving a message on my cell phone. How he expected me to read this note unless I'd happened to stop home, I don't know.

I set my flea market purchases down, pulled up "Kunes Medical Associates" on the computer and skimmed Birch's bio. He'd done his residency at Hahnemann University Hospital, and then after his fellowship, he'd gone into practice

with nine other doctors in Langhorne before he'd opened
his own office. I typed the name of the practice into the
search menu, wrote down the address on a scrap of paper,
and shoved it in my pocket.

With any luck, someone who had worked there back then
would still be on staff, and I'd find out some more information on both Birch and Ardine. I didn't hold out much hope,
but it was all I had.

I added a line to Joe's note that I was taking the car and
I'd see him for dinner.

Forget the bike. Langhorne was too far.

The group practice was easy to find—a modern, one-
story building on the perimeter of the Langhorne Hospital
grounds. I parked and walked up to the entrance. The balmy
air from this morning was gone, and I zipped up my windbreaker against the sudden chill.

Pretending to be checking messages on my phone, I lingered, watching the reception desk through the plate glass
window. I wasn't exactly sure of the time line, but if Birch
joined the practice when he was in his early thirties, it could
be close to fifteen years ago now.

One middle-aged woman with frosted blond hair piled
high caught my eye. Even from here, I could see she had
deep dimples and wore lots of makeup. Her white silky shirt
was a size too small and the buttons strained, puckering the
material against her generous bosom. She looked like she
was in charge of the others. She was certainly talking a lot,
which was a good sign, so she was the one I headed for first
when I approached the desk.

"Hi. I'm—um—looking for a woman called Ardine
Smalls," I said. "I heard she works here?"

"Oh, God, she left here ages ago, honey. Why are you
looking for her?"

"Well, she's become rather friendly with a friend of mine.
In fact, he's spending a lot of time with her."

I crossed my fingers inside my pockets. Ardine *had* been spending a lot of time with Angus. It wasn't a total lie. "And—um—I just wanted to ask her to lunch. Get to know her a little better, if you know what I mean . . ."

I let my voice trail off, hoping there was a wealth of meaning in what I wasn't saying.

She looked at me, her eyes outlined with blue liner suddenly shrewd. "I do know what you mean." She grabbed her wallet and shrugged into a fake fur coat. "I'm on my way to pick up lunch for the girls. You can come with me if you want to chat on the way. What's your name, honey?"

"Daisy. And that would be great, thanks."

"Marge. Nice to meet ya."

Hardly able to believe my luck, I scurried after her. She smelled good, like a very expensive talcum powder. "Have you been here long, Marge?"

"Oh, yes, I helped Dr. Wilson open this practice. It was just him and me at first, you know. Then he took on more associates, including Birch Kunes. I've been here for almost twenty years now. Hard to believe."

"So you worked with Ardine? You remember her?"

"Yes, I do. Strange little thing." Marge shook her head. "I think Birch only gave her a job because he felt sorry for her."

We crossed a wide pavilion with stone benches and tables and a canopy of wooden beams overhead. In the summer this would be a pretty spot for people to sit and have lunch, but in late September the wind was slicing across the open area, and Marge and I hurried across to the doors that led into the hospital.

Once we were walking through the cafeteria, she turned to me and lowered her voice. "Don't repeat this, honey, but I heard she was forced to leave the hospital because of a messy affair."

"An affair? Seriously?" I couldn't picture the nerdy Ardine having a steamy liaison.

"Oh, now, see, I'm using the wrong word. It was more of a messy *situation*."

Marge approached the counter and called out a rapid-fire list of five different sandwiches with a multitudinous list of toppings and breads. The woman behind the line took it in stride.

Maybe the office ordered the same thing every day so it wasn't as confusing as it sounded to me.

"She developed this obsession for one of the doctors." Marge lowered her voice, glancing around every few seconds to make sure we weren't overheard, as if she were some kind of zaftig Russian spy. "She sent him love letters, called him all the time, the whole bit. Practically *stalking* the poor guy."

I ordered a large coffee and we shuffled along with a line of people toward the cash register.

"Eventually she was dismissed and came to work for Birch." Marge grabbed a pile of napkins and plastic utensils and shoved them into the paper bag filled with sandwiches. "I guess she's getting crazy over your friend now, right? That's why you're here?"

"Something like that, yeah," I mumbled as I emptied a couple of creamers into my cup.

We paid, left the cafeteria, and opened the main doors to brave the elements again.

"When Birch left to open his own practice, he didn't ask Ardine to go with him," Marge yelled at me above the rush of the wind. "My boss let her go soon after that, using the excuse that there wasn't enough work for her. She was a bright girl, but too weird."

We skirted the tables, and I cursed silently as hot coffee slopped over my fingers.

"She didn't get along with everyone else and it made things uncomfortable. He gave her a good recommendation, though. I think she got a job with a medical supply company in the end."

"Oh, okay, thanks," I said, as we neared the office building. "I'll try to track her down that way. Thanks so much for all your help."

I said good-bye to Marge and retraced my steps to the pavilion. Even though it was freezing outside, I needed a quiet space to collect my thoughts.

Did Ardine do the same thing with Birch? Develop some kind of crazy obsession over him that spurred her to kill his wife? I shook the droplets from my fingers as I sucked down a gulp of the hot, bracing liquid. But Ardine had been at the house when Birch and Angus were cleaning out the garage. Everything had seemed perfectly cordial between them. I hadn't noticed any tension then, or at the auction.

Not to mention the fact that Bettina should have been her target now if that was the case.

Serrano said Ardine had an alibi for Harriet's murder because she'd been at the conference hall all day preparing her exhibit. But I'd seen more than a few women at the show with shoulder-length gray hair and somewhat frumpy attire. It might have been easy to mistake Ardine for someone else from the back.

With her nursing background, she'd know how to operate a remote for an insulin pump. But why on earth would she want to kill Sophie, too?

I shivered inside my windbreaker, clasping the cup for warmth. I'd just taken another sip when Marybeth Skelton hurried out of the hospital doors.

She didn't glance in my direction as she headed for the parking lot, but even from this distance, I could see she had a big white bandage on her right hand.

I choked on my mouthful of coffee. What the heck was *she* doing here in Langhorne? Why not go to Doylestown Hospital? It was much closer to Millbury and Sheepville.

Unless she'd deliberately picked a place that was so far out of the way she wouldn't see anyone she knew while being treated for a nasty cut. From a wine bottle, for instance.

I fumbled for my phone and when I got Serrano's voice mail, I blurted out my findings on both Ardine and Mary-beth.

I hurried to the Subaru, eager to get out of the bitter chill, and drove back to Millbury. When I reached the house, I'd barely opened the front door before Joe came rushing out.

"Glad you're here, Daisy. I need to get to the hardware store for some more supplies before it closes."

Bemused, I waved good-bye as he hopped into the driver's seat.

"Looks like it's going to be raining cats and dogs here soon," he called as he drove off down Main Street.

I went into the sunroom and gathered together my finds from the flea market. I wanted to give Laura the skeleton keys before she left for the day.

Cats and dogs.

Holy crap. Cyril's cat! When was the last time I'd fed him?

A chill ran through me as I struggled to remember. Sunday? Yes, Sunday, that was it. And now it was Tuesday afternoon. Cyril had said he'd be fine on his own for a couple of days, but still . . .

I was a horrible person and a worse pet sitter. I'd go see the little guy right now.

I raced down to the store with my armful of vintage treasures. Laura was just about to lock up, so I gave her the antique keys and told her I'd see her on Friday.

After she left, I put the squid vase in the front display window and was scurrying to set the linens down on the Welsh dresser when I tripped over the sad iron.

Aargh!

Stars danced around inside my eyeballs and I huffed out a long series of agonized breaths. As if that could seriously dull the almighty pain that stabbed through my big toe. I'd be lucky if the damn thing wasn't broken.

Why wouldn't someone buy this stupid thing already? And why the *hell* did Laura keep moving it around?

My toe throbbing, I hopped around some more, conjuring up all the choice words I could remember from my days in the high school teachers' break room.

Alice didn't exactly raise her eyebrows, but I could clearly see the reproof in her eyes.

"Sorry, Alice," I gasped. "It's just that I've banged my toe on this freaking thing for the last time. I can't take it anymore."

I know. I'd bring it with me to Cyril's. It would feel at home there with the other old crappy rusty things. Screw the five bucks I might get by selling it. It wasn't worth all this agony.

I dumped the offending item in my bag and tentatively tried taking one step, and then another. The sooner I got back home and put some ice on my foot, the better.

The walk to the salvage yard took a lifetime. The sad iron skulking in my pocketbook had increased its weight by at least a hundred pounds and the strap cut savagely into my shoulder. This had to be the most ludicrous idea I'd ever come up with.

Finally I opened the door to the trailer, set my bag on the kitchen floor, and picked up the container of dry cat food.

I knelt down and poured some kibble into the dish and suddenly my heart almost stopped as I heard the magnificent sound of a cat purring.

I didn't move. I didn't breathe. The tiny black cat padded closer to the bowl. He paused to rub slightly against my side before he delicately lowered his head and began to eat. I smiled as I heard the soft crunching noise between his little teeth.

I'd never heard anything so wonderful.

I hadn't killed Cyril's pet. *Thank God*. He even had some water left.

Cyril and Martha were due to come home tomorrow, and it wouldn't be a minute too soon for me. I missed them both, more than I'd ever imagined.

I watched until the cat had eaten about half of the food, and refilled the water bowl with fresh water.

"See you later, His Nibs," I whispered, and picking up my pocketbook, I let myself out. I locked the door and turned around to see Ardine Smalls standing in the semidarkness.

"Hi, Daisy."

I tried to swallow in order to be able to speak, but I couldn't.

She grinned, showing those horse-like teeth. "Marge called. Said you were poking around, asking all kinds of questions about me."

Shock loosened the wedge in my throat. "Marge? But she seemed so . . ."

"Like your best friend, right?" She stepped over a grappling hook and came closer. "Yeah, Marge is anybody's best friend for the right price. We have a real sweet deal going on. She sends me patients, and I give her a cut of the commission."

Ardine wrinkled her nose as she looked around. "It should be easy enough to hide a body somewhere in this pile of junk," she murmured, as if to herself.

She took a long syringe out of her old-fashioned purse. God knows what was in it. All I knew was that if I let her get close enough to stick me with that thing, I was toast.

My heart bounced. "You killed Harriet and Sophie." It didn't seem worth beating around the bush.

"Yep, and now I'm going to get rid of you, too."

There was only one clear path up to the trailer among the piles of miscellaneous salvage, and she was standing in it.

To my right were stacks of oil drums and the cap to a pickup truck, and to the left was an avalanche of iron bed frames, bathtubs, and stacks of wooden shutters. If I tried climbing over that lot, I'd be a slow, easy target.

Going back into the trailer wouldn't work either. It would take too much time to unlock the door.

I stared into her eyes and realized how completely crazy she was. *But how could she kill me? We'd become friends, sort of.*

"Why, for the love of God?" My breath was coming in short puffs, but I tried to keep my expression calm.

Ardine waved the syringe in the air. "Harriet and I were best friends once. Bestest friends. But when she met that bitch, Sophie Rosenthal, she discarded me like a used prophylactic. I couldn't believe it. So I took Sophie down. I thought once she was out of the picture, things would go back to the way they were, but Harriet still wanted nothing to do with me."

I glanced up the lane that led to the salvage yard. Even if I somehow got past her, I'd never make it to the main road. Ardine was an ungainly runner, but she was used to running, and much younger than me.

"So you snuck into Sophie's house, paired up the second remote—"

"While she was in the shower, and then I climbed out the window. Instead of shutting it all the way, I left it open a crack so she'd notice the cold air and shut and lock it from the inside."

"You're so clever," I said.

It's often the guys who are too nice, too helpful, that you need to consider. Serrano's words came back to haunt me. Hadn't she been such a great help the day we found the stuff at Harriet's house?

"Don't patronize me, Daisy." Ardine's voice was frigid, completely missing its usual nerdy tone. "I realized you were getting close. Too close to figuring things out."

So you threw me the information about the serial number to disarm me.

"And Chip? Why did you kill him?"

She wrinkled her nose again. "I didn't. Must have been someone else."

"But you planted the remote in his apartment, right?"

"Yeah." She smiled, a hideous smile. "Angus gave me the idea when he said that whoever found the remote would find the killer. And once Chip conveniently turned up dead, well, that wrapped things up very neatly. Except for one loose thread. *You.*"

"How did you get into his place?" I wasn't sure why I kept her talking. It was the classic trite ploy you see in the movies, but I guess I didn't feel like dying right that minute.

Raindrops began to fall, misty against my skin. How long before Ardine decided she didn't want to get wet and ended this little chat?

I was also clinging to something else Serrano had said, which was that the two other killings were "hands-off." Did she really have the nerve to kill me face-to-face?

"I rocked the Audi, and when the alarm went off and he came running down to see if someone was stealing it, he left his apartment door open," she said. "I didn't have time to find a great hiding spot, so I just tossed it in the bathroom cabinet."

As she talked, I scanned the yard in the fading light, trying in vain to see a way through the rusty obstacle course.

Suddenly I had another horrible thought. "Ardine, did you kill your mother, too?"

She grinned. "I told you, she tripped and fell down the stairs. Now, I might have loosened the banister some . . ." She took another step closer, her arm raised with the deadly syringe, and her face twisted into a snarl. "The old witch was always after my money, always putting me down."

Another hands-off killing. Serrano's cool, detached voice

seemed to be speaking inside my head. *She doesn't have the guts to do you in. You can take her, Daisy.*

Out of the corner of my eye, I caught a glimpse of twin pricks of light in the gathering fog. Cyril's cat was creeping along the top of a nearby bed frame, his eyes like flat green glass, muscles slithering in perfect unison as he stalked closer.

Control your breathing. Get ready.

Suddenly he dove past Ardine, a black flying shadow.

She screamed. "What's that? A bat?"

I swung my pocketbook holding the hefty sad iron in a wide arc, bashing Ardine in the ribs. She moaned and staggered, but didn't fall, still holding the syringe, still intent on stabbing me.

In that split second, I remembered hearing once that women were always afraid to hurt someone, even in a fight. Another body blow wouldn't do much to stop her, but even so, I hesitated.

Daisy, she killed three people for Christ's sake! Serrano was practically shouting inside my head now.

I gritted my teeth and kicked Ardine Smalls in the crotch.

"Aargh!" With an unholy yowl she crumpled to the ground and I hauled the bag back again and gave one final smash, whacking her in the head and shoulder.

I didn't wait to see how much damage I'd done as I threw the bag down and leapt over her. I ran harder than I'd ever run in my life, dodging old tires and engine parts as I headed for the road. I couldn't hear the sound of footsteps behind me, but I didn't dare look back.

In a couple of minutes, I was heaving for breath, and soaking wet from the rain. Halfway to the intersection with the main road, I slowed to a stagger, but I kept going, my lungs screaming in my chest. I prayed that I'd knocked Ardine out long enough to keep her down until I could reach the road and relative safety.

I'd almost made it when a car going about eighty miles an hour came flying into the lane, illuminating me in its high beams. It swerved and came screeching to a halt, spraying mud all over me.

A few seconds later, Serrano appeared through the fog and wrapped me in his arms.

I clung to him, trying to tell him about Ardine and the syringe, but all that came out was a garbled mess.

Serrano's clipped voice cut through my incoherent babbling. "Calm down, Daisy. Where is she?"

I pointed toward the trailer with a shaking finger.

"Get in the car."

"I'm all muddy."

"*Come on.*"

I hobbled around to the passenger side, got in, and he took off at high speed. I gripped the armrest, thrown back against the seat as we nearly went airborne bumping over potholes. Behind us, I could see headlights in the wing mirror from two more cruisers pulling into the lane.

Serrano slammed the brakes on when the piles of salvage blocked our way and jumped out of the car, gun drawn. "Stay here, Daisy."

The other officers followed him, splashing through mud, and I watched as they all ran over to where Ardine lay on the ground, not moving.

Holy crap. Had I killed her?

Despite strict instructions to the contrary, I got out of the car. Serrano glanced at me, but didn't tell me to go back as I stumbled up alongside him.

I gasped as I stared down at the body of Ardine Smalls, the deadly syringe still clutched in her hand, but now sticking out of the side of her neck.

Chapter Twenty-two

A few hours later, after a visit to the station to give my statement, and then a long hot shower, I was ensconced on our leather couch in the study, my foot bandaged and propped up on the steamer trunk. The toe wasn't broken, just badly bruised. Eleanor and Serrano sat facing me on the other couch.

Joe was at the bar cart, fixing drinks. A bottle of Belgian beer for Serrano, an ice-cold Beefeater martini for Eleanor, and a glass of merlot for me.

"So, Serrano, how did you know to look for Daisy? How did you know she was in danger?" Eleanor asked.

"That hair I pulled off Ardine's coat?" He nodded at me. "We'd found a few dog hairs at Harriet's house, but of course she didn't own any pets. I got the lab result back this afternoon and it was a match. Told you the killer always leaves something behind."

He took a sip of his beer. "Then I got your message,

Daisy, and everything came together for me. I called Joe and he said you'd probably gone to feed the cat."

He chuckled. "What do you call that iron thing again that you planned to drop off at Cyril's? We might have to institute a new standard-issue weapon for the department."

I glanced at my bag sitting on the floor. "A sad iron," I mumbled.

Eleanor narrowed her gaze at me. "You were getting rid of my gift?"

"Yes, sorry, I was, but I guess I should keep it now. After all, it did save my life. Actually it was Cyril's cat who really saved me. He distracted Ardine so I could get in a good enough shot to whack her with it."

The corners of Serrano's mouth quirked up. "I would have loved to have seen that."

"What the heck was in that syringe anyway?" I asked.

"A powerful muscle relaxant. Part of the cocktail they use for lethal injections. The part that leads to respiratory arrest."

"Is there any kind of antidote?" Eleanor asked.

"There is, but it would have to be administered within a couple of minutes. If she'd stabbed you, I don't think you'd be sitting here right now, Daisy."

I took a large gulp of my merlot. And then another.

Joe shook his head. "I know this is going to sound weird, but poor Ardine. She had such a sad little life. Why did she have to kill herself?"

"She knew," Serrano said. "Three murders and one attempted? It would be a case of simply throwing away the key, if not the death penalty. She just beat us to it."

Eleanor popped an olive into her mouth. "I always thought she was wickety-wackety-woo."

There was a hard knocking at the front door. Jasper leapt to his feet, barking. Joe went to answer it, and then a few moments later, PJ Avery sauntered into the study.

"Saw the Challenger outside," she said to me. "Figured you were getting yourself into something interesting."

She nodded at Eleanor and Serrano in curt acknowledgement.

"Well, that's convenient," I snapped, "because I wanted a word with you anyway."

"Yeah?"

"Yeah. What's with printing all that crap in the paper and inferring that I said it? And what's with the *elderly* bit?"

"Sorry. Drama makes for a better story?"

I glared at her, but suddenly, in a peculiar way, I felt like I was looking at a younger version of myself. Cocky and ready to take on the world, consequences be damned.

My daughter, Sarah, and I were nothing alike, but in PJ I recognized the same reckless passion I'd been fired up with in my youth. Heck, I was still like that, barging ahead without sufficient regard to my own safety. Was it possible that I could somehow help her not make the same mistakes?

"What's your poison, PJ?" Joe asked cheerfully, pointing to everyone's drinks.

I shuddered. "Joe, please."

"Sorry."

PJ shoved her hands in her pockets and rolled forward on the balls of her feet. "Tequila. Rocks. Lime. Salt. Thanks."

Joe grinned at me, but he hadn't even picked up a glass before the doorbell rang again in a long burst. I heard a commotion in the foyer, and Martha and Cyril came rushing in.

"Well, this is a fine state of affairs, I must say." Martha couldn't get out any more than that before, overcome, she enveloped me in her arms. I hugged her back, as much as I could from my seated position.

"What are you guys doing here?" I managed. "Aren't you supposed to be on vacation until tomorrow?"

Martha sniffed. "Well. It appears that there has been an

inordinate amount of murderous activity in this village so we came back early. Not that my two *best friends* bothered to let me know, mind you. And now come to find out, there's a *party* going on."

Joe handed Cyril a Newcastle Brown Ale and gave PJ her tequila on the rocks.

"Martha, I'm so glad you're back," he said to her. "I have a bottle of Veuve Clicquot in the fridge that I've been saving for a special occasion, and I'd love an excuse to open it. Will you have a glass with me?"

God, he was good.

Somewhat mollified, she said, "That sounds delightful. Thank you, Joe."

He hurried off into the kitchen.

Cyril took a swig of his beer. "Aye up, so old Chip fell off his perch, did he?"

I nodded. "In a manner of speaking."

"Let me tell you, I am not planning on going away again for a *very* long time," Martha declared. "Of course, I enjoyed being with my dear Cyril for those few precious days, but it's just so hard to catch up."

Cyril winked triumphantly at me and I stifled a chuckle.

Joe came back in, opened the champagne with a gentle hiss, and filled two flutes.

After everyone had their drinks, I had to repeat the whole story that I'd already told to the police and then again to Eleanor, while PJ took a notepad out of her back pocket and scribbled furiously. We still called her PJ in spite of the fact that her name was really Margaret Jane, but she seemed to prefer it.

Cyril made me tell the part twice about his cat diving in front of Ardine to distract her. "Good old His Nibs. Ah'm right chuffed about that." He pointed his beer bottle at me. "And yer a jammy dodger."

I wasn't quite sure what he meant, but I think the gist of

it was that I was lucky I'd dodged a bullet. Or a lethal syringe, to be precise.

"I allus thought that Ardine were a rum 'un."

"Yeah, spooky," PJ said.

"What about Marybeth?" I asked Serrano. "Did you get a chance to follow up on that?"

His bright blue eyes were full of amusement. "Daisy, I don't think we even need a police chief now that we have you. Yes, I interviewed Marybeth Skelton this afternoon. Right after she got back to her office. At first she said she cut her hand while preparing a meal. But then one of our guys talked to the cleaning woman who couldn't wait to rat on her. Marybeth mustn't be very nice to the help. She said that Marybeth never cooks."

He took a careful sip of his beer. "So while you and I were dealing with Ardine, they interviewed Marybeth again, and this time she folded like a cheap card table."

"Why'd she do it?" PJ's tone was razor sharp.

"Chip informed her, via a text message, no less, that he was cutting her out of the waterfront deal. He was giving the brokerage to a younger real estate agent. Some woman he was dating. Marybeth went down to the park because she knew he liked to hang out at the old mill. In a fury, she hit him with a wine bottle. Said she never meant to kill him, just knock some sense into him, but apparently her golf swing is pretty powerful. In the process, she managed to cut her hand."

"Jeez," I whispered. "She finally snapped. One last real estate deal gone wrong."

"He managed to get away from her, ran bleeding through the woods, and eventually collapsed and died on the giant pumpkin. Marybeth drove to Millbury and threw a different wine bottle into the pumpkin patch. One that she'd carefully picked up using a plastic doggie bag from the supply container they provide at the park. None of her footprints would be in the pumpkin patch, either. Quite clever, if you think about it."

"Class, today's lesson is . . . be nice to your cleaning people," I said.

Serrano chuckled as Joe came over and refilled Martha's champagne glass.

"Thank you, Joe. Oh, impromptu parties are simply the best, aren't they," she declared, eyes sparkling. "Who knew murder could be such *fun*?"

PJ swiped at her eyes and downed the rest of her tequila in one swallow.

"Hey, PJ, are you okay?" I asked.

She glared at me. "I know Chip was a jerk sometimes, but he was the only one left." Her voice choked up. "Everyone's gone now."

Martha was immediately remorseful. "Oh God, that was thoughtless of me. I'm so sorry, my dear."

PJ's bony shoulders slumped. "I'm all alone in the world."

"No, you're not. You have us," I said firmly. "Come here." I patted the sofa and she hesitated for a moment, but sank down next to me. I slipped my arm around her, and Jasper laid his head on her knee. Joe handed PJ a box of tissues and plucked the empty glass out of her fingers for a refill.

"You know, I've been noticing something lately," Eleanor said. "About doll collectors, and pumpkin growers, and Romeos who sing under your balcony at night. Isn't there a lot of obsessive behavior in the world?"

I could certainly attest to that. "I wonder how poor Sam's doing?"

"Oh, he's okay," Eleanor said. "I saw Dottie yesterday. She went with him to the weigh-in, just to see the other giant pumpkins and talk to the growers. They were all comparing sizes, and joking about whose is the biggest and so on." She winked at me. "Anyway, the other guys felt so bad for Sam that they each gave him some of their prize-winning seeds.

Next year, look out. There'll be rampant pumpkin sex all over the place. Dottie said Sam is already drawing diagrams and figuring out which ones to mate together."

There was another knock at the door.

"Boy, it's like Grand Central in here tonight," Joe said as he went to answer it. A few seconds later, he was back with Birch Kunes and Bettina Waters.

"Hi, Daisy," Bettina said. "We heard what happened, so we stopped by. We wanted to make sure you're okay."

"I'm fine, thanks. Just glad it's over, and all the killers are either dead or locked up."

"How about a drink?" Joe slapped Birch on the shoulder.

"Sure. Thanks. Those beers look good."

"Bettina?"

"Just a ginger ale for me, please."

"I heard the house is sold. Congratulations," I said. "But wait—what happens now that Marybeth is out of commission? If you'll pardon the pun."

Eleanor rolled her eyes.

"One of the other real estate agents in the office will handle the sale until closing," Birch said. "Angus is taking the rest of the furniture that we left for staging out in the next day or two. He'll auction it off next Saturday."

"Speaking of houses," I said, "you should see the fantastic job that Cyril did on the dollhouse for Claire."

Joe brought it in from the living room and set the restored dollhouse down on the steamer trunk to a chorus of various oohs and aahs.

Cyril hung his head, a slight flush on his cheekbones.

I explained how he'd added new shingles to the roof, repaired all the woodwork and balustrades, and refinished the floors.

"It's absolutely perfect," Martha declared, "and ready in time for Claire's birthday, too. She's going to love it."

"Let's plug it in and see if it works," Eleanor said.

"No!" Birch, PJ, and Serrano all exclaimed in unison.

I laughed. "It's okay. Joe did the lighting. It's safe."

Joe plugged it in and the three fireplaces flickered to life as well as the sconces on either side of the mirror in the parlor. Every room was decorated and accessorized now, including the dining room, where Joe's table gleamed in the light from the tiny chandelier above. The pretty lilac siding and yellow gingerbread trim were softly illuminated by the outside carriage lamps, and the hanging plants on the porch made it look like a welcoming, happy place.

"Enchanting." Eleanor raised her martini glass in a toast.

Joe came over and hugged me, and I whispered in his ear, "Thank you. For everything."

I showed everyone the fainting couch, carved rosewood bed, marble-topped parlor table, and Chippendale desk. "These things were already in the house when I bought it. Sophie would have a stroke if she could see my toaster oven, plus the upcycled things I'm going to make with Claire. She and Harriet were fanatical about being historically accurate."

I picked up the Chippendale desk. "Look at the workmanship on this piece, for instance. Every drawer has mortise-and-tenon construction, and each one of them actually opens . . ."

I tugged on one of the drawers. "That's odd."

"What's odd?" Serrano leaned forward.

"This middle drawer doesn't open. Why would you make all the rest of them functional except for this one?"

PJ peered at the desk. "Hey, you know what else is funny? Sophie had a desk in our living room that looked exactly like that. I mean, a real, life-sized version."

I sucked in a breath. "PJ, do you know where that desk is now?"

She shrugged. "No idea. Guess Chip got rid of it."

"Or maybe it's still at Sophie's house, knowing Marybeth's

penchant for staging," Birch suggested. "A nice piece like this would look great for showings."

I struggled to remember the scene when I'd peeked in the window to see Marybeth and Chip arguing. There was certainly furniture in the room, but I couldn't be sure if there was a desk there or not.

Serrano and I looked at each other, the now familiar spark of understanding zinging between us.

He was already moving off the couch when I said, "Serrano—let's go!"

Chapter Twenty-three

"Where are we going?" Eleanor grumbled. She didn't like to be separated from her Beefeater martinis.

"Sophie's house," I yelled over my shoulder, hobbling toward the front door.

Bettina took Birch, PJ, Martha, and Cyril in her car, and Serrano, who'd barely drunk a quarter of his beer, drove Eleanor, me, and Joe.

Serrano called the real estate agent who was handling Marybeth's listings and asked her to meet us at the house.

When she arrived and unlocked the front door, we all raced past her into the living room and stumbled to a halt in front of the actual Chippendale desk. I pulled on the drawer that corresponded to my miniature, but it was locked, and no sign of a key.

"Damn it." I ran a hand through my hair. "Now what?"

Cyril pulled a hairpin out of Martha's red hair, watching spellbound for a second as a curly red tendril fell free. He bent down, wiggled the pin inside the lock, pushed against the other drawers for a minute, but it was still stuck fast. He bent down, took the pin out, licked it, and stuck it in again.

"This clue was staring us in the face all along," I said, watching him work. "God, I've been so stupid. Harriet would have picked up on this in a second if she'd bought that dollhouse."

"What do you mean?" Eleanor asked.

"A Chippendale desk is not the right time period for a Victorian house. It was made about a hundred years earlier. To historically anal Harriet, this would have been a giant red flag."

"Aye up now, I beg to differ. That's not quite true." Cyril swiveled around and pointed the pin at me. "According to this book on dollhouses ah'm reading, there were all kinds of furniture styles in the Revival period that hearkened back to the past. A desk like this would be perfectly acceptable in an 1860s Victorian home."

"Oh God, all right, fine, fine. Just focus, please," I begged, waving his attention back toward the desk.

Cyril wrestled with the drawer for a few more minutes, and finally it broke free. The drawer itself was empty, but when he turned it over, an envelope was taped to the underside.

"You're a man of so many talents." Martha beamed at him.

Cyril handed the envelope to Serrano, who opened it carefully.

"Appears to be the last will and testament of one Sophie Rosenthal," he said. There was silence for a few moments as he scanned the document.

"Why would Sophie go to such lengths to hide it?" Martha said. "Why not just give it to Harriet?"

PJ shook her head. "Chip was always skulking around, watching her at the end, perhaps suspecting she might pull something like this."

"Maybe Sophie was planning on giving her the dollhouse but never got the chance," Eleanor said.

I couldn't take the suspense anymore. "What does the will *say*, Serrano?"

He looked up from his perusal. "Basically she gave this house and some miscellaneous possessions to her nephew, Chip Rosenthal."

At the outer fringe of our group, I could see the real estate agent breathe a tiny sigh of relief. It might have made things a bit tricky with the closing if the will had said otherwise.

"And the fifty prime waterfront acres along the Delaware River to one Margaret Jane Avery."

"My God, PJ, do you know what this means?" I exclaimed. "You're a millionaire."

"Woot!" PJ gave a jump and high-fived the air.

"Oh, yes, and to her beloved Millbury Historical Society, Sophie gave the commercial building on Main Street that currently houses a sewing notions shop," Serrano said.

Martha swept me up into a bone-crushing hug. I grinned over her shoulder at my good friend and new landlord.

Eleanor Reid, president of the Historical Society.

Turn the page for a sneak peek at
Cate Price's next Deadly Notions Mystery

Lie of the Needle

Coming soon from Berkley Prime Crime!

It wasn't every day you had the opportunity to see the best-looking men of your acquaintance naked. Almost never, in fact. And after tonight, I doubted I ever would again.

The shooting for the 'Men of Millbury' calendar had been going on all week in the carriage house of Ruth Bornstein's estate. The gorgeous fieldstone building was serving as both a studio and temporary living quarters for the high-fashion photographer she'd lured from California.

The Millbury Historical Society, of which I was a member, was desperately trying to save an old farmhouse once inhabited by one of the founders of our quaint nineteenth-century village. The current owner was entertaining bids for the property and accompanying twenty acres situated in bucolic Bucks County, Pennsylvania, and the Society was up against a local builder who was intent on putting up a slew of cookie-cutter housing unless we could stop him.

We'd gone the bake sale route. Now we needed some serious cash.

"Having fun, Daisy?" Mr. February, who also happened to be my very handsome husband, Joe Daly, came over and wrapped his arm around me.

I grinned and leaned into his embrace.

Not only did we want to save the character of our beloved Millbury, but the rambling farmhouse would be turned into a community center, providing badly needed recreation space for the local children.

Somehow my best friend, Martha, secretary of the Society and a fiery redhead, had convinced these twelve brave souls to take it off for the sake of historical preservation. Perhaps the fact that it would benefit the children had been the motivating factor for these guys, and not so much Martha's salesmanship or, should I say, relentless arm-twisting.

"It's crazy out there tonight," Joe said to me. "Think you might need a couple of bouncers for the next guy."

There was high excitement in the air. Tonight we would see the crème de la crème.

Dark and dangerous Detective Serrano, in the flesh.

Literally.

Although these guys weren't completely baring it all. Depending on the way they made a living, the photographer had used a discreetly placed object to cover the family jewels, like a fire helmet, a barbershop chair, or a farming implement.

We were working in the garage of the carriage house, which was still a beautiful space with its heavy wooden timbers overhead and whitewashed walls. It was even heated, which was a definite plus on an early winter's night. The building looked like an L-shaped barn, with the long part being the garage with its three wide mahogany doors. In the summer, swathes of orange daylilies grew along the sides of the house, which was half fieldstone on the bottom and light green siding above.

It would certainly have been easier to produce this calendar in the summer when we could have used outdoor locations, but seeing as it was early November, the clock was ticking to get it printed and into the stores in time for Christmas.

By the way, I'm Daisy Buchanan, the fifty-something-year-old proprietress of Millbury's antiques and sewing notions store Sometimes a Great Notion. Actually I'm fifty-eight, but fifty-something sounds better. I'd kept my maiden name of Buchanan when we married. Joe was secure enough in his masculinity that he didn't have a problem with that, or about sitting bare-bottomed on his lovingly restored vintage bicycle.

The shooting had been going on since last Wednesday, with one or two guys each day. Joe had had his turn on Monday, and yesterday the local butcher brought a string of fat Italian sausages with him as his prop, which caused more than a little hilarity.

All in all, this project had been a lot of fun. Our models had been pretty good-natured about the whole thing. Privately, I think they'd quite enjoyed the fuss.

Some of them, like the firefighters, had been filmed in situ, but for the rest we'd created a set inside the garage.

Tonight Joe had helped us by hauling in bales of hay and stacks of gourds because first up under the lights was Mr. October, a former mailman whose hobby was growing giant pumpkins. He was in his early sixties now, but still in good shape thanks to years of extreme gardening.

The plan was for him to hold a pumpkin in front of the essential bits, and there was lots of cheerful ribbing going on.

"Hey, that's a mini pumpkin!" Sam yelled, still fully

clothed, as Martha gave him his prop. "I'm gonna need a bigger one than that!"

Eleanor Reid, president of the Society, and my other best friend in the world next to Martha, sidled up to us, her gray eyes sparkling with anticipation. She wore her usual all-black attire—a long-sleeved baseball shirt and yoga pants—which actually seemed to fit with her role as photographer's assistant. Her white hair was cropped mannishly short.

Eleanor owned a store across from mine on Main Street called A Stitch Back in Time where she restored and restyled vintage wedding gowns. She only worked whenever she felt like it, which wasn't very often, but in some mysterious manner she always seemed to maintain an exceedingly comfortable lifestyle.

Enough to put gas in her red Vespa and chilled Beefeater in her martini glass anyway.

"There's a huge crowd outside those garage doors," she said to us in her husky voice. "All kinds of women from the village, not just from the Historical Society. Like a rock concert or something. Far out. I feel like I'm back in Woodstock."

I could feel the tension building, like the pressure in the air before a summer thunderstorm. The mailman was nice enough to look at, but it was nothing compared to the main attraction.

Detective Serrano was a transplanted New Yorker, like Joe and me. He was the hottest, most exciting import into Millbury in years and he spent as much time fending off the local females as he did catching criminals. Somehow I'd become a bit of an amateur sleuth, thanks to my, um, inquisitive nature, and I'd helped him solve a couple of cases, whether accidentally or on purpose.

Martha had finally given Mr. October a large enough pumpkin to satisfy his manly ego, and she swept over to us, carrying a clipboard, and trailing Cyril Mackey in her wake.

I wasn't sure what the clipboard was for, seeing as we only had two models to keep track of, but I didn't dare ask.

She was wearing a gold lamé wrap shirt, harem-style pants in a Japanese black and gold design, and high heels. The shirt gapped dangerously over her impressive curves and I hoped the little snap fastener at her cleavage was up to the challenge, ready to give his all for God and Country. Her bright red hair was twisted up into a thick knot, showing long shimmering earrings. If need be, the photographer could always use her as another light reflector.

"How did you ever talk these guys into this anyway?" Joe asked her. "I mean, I know *I* was a pushover, but it can't have been that easy with everyone."

"Well, some were easier than others," she said with an arch look at Cyril.

Cyril was the cantankerous owner of the local salvage business. He was originally from Yorkshire, England, and until recently, a bit of an outcast whose wardrobe left a lot to be desired. The village was still intrigued as to how he and Martha, a wealthy widow, had embarked on their strange and precarious new romance.

He glared at her. "I still don't know how I feel about taking my kit off in front of a bunch o' gawping women."

"Come on, man, be a sport," Joe said. "We've all sacrificed our pride for a good cause."

Cyril took his tweed cap off and ran it through his thick gray hair before jamming the cap back on his head. "I know, and that awd bugger what owns the place has already scarpered to the bloody Outer Banks. So I hope a lot of people buy this damn calendar and right quick."

Cyril was correct that the current owner of the historic property had no real emotional attachment to Millbury anymore. The only thing he cared about was getting a nice fat check to fund his retirement. He'd simply sell to the highest bidder.

Joe clapped him on the shoulder. "Well, Cyril, after tonight you're the last one, and then the ladies can get it into production."

At that moment, the photographer, Alex Roos, strolled past our group, one hand on a slim hip. "People, people, how's it going?" he said, showing capped teeth that were startlingly bright against his tanned skin. He wore black jeans, a long shirt with billowing sleeves that made him look a bit like a pirate, and pointed emerald green snakeskin boots.

Ruth Bornstein, the owner of this estate, who had more connections than a crocheted shawl, had talked him into doing the shoot for a cut-rate price. She was also providing his room and board for free, which was her contribution to the cause. Even without knowing he was from California, it was clear to see he was an exotic bird amongst a flock of country fowl.

His hair was cut in a Mohawk style, about an inch long, like the bristles on a silver-backed antique brush, and so blond it was almost white. The way some fair-skinned children get after a summer spent playing outside. And like a soft brush, it seemed to invite the touch of your fingers.

Roos had caused quite a stir himself around these parts during the week he'd been shooting. It was rumored he'd had almost as many liaisons as there were months in the calendar, including a dalliance with one of the married women. There was more than one jealous significant other who would be glad to see the back of him when he left town.

He winked at the local librarian who was doing a last minute polish of the carved pumpkins near us. In spite of his affectations, I had to acknowledge that he did have some charm. But give me Joe's wholesome good looks or Serrano's brooding, debonair appearance any day.

"Today's cock, tomorrow's feather duster," Cyril muttered. He looked as if he would have spit on the ground if he was back in his junkyard and not in this garage that was nicer than a lot of people's living rooms. "And I don't know about being alone with that fancy pants bloke, neither." He nodded toward Roos, who was busy setting up his camera. "Think I dassent turn my back to 'im."

Joe cleared his throat. "So, Daisy, where's Serrano?"

"Mr. July should be here any minute," I said confidently, not even bothering to check my watch. Serrano always showed up on time for his rendezvous.

The librarian inhaled as if she could already catch a hint of his intoxicating aftershave in the air. "Ah. The hot detective. Every woman's fantasy."

Martha shook her head. "No. Trust me, dear. At our age, it's a fantasy to have someone *cook* for you every night. Like Joe does for Daisy."

My husband had blossomed into quite the gourmet cook, seeing as the tiny village of Millbury didn't have a restaurant, only a diner that closed at 3 p.m. He'd convinced me to take early retirement two years ago from teaching high school and we'd moved into our former vacation home, a Greek Revival on Main Street. Joe had settled comfortably into country life, but it had been harder for me, and when I bid on a steamer trunk full of sewing notions at the local auction, it had been the inspiration to open my store. And my salvation.

So not only was I a resident, but as a store owner in Millbury, I was doubly interested in what happened to our little village.

Mr. October headed for the changing area that we'd set up with a wooden screen in the back of the garage. No one else would be allowed to stay for the actual shooting, except for the designated photographer's assistants—Martha, Eleanor, and me.

"There have to be *some* perks of sitting through the

insufferably dull Historical Society meetings," Martha had declared when she'd made the arrangements.

Everyone else left, our model came out with a towel wrapped around his waist, and shooting began.

To protect his modesty as much as possible, we kept our backs turned until he was posed with his strategically placed pumpkin, and only came forward when requested to reposition an item on the set, or to hand Roos a roll of film.

After the photographer was satisfied with the shots, and the mailman was dressed once more, we opened the garage doors. Joe loaded the bales of hay back into Cyril's truck. I swept the garage and the others removed the pumpkins.

"I'm going to catch a ride back to Millbury with Cyril, so I can let the puppy out," Joe said, as he kissed me good-bye and handed me the keys to our old Subaru station wagon. "See you later."

As I watched Joe and Cyril pull away in the truck, I blew out a breath against the guilty flutter in my chest for the imminent arrival of our next model.

Eleanor had borrowed a fake brick wall from the local theatre and the plan was to back the detective's Dodge Challenger on an angle into the garage and create the illusion of a grimy alleyway with a couple of garbage cans and some moody lighting. Serrano would stand partway behind the open driver's door, pointing his gun at an imaginary assailant.

"Now, aren't you glad we talked you into joining the Historical Society?" Eleanor said, as we maneuvered the wall into place.

"Yes," I answered dutifully, grunting as I pushed.

"Well, it was about time you joined, seeing as you were a history teacher after all," Martha said, peering at us over her clipboard.

Okay, Tom Sawyer.

"You know, it's been quite a week so far," Martha continued. "Starting with the cute little barber. Even though he was the first to take his clothes off, you didn't have to ask him twice."

"The man's an exhibitionist," Eleanor sniffed.

The Millbury barber had had a crush on Eleanor for years, but she'd never taken his pursuit seriously.

"I must say I'd never realized how well built he was," Martha said. "I mean, he's short and everything, but very nice-looking. Especially with his clothes off."

"I suppose." Suddenly Eleanor brightened. "Hey, remember when Angus mooned us?"

"Ew, yes!" I said. Our irrepressible auctioneer had loved every second of his fifteen minutes of fame.

The powerful sound of a muscle car rumbled up the driveway and we quickly opened up the first garage door. We stepped out of the way as Serrano executed a swift three-point turn and slid the gleaming black vehicle into position in one smooth move. He got out, and with a respectful nod in our direction, headed over to talk to Roos, exuding authority with every movement. I could see there would be none of the usual banter like when he stopped by my store in the mornings for coffee and baked goodies.

Tonight was a necessary evil he obviously wanted to get over and done with as quickly and efficiently as possible.

He was wearing a dark gray suit which complemented his closely cropped salt-and-pepper hair. He had the perfect muscular-yet-lean physique to wear a suit, and wear it well.

Eleanor narrowed her gaze in Serrano's direction. "God, I can't wait to see that man with his shirt off."

Neither, apparently, could the crowd of women waiting outside, who had rushed into the garage now and were leaning against the car, trailing their fingers over the warm hood, cooing over it, huddled together and giggling in feverish anticipation.

Serrano's ice blue eyes surveyed the scene, taking in everything, missing nothing.

"It's a good thing it's cold enough to wear gloves tonight, or he'd have a heart attack at the fingerprints on that paint-work," I murmured.

To say that Serrano was slightly anal was like saying Philly sports fans were somewhat enthusiastic about their favorite teams.

We shooed everyone out again with some difficulty and I closed the doors to a chorus of groans. While Serrano took his jacket off and laid it carefully on the backseat of the car, Alex Roos adjusted the lighting. Martha dusted the car with a sheepskin cloth and Eleanor and I pulled the garbage cans into place.

We stood back to admire our tableau.

Suddenly I spotted faces through the row of windows at the top of the garage doors. The groupies must be giving each other piggy backs to try to peek inside.

I got up on a stepladder and Martha handed me pieces of black paper that I taped carefully over the small square panes so that not a crack of light shone through.

The stage was finally set.

"Okay, ladies." Roos clapped his hands. "I think I can handle it from here. Good night. Thanks for your help."

Eleanor sucked in a breath, but we couldn't really object, not with Serrano standing right behind him. The photographer had obviously been given strict instructions to clear the scene.

One by one we trailed glumly into the house.

"*Damn* that Roos. Now *we* can't see anything either," Eleanor grumbled as I pulled the door to the kitchen closed behind us. "What a spoilsport. And why the hell did you have to be so efficient and cover up all the windows, Daisy?"

The tastefully remodeled carriage house had the same heavy ceiling beams as the garage, but the whitewashed walls and exposed stonework were softened with paintings of rustic subjects like a folk art pig, and there were top qual-ity Persian area rugs covering most of the stone floors. It was a simple layout. A huge sleeping loft and a sitting room above, and a good-sized living room, dining room, and kitchen with walk-in fireplace downstairs.

Ruth was at the maple wood kitchen counter making a fresh pot of coffee and she grinned at our downcast expressions. "Don't despair, my friends. All is not lost."

She made a beckoning motion and we followed her to an alcove off the kitchen that was set up as an office. It also housed a closed-captioned TV system. Ruth poked the power button on the computer monitor and it flickered into life, showing a quadrant of pictures of the front of the house, the back door, the main gate, and the interior of the garage.

There was quite a bit of pushing and shoving so we could all get into a good viewing position before the show started.

We didn't have long to wait.

Serrano didn't bother going back to the changing area to don a robe or a towel like the other guys. He simply pulled off his tie right where he stood and stripped off his shirt while we held our collective breath.

Even in a grainy black and white image, the hard-muscled body was awe-inspiring.

"Good *God*," Martha said.

The nighttime gray hues accented the rippled stomach and strong biceps that flexed as he moved, like a prowling mountain cat that wastes no energy, but is a focused, tightly coiled killing machine.

I swallowed, but there was no moisture left in my throat.

As Serrano slowly reached for his belt buckle, he glanced in the direction of the security camera, and it seemed as though his eyes met mine.

Roos tested his light meter near Serrano's face and the resultant flash made my heart bounce.

With shaking fingers I turned the monitor off. "We shouldn't be spying on the man like this. We're just a bunch of sick old women getting our jollies."

"And you're jolly annoying." Eleanor pouted and slumped back in a chair, crossing her arms over her narrow chest.

"Daisy, why don't you come up to the house with me and visit with Stanley while the shoot is going on," Ruth urged.

"Okay." My heart was still racing.

"We'll clean up here when it's all over, dear," Martha said to Ruth. "Don't you worry about a thing."

As we left the room, I thought I could hear the whir of the monitor starting up again.

I grabbed my coat from the kitchen and Ruth and I walked the short distance up the curving driveway toward the magnificent main house.

The original section was from the eighteenth century with random width floors and fireplaces in most of the rooms. It had been added onto over the years and the newer wings had the same sage green siding as the carriage house. The carefully tended rose gardens, tennis court, and pool were situated behind the house, and open verdant acres rolled away in every direction with breathtaking views of the countryside.

Ruth's husband had been diagnosed with Alzheimer's a few years ago. Before his illness, Joe and I used to join the Bornsteins occasionally for dinner during the summers when we vacationed in Millbury. Stanley Bornstein had been a successful chemist for one of the large pharmaceutical corporations based in Montgomery County. He'd made a fortune for the company, and for himself, and had retired about seven years ago in his early fifties.

I'd always thought of him as a highly intelligent, fascinating man. Brilliant, in fact.

And now he barely knew his own name.

Ruth took a deep breath before we headed upstairs. "Daisy, you haven't seen Stanley in a while. I don't want you to be upset, but he—well, he's gotten much worse lately. He probably won't recognize you."

"That's okay," I said, and smiled up at her in reassurance. I'd never seen the tall, elegant Ruth not perfectly coiffed, and tonight was no exception. She wore an ecru flowing sweater coat over a silk top and dress pants, together with a necklace of intertwined gold rings. Her bobbed hair was dyed a rich chocolate brown and her dark eyes were enhanced with eyeliner of the same shade.

She'd always looked years younger than her husband, even before he got sick, but in the light cast by the chandelier in the foyer there were fine lines of exhaustion drawn around her eyes and mouth that even the most expensive night creams couldn't erase.

We passed a guest bedroom on our way, and I caught a glimpse of some of Ruth's things. When we walked into the master bedroom, I could see why. The imposing cherry four poster bed was gone. It must have been dismantled and stored somewhere else and was now replaced by a metal hospital bed.

I'd steeled myself to be prepared, but I had to press my lips together to hide my shock at Stanley's wasted appearance. He'd always been a slim guy, but now he was incredibly thin, his cheeks sunken and gray hair standing up in wisps on top of his head.

His hands looked like little bird claws resting on the starched white sheets.

"Stanley, Daisy's here to see you," Ruth said.

He didn't turn his head.

It must have been six months since I'd last seen him. At that time he seemed to know who I was, although he couldn't quite follow the thread of the conversation. He kept asking Ruth about someone named Charlie. Turns out that Charlie was the cocker spaniel he'd had as a kid.

There were sheets covering the mirrors on the dressing table and also draped over the closet doors. Ruth followed my gaze. "Sometimes we see imposters in the room," she said softly.

I bit my lip and nodded.

An array of medicines stood on the bedside table, and a nurse was sitting in an armchair next to the bed, knitting a pink and orange scarf. She got to her feet with a grunt.

"He wouldn't let me change him, Miz Bornstein," she said, pursing her full lips together.

"I'll do it, Jo Ellen," Ruth said gently. "You were right not to push matters. Evenings are always the worst time."

Stanley coughed, a painful dry wheeze.

"His cold is getting real bad again, too," the nurse said, shaking her head. "Doctor was here earlier to do his blood work and said he's probably gonna need another course of antibiotics."

"I'll pick up the prescription tomorrow." Ruth walked over to the table and trailed a graceful hand over the bottles. "Did you give him his meds?"

"Yes, Miz Bornstein."

"And did you sign off on the chart?"

"Yes, ma'am."

The nurse glanced at me. She stopped short of rolling her eyes, but she may as well have. I gathered they'd been through this routine many times before.

Ruth touched a hand to my shoulder. "Daisy, I'll be right back. I'm just going to see Jo Ellen out."

They walked out of the room and I sat in the chair next to the bed. Even though I didn't know much about how to deal with a person afflicted with Alzheimer's, I knew I should talk to Stanley as normally as I could. If there was a part of him that could still comprehend, I wanted to respect his dignity.

I tried to ignore the faint odor hanging in the air that reminded me of teaching school in the early days, when some of the little kids didn't always make it to the bathroom on time. I wondered how long he'd been lying here like that.

Surely Ruth paid the nurse well enough that she could have handled the task, unappealing as it admittedly was.

I struggled to think of something to say.

Throughout the house there were hundreds of books. He'd been such a vibrant, educated man. There were even two bookshelves on the back wall of this huge master bedroom.

I'd always relished our conversations about novels we'd enjoyed, the current state of world affairs, and even news of his chemical research. He had a way of explaining things that made it easy to understand.

We also shared a passion for quirky historical facts.

"Hey, Stanley, did you know that Charles Dickens always faced to the north when sleeping?" I said to him, hoping to see some sort of familiar answering spark in his eyes.

"Or that ketchup was sold in the 1830s as a *medicine*?" He used to tease me about my penchant for putting the tomato condiment on anything and everything.

He stared unblinking at the ceiling.

Never mind not recognizing me, it was as if he couldn't hear me at all.

I sighed, remembering one time when the four of us had gone out to dinner, right before he retired. Stanley insisted on taking the bill when it came to the table because Joe and I had treated the time before. But then he took so long figuring out the tip that Ruth pulled out her own credit card. Stanley was furious at his wife and it was an uncomfortable scene, to say the least. She'd excused the episode afterward by saying he'd been under a lot of stress at work.

Now I wondered if Stanley had retired because he'd had a premonition that something might be going wrong.

His thin fingers plucked restlessly at the sheet and he turned to look at me.

"I know you." His face crumpled and he started crying.

"It's your birthday, isn't it? That's why you're here. And I forgot your birthday."

"No, no, it's not my birthday. It's okay. Really."

"Card. I should have bought you a card."

I tried again to tell him it wasn't my birthday, but he wouldn't be consoled. In fact, the more I protested, the more agitated he became. Desperate, I looked around. There was a small writing desk near the window with a stack of expensive cream-colored writing paper.

"Okay, you know what, Stanley? You're right. It *is* my birthday. So let's make a card. What should I put on it?"

But he lapsed into silence once more.

I knew he liked dogs, so I drew a stick figure of a dog that looked a bit like my golden retriever mix puppy. I added a bunch of flowers and wrote *Happy Birthday* inside.

I came back to the bed and sat next to him. "Look. Here it is. Do you want to give it to me now?"

I held it out, but he suddenly gripped my wrist so tightly that the paper dropped from my fingers onto the white sheets.

"Help me, Daisy," he said in a hoarse whisper, his eyes focused and very bright. "She's trying to kill me!"

The Millbury Ladies' Home Companion

Decorate a Dollhouse on a Dime

You don't need to spend a lot of money to decorate a child's dollhouse. Many items that you have lying around the house can be cleverly repurposed into furniture or accessories. Here are just a few fun ideas that will work with variously scaled dollhouses:

- Make a cute bistro chair out of a champagne cork holder. Clip, remove, and straighten the bottom wire from the "cage." The cap is now the seat and the four twisted wires are the legs. Form the center of the straight wire into a circle design, and reattach to the two back legs to make the back of the chair. Voila!

- A stack of matchboxes makes a great chest of drawers, with the addition of brass paper fasteners for drawer pulls.

- The tiny plastic stands that come in pizza boxes are ready-made doll's tables, especially when covered with a cloth.

- Small doilies are perfect for tablecloths and bed-spreads.

- After Eight mints have an ornate clock design on the wrapper to decorate your doll's grandfather clock.

- Empty eye shadow containers make good serving trays or picture frames.

- Use the metal palettes that held the eye shadow itself for baking trays in the oven.

- Buttons can be used as plates, and beads as vases or bottles.

- Empty toothpaste caps can also serve as vases.

- Coat buttons, or buttons covered in fur, make nice little throw pillows for the sofa.

- Think of using empty thread spools for table bases, stools, and perhaps a plant pedestal.

- Small candy boxes, like Russell Stover chocolates, make the ideal doll's bed. Glue on wooden beads for the feet.

- Empty creamer containers can be repurposed into lampshades, and a golf tee is a good lamp-shade base.

- Use thimbles for flower planters, and lids from narrow hair spray bottles for trash cans.

- A beer cap can now be the top of a barstool.

- Cut down birthday cake candles for doll-sized candles.

- String together bits of old jewelry for pretty chandeliers.

- Popsicle sticks laid side by side make a great hardwood floor.

- An empty, clean applesauce cup might find new life as a laundry basket.

- Paper clips can be re-twisted into tiny clothes hangers.

- How about wrapping paper for wallpaper?

- Postage stamps or miniature pictures from magazines can be framed with toothpicks for your doll's artwork.

- Foil, cut in either a rectangular or oval shape and pasted to the wall, makes a good mirror.

- A drinking straw is an easy curtain rod, with fabric scraps or old handkerchiefs for curtains.

- Wine corks, empty egg cartons, and cardboard paper towel rolls are all good items to save for future projects.

- So think small and let your imagination be your guide!

Trick or Treat? A Mini Pumpkin Wreath

- Cover a 20-inch foam form with sheet moss, using a glue gun.

- Wrap a 3-inch-wide burlap ribbon over the wreath to make a hanger long enough to reach the top of the door and allow the wreath to hang at eye level.

- Insert wooden florist picks into the bottoms of mini pumpkins and/or little gourds, and hot glue the connections.

- Once the glue has cooled, stick the pumpkins and gourds into the foam.

- Fill in the gaps between the pumpkins and gourds with more moss, securing with the glue gun. (You could also use putka pods, which are dried seed pods that look like tiny pumpkins, but glue them directly onto the form. You may need to do two layers of putkas to cover the gaps where the moss shows through.)

- Attach the burlap ribbon holding the wreath onto the top of the front door with an upholstery tack.

- This rustic wreath could also be used as a lovely candle ring for Thanksgiving Dinner.

Out, Out, Danged Spot!

This is Eleanor's secret recipe to bring back water-stained (and otherwise-stained) fabrics.

> HOT HOT HOT water
> 1 cup of laundry detergent
> 1 cup powdered dishwasher detergent
> 1 cup bleach
> ½ cup borax

Mix all items together in the smallest container that will hold them. Soak for a minimum of 30 minutes, or longer for even better results.

You can omit the bleach the first time you soak and see if it works. If it doesn't, then you can try the bleach. (Unless the item is silk—then no bleach, ever!)

Sausage, Cabbage, and White Bean Soup

A delicious, hearty, but relatively healthy soup for a cold winter's day.

> 4 tablespoons olive oil
> 12 ounces fully cooked chicken-apple sausage (about 4), halved lengthwise, then cut crosswise into ½-inch-thick slices (You can also use Italian turkey sausage)
> 4 cups thinly sliced green cabbage (about ½ small head)
> 3 leeks (white and pale green parts only), washed well and halved lengthwise, then thinly sliced crosswise (about 3 cups)
> 2 cups sliced baby carrots

2 tablespoons tomato paste concentrate
2 tablespoons chopped fresh Italian parsley
1 tablespoon chopped fresh rosemary
8 cups low-salt chicken broth
1 15-ounce can cannellini beans, rinsed and drained

Heat 2 tablespoons of the olive oil in a large pot over medium-high heat. Add the sausage slices and sauté until brown around edges, about 5 minutes. Add cabbage; sauté 2 minutes. (I never know what to do with half a head of left-over cabbage, so sometimes I use the whole head of cabbage in this recipe.)

Transfer to a bowl. Add the remaining 2 tablespoons of oil to the pot and heat. Add the leeks and carrots and sauté them until soft, stirring occasionally, about 5 minutes.

Add the tomato paste, parsley, and rosemary to the carrots and leeks and stir 1 minute. Add the broth, sausage-cabbage mixture, and beans and bring to a boil. (Depending on your taste, you may want to add a tad more tomato paste.)

Reduce heat and simmer until vegetables are tender, about 40 minutes.

Season to taste with salt and pepper. (Taste it first, though. Surprisingly, you may not need any!)

Note: If you don't have fresh herbs on hand, the world will not come to an end. Use 2 teaspoons of dried parsley and 1 teaspoon of dried rosemary as a perfectly fine substitute.

Martha's Marvelous Madeira Cake

A classic English cake, similar to a moist pound cake, flavored with your choice of lemon or orange. Perfect for afternoon tea! Serve with some fresh fruit on the side.

1½ cups all-purpose flour
2 teaspoons baking powder
1 cup sugar mixed with 2 tablespoons lemon rind (from 2
    small lemons) OR the rind from one big orange
½ cup vegetable or canola oil
1 cup (8 ounces) plain Greek yogurt
2 eggs

Preheat the oven to 350 degrees.

Grease a loaf tin with butter or cooking spray. Dust with flour and shake out the excess.

Mix the flour, baking powder, and sugar mixture together in one bowl.

Mix the oil, yogurt, and two eggs together and then combine with the dry ingredients.

Bake at 350 degrees for 50-60 minutes or until golden brown on top and a skewer inserted into the center comes out clean.

If you like, make a glaze for the top with 1 cup of confectioners' sugar and 2 tablespoons of lemon juice. It's also delicious sliced and toasted for breakfast.

Lackluster Silver?

First, a simple chemistry lesson from my high school teaching days:

Silver tarnishes because it undergoes a chemical reaction with sulfur-containing substances in the air to form silver sulfide, which is black, and darkens the silver.

One way to remove the tarnish is to use abrasive, toxic polishes that take off the silver sulfide, but the problem is they also remove some of the silver along with it. Or, you can "reverse" the chemical reaction to turn silver sulfide back into silver (without removing any of the silver) by using the following items you probably already have in your kitchen: a pan, aluminum foil, baking soda, and water.

- Place sterling or plated silver in an aluminum or an enamel pan large enough to immerse the utensils. If using an enamel pan, place a sheet of aluminum foil in the bottom. Make sure that the silver touches the aluminum. They must be in contact with one another for the electrochemical reaction to take place.

- Sprinkle ½ to 1 cup baking soda over the silverware. Use about one cup of baking soda for each gallon of water.

- Keeping the pan in the sink to minimize splashing, pour in enough boiling water to cover the utensils. The mixture will froth up, which is why it's a good idea to do it in the sink.

- If the silver is only lightly tarnished, all of the tarnish will disappear within several minutes, and be transferred to the aluminum foil. If it's badly tarnished, you may need to repeat the process.

- When the tarnish disappears, remove the silverware, rinse, dry, and buff with a soft cotton cloth.

Note: This process will remove ALL the tarnish, and even tarnish in crevices that polishing normally doesn't remove. If you have a piece where the dark contrast in the crevices adds to the beauty, you may not want to use this method on that particular piece.

About the Author

A Dollhouse to Die For is the second in Cate Price's series of cozy mysteries featuring the proprietor of a small-town vintage notions shop. Her debut mystery, *Going Through the Notions*, is also available from Berkley Prime Crime. Visit her online at cateprice.com.

FROM NATIONAL BESTSELLING AUTHOR
CAROLYN HART

Death at the Door
A DEATH ON DEMAND BOOKSTORE MYSTERY

Annie Darling—owner of mystery bookstore Death on
Demand—has a dual murder to solve: a local doctor
and the wife of an artist. Someone may be trying to
frame the artist, and Annie must discover who wanted
both victims out of the picture.

PRAISE FOR CAROLYN HART

**"Hart's work is both utterly reliable
and utterly unpredictable."**

—**Charlaine Harris, #1** *New York Times*
bestselling author

**"One of the most popular practitioners
of the traditional mystery."**

—*Cleveland Plain Dealer*

carolynhart.com
facebook.com/TheCrimeSceneBooks
penguin.com